Praise For
OTHER PEOPLE'S KIDS

"A gripping, cozy drama about the careers and lives of teachers. Written by a career educator, this story offers a rare glimpse into the complex lives of teachers, engaging readers in a middle-aged coming-home narrative and inviting them to reflect on the struggles faced by contemporary teachers nationwide. Culbertson's prose is enthralling without being melodramatic and witty without being overly lighthearted. Every character is lovingly constructed with empathy and imbued with complexity, making them relatable and likable. Readers will get lost in the story and come away having learned a few of the hard lessons that our teachers were trying to impart all along."

—Kirkus Reviews

* * *

"In *Other People's Kids* Kim Culbertson writes with empathy and humor, complexity and insight, about a cast of characters impossible not to fall for. But the greatest magic of this novel is the glow that growing to know them will cast over your own life, making you view those around you—and maybe even yourself—with a bit more generosity. This big-hearted, sweet-souled, tenderly funny book is just the balm we've all been wishing for."

— Josh Weil, California Book Award-winning author of *The Age of Perpetual Light*

"At a time when teachers are finally getting some overdue recognition as our culture's unsung heroes, Kim Culbertson gives us an intimate view of a profession and its practitioners so often taken for granted. With precise detail, subtle drama, and surprising humor, she creates complex characters we want to spend time with and learn from, both in and out of the classroom; they may not want their students to know it, but her educators are fully alive and frustratingly, stubbornly, lovably human. *Other People's Kids* is a warm, vital, intricately structured, and beautifully written novel about a small community in the midst of change and the people most likely to hold it together."

—SCOTT NADELSON, OREGON BOOK AWARD-WINNING AUTHOR OF *Between You and Me*

* * *

"As a daughter of educators and longtime fan of Kim Culbertson's YA, it was a joy to journey into her first adult novel. She has such a knack for creating characters we know and sympathize with, who make us tear up and laugh out loud. Everyone should pick up a copy!"

— BRITTANY BLAKE, LIBRARY (GODDESS) TECH AND FORMER INDEPENDENT BOOKSELLER

* * *

"The characters in Kim Culbertson's novels always feel truthful and grounded, and *Other People's Kids* is no exception. Instead of cynicism, she offers a genuine and honest look at humans and all our messiness, writing adult characters that feel wonderfully familiar. So familiar, in fact, that I wanted to curl up with this book and a glass of wine and read about their lives, just like I would catch up with a good friend over a meal.

Kim understands our desire for connection, and that sometimes real connection comes from the people who knew us first, before we grew up and moved to far-flung cities and studied at fancy schools and chased the dream job, only to become disillusioned and jaded. Because the people who "knew us when" can restore our core self and not care that we screwed up along the way. They know there's hope for us yet. And I think that's something we could all use reminding of."

—LORETTA RAMOS, TELEVISION PRODUCER, *American Gods*

"In *Other People's Kids*, Kim Culbertson deftly weaves the stories of three educators, each at a crossroads in their lives. Faced with tense family dynamics, broken romantic relationships, not to mention troublemaking students and their exasperating parents, Culbertson's characters come to life on the page, their flaws and complexities written with compassion and humor. In a time of so much uncertainty, *Other People's Kids* offers a moving, hopeful story of what it means to come home."

— DARIEN GEE, NATIONAL BESTSELLING AUTHOR OF *Friendship Bread*

* * *

"The pages of Culbertson's winsome and wise novel turn swiftly, even as they offer ongoing and profound ideas about life choices. Choices that may have led to dead ends—or to surprising places. A novel packed with joy, loss, regret, love, fury, and redemption, its compelling characters and delightful writing make this an engrossing and inspiring read."

— SANDS HALL, BESTSELLING AUTHOR OF *Catching Heaven* AND *Reclaiming My Decade Lost in Scientology: A Memoir*

OTHER PEOPLE'S KIDS

A NOVEL

KIM CULBERTSON

Sibylline PRESS

AN IMPRINT OF ALL THINGS BOOK

Copyright @ 2025 by Kim Culbertson

All Rights Reserved. Published in the United States by Sibylline Press, an imprint of All Things Book LLC, California. Sibylline Press is dedicated to publishing the brilliant work of women authors ages 50 and older.
www.sibyllinepress.com
Sibylline Press
Distributed to the trade by Publishers Group West

ISBN Trade: 9781960573438
eBook ISBN: 9781960573490
Library of Congress Control Number: 2025933375

Cover Design: Alicia Feltman
Book Production: Sang Kim

This book is a work of fiction. Names, characters, places, and incidents are either a product of the author's imagination or are used fictitiously. Any resemblance to actual persons, living or dead, is entirely coincidental.

HUMAN AUTHORED: Any use of this publication to train generative artificial intelligence (AI) technologies to generate text is expressly prohibited.

For Peter and Ana, always

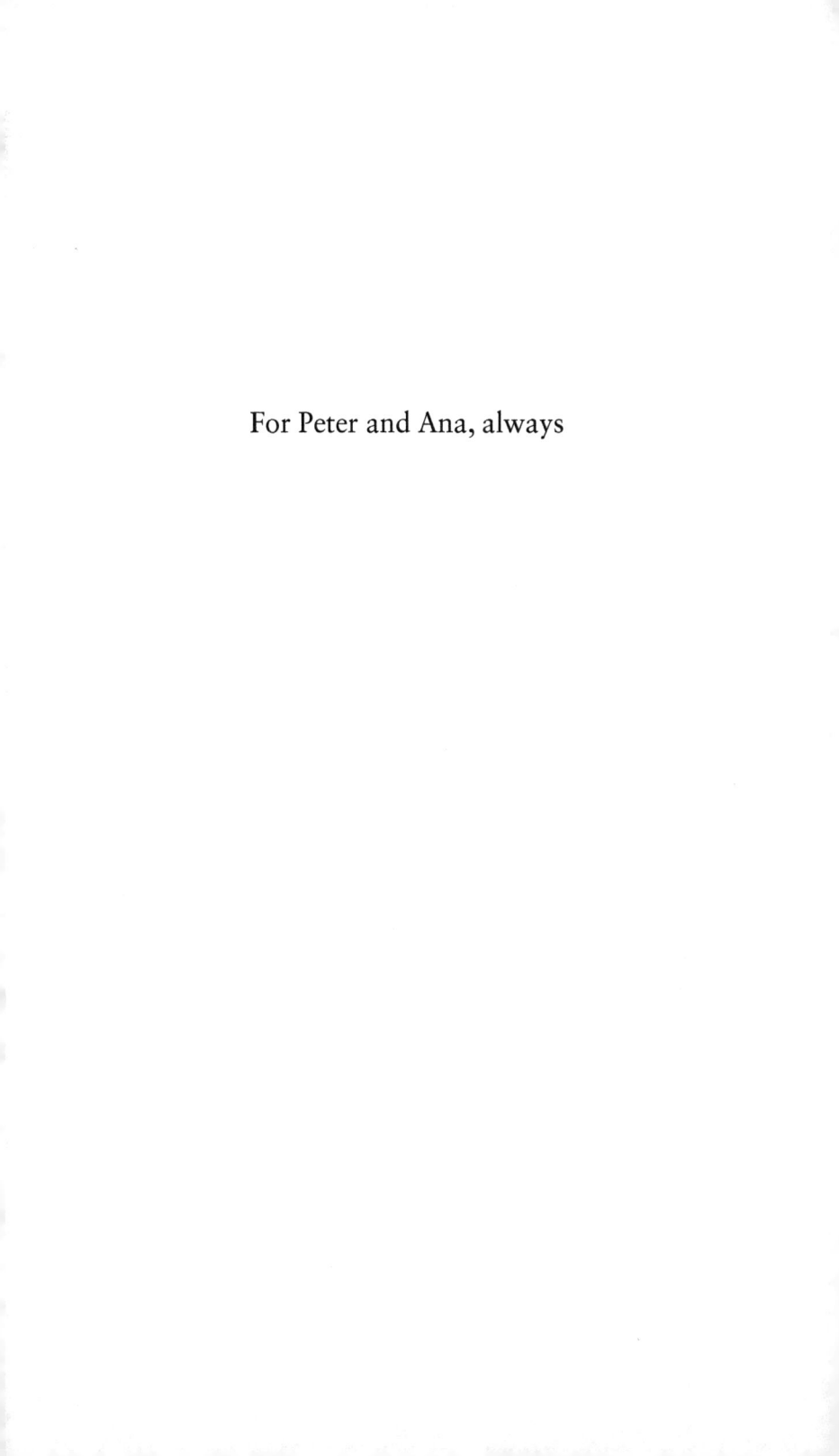

OTHER PEOPLE'S KIDS

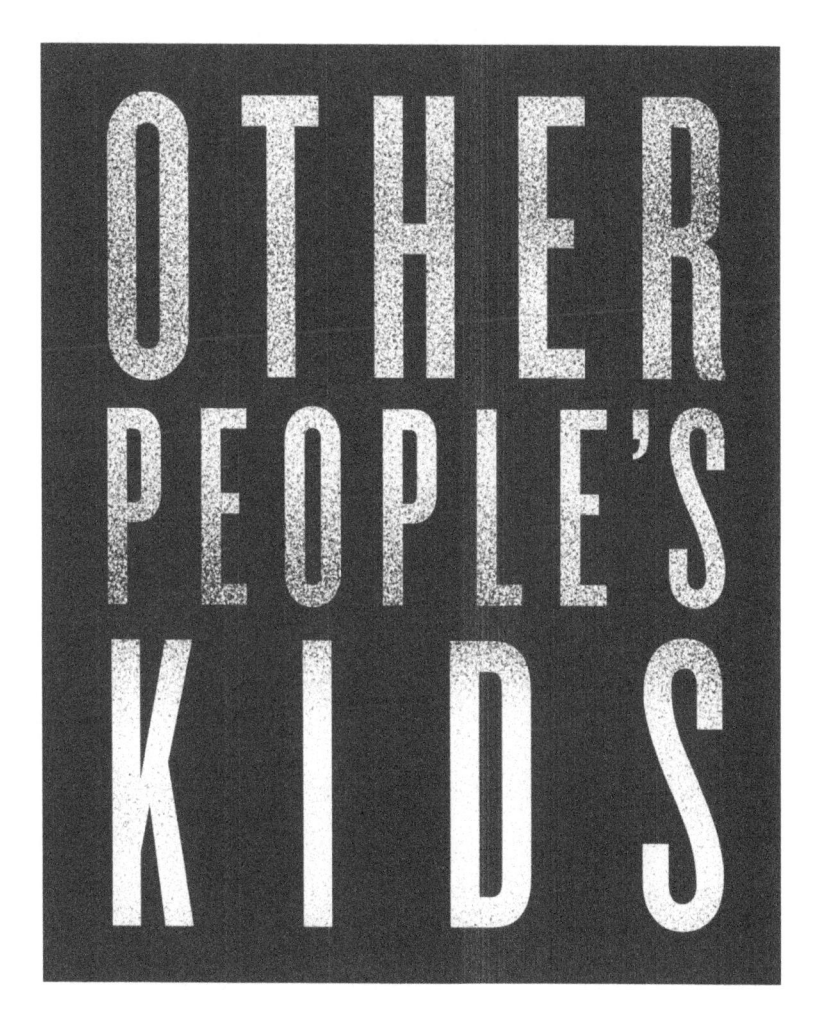

A NOVEL

KIM CULBERTSON

2022-2023
SCHOOL YEAR

PART ONE

Even when we run away,
we're going home.

—Sunset Dark

CHELSEA

CHELSEA PEERED THROUGH THE FOGGY Marin twilight at the figure approaching her from the other side of the parking lot. Broad-shouldered. Dark overcoat. Expensive haircut. Beyond him, she could just make out one last shot of light along the rim of the Bay, the city lights starting to blink on through the haze. Maybe if she hadn't paused to watch that thin, glowing band, had just slipped into her car and ignored the way the man picked up pace as he moved through the gloaming, she might have avoided it all. But she'd always been a sucker for transitions and that lingering streak of light was no exception. So, even though she hurried to wiggle the key into the tricky lock of her silver 2012 Volvo, the man closed the distance across the parking lot before she could get the door all the way open.

"Ms. Garden?"

She tossed her bag of grading, her uneaten lunch, and her water bottle across the driver's seat where it tumbled into the empty well of the passenger side. She had one of her headaches again, the kind that grew from the outer edges of her eyes until it lodged its fangs into the nape of her neck.

Again. "Ms. Garden?"

She kept her chin tipped down, pointed toward the door, the exit. "I think it's better if we don't talk anymore right now, Mr. King-Jennings." She tried not to trip on the hyphenated name, tried not to let him hear the shake in her voice. Chelsea hated that quaver, betraying her time after time in meetings with the high-powered parents who sent their children through the doors of her Grove Prep classroom year after year. Besides, that hyphen was such a crock. Implied compromise, a willingness to recognize another perspective.

Mr. King-Jennings held up his gloved hands, as if assuring her he didn't have a weapon of some kind, as if his complaint against her hadn't been weapon enough. "Just a minute of your time?"

"It's really best if we follow the plan the way Ms. Alexander explained it. Best for everyone. Especially Chance." *Who the hell names their kid Chance anyway?* And if it was short for Chancey, well, that was just worse.

"If you'd only listen to reason—?"

Isn't that what she'd been doing for the past hour? Listening to reason. After reason. After reason. More like excuses, if you wanted Chelsea's professional opinion. Which no one did.

"I really have to go. I'm late—"

"It's just this grade. You'll ruin his chances for Cal, for any of the Ivies. Is that what you want?"

Chelsea pressed her fingertips to her temples, leaning vaguely into the open doorframe of her car. If she could just get in and drive away. Stone was in the city at a dinner with clients. She'd have the whole night to herself.

If she could just go home to her studio apartment with its slice of water view and pour a glass of white wine, take off her shoes, turn on the Warriors game. She had done so well in the meeting, holding her tongue, nodding along to the conditions Sheryl Alexander, Grove's Executive Director, had laid out like Sunday dinner for one of her biggest donors.

Chance would take a B+ in the class. There would be no

mark on his record, everyone had agreed, politely sipping coffees from the bone china cups Ms. Alexander's assistant, Beth, had brought in on a silver tray. This wouldn't impact his applications for next fall.

She tried again. "Ms. Alexander decided—"

"But if you talked to her, if you told her this isn't Chance, only a one-time thing—?"

"But it's not, is it?"

"Excuse me?" Mr. King-Jennings didn't step back so much as shift his weight into the heels of his calfskin loafers. "What did you say?"

She'd heard it only after she'd said it, instantly blaming the headache, but it was out there now. The truth. Men like Mr. King-Jennings didn't like the truth when it didn't suit them. She forced herself to look at him, at his dark eyes, at the deepening line of shadow along his chin.

"A one-time thing," she repeated. "He just got caught this time, right? Be honest, Mr. King-Jennings: We both know his tutor has been writing his papers all semester."

"How dare—!"

"I have to go now."

At first, his grip was more reaction than threat, but Chelsea felt its weight on her upper arm as if he'd taken her by the throat, as if all the heat of a bonfire concentrated suddenly in the clutch of his leather driving glove. She knew it then, knew she shouldn't have waited to watch that end of light, should have gone home, poured wine, taken some Advil, heated up the leftover Carbonara from Fred's Bistro, flipped on the game.

But that's not what happened.

* * *

Chelsea held a cold pack to her bruised head. Every few moments she pulled it away to palpate the cut above her eyebrow. It had already stopped bleeding. She wouldn't need stitches, though Beth had applied a butterfly stitch to be safe. Sheryl Alexander didn't look at Chelsea as she spoke to Mr. King-Jennings on her office phone.

In fact, she had swiveled her chair away, staring out the window as she listened and occasionally said, "Right. Right. Okay." Chelsea could hear, faintly, the deep buzz of the man's voice on the other end. She tried not to think of a rumor she'd heard a few years ago. Apparently, Mr. King-Jennings had confronted one of the science teachers about a grade for his oldest child, red-faced, with a copy of the student's transcript saying, "Does this look like a fifty-thousand-dollar transcript to you?" Rumor was the science teacher changed the grade.

More murmuring into the phone from Sheryl.

Adjusting her cold pack, Chelsea felt eight years old, reminded of the time in third grade when she'd plunged through a faulty play structure and sprained her knee. She'd waited in the nurse's office until her mother arrived. Glancing into the little room where Chelsea sat on a white-sheeted bed with a cold pack on her knee, Judy Garden had asked the nurse, annoyed, "What has she done?" as if Chelsea had somehow been responsible for the spongy section of structure that had collapsed and taken her with it.

"I understand." Sheryl ended the call, swiveling back to face Chelsea. "Mr. King-Jennings feels awful about your misunderstanding."

Misunderstanding.

Chelsea cleared her throat. "Actually, Sheryl, he shoved me into my car door and split open my forehead. I'm not sure how that's a misunderstanding?"

Sheryl pursed her lips, folded her hands in front of her. "That's not what Mr. King-Jennings said happened." She attempted to hold Chelsea's gaze, but soon dropped hers to her phone where texts seemed to keep blooming, one after the other, on the screen.

Chelsea sighed. Sheryl had mostly been a good boss, organized, clear. She could even be fun, occasionally. Chelsea had seen her laugh with a glass of wine at the annual fundraiser or play frisbee with some students at the back-to-school beach day. Mostly, though, she'd always seemed a bit removed, tucked away in her office. Official, if slightly nervous, most of the time. As if at any moment, Grove could lose all its funding and she'd have to apply to a public school. Most public schools didn't have offices with this view, these wood-panels and decor, an assistant who brought coffee in bone china cups on a tray. What people would do for linen curtains and a slice-of-sea-view.

Beth poked her head inside the door. "Um, your—," she cut her eyes to Chelsea, then back to Sheryl, "—attorney is on line one."

"Thanks, Beth." To Chelsea, she said, "I need to take this. I think it's best if you stay home until after the holiday. We'll get someone to cover your classes tomorrow. It will give you time to clear your head."

"Time for me to remember things differently, you mean?"

Sheryl's hand hovered over the phone cradle. She looked tired. Her cell continued to buzz with texts. "Chelsea." She paused, sighed—Chelsea heard her fate in that sigh—and leaned forward, her expression full of the inevitable.

In a low voice, she said, "Last year, the King-Jennings gave over $100,000 for the library renovation. They have two more children in middle school. Their oldest son went here. He's at Cornell." She closed her eyes, rubbed them.

Chelsea had never felt a room spin before. Even the few times she'd been good and properly drunk, she had always thought it was an exaggerated cliché.

It was spinning now.

* * *

In the hall, she found Amanda Wang waiting for her. "Chelsea? Ohmygod, your head!" Dressed in a Grove Water Polo sweatshirt and jeans, Amanda looked even younger than her twenty-seven years. "What happened?" She lowered her voice. "I heard Beth talking just now. You fell?" She looked worriedly at Chelsea's forehead. "Do you need me to take you to the hospital?"

Chelsea's head was pounding, the world still wobbly. Maybe she should go to the hospital? Did she have a concussion? She let her friend lead her outside to the front of the school. Once they were out of earshot, Chelsea explained what happened, including the conversation with Sheryl.

Amanda's eyes kept widening until she blurted, "Asshole!"

"Which one?"

Amanda frowned. "Remember when I pulled Chance out of the game against University last year because he couldn't even hit water while in it?" Amanda coached both of Grove's water polo teams. "His dad flipped. So did his mom. Neither side of that hyphen can handle not being in control of the universe. That kid is in for a world of hurt someday."

Maybe, thought Chelsea. Though she imagined he'd simply follow both of his parents into finance like an Italian-suited duckling. But aloud, she said, "Seriously."

Amanda was young, had put herself through UCLA undergrad and a teaching Masters in five years. It was just her third year in the English department with Chelsea; she had perhaps another decade before she realized that most of these kids ended up fine or better because their parents made sure of it. They had to have something noteworthy to submit to the *Grove Alumni Newsletter*.

Amanda put a tentative hand on Chelsea's arm. "What are you going to do?"

Chelsea studied the leafy line of trees leading up the Grove driveway, the burnt oranges and reds. It was such a beautiful school. "Sheryl's getting my classes covered tomorrow. She wants me to take the Thanksgiving week to think about my intentions. Longer if needed."

"What the hell does that mean?"

She prodded her forehead again, wincing. "Pretty sure it means that if I'm thinking of suing the King-Jennings, I can start looking for a new job."

"She can't do that!"

"They give a lot of money to Grove. And they have two more kids on the way."

"He shoved you into a car door!"

"Says me."

Amanda tucked both hands in her pockets, her eyes dropping to the cement at their feet. She might be young, but she wasn't an idiot. "Shit, Chelsea."

"Yeah."

* * *

Chelsea heard Stone let himself into the apartment with his key. She pulled the duvet over her head. "I'm sleeping." She felt him sit on the edge of the bed, could smell his musky cologne.

"You didn't pick up. I was worried."

Even through the duvet, she could tell how dark it was out. "How was the dinner?" she mumbled.

"Like all the others. What happened? You sounded panicked on your message, scared the shit out of me." He pulled the covers back, and Chelsea was relieved, at least, that he visibly gasped. "Jesus!" His hand shot out to her bruised forehead. "He pushed you?"

"He definitely pushed me."

"Fucker. Leila was with me at dinner. Say the word and she'll be all over that shit."

The last thing Chelsea wanted right now was to involve Stone's wife, even if she did have a fancy law degree from a fancy school. "That's generous of her." She and Leila didn't see much of each other, but she'd been supportive and kind toward Chelsea throughout her six years with Stone. Leila and Stone were the kind of model polyamorous couple who gave workshops about how much of a model polyamorous couple they were. Leila had a girlfriend Chelsea had met a few times at Workshop. And Stone had Chelsea.

She'd always tried to be as calm and kind to Leila as Leila was to her, attempting to tamp down the blooms of jealously or irritation that neither Stone nor Leila ever seemed to exhibit. Well, at least not the jealousy part. They could both get irritated, but mostly with each other. Over the last year, Chelsea had started to believe they were just better humans than she was. Or just lacking most usual human tendencies. It was quite probable they were androids.

"I'm not sure what I want to do yet."

Irritation rippled his features. He left the bed, crossing the room to the fridge. He pulled out a bottle of white wine, helped himself to a glass from the cabinet. He took a long drink before responding. "Chelsea, we've talked about this. You're too passive. You have to stand up for yourself. You should go back to Workshop. Leila's leading one on compassionate self-talk in Big Sur for the Thanksgiving weekend. I'll see if there's space."

Chelsea resisted pulling the duvet back over her head. That was Stone and Leila's answer to everything. Anxiety at work. Go to Workshop. Money stress. Go to Workshop. Jackass entitled parent shoves you into a car door? Go to Workshop. She had no interest in spending $750 so she could waste a long weekend learning to speak *gently* to herself. Even with the ocean view and vegan chef. She'd rather read a book and eat cheeseburgers. "I'm not really in the mood for you to patronize me right now."

"That's not what I'm doing," he said, adding a unironic patronizing sigh.

"I'll figure it out."

"Will you?" He was using his soothing yogi voice that used to relax her and now made her want to start throwing any nearby sharp object. Directly at him.

"Stone." She tried to remember when even saying his name had sent a shiver through her, and was surprised to realize it had been years. *Years.* "Just let me figure out what I want to do."

"He had no right to touch you, much less push you. You should be taking pictures, documenting it, instead of hiding in your bed. You should be pressing charges immediately."

She bristled. Stone slipped so easily into directives. "Not if I want to keep working there."

He poured himself more wine. "Why, for fuck's sake, would you want to keep working there?"

"I don't know what I want."

He snorted. "Well, there's nothing new."

She shot out of bed. "How about this, then. I want you to leave!" She steadied herself with a hand on the side table, her head throbbing, trying to catch her suddenly quick breath.

Infuriatingly, he just raised his eyebrows. "Go to Big Sur. I'll call Leila right now." He fished his phone from his pocket.

"Don't call her!" She grabbed both the bottle of wine and his half-finished glass, sloshing some over the side.

He took a step back. "Chelsea."

"Out!"

As he slunk toward the door, she called after him. "Besides, I won't be here for the break. I'm going home." She almost laughed at his genuine look of confusion, at his glance around the apartment. "No, *home* home. To Imperial Flats."

EVAN

Evan Dawkins pulled the locked door closed and leaned against it.

Haven Tully had taken roughly a year and a half to pack up her cello—untightening her bow, tucking her rosin into its special pocket, wiping down the body of the instrument, settling it gently into its soft backpack case. Endlessly, it seemed, she zipped the case all the way around, kneeling on the carpeted floor of the music room, her long hair in her face. Once, when he'd first started teaching her, Evan had offered to help, but she'd visibly shaken as he held the neck of her cello, audibly winced as he'd quickly zipped—and caught—the case's zipper in a way that clearly pained her.

In his many years on the road, Evan had worked with enough crazy musicians to know that sometimes you just had to let them get through all their shit. Besides, it was Friday. He had time. Fridays had changed shape on Evan over the last few years. In his former life, Fridays had been the start to a long weekend of gigs, blurry with scotch and late nights. But since he'd moved back to the Flats, it meant a quick trip to the gym, some take-out or canned soup with his dad, and asleep by nine. Frank turned in before eight and was up off and on throughout the night, so Evan had to grab sleep where he could.

"Haven! Oh my god, what is taking you so long? We have Civil Issues Club, like, ten minutes ago!"

Evan looked to where Ashleigh O'Hare stood in the doorway of the band room. He didn't know her very well. She was a senior, had been in band last semester (violin) when he'd first arrived at Imperial Flats High, but hadn't taken band this year because she needed to add another AP class to her already AP-heavy schedule.

"Hi Ashleigh."

"Hi Mr. Dawkins. Haven, come *on*! You and that stupid cello." Ashleigh disappeared from view, and Haven hurried to catch up with her.

Evan finished submitting his online attendance, shut down his laptop, stuffed it into his bag, and headed out the band room door, tugging it twice to make sure it was locked. Some asshole had raided the computer lab last weekend and stolen more than $5000 worth of equipment. That's a low brand of loser who steals from a school. Not that the music room had much worth stealing.

"You heading to the gym?"

Evan turned at the voice. Dean Moreno was locking his classroom outside the B Building. He and Dean were two of the handful of male teachers at Imperial Flats under the age of sixty, so they'd taken to hanging out more than they probably would have in any other situation. "Yeah, heading there now. You?"

Dean shook his head, pocketing his keys. "Review board with Nora."

Evan checked his watch. Pretty late on a Friday for a review board meeting.

"Text me when you're done. We can grab a beer or something." He said this last bit just as Mrs. Eklund stepped out of her own B Building door and began to lock up. Evan was forty-five years old and clearly allowed to grab a beer with a colleague, but he felt the same sort of disapproval in her gaze as he'd felt when he sat in the back row of her English class almost three decades ago. Dean raised his eyebrows behind the thick frames of his glasses before heading off toward the admin building.

Mrs. Eklund rolled her wheeled carry-on toward the parking lot, so Evan fell into step beside her. "Big plans for the weekend, Mrs. E."

"You can call me Martha."

He really couldn't. Evan nodded to her bag as she maneuvered it down the ramp. "You taking a trip?"

"Oh, heavens, no. I have two freshman lit this year and three juniors. That's too many essays to carry anymore."

"You should have them use an online drop box. Or Google Classroom."

She waved this off as if he'd suggested she run for congress. "Old dogs, and all that, young man." She veered off toward an aging blue sedan under a pine in the far corner of the lot, her white hair lifting in the sudden crisp wind.

Evan shivered. If he was still here in ten years, maybe he could get one of the school buses to run him over.

* * *

Usually, Evan tried to get into the gym and out again without talking to anyone. Friday afternoons were good for that. He kept his eyes down and his earbuds firmly in place as he headed for the treadmill to run out his week. Sometimes, he managed a few free weights, maybe some stretches if he could find a quiet corner upstairs where they stored old yoga mats and step class contraptions. Mostly, he tried to avoid people he knew, which in Imperial Flats was like trying to maneuver through one of those laser traps from museums in spy movies: each tentative move one way or another could trip a conversation that led to red-laser strands of questions. *How's your dad? What happened with the band? Can I ask you a question about my son's instrument assignment?* He never used to see his own teachers outside of school when he attended Imperial Flats, and it took him less than three months of teaching there to realize they'd been hiding.

Most Fridays he was lucky. Not this one, though.

This one ran him smack into Lindley Watson. "Evan?"

He stepped off the treadmill, mopping up sweat with one of the threadbare, over-bleached white towels they provided in stacks in the locker room. "Oh, wow, Lindley, hey." The last of his Ghosts of Girlfriends Past. Well, second to last. Only he never counted Chelsea Garden. She got her own category.

With the exception of her real estate headshot slapped on the grocery carts at Imperial Market, Evan hadn't seen Lindley Watson since he left town at eighteen. She was mostly the same as she'd been then, a little curvier, crow's feet around her blue eyes, but still the tall, fit Lindley he'd dumped two days before graduation.

She folded her arms across her chest, her stare accusatory, but trying to appear otherwise. "I heard you were back."

"Yep."

"And teaching at IF?"

"Guilty."

"Oh, Evan."

He was used to this particular head-tilt, this look of pity, so he went with his usual story. "The band room was the only place I felt at home in high school, so it's nice to provide that for other kids now." A cowardly defense. Not so much advocating for the place itself, instead positioning his role there like he was the high school equivalent of a fucking sanctuary state. Pathetic, really. Not to mention pretentious. But he did it mostly because it got the exact response Lindley was giving him now, her face brightening with understanding, the judgment slipping momentarily from her features.

"Actually, that makes sense. Like swim team for me."

"Right." He was hit, then, with an olfactory flash of her, of blonder hair smelling of chlorine, then a memory of her in tears near her locker. Guilt chewed through his gut. Nothing had been wrong with Lindley Watson. She'd done nothing to deserve how he'd treated her. None of them had. Only with Lindley it had been the most terrible of all of his breakups. Even if he hadn't cheated. With his track record, she would have expected that.

No, that day he'd told her something worse. Not just that he didn't love her, but that he was in love with someone else. Evan was ashamed now of how casually he'd said it, as if Lindley would be thrilled for him, at his sudden capacity to admit to being in possession of a heart. Of course, she hadn't been remotely happy for him. He could still see in vivid detail the way her face had collapsed into tears. He wanted to tell her now how it hadn't even mattered, how he hadn't been loved back, but Lindley already seemed to be looking for an exit.

Besides, for all he knew, Lindley Watkins hadn't thought of him in years, wasn't looking for an Evan Dawkins' apology.

Inching toward the women's locker room, her eyes still brimming with pity, she added, "I was sorry to hear about your dad."

Evan also had a stock answer for that specific sympathy. "I'm just glad I can be here for him." And she, like almost everyone, gave him a nod, a pass. Because of why they thought he'd come home.

If only they knew how full of shit he was.

NORA

NORA DIDN'T SEE HIM AT first. Sitting with his back against the wall behind the door of her office. She had stepped out, just for a minute, to heat up the tea that had gone cool in her mug three times already this afternoon. Some fruity blend with chamomile a student had given her last year that she'd found wedged in a side drawer of her desk. Upon return, she took two or three sips before noticing Dean. Back against the wall, elbows to knees, fists to forehead, like a post-race runner.

Dean Moreno was that certain brand of English teacher who favored heavy-framed black glasses, jeans, and something plaid over an ironic T-shirt. Still had a bit of teenager in his face, even at thirty-two. He'd been teaching at Imperial Flats for—Nora thought for a moment – maybe six, maybe seven years? A good teacher. Cared about the kids, sat on committees, volunteered to take students to Ashland each year, asked to go to professional development workshops. Nora had seen his car parked many a Saturday in the tree-shaded lot.

"Dean?" She set her tea on the conference table and peeked at the slim silver watch on her wrist she insisted on checking instead of her phone. 4:11. "You okay?"

"We have the Smiths at four-fifteen," he mumbled, taking off his glasses, rubbing his eyes.

"What kind of jerk schedules a review board at four-fifteen on a Friday?"

A flicker of a smile. "You."

"Oh, right." Nora studied him. He and his wife had their second baby awhile back, maybe six months ago. "How's Travis? Sleeping any better?" she asked, extracting the file for the Smith family from the pile on her desk. One of the many files for this particular Smith family.

"Pretty much through the night now."

"Dean?"

"Yeah?"

"I think it was the Ancient Egyptians who invented this device called a chair—"

Another flicker-smile. No movement, though. Outside, the sky crept toward an inky November evening. It might even rain. Nora's body thrummed with a deep sort of ache that only Netflix could cure. Netflix and a Lucky's Pizza Skinny Crust Garlic Chicken. And that bottle of Zin she'd been saving for a Friday night like this. She flipped through the folder, still half-watching Dean survey the floor between his knees. He was not the first teacher to sit like this in her office in the last two decades. He would likely not be the last.

"Can I get you something? Tea? Coffee? A Murphy bed?"

"I think I'm done, Nora."

It was also not the first time she'd heard this from a teacher sitting on the floor. She would not let that spark of ache she felt at hearing those words catch; she would douse it instead with a studied patience. She dropped the folder on the desk and gave him her full attention. "Okay." Over the years, she'd learned not to argue, not too ask many questions, not to jump in too soon. Not to take it personally. She was still working on that last part.

"I've been thinking about quitting at the end of the year. Teaching. Education. I'm so tired."

Nora knew this. *Saw* it, really, each day, because teachers wore this kind of tired visibly. Most of her faculty lurched around like extras from a zombie movie. Everyone, so tired. And Dean had weathered the pandemic smack in the middle of his tenure here. Most of them hadn't fully recovered from more than a year in Zoomland, that strange masked-year that followed. She certainly hadn't. Still, this was a longer conversation.

"We should probably be sitting in chairs when Gloria Smith gets here. As you know, she enjoys any chance to point out our deficiencies."

"Okay, sure." Dean hoisted himself off the ground and motioned at the space where he was sitting. "I was partly hiding."

"Hiding?"

"Not from the Smiths." He paused. "I gave Ashleigh O'Hare a B+ on the first draft of her *Hamlet* essay."

"Oh, boy."

"Yeah."

"And now you have the Smiths. Big Friday for you." Nora moved to the hallway and peered through the floor-to-ceiling glass windows at the empty campus, at the stretch of field beyond that met, eventually, with the rural highway that formed the arthritic spine of Imperial Flats, the far mountains blurred today on the horizon. "I think the coast is clear."

Nora watched Dean settle, finally, into a chair at the conference table and pick up the file marked Davis Smith.

At IF High, each staff member held around thirty students to advise during a special period once a week. Nora knew he hadn't been thrilled to see Davis on his roster last August, though of all the Smiths they'd had at IF, Davis seemed at first like the quietest, maybe even the easiest. She'd hoped through some sort of evolutionary trickle he might have at least *diluted* genetically. But this was the second review board this year and it was only November.

Dean glanced up from the file. "So, what's the verdict?"

Nora frowned. This particular family hit their drama quota years ago and this latest episode was working her last nerve. She actively tried not to hold Davis accountable for his four older siblings, who had, over the years, racked up a combined sixteen suspensions, seven vandalism incidents of varying degree, and too many failing grades, tardies, and absences to commit to memory. Not to mention the one expulsion. Now Davis, the second youngest of the six Smith kids, appeared to have set a trash can fire outside his history class yesterday. Probably on purpose.

Of course, Nora knew it was definitely on purpose, but she had to at least listen to the kid. And his bleach-blonde, big-eyed mother who always, oddly, reminded Nora of a pogo-stick. G-L-O-R-I-A! The quiet, brooding father had only materialized once in ten years, at the expulsion hearing for Daryl, the oldest, who had been expelled for bringing a jug of vodka on campus and selling it by the swig behind the cafeteria. Nora had always felt it was the weakest, but most obvious, of his overall infractions during his tenure at IF High.

"Nora?" Elaine Frink appeared at the office door, clutching a single sheet of paper, tucking one of her ever-eager curls behind her ear. "Just wanted to give you that letter from Rebecca Carey. You said you'd get back to her about the dress code issue with her daughter." She frowned at the wall clock, adding, "Before the end of the week." She handed off the letter, vanishing quickly back down the hall, her crisp cords swishing in her wake.

Nora deposited the letter onto the growing pile on her desk and caught Dean's eye. "If only trash can fires were as simple as dress code."

Dean's smile finally broke through. They both knew nothing had more rabbit holes than dress code.

Nora handed Dean the trash can fire statement from the history teacher, Jack Winter, and the one Davis himself wrote yesterday. His smile vanished as he read. Jack had been Dean's mentor when he first started at IF, and he'd been old and bitter then. Dean glanced at Nora. "Davis claims the fire was already there when he went to throw something away?"

"Was that something a match?" Nora's eyes flicked toward the door. Toby Cameron, a board member, recently mentioned that her sarcasm wasn't a welcome addition to their meetings. Still, Nora knew it was the only thing getting her through the week. Well, that and the Zin-pizza-Netflix trifecta awaiting her at home.

Dean didn't lift his eyes from the report. "Davis asked to use the pass and the next thing Jack found was a blazing garbage can?" Nora nodded. Dean dropped his forehead to the table, an inverted shadow of the earlier back-to-wall. "Happy Friday to us all."

"You could try talking to Jack, get more of the story?"

"Jack hates me."

Nora suppressed a smile. "He doesn't hate you. He's just not interested in being part of anyone's Adopt-a-Boomer sensitivity training program."

Dean frowned. "I was just trying to explain to him about using a kid's preferred pronouns."

Nora gave him a knowing look and moved to her desk phone, clicking her lacquered nails against the plastic receiver until Elaine picked up. "Any sign of the Smiths?"

Elaine didn't pause in whatever she was typing on the other end of the phone. "Not yet. I texted Gloria but haven't heard back."

Nora settled the receiver back into its cradle. "Maybe they won't show."

Dean's eyes darted to the clock. "Your clock is broken."

"I have a maintenance order into the county so I should have a working clock in, oh, five to six months."

"Just in time for summer." His gaze returned to the folder. "Sometimes I feel like I'm always waiting for summer. Holding my breath until the next holiday. Because that's the only time I feel like I'm not holding my breath, like I'm not living in a state of overwhelm. I never thought I'd feel like this. I used to criticize teachers who felt like this." He shot her a chagrined look. "I used to wonder why they were even still teaching."

Nora settled into the chair next to him. "We've all felt like that at one point or another."

"But I've felt it since school *started*. Even before that. Like I haven't taken a deep breath, not a real one, in years."

"Take one now."

He rolled his eyes in a way that would annoy him in his students. "You know what I mean."

"I do." And she did.

Seven or eight years ago, Nora had attended a weekly yoga class at seven on Monday evenings because it fit into her schedule, and she liked the tall, angular teacher with the silver-spiked hair. Almaya. A name Nora had never seen before, and she'd seen a lot of class rosters over the years. At each class, Almaya read them a short passage and they would practice breathing. At first, Nora had balked at the idea of *practicing* something you did naturally each day or you died. But for months, ever the good student, Nora had closed her eyes *like resting butterflies* and *felt* her own breathing.

It had dawned on her during those long Monday evenings that when she allowed herself to settle into the practice, into the awareness of the practice itself, she had connected with some sort of mysterious pool at her center, even for just a moment. But then Almaya had moved back to Maui, and her replacement, a tattooed sprite with a broken-glass voice and an even sharper agenda, had driven Nora to change IF's monthly board meetings to Monday evenings that year. "Sorry," she'd told her, rolling up her mat for the last time. "I have a board meeting." She hadn't found another class she liked and then the current of school had simply swept her into the next few years.

But she knew what Dean meant about breathing.

"Mr. Moreno?"

Nora and Dean started, turning toward the voice in the doorway.

Ashleigh O'Hare. Senior. Championship runner. Student Body Treasurer. Applying to twenty colleges and counting. Nora knew she should be proud of Ashleigh's focus—so few of their kids went to four-year schools, much less applied to the tier of schools Ashleigh had her eye on—but there'd always been something about her that rubbed Nora wrong. The self-absorption, most likely. And the entitlement.

"We're in a meeting, Ashleigh." Nora used the voice she normally reserved for truancy and not an above 4.0 G.P.A honors student.

Ashleigh showed no sign of leaving. "If I could just talk to Mr. Moreno for a minute about my essay."

Dean swallowed. "It's a rough draft, Ashleigh. You have to make room for it to get better. Just please read my suggestions."

She tucked a lock of straight brown hair behind her ear. "I understand that, Mr. Moreno, but the rough draft is still worth 35 points and these four points will impact my overall grade."

"I understand how the math works."

"I can improve my work without my grade suffering. I completed the assignment."

Dean's eyes flicked to Nora, then back to Ashleigh. "What's my rule about talking to me about grades?"

Ashleigh's eyes fell to the top of her Uggs. "We have to wait twenty-four hours before discussing a grade with you."

"Has it been twenty-four hours?"

"No."

"It's not an arbitrary rule. I want you to look over the paper and take time to think about my comments before talking to me about the grade."

"With respect, Mr. Moreno, most students won't care about their grades in twenty-four hours. You do it to save yourself the trouble." Dean's shoulders visibly sagged. Ashleigh noticed, moved in for the kill. "Besides, it's Friday. I wouldn't want to bother you on a *Saturday*."

Nora had heard enough. "I think you've made your case, Ashleigh." She pushed back the chair, stood, and crossed to the doorway. "Mr. Moreno answered your question. He'll talk to you on *Monday*. I appreciate your advocating for yourself, but as I mentioned, we're in a meeting. In the meantime, look at the essay, at Mr. Moreno's notes, and see where you can improve it."

Ashleigh opened her mouth again, but she didn't say anything. She knew she'd lost this particular battle. After a moment, she said, "I'll come to class early on Monday."

"Looking forward to it," Dean muttered.

Nora shut the door behind her. To Dean, she said, "No matter what, do not give her those four points. You can direct her mother's phone call to me."

"Thanks." He picked at the edge of the folder. "You know, I used to think the Davis Smiths of the world would wear me down. But the Ashleigh O'Hares are a close second."

"Nonsense." Nora sat back down next to him. "She'd never settle for a silver medal."

Grinning, he met her eyes. "Maybe I should have taught elementary. At least then you can just blame the parents."

"Oh, I still do that," Nora insisted.

"How do you keep at it, year after year?"

His face was such a pure blend of earnestness and injury, Nora almost reached out to him, almost brushed the stray lock of hair from his eyes, like she would have once with her son, long ago, when he was still a tender-hearted nine-year-old with too-big feet and endless *Star Wars* trivia at quick release. But she didn't. She just watched him wait for her answer as if it might get him over this particular wall. Under the table where he couldn't see it, she let the heel of one of her pumps slip off, dangling the shoe from the front of her foot.

An idea bloomed. "I see you with Evan Dawkins quite a bit."

"Yeah, we might grab a beer later."

"Go now."

He perked up. "Really? But—"

"I'll deal with Gloria if she actually shows up. It's the weekend. Try not to think about any of this until Monday."

"I have three parent emails to reply to—"

"They can wait until Monday."

After he left, Nora carried her tea, cold now, to the window. She could just make out Dean moving across the parking lot toward his car, already checking his phone, pausing to type something. Nora hoped it wasn't a response to a parent email. Unlikely. She knew teachers like Dean were either all in or all out. It took her a full minute to pull her eyes away from his hunched form, still typing, in the fading light of evening.

※ ※ ※

Nora pulled into the Imperial Flats Market parking lot. She usually avoided it at all costs on a Friday evening when she'd see too many of her students and their families, but she'd had her heart set on that bottle of Zin only to discover it had gone off. She would not be without wine this evening. Besides, she could pick up her pizza from Lucky's on the way back. She'd changed into jeans and a lightweight down jacket, pulled on a pair of Uggs, and knotted her hair into a twist. She would run in and run out. The wine. And a carton of eggs. She was out of eggs and she wanted to make a frittata for dinner tomorrow night if she didn't meet up with Dani at the restaurant.

Inside, she grabbed the eggs and made it to the wine aisle without seeing anyone she knew, perhaps an Imperial Flats Market first. She was choosing between the two bottles of Zin on sale when she heard a familiar voice beside her.

"Spend the money and get the Frog's Leap. You won't regret it."

She turned to find Toby Cameron, a school board member, holding a bottle of white wine and a tub of olives. Her face heated, remembering the tense words they'd exchanged at the last meeting. Over the cafeteria menu, no less. Sometimes, Nora felt like Toby just argued with her for the sake of arguing.

"Hi, Toby."

He was dressed in jeans and a zip neck sweater, more casual than she was used to seeing him. "Happy Friday."

She motioned to his wine and olives. "Date night?"

He shifted his gaze over her shoulder as he answered, "Just dinner with some friends." He eyed her carton of eggs. "Big plans this evening?"

She felt an unexpected flood of nerves, and gave a short laugh, "Oh, you know—just a hot date with Netflix and this frog apparently." She held up the wine bottle. "And I was out of eggs."

"I've been living on omelets and wine, so believe me, no

judgement here." He smiled, and Nora realized for perhaps the first time that he had a nice smile.

She started to respond but caught the eye of one of her students as she passed their aisle. Alicia—something. The girl looked quickly away. It must be like seeing a giraffe in the middle of the street, catching sight of your principal in the wild. And she always felt a little caught out being spotted by students in the booze aisle. She smiled again at Toby. "Well, have a great dinner. Thanks for the wine suggestion." She moved in the direction of the checkout.

"Nora?" She turned back to him. "I think I was too hard on you at the last meeting. About the cafeteria stuff?"

"Oh?" She tried to look surprised. "Were you?"

He looked like he wanted to say something else, his features clouding, but hesitated, saying finally, "I'm sorry I pushed so hard. I—" He glanced down at the olives in his hand as if just noticing they were there. "Anyway, sorry."

She flushed, unused to board members apologizing to her in the middle of the grocery store, and managed to bobble out, "Okay, well, thanks. Sure. Don't worry about it," before a long-serving Choir Booster mom called out a hello as she passed her.

Nora turned to nod to the parent, and when she'd turned back, Toby had gone.

CHELSEA

The Stop-N-Shop was gone. And not in that way where it was now a beauty salon or a deli or an upbeat pet-grooming place with pink, laughing poodles painted on its windows. It was just gone. A slab of concrete and a black patch of asphalt where the single gas pump had been. Chelsea pulled the Volvo over that darker area now, her pulse quickening. Another left-left-right and she'd reach her uncle's peeling ranch-style house near the end of Macintosh Road. Or at least she assumed it would be peeling. It had needed a paint job when she had been home last. She ran the math in her head. Jesus, had it really been over six years?

Her phone pinged, sending a ripple of dread through her stomach. It was probably Mr. King-Jennings again:

let me explain
things got out of hand
no harm done

Only he was wrong. Harm had been done. She just didn't quite know how to give it a name yet. She hadn't made any decisions about next steps despite the articles Stone and Leila kept sending her about victim-shaming. And standing up for herself. And litigation options. She touched the yellowing bruise above her eye and risked a glance at her phone.

Sometimes relief felt like love.

Amanda Wang: *Do you need me to come with you?*
She texted back: *I left already*
Amanda: *got it—let me know if I can do anything!*

Chelsea hearted the message as another one came in. This time, it was from her Uncle Kyle: *You still a vegetarian?*

She texted back: *Some days—not if there's bacon. Why pick a side?*

UK: *My life motto! Where r u?*

She paused, gazing at the line of pines on the horizon heavy with storm clouds, then typed: *still a bit out—*

UK: *c u soon!!!*

She'd told her uncle this was a visit for the holiday week, but his overuse of exclamation points suggested he knew something was amiss. And why wouldn't he think that? It wasn't the first time she'd run to him when everything had gone wrong. She slipped her phone into the open pocket of her school satchel, cavernous with the absence of its usual pile of school paraphernalia. Sheryl Alexander thought it best to leave all her materials and papers at school, just in case. Just thinking of the way Sheryl had said *just in case* tied Chelsea's stomach into a double-knot.

Chelsea wasn't quite ready to face Kyle, so she pulled out of the bulldozed Stop-N-Shop, and, instead of taking a left toward Macintosh, turned right past the high school, into downtown. She would just drive for a bit. Past the empty parking spots outside of Charlie's Bar that would be full before five. Past Faraldo's Hardware, its plastic white and red sign cracked. Past the tattoo parlor and the library and the Burger Barn. She'd spent many teenage hours at the Barn, eating curly fries and reading novels well past closing while Buck, the owner, swept around her feet.

Imperial Flats was not one of the gold mining towns of the Sierra Foothills often featured in *Via* or *Sunset* magazines. It didn't have a thriving artist presence or a strong local community theatre or an independent bookstore that the residents rallied around because they understood how special a bookstore could be to the soul of a town. It was a place you escaped from if you kept your head down in school and didn't get pregnant, or maybe you could shoot a ball into or through whatever hoop or goal got you noticed for those sorts of things. The people who stayed either had that strong civic spirit Chelsea found exhausting, or they had no other options. Mostly the last one.

Imperial Flats had litter clogging its gutters and cheap food and a market that sold a combo macaroni and potato salad made with mayonnaise and pickle relish called Best of Both. Nothing here—not the diner, the carwash, the market—was an ironic nod to another time. It was just outdated, out of touch, old.

She missed it sometimes.

* * *

Uncle Kyle's house had fresh paint and then some. Some landscaping. Some new trim. An entirely rebuilt carport with twisting vines crawling its trellis-edged sides that might flower in the spring, a beige Ford sedan with a Carmax sticker sitting in its shadow. It was so utterly transformed that Chelsea drove past it before U-turning and pulling in along the front curb behind her uncle's aging BMW. In fact, now it had an actual front curb with a stained gray cement sidewalk, a shade darker and richer than average concrete. This was Diego's influence. Kyle couldn't match his socks, much less pick out the sage green paint of the house and its rich ivory trim.

Chelsea turned off the car, watching Diego through the kitchen window, his back to her, most likely chopping or mixing whatever they'd eventually eat for dinner. He was often cooking or baking something and had been working for a caterer in Marin County the first time Chelsea met him. Ten years ago, Kyle and Diego had connected online, bonding over a mutual interest in rare books. During that first year, Kyle had traveled on weekends to the city to see Diego and Diego made trips to Imperial Flats to see Kyle. Diego had accompanied her uncle the dozen or so times he met Chelsea for dinner in San Francisco or Marin. He was fine-boned and quiet to Kyle's round cheerfulness, and Chelsea had liked him instantly, his sweetness always ripening the air around her, setting her at ease.

Diego studied art and practiced yoga and knew a thousand things about cheese. That he would eventually move permanently to Imperial Flats instead of insisting Kyle leave his law practice and move to the city always made Chelsea imagine he was harboring a dark secret of some kind, even if it undoubtedly had more to do with rent and traffic.

She couldn't bring herself to open the door, instead dipping her head to the steering wheel, which was never as comfortable as it looked in the movies even without an injured forehead. She was a cliché. The sort she would frown at in the novels she read. Forty-five-year-old woman flees her city life, taking up sanctuary in the small town she thought she'd left for good. Ugh. If this were a Netflix Original, she'd skip right by that tired trope.

She wasn't even leaving an extraordinary job. She wasn't in film or eco-resort management. She hadn't been traveling as a photojournalist or international food critic. She didn't even have a half-finished novel in a file on her laptop. In the twenty-seven years since leaving Imperial Flats, she'd been a student, then a bartender/SAT tutor/caterer with some grad school sprinkled in until finally spending the last fifteen years as a high school English teacher, briefly at public schools and then at an overpriced, mid-range prep school three hours south of her hometown. No marriages. No kids. She was well-read and well-hiked, but that was about it. The list of her life's triumphs felt shockingly short.

At the tap on the window, she looked up into the concerned face of her uncle. He stood in the street, his long arms crossed, and waited for her to get out of the car.

"Promise we won't bite you," he said. Then, as she stepped out of the car, he took stock of her face. "Geez, you take up prizefighting?" He reached gingerly toward her forehead.

Turning, Chelsea scrounged for her bag in the passenger seat, noticing too late a smudge of chocolate on the left thigh of her jeans. She had eaten the entire sack of chocolate covered pretzels she'd bought at a gas station on Highway 80 during the drive up, the sort of food she always felt the need to hide when she was anywhere other than Imperial Flats.

Inside, she blinked in the dim lighting, shocked to find her parents sitting on a teal suede couch amid half a dozen throw pillows. Her uncle tugged at her arm, and as she moved with him into the room, her parents both stood in unison, her mother holding a white fuzzy pillow as if it were a delicate dog. The sedan. She should have known Diego would never own a car in any shade of beige. They had both aged, Matt and Judy Garden, and the shock of it, of the white ropes through her mother's short, dark hair, of her father's thinness, his plaid shirt a size too big, caught her breath in her chest, turned her limbs liquid.

"Hi," her mother started, a word small and informal and insufficient for holding the sum of their history in its sad syllable. Then, her gaze the beeping scan of a metal detector, she added, "What on earth did you do to your face!?"

Judy Garden had always made a habit of immediately zeroing in on Chelsea's flaws—a pimple, a frizzy lock of hair, accidentally mismatched socks—anything Chelsea was hoping people would simply not notice or have the courtesy not to comment on.

Ignoring the question, she said, "Hi Mom." Her eyes slid to her father. "Dad."

"Chels-bells." His face flared with the pet name, the way it slipped out after all this time on the wake of his nerves.

But her mother wasn't going to let it go. "Chelsea, what did you *do*?"

"Fell into my car door." Not technically a lie, even if it would give her mother an opportunity to raise an eyebrow—yes, there it went—over Chelsea's inability to outgrow her childhood klutziness. Something that had always felt like an affront to her graceful mother, as if Chelsea tripped over side-tables and ran into doorjambs only to goad her, to remind her how sloppy genes could be.

"Same old Chels," her uncle tried, but Chelsea narrowed her eyes at him until he dropped her gaze. She would deal with him later.

Her father pushed at the nose of his glasses with his index finger, the familiar gesture washing through Chelsea, that gesture while reading books on the edge of her bed, that gesture while watching her play basketball, that pushing of the slipping glasses while making sense of Chelsea's Algebra II or Economics homework. That gesture on the front porch of her childhood home as she pulled her car away from that last terrible fight with Judy six years before when she'd refused to let Stone come into the house.

"Not while he's married to another woman," Judy had hissed, peering out from the crack in the door.

Chelsea had pleaded with her, trying to explain, again, what polyamory meant until her father came out onto the porch. "Just let her cool off," he'd suggested, pushing at those frameless glasses. "You know how she gets once she's set on something."

Chelsea knew all too well. Her father had shifted uncomfortably, adding, "and she just doesn't believe in—all *that*." He'd waved off Chelsea's lifestyle as if it were in fact something one must believe in, like unicorns. Or God.

So she'd left. Then, somehow, time-to-cool-off became more than six years. At first she'd just seethed, and then the pandemic made no-contact a moral high ground she'd scrambled up. Eventually they'd started talking on the phone every few months. Tried Zoom once before Judy pronounced it ridiculous. But no in-person. And they never talked about Stone.

Now she looked at her quiet, patient father, who still taught a science class at the community college one town over, realizing she might be most disappointed in him, still feeling the sting of his passivity as he waved goodbye to her on the porch that day. Why wouldn't he just let them in? It was his house, too. What did *he* believe?

"I'll get some ice." Her mother abruptly returned the white cushion to its brethren on the couch.

"Oh, I don't need—" But it was no use, off her mother went, buoyed with purpose, returning in minutes with ice wrapped in a vermillion kitchen towel.

Diego sailed into the room after her, smelling of garlic and lime. "Chelsea!" He kissed the side of her face, pushed an emerald iced-filled glass of red liquid into the hand that wasn't pressing the towel to her eye. "Sangria, darling." Bless, Diego. "Come see what I've cooked up for us."

He motioned for her to follow him into the kitchen, her mother already complaining behind them that it was awfully early to start drinking, for heaven's sake.

* * *

Diego served dinner in the sun parlor. Because the back patio had been framed and fitted with removable glass windows and was now called the sun parlor.

Uncle Kyle beamed. "We eat out here year-round now."

Chelsea soaked in its beauty: wide stone tiles, potted plants, a sleek, honey-hued wood table with eight cushioned chairs in a plush, mulberry velvet. A wooden ceiling fan sat in the center of the slanted roof over the table and tiny, recessed lights shone like stars.

Diego poured sangria into more jewel-toned goblets, setting them in front of Judy and Matt. "I love it when it's snowing." He headed back into the kitchen.

Chelsea drank from her second glass of fruity wine. "You guys have done so much work."

"The best part," Uncle Kyle said, "is that we finally turned the back room into an actual studio apartment. Bathroom, kitchenette, its own entrance. We might Airbnb it." He cut his eyes to Diego who gave an enthusiastic nod as he came back through the doorway, his hands full of platters. Chelsea didn't have the heart to suggest that no one would vacation in Imperial Flats on purpose.

Diego made tapas for about twenty people instead of five and, as he sat the last of the platters in the center of the table, he murmured, "*Voila!*"

"Mmm, looks great, D." Kyle hurried to pile his plate with olives and cheese and bacon-wrapped dates.

Judy frowned at the food. "Do we just—?" She twisted her napkin in her lap and glanced at Matt, who shrugged, and finished, "—take a little of each?"

Chelsea's parents had done this for as long as she could remember, handed off their sentences to each other like relay runners.

"Small plates." Diego settled into the chair next to Kyle.

"Take some of each, or whatever you'd like." He spooned a piece of marinated white fish onto his plate.

Matt poked at the fish. "Is that raw? I'm not really a sushi eater."

"Not exactly raw. It's ceviche."

Matt tested a tiny bite of fish on the end of his fork. "Mmm, good."

Diego nodded, beaming. "Try the marinated vegetables." He pushed a ceramic platter toward Matt.

Chelsea bit into one of the stacked corn cakes, her mouth bursting with spices. "Oh, Diego—what is this one?"

"Spicy polenta cake."

"Amazing."

"Why are we here?" Judy cut in, her plate still bare, her Sangria untouched. Judy was famous for getting to the point, but this might be a personal record. She looked pointedly at Chelsea. "Did something happen with *that man?*"

Chelsea couldn't help it: she flashed on Mr. King-Jennings, the clench of his gloved hand, *the push*. Her body remembered it as if it were still happening and she quickly set her glass down before it spilled. Of course, her mother knew nothing of it. Mr. King-Jennings wasn't the man she was referring to, sitting there under the warm glow of Diego's hidden stars.

"A family can't get together and have tapas?" Kyle tried, half-heartedly.

"Try the bacon-wrapped dates, Judy," Diego added. "You'll love them."

She frowned at the dates. "I don't understand this meal. Is it a gay thing?"

"Mom!"

Diego chuckled, draping his arm across the back of Chelsea's chair, giving her shoulder a quick squeeze. "It's more of a Spanish thing."

Not to be deterred, Judy pointed her original question again at Kyle. "Why are we here really?" Normally, the resemblance was hard to see between the siblings, Kyle ten years younger and round where Judy was angular, Kyle tall and long-limbed, and everything about Judy compact. But both had the same arch of brow when they wouldn't back down from something, even if Judy's had the practiced height of a disapproving, much-older sibling. Now even Kyle was no match for that more seasoned eyebrow; giving up, he glanced helplessly at Chelsea.

Chelsea twisted her napkin in her lap. "I wanted a break from the city."

"Thought you city folk chose Napa or Big Sur for that?" Her father had a habit of laying the bumpkin on thick when he thought he could charm his way out of an uncomfortable spot. Except Chelsea knew he had a Masters in Molecular Biology from UCLA, so who was he actually kidding with the *city folk* comment?

She forced her shaking hands to smooth out the napkin in her lap. "I wanted to come home."

Judy turned the eyebrow back on Chelsea, its original target. "Is that still what this is?" If eyebrows had superpowers, her mother's would rival any in the Marvel Cinematic Universe.

Chelsea's headache threatened to re-bloom behind her eyes. "I think wherever you come from is home."

Judy took the tiniest sip of Sangria. "If you say so."

* * *

Later, Kyle knocked at Chelsea's door while she was brushing her teeth. He leaned his long frame against the jamb, a damp dishtowel still over his shoulder. "That went well."

Chelsea spit foam into the sink and washed it down. "You ambushed me."

"I can't keep waiting for the Garden family to bury the hatchet. We'll never have Christmas together again."

"I've never liked that expression—bury the hatchet. A history teacher at Grove told me it came from the supposed end of war between the settlers and the Native Americans, so it always feels more like a ceremonial lie than a true peace offering." Chelsea pointed at a silver tray of assorted travel size lotions, shampoos, and soaps from the back of the sink. "Am I allowed to use those?"

"Please do. He bought about a thousand of them." Kyle watched as Chelsea applied mint lotion to her arms. "You know, sometimes a show of peace is the first step."

She capped the bottle. "Always the optimist."

Kyle pulled the towel from his shoulder and wound it absentmindedly around the other hand. "Speaking of an ambush, I'm sure you've heard Evan Dawkins is back in town."

Chelsea hoped he couldn't see the sudden wave of goosebumps spreading across her skin. She rested a hand against the white porcelain sink. "Like, *back-back*? Living here?"

"He's teaching music at the high school."

Evan Dawkins. Living back in Imperial Flats. So apparently hell had, in fact, frozen over. "I guess I haven't been on Facebook in a while." Or for years. As if her homecoming wasn't already full of clichés, she could now add Evan Dawkins to the elevator pitch.

Kyle searched her face before asking, "Will Stone be joining you for the break?"

"No." She hesitated, then said what she'd been feeling for months out loud for the first time. "I'm not sure I'm going to keep seeing him."

"Oh, really? Why's that?" Kyle had probably tried to sound casual rather than bitchy, but it came out more the latter.

"Not you, too."

"I'm not judging your whole arrangement, love. I just don't see him making you very happy as of late."

He knew her too well. She wasn't happy with Stone anymore. When she had first started seeing Stone, it had been thrilling and alternative and even a simple text from him had sent a shot of heat through every part of her body. For the first couple of years, she'd basked in the hot glow of him, this gorgeous, open-minded, polyamorous man. And she adored the beautiful Sausalito studio he rented to her on the cheap while he lived in San Francisco with his equally open-minded, gorgeous, polyamorous wife.

The relationship had been playful, sexually adventurous. Chelsea had felt brave and shocking and vitally autonomous. She'd always had a tenuous relationship with partnership, had never wanted marriage or even too demanding of a long-term boyfriend. Teaching kept her busy; she had friends and book clubs and colleagues. Her relationship with Stone, their quick hook-ups in the studio or at his office in the city, their long walks on Mt. Tam on Sunday afternoons, their weekends in Santa Fe, or Portland or L.A. at seminars and festivals, that time they spent thirty-six straight hours in bed and only got up to eat and pee and take one gloriously steamy, environmentally irresponsible shower. For a long time, it had been exactly what she needed, perfect even. She'd never wanted the traditional life of her parents and brother, and, with Stone, she had the lifestyle to prove it. Or so she used to think. Now she just felt exhausted.

Kyle studied her for a moment, seemed on the verge of saying something else, but then simply, wisely, asked, "You need anything?"

Grateful, Chelsea pulled off her socks, wadded them in a ball, and jammed them in her bag. "Nope."

"Three hundred travel-sized lemongrass hair conditioners perhaps? More pillows?"

Chelsea eyed the bed, piled with no less than a dozen multi-sized pillows in silky, velvety shades of slate-blue and cream. "Can he spare some?"

"He harbors dreams of a bed and breakfast by the sea."

"Did you remind him he lives in Imperial Flats?"

"Sleep tight, Chels."

* * *

Imperial Market hadn't changed much since it was built in the late 1960s, a boxy ivory building with raised signage and a wide cement walkway crumbling at its edges into the parking lot. As Chelsea stepped through the whoosh of the sliding door, she imagined it might even still be the same stale air that had always circulated, its pseudo-damp smell grown from its beige walls, cracked linoleum floors, and refrigerated cases. As expected on the day before Thanksgiving, the store was packed, everyone hurrying with carts heaped as if they had simply forgotten until this very moment that tomorrow they would need mounds of food for incoming family. People scurried down the aisles, their eyes wide with manic determination.

"Excuse me." Someone slipped past her as Chelsea squinted at the Post-It in her hand, at Kyle's spidery writing. *Ginger. Orange juice (fresh!). Lemons.* Diego had everything else.

She grabbed a handbasket and tried to ignore "End of the Line" crackling through unseen speakers above her as if even Imperial Market's song rotation was designed specifically to mock her. She dropped a bottle of Tums into the basket and started to head in the direction of juice when a voice stopped her.

"Chelsea?"

She turned and found herself staring into Evan Dawkins's middle-aged face, her heart time-lapsing him into the present, taking him through the decades from the green-eyed teenager with the flop of hair that always fell into his eyes to this older, still green-eyed, closely-cropped-going-gray-haired man. *Handsome* man. Damn it. He'd just gotten better looking, the bastard. "Wow, Evan. Hey."

"I heard you were back."

"For Thanksgiving." Only even as she said it, she tasted the coppery tang of a lie. How many times had she called him a liar graduation night? Probably six. One for each can of Coors Light she had thrown through his window. Coors fucking Light. Mortifying. The only upside was he hadn't been there to hear or see any of it. He'd been long gone.

He switched the basket he was carrying from one hand to the other. "Jesus, you look great."

Still sending electrical currents through her gut. *Fucking asshole.* "You got so gray."

But of course he just grinned, igniting (cute!) crow's feet around his eyes. "Yeah, genetics can be a bitch." He turned the grin toward her basket, nodding at the bottle of Tums. "Provisions? I gather your parents are coming to Thanksgiving." At her surprised look, he added, "Your mom said you weren't visiting much, that things were—tense."

Chelsea tried to ignore the flare of annoyance in her stomach. "Did she?"

"Actually here, in the produce section." The amount of gossip and news exchanged over the apple bin at Imperial Market could power the town. If energy worked like that. Evan's smile widened. "Said you were being stubborn as usual."

"That sounds like her."

"Aw, Judy's okay."

"She always did like you best."

He didn't answer, distracted with something over her shoulder. "Hi Nora."

A tall, vaguely familiar woman in dark jeans and a plush ivory sweater wandered over, her own handbasket full of greens and veggies, her dark hair pulled into a high twist. "Evan, hi. Look at us with our last-minute shopping." She nodded politely at Chelsea. Up close, she was older than Chelsea first thought, thumbprint-size dark patches staining the skin beneath her eyes.

Evan stepped in. "Nora, this is Chelsea Garden, a friend from high school. Chelsea, this is our principal at Imperial Flats, Nora Delgado."

Chelsea shook her cool hand, noticing the short, perfectly polished nails. "I think you taught history when we went there?"

Evan looked stricken. "That's right, you did! I'm sorry I never put that together."

Nora waved him off. "I would only be offended if you'd been in my class."

"Chelsea teaches English at a private school in Marin." Judy had apparently given him her life story in the produce section. Well, probably only the acceptable bits. Not the part about her polyamorous relationship. Her *cult*, as Judy called it. Judy had a tendency to omit any detail that might hint she didn't have her children well in hand.

Nora's smile widened at the news. "Ah, one of us. How long have you been teaching?"

"Fifteen years. Well, twelve at Grove, where I am now. Before that I was at a public school in Marin, but kept getting pink-slipped, so I finally took the private school gig."

Nora nodded knowingly. "Still, fifteen years. Sounds like you might be in for the long haul."

"We'll see." Chelsea resisted the urge to break into the Tums bottle in her basket.

Nora nodded. "I've said that for most of my career. It's the only way to get to summer." She let her gaze slip between the two of them. "Well, I better go find some chocolate and wine to balance out all this healthy food. It was nice meeting you, Chelsea. Evan, enjoy the break." She glided away.

"She seems much nicer that Mr. Jergson." Chelsea remembered the way their high school principal had hurried through the halls in his ridiculous three-piece suits and slicked coppery hair, his walkie-talkie always alive and crackling in his hand. Mr. *Jerk*son, they'd called him.

"What?" Evan asked at her flicker of a smile.

"I was just thinking about how we used to call him Mr. Jerkson."

He grimaced. "Our wit knew no end."

"We were hilarious." Only she suddenly wondered if he knew they called him that. She hoped not. She would never want to be principal of a high school like Imperial Flats. Or any other, for that matter. Of course, right now she had no idea what she wanted anymore. Except not being pushed into a car door with seemingly no consequences would be a nice start. She brushed her fingers across her fading bruise. Even with the foundation she'd applied, she was sure it beamed through like a neon sign.

But if he noticed, there were too many years gaping between them for him to comment. He simply said, "It's really good to see you." Her eyes darted to the stacks of generic soda on the end-cap. Was it good to see Evan? She couldn't tell, her battery had run so low she couldn't register much of anything except possibly building a fort inside those soda packs and living there until Christmas. When the silence kept elongating, he added, "What are you doing after you shop? You want to get a drink? We could meet at that new brew pub on Main?"

She imagined sitting across from Evan in a dark booth and her stomach flipped against her better judgment. "Imperial Flats has a brew pub now?"

"A lot has changed around here."

* * *

Gold Rush Brew didn't have any booths. It had wooden picnic tables. Chelsea was relieved to see the place was half-empty. She barely wanted to sit on a bench with no back, much less have to make small chat with random strangers at a shared table. She scanned the room for Evan. He sat with his back to her at a table near the bar, scrolling on his phone, a pale beer already half gone in front of him. She had run her groceries back to Diego before coming to meet Evan. And she might have applied some make-up.

Now, she slid in across from him. "What, you didn't get me one?"

He tucked his phone into his back pocket and flashed her the same dismantling smile he'd used to his advantage on pretty much everyone in high school. "I wasn't sure what you wanted. And they don't have Coors Light."

"Oh, that's how it's going to be?" She tried to sound playful, even as her cheeks heated with the memory of it. Chelsea fiddled with the tiny chalkboard menus, remembering the eve of graduation, hurling those beer cans through Evan's bedroom window. She could still hear the glass shattering, still picture the panicked look of his stepmom, Peggy, when she came running out onto the front porch. It was the finale of a long, exhausting story, one Chelsea wished she could just shake and erase like an Etch A Sketch from her mind. And yet, here she was. Sometimes, though, when she let herself, she felt secretly proud of those cans, of the girl who threw them.

"What else can I get you?" A waitress appeared at their table. Early twenties. Pink hair, tats on both arms, nose ring. The chalkboard menus and now this waitress. Somewhere in the last six years she'd missed the hipster invasion of Imperial Flats. Without looking at Chelsea, the waitress widened her smile at Evan. Chelsea calculated how many steps would carry her out of the bar and back into her car. Thirty? Eighty?

Evan examined a chalkboard. "Can we get the appetizer platter and whatever this lovely person wants to drink?"

"I'll take the stout."

Pink Hair nodded and headed to the bar, minutes later depositing a frothy dark beer in front of Chelsea.

"The opposite of Coors Light," Evan said. "Cheers." They clinked their glasses. "You know, I never understood why you threw those beer cans in the first place."

Chelsea gaped at him. "Seriously?" He shrugged, nodding to the waitress as she set down a platter of various fried items. When they'd each dunked a zucchini into the pot of homemade ranch and tried the sweet potato fries with the cranberry dipping sauce, Chelsea asked, "You honestly don't remember?"

"Remember what?"

"Wow." She shook her head, trying to hide her shaking hands in her lap.

"Is this about me not going to graduation?"

"I don't care about you not going to graduation."

"Then what?"

She drank a quarter of her beer before setting it down. "Let's see if this rings a bell: 'Hey, Chelsea, can we meet at the lake after graduation? I need to talk to you, we need to sort this out, we can blow off grad night, drink some *beer*—'" She stopped at his blank expression. All these years, and her grand cans-through-the-window gesture hadn't even landed. She didn't even have that anymore. "Well, that would've definitely made it more confusing. Sucks when the symbolism gets lost."

She couldn't help it; the memory flooded her. As much as she'd tried for years to expunge it from her brain—the image of sitting on that flat rock, looking out at the haze over the lake, at the muddy edges of its shore, waiting for him—she couldn't quite erase it. Even with his grand proclamation of love the day before, it turned out he'd meant more to her than she had to him.

Evan dropped his eyes and, maybe Chelsea imagined it, but he seemed squirmy on the bench even as he continued to feign innocence. "I had to get out of here, Chels, you know that. I had to leave."

She stared at the foam evaporating on the surface of her beer. "I guess I owe Peggy an apology."

"Wait." He reached across the table, took hold of her free hand. At least it wasn't the greasy one. "Are you mad?"

She tried to ignore the creeping headache. "Oh, Evan, it was a long time ago." Except she must be. Mad. She'd been trying to let it go for years, but it always resurfaced, the anger always ready to ignite. It had turned up in therapy. Turned up in yoga when they were supposed to be releasing that which no longer served them. She'd let other things go, but somehow this particular wound refused to heal, year after year. Several of her therapists had thought it had to do with closure, but that just seemed obvious and unhelpful. Looking past him out the floor-to-ceiling windows, she watched people walk by on the street outside, under the bare limbs of maples planted in dirt squares along the sidewalk. She knew it was petty, to hold onto things from high school. It's not like she didn't know how stupid she was being. She pulled her hand away.

Looking worried, Evan cast around for another topic. "How's your brother?"

Chelsea knew how to play the small talk game. Her mother had raised her on its merits. "Fine. Manages a bank back east. Three kids. Stay-at-home wife. Kelly."

"So he lives on It's-Still-1957 street?" He raised his glass.

Chelsea clinked her glass against it. "He's always been the good child."

"Judy told me she doesn't think he could possibly have moved farther away."

Chelsea widened her eyes in mock surprise. "Outrageous. There are six other continents!"

"Poor Judy."

Chelsea fell silent. Evan's expression held an echo of the distant look he used to get in high school when people talked about their mothers. Evan's mom had died when he was eleven. Cancer. Peggy had moved in when he was fifteen, worked overtime to play catch up but there had simply been too much ground to cover. Still, he had always played the dead mom card when it came to her and Judy. Why couldn't he ever just let her be mad at her very-much-alive-and-annoyingly-controlling mother?

She took a long drink before asking, "How is Peggy?"

He frowned. "I hear she's good."

"She's not with your dad anymore?"

He signaled for another round. "Not for about a decade now."

They would have to do this at some point. It might as well be now. Fill in the more than two and a half decades they were out of each other's lives. There were certain things that once belonged to them that no longer did. Things that had been theirs weren't theirs anymore. It happened to so many people, throughout time, across cultures, Chelsea knew she had no right to grieve their small story in particular as if they were special. They weren't. But she felt it anyway, that wash of grief for not knowing even the simplest of things about Evan now when she used to know so much. As a teenager he ate Sour Patch Kids mixed into his strawberry yogurt, had an almost allergic reaction to Pearl Jam, and housed a secret love for John Hughes movies even if he pretended not to with most people. Especially the goofy ones, like *Planes, Trains and Automobiles* and *Mr. Mom*. What movies did he watch now? Did Eddie Vedder's voice still make him want to stab out his own ears?

"I'm sorry about the band," Chelsea offered, finally, when their new beers had arrived. After all, he'd brought it up. Well, he kind of brought it up.

To her surprise, he laughed. "Right, the fucking band."

During sophomore year at Imperial Flats Evan had started a band called Sunset Dark. They played a strange blend of styles, Americana laced with grunge laced with brass. They had all been geeky band kids growing up, classically trained. Sunset Dark started like any band: a garage, some private houses, a few local venues, but then they had branched out to Sacramento and Tahoe and even wider. By senior year, they had weekend gigs as far as San Jose and then in the years following high school, *Rolling Stone* included them in a bands-to-watch round-up and they grew bigger. And bigger.

They played venues in San Francisco. Los Angeles. Then, rumors of a record deal. But Evan had a falling out with his bandmate, Denny Bliss, and before any ink found a contract, Evan gave the rest of the band an ultimatum. Him or Denny. They chose Denny. Lawyers got involved. Evan got some sort of piddly buy-out and he walked away. A couple of years later, Sunset Dark exploded. In a few more years, they were selling out stadium tours. Chelsea watched a documentary about them on Netflix a couple of years ago. She wouldn't admit it to Evan, but she had five or six of their songs on her regular Spotify rotation.

"It's okay." He waved off her concerned look. "No, really. I'm okay. Want to know what I learned after ten years of therapy? That band is not my band. And I'm okay." His expression soured enough to show he would need another decade of therapy before any of that was true.

"*You* named them."

"It's a stupid name. Sunset Dark? What a bunch of assholes we were." He fiddled with a half-eaten onion ring on the plate in front of him.

"Do you talk to any of them?"

"Denny never returned any of my emails. After a while, I just stopped trying. A guy's gotta have some pride."

"I'm pretty sure Denny Bliss never reads his emails. He probably has, like, twenty people for that sort of thing. Besides, I heard his third wife left him already." Chelsea gave it a beat. "I think it was getting in the way of her Girl Scout Cookie sales. She was, like, a top-seller."

Evan burst out laughing, his green eyes lighting as they caught hers. The 19-year-old supermodel Denny married last year was young even for Denny standards. "Wow, that was classic Chelsea Garden. Thanks for that." He shook his head. "Full disclosure: there's not enough therapy in the world to take away all the bitter."

"Of course not. Gandhi would chuck Denny off his yacht."

Evan ran his hand through his hair. "At least they're not allowed to play 'Sunlight Girl' and that was our all-time best song anyway."

She didn't point out that he said *our*. "Well, that's something."

"Yes."

She watched him take another gulp of beer. "And now you're teaching at Imperial Flats. Connect those dots for me."

He winced, setting down his glass. "Well, I was basically on the ten-year plan at Sonoma State in my thirties and finally managed to get my credential during Covid when all my paying music gigs dried up." He drained the last of his beer. "Then my dad got sick."

"I heard that. I'm so sorry, Evan."

"Yeah, for a while I tried to commute up here to keep an eye on him, but he really can't live by himself full-time anymore. So, when the music teacher job came up last year, I jumped on it."

"And now you're home."

"Home. Right." He ate the last sweet potato fry. "And so are you."

"I'm not, not really. Just taking a little break."

"For Thanksgiving?"

"Maybe longer." Hearing it out loud suddenly made it true.

"Want to order more food and tell me about it?"

She shook her head. She wasn't ready to get into what was next for her, especially not with Evan. Not right now. Should she sue Mr. King-Jennings like Stone and Leila thought she should? Should she look for a new teaching job? Or should she just quit education, move to a far-flung British isle, and waitress at a seaside restaurant? (Now she was just stealing ideas from the novels she read). Because she truly had no idea. And sitting here was only making her more anxious.

She wished she could blame the fizzy mess of her stomach on the beer and fried food.

"I should probably get back. Diego was making an elaborate breakfast dough of some kind when I dropped off the groceries, and I feel like I should help him."

"Because you know something about elaborate breakfast dough?"

"Not really."

He waited for her to say more, then held up his credit card to flag the waitress. "Okay, but we're doing this again soon. We didn't get to talk about you at all. Next time, it's your turn." Surprised, Chelsea watched him sign the check, waving off her offer to help. The lines around his eyes seemed suddenly mysterious. The old Evan would never have noticed they hadn't talked much about her. And he sure as hell wouldn't have paid the bill.

EVAN

Evan eased his aging Honda into park along the curb. As he turned off the ignition, his eyes strayed to the window where Chelsea had done all that damage with the beer cans years ago. His dad had been so pissed, his voice raging through the pay phone from the lot of some club where Evan was supposed to play the first gig of his adult life.

"Goddamn beer cans!" Frank had shouted. "Fucking glass everywhere! Your friends better fucking pay up!"

Evan knew it had been Chelsea, but he hadn't wanted Frank to find out, so he'd sent money home to cover the damage. A third of what he'd saved up to make it through the summer. Earlier, at Gold Rush, he'd tried to play it off like he couldn't fathom why she might have done something like that, like he couldn't even *remember*, but of course he knew, of course he remembered. He'd been carrying it around his whole adult life, all that broken glass rattling around in his psyche. He'd earned every one of those cans.

As he slammed the car door, he heard the clang of a shovel hitting stone and realized his dad was in the side yard again. He crossed the lawn and rounded the corner where he found him leaning his weight onto the blade of a half-buried shovel.

"Whatcha up to, Dad?"

Sweat dotted Frank's flushed face, a few strands of white hair floating about his head with the exertion. Four fresh mounds of dirt dotted the lawn around him. He must have been at it most of the hour Evan was at the bar with Chelsea.

"Fence," Frank wheezed. "Gotta get it in before the roses bloom or the damn deer will be at 'em."

Evan had discovered it was better to play along than try to explain they'd lost the roses years ago. "Yeah, good idea. But take a break for dinner, okay? I got your favorite soup at the store today."

Frank took another pass with the shovel. "Goddamn it, gotta—*oof*," he paused, one foot on the blade, breathing heavily. Evan waited. This could go several different ways, escalating until Frank started yelling and throwing the shovel, or he could decide to stalk off down the street, which would take at least a half hour of coaxing to get him back inside. Or he could give up. Evan never dreamed there'd be a day when this last option was the one he'd root for, but he couldn't ignore the shimmer of triumph that surged through his body when Frank left the shovel half-buried and followed him inside.

In the kitchen, Evan opened a can of soup and poured it into the waiting pan. It was the only thing his father would eat for dinner. Progresso chicken noodle soup. He'd managed to find a low sodium version that Frank wouldn't hurl across the room, but he worried about the daily diet: Grape-Nuts for breakfast with half a banana and two percent milk. For lunch, a ham sandwich (white bread, slice of American cheese, yellow mustard) with Fritos. Soup for dinner with Ritz crackers. Every damn day. And two fudge pops in front of a rotating variety of cop shows or, paradoxically, a select group of animated children's movies.

Peggy had been the one to let him know how bad things had gotten. She was such a peach, had continued to check up on Frank for the past decade even if she couldn't bear to live with him anymore. Who could blame her? Evan was only here because of a gluey mix of filial guilt and lack of finances. It pained him to admit it, but he needed this particular roof over his head. Mid-life was thick with irony. He couldn't have run faster from this house as a teenager, appalled by the cheap motel art on the walls and outdated carpet. It had a white picket fence, for Chrissake. He'd been arrogant and young enough to see his small-town life as a prison instead of what it really was: secure, easy, privileged, even in its lower-middle-class shabbiness, even with the specter of his father's unspoken grief in every corner. The cabinets had been stocked with food. The electricity was never shut off. His dad was a regular brand of asshole, but he'd always had a job, had always made sure Evan had stuff.

Chelsea had pointed all of this out in high school once. He'd been smoking a cigarette in the backyard, bitching about some fight he'd gotten into with Frank about wanting a new amp for his guitar and she'd cut him off.

"Do you ever get bored with what a cliché you are?" Chelsea could say those sorts of things and make them sound like love letters. He didn't know how she did it. Walking away from the pub tonight, he'd had to stop suddenly and lean against a bike rack, his chest tightening. Seeing her had been like opening a locked box from under the bed and finding—what? A stack of cash? The coil of a snake? Whatever it was, Evan hadn't felt it in years.

"Dinner!" He set the cracker box on the table, then distributed the soup into a pair of blue bowls, making sure not to give his dad the one with the chip. He settled into his designated chair. He wasn't hungry but didn't feel like fighting a battle about it tonight. His dad didn't understand that Evan might have eaten somewhere else.

Frank padded into the kitchen and took a seat. "Smells good."

Same thing every night.

Cliché or not, Evan might lose his fucking mind.

* * *

Evan wasn't anywhere near sleep when the text lit up his bedside, but it startled him. He scrambled for the phone. Violet. She wasn't supposed to be using her phone this late, but Evan still grinned at the puppy meme she sent. He texted back: *you should be sleeping*

Vi: *Puppy in a bow tie!!!!!*

He scooted back against the headboard, texting: *Very cute.* And then: *Go to sleep*

Vi: *Night daddy!!!!!!!!!!*

He sent her a heart emoji before pulling up Lauren's number and typing: *why the fuck is our nine-year-old daughter texting me at midnight?*

Then he deleted it. He didn't have the energy to fight with Lauren tonight. He set his phone back on the nightstand, watching a slow, curved stripe of headlights move across his bedroom window, the neighbor's car pulling in next door. She came home at almost the exact same time each night, after her shift at the pizza place where she waited tables. Evan was often awake for her return. During the day, he stayed busy with school, with Frank's schedule, with the gym or running or playing his guitar, even if that was rare lately. At night, though, he couldn't settle. The night hours tangled him in the seemingly endless loose ends of his adult life. Not just the band, his whole dodgy career. Not to mention the disintegration of his relationships. Including what was likely his most important: Violet. Why hadn't he told Chelsea about Violet?

Everyone assumed the worst thing to ever happen to Evan

had been Sunset Dark. And, sure, that was awful. But that was public shame. There was even a Netflix documentary about it he had declined to participate in or even watch. On good days, he could almost imagine it had happened to someone else. And because it was so long ago, because in certain circles he could glibly play it off as not his fault or that he didn't want to sell out, it was a distant pain, the throbbing of an old injury that only flared when the weather got particularly dreary. It was nothing compared to Violet.

Of course, he'd tried to create that same bubble of explanation (excuses) around her, too. He'd been traveling so much for his music, focusing on his career, trying to scrape a college degree together here and there, all the time sending as much money as he could manage to Violet's mother. Things had been so difficult with Lauren from the start. She'd never made things easy. And they'd only been kind-of-together for about six months when she got pregnant. But the truth was, all these years he'd accepted her version of who he was to Violet. Had let it be the reason he missed holidays or forgot what grade she was in. He was busy leading a musician's life. Feast or famine. You took everything or you ended up with nothing. At least, that was what he told himself during those years on the road. Industries loved their own mythology.

The truth was he had neglected Violet. And, maybe, to a certain extent, Lauren. During their battles, Lauren liked to trot out her half-finished psych degree. They'd met in an undergraduate writing class at Sonoma State, both on the decade plan like so many adults with jobs and kids or a certain brand of aimlessness, but whereas Evan finally finished both his undergraduate degree in music and his teaching credential, she never finished anything. Which had somehow also become Evan's fault. Each fight had been a variation of why-Evan-was-an-egomaniac-with-fucked-up-priorities.

In the last of these fights, standing in the pale evening light of her kitchen, after Evan had driven four hours through traffic to Santa Rosa for what he thought was Violet's ninth birthday party only to discover he'd gotten the days mixed up and the party had happened the day before, Lauren had offered a scalding summary of his life as she'd scrubbed a pan that had long ago been clean:

"You have only, ever, been in service to yourself, Evan. You have only, ever, worked toward advancing your own needs and your own career and never the needs of the people who love you, who need you to pay attention!" Her auburn curls kept escaping the messy bun on top of her head as her rage escalated the way it always did.

"Your outlandish ego fucked things up with Denny, and then it continued to fuck things up with every other professional environment you found yourself in. You were so busy trying to prove yourself, so busy name-dropping that you met *someone* at some *special* club, making sure to tell us they mentioned how talented you are, how cool you are. As if we should all just believe these accounts when we saw no proof of it in real-time. You were always trying to tie yourself up in all this exterior specialness. But even that wasn't enough, right? That manager was an idiot. That band had sub-par musicians. That club didn't pay enough. It was always something."

She had turned then, fixed her furious dark eyes on him. "But you never stopped to ask if that something was you." Before he could argue, she started back up. This was Lauren's shining strength: her sheer fucking stamina.

"You're going to wake up one day and look around at your life and realize you spent all your time chasing the wrong things." She had more to say, he knew she did, but he'd heard it all before, and by then he was already in his car, getting on the freeway, heading back to Imperial Flats.

He thought now of his father asleep in the room down the quiet hall and he clamped two hands over his churning stomach. After everything he'd gone through with Frank, he'd somehow still managed to become a second-generation regular brand of asshole to his only child. Probably eighty percent of their relationship was composed of texting YouTube videos and memes and now she was nine years old.

How had he let this happen?

* * *

Thanksgiving morning, Evan got up early and laced up his running shoes. He ran toward the high school, making several loops around the track before heading up into the hills behind the school and cutting down through the ranch-style houses on the other side. Eventually he found himself running the length of Macintosh Road. Chelsea's uncle lived on Macintosh. As he slowed to a stop by Kyle's house, he tried to think of this route as accidental and not as the blossoming of a latent stalker-instinct.

"Evan?" Kyle was on his porch in a pair of pajama bottoms and a Cal sweatshirt, a rolled-up newspaper in his hand.

Evan hadn't seen him. "Oh, hey—Happy Thanksgiving!" He feigned some runner stretches, like he had just happened to stop his run to stretch out a quad, that he had stopped in front of this particular house by pure accident. He was pretty sure Kyle wasn't buying it.

Kyle took several steps closer. "She's sleeping right now."

"Right, sure. It's early."

Kyle squinted at him. "You guys doing a holiday concert this year?"

"December fifth." Evan thought the jazz band was doing a particularly good job, especially since he only had eleven students in that class. "We'll be in the Little Theatre."

Kyle tapped the paper against his thigh. "It's great you're doing that. The kids are lucky."

Evan shrugged, uncomfortable. He wasn't sure they were all that lucky. Their instruments were falling apart, and they were still wearing the same tuxes and black dresses from the late 1990s. It made Evan alternately sad and furious. He'd actually reached out to Denny at the end of last year just to see if he'd donate something, anything. He'd been the bass in the jazz band for four years after all. But nothing. What a dick.

"You got plans today? You want to come in for some cinnamon bread? Diego made it."

Kyle's offer was tempting, but his sympathetic look was killing Evan. "I'm with my dad today, so we're set. I should probably take off, trying to get in five miles before he wakes up."

Kyle gave him a wave with the newspaper. Definitely not buying it.

As Evan set out toward home, a memory of being with Chelsea in Kyle's backyard crept in. Fall of senior year. Out past the patio on a patch of damp grass under the stars. She'd just broken up with some jerk from the soccer team, a tall blond who fancied himself a drummer in his spare time, even if Evan knew better. Chelsea'd been crying because she'd caught him at a party in a bedroom with some dark-haired, doe-eyed girl, who Evan thought seemed like a blurry photo-copied version of Chelsea. Evan had picked her up and driven them to Kyle's, who was away for the weekend. They'd grabbed a couple of wine coolers from the fridge and a blanket and stretched out under the stars.

As he ran, Evan remembered how the starlight had magnified the streaks of tears on her cheeks. He'd been rubbing her back the way they did for each other, so much touching and cuddling and nearness, but never anything more, never anything that could tip into that overtly sexual area they were always willing to venture into with other people but never each other. Except that night, in Kyle's backyard, he'd found himself wiping away her tears, then kissing them, and then they were on the ground, and her body was warm across his and he was kissing her mouth and she was definitely kissing him back, and his hand was under her shirt. He'd always loved Chelsea's body, definitely more than you're supposed to love a friend's body, but he'd tried to chalk it up to admiration. All her muscular curves and long hair and her soft skin, like swimming in water one degree warmer than your own body. No one had skin like Chelsea's.

But then a light had gone on in the neighbor's yard. The old lady who lived next door had thrown open her window, peering out at them. "Hey, hey!" she'd shouted, and they'd scooped up their blanket, their empty bottles, Evan cracking up, Chelsea muttering *holy shit holy shit holy shit* over and over as they'd hightailed it back to Evan's car. She never brought it up, so he didn't either and then it was just this thing neither of them talked about for the rest of the year.

He stopped in front of his house, breathing hard, leaning over to grip the top of his knees, knowing this wasn't the first time over the years he'd thought of the starlight on her cheeks that night, knowing he'd spent too many years searching for something, anything, that felt like her skin.

* * *

"Happy Thanksgiving!"

Violet's voice had the same effect on him every time. His chest squeezed; his head began to throb. Regret was such a sticky, physical thing.

"Hey, kiddo." He swallowed and pushed the sliding door open, stepping onto the back patio, leaving his dad watching the flickering light of the TV behind him. "You at Grandma's?"

"Yeah. Grandpa didn't start shouting until after dinner. Mom said it was a personal record for him."

He smiled, could hear Lauren's voice in his daughter's, could faintly make out the sounds of Lauren's family in the background of the call. His smile soured. "You hanging in there?"

"Oh, sure."

After each of the two Thanksgivings he'd spent with Lauren's family, he'd felt battle-weary. At the first one, he'd narrowly missed getting hit in the head with a stemless wine glass her sister Cassidy had thrown. Not at him. At her husband. She had terrible aim. And, at the second holiday, he'd taken eighteen-month-old Violet out for a walk after Lauren and her father had spiraled into a screaming match about Lauren's "questionable financial decisions," and Evan had made the mistake of partly seeing her dad's point. Needless to say, he didn't miss dinners with Lauren's family.

Honestly, he didn't miss Lauren, which probably made him the terrible person she was always accusing him of being. But he missed Violet the way you noticed an absent front tooth.

"Dad?"

"Yeah?"

"Mom said I'm going to live with you now."

Evan froze, his eyes scanning the bare yard. "Wait, what?"

Violet sighed in that way children with messy parents do. Too old for her age. Too aware. "She said I'm going to live with you. When? Can I come now?"

Fucking Lauren. They'd been discussing it more over the last few months. If you could call what Lauren did *discussing*. Now that he wasn't on the road anymore, now that he had a house and a steady job, maybe he could take Violet for a while? Scratch that. There'd been no maybe. He'd just never thought she'd actually let Violet live with him. She was too controlling, too mercurial. But Violet wasn't happy at her school, had been asking Lauren for a change.

"Let me check on that, okay, sweetie? Could you put your mom on the phone?"

Violet called out loudly, then some shuffling, the slamming of a door, then Lauren came on with a "Yeah?" like she had no idea why he was asking to talk to her.

"What the actual hell, Lauren?"

"Happy Thanksgiving to you, too." He heard her exhale. She'd lit a cigarette. She must be outside now. No way her mother would let her smoke in the house.

"Vi said she's going to live with me?"

"Sure, we talked about it."

"But we hadn't decided anything."

"We did." Another exhale. "Are you fucking backing out?"

"I can't back out of something we never agreed to in the first place!" Evan cut his gaze to his dad, who had clearly heard Evan's outburst, had tipped forward in his chair, was watching him now with a worried expression. Evan waved at him, tried to smile. He knew better than to argue, knew to just play her game. "Fine, Lauren. It's probably best if we wait until after the holidays so she can settle in after the break."

"You don't think I know that? Like I would pull her out of school before break?"

"Right. Mother of the Year. Sorry."

"Fuck you, Evan."

"Fine. We can talk details at Christmas."

"We're going to be in England for Christmas."

"England?"

"The *country*."

Evan's heart began to whirl. "I know what England is."

"Good. Because I'm moving there." A pause. "I met someone." And suddenly it all made sense.

NORA

Nora always hated fighting with her ex (she had enough conflict at school), but she especially resented fighting with him on Thanksgiving. It seemed so obvious. Besides, their son was spending the break with his girlfriend's family back east, so why was she even tolerating this phone call in the first place? Wasn't one of the best things about divorce *not* having to fight on a holiday?

"I'm not sure what you want me to do about it," she repeated for what must have been the fifth time, adjusting her position on the floor where she was attempting to stretch out her aching back. Too much time in front of the laptop.

"Maybe I don't need to be paying for his phone if he can't be bothered to text me back on goddamn Thanksgiving!" Craig had a terrible habit of drumming his fingers on the side of his phone when he was frustrated. It was what a migraine sounded like. "I'm sorry if I thought his mother would understand."

When had Craig gotten so petty? These last few years, she barely recognized him anymore. "It seems to me like you're letting it ruin your day. Aren't you in Maui? What does Sarah think about this call anyway?" Last Nora checked, Craig's new wife didn't much like it when he ran to Nora each time he wasn't getting what he wanted from their twenty-year-old son.

"She's at the spa."

Nora picked some lint from the knees of her leggings. She'd gotten better at pushing aside the stab of disgust that shot through her every time she thought about Craig and Sarah, but she wasn't interested in hearing how luxurious his life was with her. Sarah was sixth-generation small-town privilege. With their many properties and large patches of land holdings all over the county, it seemed like the Crocker family owned half of Imperial Flats.

"Craig, I have to go." If she hurried, she could change into her dress and still make it in time for the appetizers at Romano's. Dani Romano had been one of Nora's favorite students when she'd taught Government at Imperial Flats decades ago. Dani had been a senior during Nora's first year at IFH. Her family owned Romano's Italian Restaurant, had for three generations, and now Dani managed it. What had started as a few coffee dates between a teacher and her former student had grown over the years into one of Nora's most cherished friendships. Each year, Dani shut down the restaurant on Thanksgiving and invited family and close friends to an enormous multi-course meal, just as her parents had for decades. It was one of the highlights of Nora's year.

"I'm late to Thanksgiving," she added.

"You can't be late to a Romano's Thanksgiving. It's just one continuous free-for-all. They won't even notice when you get there."

Another plus in the divorce category was supposed to be attending Romano's Thanksgiving without Craig complaining the entire night. At least now, she could hang up on it. "Bye, Craig."

* * *

Nora closed her eyes for a moment each time she stepped into Romano's Italian Restaurant, to breathe in the mix of oregano, red wine, and lemony furniture polish that had settled into each nook of the place over the last half-century. She paused for longer than usual this time, breathed in, out, then in again. Lately, Nora craved longevity most of all.

When Leo had left for college in Ohio after high school, she'd felt a crush of sadness and pride and relief. Together, she and Craig had raised this human up to eighteen, a human who read the *New York Times* and cared about things like composting and jazz and going to college to study economics. Sure, during his high school years he'd been prone to dark silences, and she'd felt in constant competition with his phone for his attention, but these triumphs were a feat in a place like Imperial Flats. She was proud of him. Then, Craig had come home that same September after Leo'd gone and said he was leaving, too, that he'd fallen in love with Sarah Crocker, that he wanted to marry her. Nora hadn't realized he even *knew* Sarah Crocker. He was sorry, he'd told her. It had just "happened," as if falling in love was like a fender bender, a momentary lapse of attention.

And then Craig was gone, too, and Nora found herself alone in the sprawling house. Her son gone. Her husband gone. Even her sweet spaniel mix had died several months later of cancer because apparently the universe was just doling out its Nora-related shit all at once.

Now somehow Leo was almost halfway through college and her husband was calling from Maui with his new wife and she was at another Thanksgiving as a single woman. This year, though, she might be okay. She was breathing. For a long while, she hadn't been sure she'd make it through. The year following Craig's announcement and the divorce was a murky time that had reminded Nora of the first year of Leo's life, when the birth of that tiny, wrinkled creature had twisted her world into knots. She'd never felt so helpless, so confused, as she had staring into Leo's tiny newborn face. How could she have spent years teaching 200 teenagers a day, but ten pounds of brand-new human made her doubt every choice? Leo barely slept for a year, and so Nora had barely slept for a year. Craig would come home from his engineering office to her sobbing on the blue couch, Leo howling in her lap.

That year, though, with both men gone, she realized there would be no one to come home to find her in tears.

Except Dani had come. She'd arrived with lasagna, with Caesar salads, with wine, with chocolate. "My family feeds a crisis," she'd explained, pouring jeweled liquid into glasses, then humming to herself as she washed dishes while Nora sat at the breakfast bar, staring blankly into the emptiness of her future.

"Nora!" Dani hurried across the room, a full glass of wine at the ready.

"Sorry I'm late. Craig called from Hawaii."

"Ugh. No-*mahalo*." She pushed the glass into Nora's hand and signaled Marco, her oldest, to bring over the tray he was passing around. "Mini roasted-tomato tarts."

"Thanks, Marco." Nora popped one in her mouth, a buttery burst of bright tomato hitting her. "Mmm."

"Dad made them," Marco beamed. "Great, right?" He waited for Nora to nod before moving away.

Dani's kids were well-mannered, hard-working, proud of their family. In his last few years at home, Leo had mostly made it a point to ignore what she did for a living. Unless he needed a hall pass or an excuse for missing a Zoom class during that last year.

"Your kids are so sweet," she said to Dani.

"To other people." Dani watched her son cross the room. "Which I guess is what we want." She chewed one of the tarts. "Just don't ask him where he's applying to college. He might bite you."

"Still doesn't want to leave?"

She shook her head. "He wants to work here, but Bert told him he can always work here. We basically forced him to apply to three state schools this month and we're working on a few culinary options. Bert wants him to get out of the Flats for a while."

Nora adored Dani's husband, Bert Jones. He hadn't grown up here, either. Dani had met him when he was hired on in her dad's kitchen. Now he was head chef. Like Nora, he'd grown up in Los Angeles, and, also like Nora, worried that the kids here ended up with a too-narrow view of the world.

"He can always talk to Leo."

"Yeah, I think they connect on Instagram and all that, thanks." Dani's eyes darted away. As much as Nora and Dani had tried over the years, Marco and Leo had never been close. Both mothers pretended it was the age difference.

Nora sipped her wine. In the geometry of teenage boys, she'd mostly found that any sense of parental control was imagined or manufactured. "It's ultimately his choice."

Dani squeezed Nora's arm. "Not if Bert has anything to do with it."

A crash from the kitchen pulled them toward the crowd of people in the main room. Everyone turned to find a sheepish James, Dani's fourteen-year-old son, emerging from the kitchen splattered in what looked like mashed potatoes. "Mom?"

Dani closed her eyes for a moment. "Excuse me," she murmured to Nora, "I have to go murder someone," and disappeared into the kitchen after him.

Nora surveyed the crowd over her wine glass, her eyes falling on a familiar face. Toby Cameron again. He caught her eye and smiled, almost nervously, and raised his own glass of wine. Interesting. Maybe this was the Toby she saw at Imperial Market when he suggested the delicious wine, and not the man who always seemed to get her back up during board meetings.

She decided to play nicely in the sandbox and moved across the room to him. "What are you doing here on Thanksgiving?"

His forced smile faltered. "You haven't heard, I guess. I thought maybe you hadn't when I saw you the other night." He cleared his throat. "Elizabeth left me."

"What?" Nora didn't bother to try masking her shock.

"A couple of months ago."

"I'm so sorry, Toby. I had no idea."

"Neither did I." He tried to play it off casually, with a quick grin, but his hand shook. He set down his wine on a nearby table.

Her cheeks burned. "And I made the crack about date night at the market—"

He waved her off. "You didn't know. I was going to see some friends. They were trying to cheer me up."

"Did they?"

"Not really."

Nora stared into her wine, speechless. The Camerons were the kind of family who sent out yearly Christmas cards with everyone, including their two Labradoodles, grinning into the camera wearing complimenting shirts, sometimes plaid, sometimes denim, in front of a fire and a meticulously decorated Christmas tree. Nora had received various versions of this card for the five years Toby had been on the school board. They sent out beautiful graduation announcements and held parties by a pool landscaped to look like a lagoon. Elizabeth Cameron seemed like the kind of woman who had already pre-ordered custom grandmother boxes on Etsy for her assumed future grandbabies. Nora would never have pegged her as the one to leave. "How are the girls?"

"Surprised, hurt. Kaylee is handling it the best, but I mean, who wants to find out her mother is moving to Hawaii with her yoga teacher?"

"No!"

"Sadly, yes. We are officially a middle-aged cliché."

Hawaii didn't deserve its current batch of Californians. "Where are the girls now?"

Toby shook his head. "Paige and Kaylee are here somewhere. And Emma's in Colorado with her boyfriend. At their condo." He lowered his voice, took a step closer. "Paige isn't even talking to Liz. Won't return any of her calls." As if summoned, Toby's youngest daughter walked by, her blond hair in a messy knot, carrying a bottle of white wine. "Paige." Toby's voice held a warning.

"It's for Bert's grandmother." Paige showed him the label, which read DOLORES. "They mix white grape juice and water in with it, so she doesn't drink too much." Nora watched her cross the room to where Bert's ninety-two-year-old grandmother sat in a straight back chair, blinking into the dim light, her hand clamped around an empty wine glass. Hanging behind her on the wall, a sign read: *Please only give Dolores HER wine!*

Nora watched Paige fill Dolores's glass halfway. She looked the most like Elizabeth of all the girls, only she had Toby's dark, heavily-lashed eyes. Somehow the combination gave her a suggestion of mystery, a faint wildness she'd always seemed like she was trying to live up to.

Nora struggled to think of something to say. "I didn't realize you knew Dani and Bert?"

Toby gestured toward Paige. "She just started working for them. And I'm in Rotary with Bert." Nora had heard through Leo that Paige had been partying a lot last year at UCSB, that she might not go back for her sophomore year.

Leo and Paige weren't terribly close, but they'd shared friends in high school. Nora gave Toby a curious look to see if he'd elaborate.

He picked up his wine again. "I don't think college will be her path. At least not right now."

"It's not for everyone."

"Her first year was—" he paused, his brow furrowing. "Rough."

"These kids have had such a difficult time reintegrating. It might take years. And last year wasn't normal. Still so much Zoom, all the masking requirements. It was a lot." Nora had said this so many times, she hoped it didn't sound rehearsed.

Toby nodded. "She decided to try again this year. We got her signed up, packed the car, and she drove down. We thought maybe if she had a more normal start, but then everything fell apart with Liz, and, well, Paige just wanted to come home." She didn't miss the flash of anger behind his eyes. Meant for Liz, she was sure, and not his daughter.

"Of course, she did. It's so shocking!"

"I'm grateful I got most of my money back."

That sounded more like the Toby she knew. Still, she put her hand on his arm. "I'm truly sorry, Toby."

She was surprised at the gloss of tears in his eyes, and he seemed relieved when Dani pushed through the kitchen door, hollering, "All right, sit down, everyone!"

* * *

Sunday afternoon, Nora had just poured a glass of wine and settled onto her couch with her current book club selection when her phone rang. She closed her eyes briefly at the ribbon of dread curling through her that came with the last remaining hours of a break. She reached for her phone on the coffee table.

Dean Moreno. Shit. "Hi Dean."

"Oh, hey, Nora, sorry to call on a Sunday."

She took a small sip of wine. "It's fine. Did you have a good holiday?"

"Er, well, that's what I wanted to talk to you about."

"Okay."

"Carrie and I talked a lot over the last few days and, well, I decided, or we decided—"

Nora waited. She could hear him swallowing some water or something. Vodka? "Dean?"

"Thing is, Nora, I haven't been happy teaching for a while; honestly, I don't think I ever found my footing again after that year on Zoom. And Carrie's parents need help at the law firm. Anyway, I decided that I'm going to leave teaching at the end of the semester and work for them, spend some time with my kids. I might go back to school, finish that law degree I started before I got my credential, I don't know yet, but I'm just ready to do something else." He ended with a whoosh of air, of relief. Nora could feel it through the phone.

She had been on the receiving end of so many of these sighs. She was starting to think they had, over all these years, lodged somewhere in her joints. Prickles of pain started behind Nora's eyes. She didn't have the energy for any more of these conversations. Who was she to convince him to stay? "I understand, Dean. Come in tomorrow after school and we'll talk about next steps."

"Right, okay." He hesitated. "I'm sorry, Nora. I know I'm letting the school down by not finishing the year, but I just—can't."

Nora clicked off the phone. *Shit.*

CHELSEA

In college, Chelsea had written a paper for a psychology class called, "A Brief History of Chelsea and Evan: A Tragi-Comedy of High School Proportions." They had been discussing "love patterns" and reading a book that mostly mined their childhoods for things that highlighted reasons they might choose certain lovers or be attracted to a particular kind of person. It was a New-Agey class, but Chelsea had secretly loved it, even as she nodded along to its naysayers who made fun of the professor with her floor-length hippie skirts and dangling macramé earrings. Over the years, every time Chelsea swapped out her laptop or updated her files, she saved that paper into a newer file, but she had never re-read it.

After driving back to Kyle's Wednesday evening, her body buzzing with the beers she'd had with Evan, with the jumble of emotions from seeing him again after so long, Chelsea pulled out her laptop and opened the file for the first time in decades. Cross-legged on the bed, she cringed a bit at that title, and then more than a bit at the first line.

**A Brief History of Chelsea and Evan:
A Tragicomedy of High School Proportions**

Chelsea Garden
Professor Beneventi

I met the love of my life in line for nachos. Actually, the whole Nacho-Line Meeting pretty much encapsulates my entire relationship with Evan Dawkins. It was fall of freshman year at Imperial Flats High School. The leaves had just started to turn gold and orange and red and the temperatures at night were finally dropping. I had a scarf on. I remember this detail because Evan commented on it. Midway through standing in the ridiculously long line for dramatically average nachos, he sauntered up with his green eyes and *that smile* and asked, "Aren't we in English together?" Then he added, in pure Evan fashion, "Nice scarf." Some girls would have taken this in stride. Cute boy. Compliment. They would have flipped their hair and flashed a coy smile back and said something charming. I am not most girls. I started to black out, mustering a response that must have been something like "er, um, oh, erp," and then staring straight ahead to try to get the room to re-focus. Evan later insisted he found this adorable, which made me want to punch him, but the real indicator that I should have been more aware of at the time was that I ended up standing in line and buying both of us nachos while he hit on Calliope Beaumont over by the pizza window. Now, I want to scream at Freshman Chelsea, "Make him get his own nachos!"

Not that Evan wasn't there for me when I needed him. Most of the time. I mean, I spent more time with him than anyone else in high school, but he was never my boyfriend. So, what was he? Best friend? Worst enemy? Sometimes he was both in the same twenty minutes. We talked and laughed and argued about *everything*. It was never much of a physical relationship (with the exception of one strange night we never discussed), but eventually it was warm and often electric, and I never felt closer to anyone than when I was curled up on a couch watching a movie with Evan. When he wasn't smoking (he was perpetually in some phase of quitting), he smelled like pine and spice and cherries. Fresh ones. Not the cough-syrup-red-candy kind. He was a musician (I know, I'm a cliché!) and I would sit on his bed and listen to him practice his guitar for hours and hours. Sometimes, I think of how many books I could have read instead of listening to Evan play that guitar. But at the time, it was magic.

We went on like this for years. Evan worked his way through endless girlfriends that never lasted more than a month or two, and he played with his band. I had some boyfriends, but I spent most of my time hiding from them in the library or on the basketball court or listening to Evan's band (they were actually good, so it's not as pathetic as it sounds). Most musicians are total snobs, but Evan taught me a lot about how to listen to all music for what I *responded* to in it. He would always insist it wasn't about thinking something was good or bad, but rather about paying attention to the way the music triggered something deeper than that in me. I think about that a lot when I read too. How does this make me feel? Me. Not everyone else. Evan was pretty much the only person in my life who encouraged me to trust myself—to be the real *me* and not just what other people wanted me to be. Once, he bought me a book of poems he found on vacation because he knew I loved lighthouses and the book had a poem about a lighthouse. That gift always felt like what love should feel like.

But things fell apart at the end of senior year. A week before graduation, we had, at the risk of adding another layer of cliché to this essay, *a moment*. Evan showed up at my house and told me he was in love with me. Pure John-Cusack-style, sans the boom box. He stood on my lawn and cried and told me that he had wasted so much time. That he had been in love with me for years. That he wanted to be with me. But he was supposed to leave with his band the day after graduation. He always had such terrible timing. I didn't know what to say. I was so happy and furious at the same time. Because I knew I loved him, too. Except the only voice I could seem to find was for my fury. I kept yelling at him, telling him I couldn't believe he was doing this to me, after all this time. He didn't give up. He said we owed it to ourselves to sort this out. So, after some coaxing, I agreed to meet him at the lake and talk things out after graduation.

Only (yep, you guessed it) he never showed up. He left with his band the morning of graduation (he didn't even go to the ceremony!) and I haven't seen him since. We haven't even talked. It's a terrible thing. To be so close to someone for so many years and then never see him again. For months after he left, I felt like a ghost, an angry ghost, the ashes of our relationship clogging my brain.

Now, though, as I sit here writing this essay more than two years after his exit, I just feel confused and sad. My relationship with Evan has pretty much made me doubt all my other relationships with guys. I've never felt as happy with any of them as I did watching movies on Evan's couch. No one has bought me a book with a lighthouse poem. Or any other books, for that matter. And I've never felt as sad at the loss of them as I did that day at the lake when he didn't come.

Why is that?

She startled at a knock on the interior door of her room, the one that led to the main house. She wiped quickly at the tears on her cheeks. "Come in."

Kyle poked his head through the open door. "Hey, I was—oh! You okay?"

"Seeing ghosts, I guess."

"Evan?"

"I ran into him at Imperial Market."

"Ah." Kyle tossed a couple of pillows aside before sitting down next to her on the bed.

She shut her laptop. "Then we had a beer at Gold Rush Brew Pub."

Kyle grimaced. "Is it too much to want a chair with a back?"

"Right!? Thank you."

Kyle put a big hand on her knee. "Can I get you something? Tea? A lobotomy?"

"Yes, please. To both."

He hurried toward the open door, but turned back again, hesitating. "I don't suppose now would be a good time to tell you we're having dinner tomorrow at your parents' instead of here?"

Chelsea collapsed back on the bed. "You are killing me."

"I know, I'm sorry. It all happened so fast. You know your mother. She's like a S.W.A.T. team."

"You better bring me tea *and* cookies with that lobotomy!" she called after him.

* * *

There were no mashed potatoes. Not even sweet potatoes. But what Chelsea wanted was Yukon Golds whipped with butter and whole milk and salt. Apparently, that was too much to ask for on Thanksgiving at Matt and Judy's.

"Where are the potatoes?" she whispered to Kyle as they stood surveying her mother's intricately laid table. The turkey waited, perfectly carved, on its silver platter next to a bowl of homemade cranberry sauce and a massive green salad in a wooden bowl.

Diego placed his lemon-ginger Brussels sprouts in an open spot on the table. "I knew your mom was doing a carb-free something-or-other, but I didn't realize it applied to the rest of us?"

"So there won't be stuffing either?" Chelsea was starting to feel desperate, a teenage whine creeping into her voice. "I'm just supposed to eat turkey and salad and Brussels sprouts!? On Thanksgiving!? No offense, Diego; they look delicious."

Diego squeezed her arm. "I'll get the bottom of this." He disappeared into the kitchen.

Kyle peered into a covered basket, his face falling. "I was hoping for rolls."

Chelsea waited. "And?"

He shook his head. "Apples."

"What the fuck?"

Judy pushed through the kitchen door, carrying a bottle of white wine, Diego on her heels. "That's not appropriate language for Thanksgiving." She began to give everyone a single inch of wine.

"Are you saving it?" Kyle took the bottle from her, adding generously to Judy's meager pours.

"Not for me!" Judy held a hand over one of the glasses.

"Mom, are there potatoes?"

"Holidays aren't excuses to let healthy-eating patterns slip." Judy lit the candles.

Chelsea shot Kyle an exasperated look. "Except that's exactly what holidays are for."

"Oh, Chelsea. You will manage without potatoes." Her mother returned to the kitchen.

Chelsea sank into the chair with the largest glass of wine. At this point, she had spent enough time in conversation with friends, in therapy, in countless workshops, to understand that this was her mother's issue and not hers. Judy had always been at war with visible things—other people's parenting or sexual choices, their houses or cars or vacations or professions. She was a gold-medalist judger of everything that didn't fit her exact specifications. And most impactful, for Chelsea at least, was that she incessantly scrutinized other people's bodies.

Chelsea's therapist had suggested it could be the result of any number of things: the byproduct of an undisclosed trauma in Judy's childhood, a fixed mindset, or an overly controlling personality. Likely, it was a combination of all of those with a hefty dose of generational culture thrown in, each acting as a vigilant soldier in Judy's battle with maintaining a singular weight, a life-long obsession with *thinness*, that she wore as a badge of self-congratulatory honor. It was just that sitting here, at her mother's potato-less table, all of that knowledge vanished in an instant, and Chelsea was a sulky, hurt teenager again. What was it about ten minutes in a room with her mother that erased all the hard work she'd supposedly done and left her feeling like complete shit?

It seemed nothing would ever erase the years spent growing up believing that her mother's fierce compulsion was a direct result of Chelsea's own unruly body. She recalled sitting on her parents' bed as a junior in high school after a day of shopping—a brutal day of Judy frowning as she watched Chelsea struggle into pair after pair of size-ten jeans.

"That can't be right," Judy had insisted, double-checking the tag. "A *ten*?" Sitting on the bed that day, Chelsea had watched while Judy cut the tags out of her new clothes. "No need to advertise it," she'd murmured, maybe to herself (God, Chelsea hoped it had been to herself), but she'd heard it nonetheless, and it had become one of those sticky childhood memories she couldn't seem to shake, no matter how many hours she clocked in therapy.

Still, Chelsea had hoped in some far reach of her heart that her long absence had changed some of this for Judy, had forced her to perhaps reflect on what might have made Chelsea need to stay away for so long. Maybe it would even inspire Judy to do something dramatic, like eat a bagel. Except it was clearly still business as usual around here.

It had taken every ounce of courage Chelsea could muster to walk up that path today.

And now there were no potatoes.

Kyle leaned down next to her, whispered in her ear. "Just get through this, and after we'll go home and eat donuts."

* * *

Chelsea wiped the sweat from her forehead and tossed the towel into the bucket next to the sink. She had managed to get most of the way through FIT HIT (all caps!) before tiptoeing through the back door of the studio and catching her breath in the privacy of the dimly lit locker room. Years ago, Chelsea would have sailed through that workout. She'd been a gym rat for two decades before deciding she preferred a yoga studio to a regular gym. It had been better for her aching joints and mental health. But over the last year she'd even slipped out of that practice, often opting for long walks in the Sausalito hills or on Mt. Tam over anything formalized.

Even here, today, she'd grown annoyed when the otherwise lovely instructor had told them they needed to work off all those carbs from last week. That it was never too early to start thinking about their beach bodies. Chelsea could only imagine one of her social justice club teenagers sprinting to the front of the room to give the whole workout class a lecture.

"You want a beach body? Take your body and go to a beach!" she could hear one of them saying. Her heart ached at the thought of them.

Yesterday, she had called early for a sub and then emailed Sheryl Alexander her resignation. Twelve years and she ended her tenure with one line: *Please find a replacement for me.* She'd felt bold, empowered. How dare they suggest she ignore what had happened to her? She'd imagined, briefly, that Sheryl would call, apologize, tell her she should come back to school immediately.

Except Sheryl's curt reply had been: *We wish you the best, Chelsea.* So much for bravery.

Today, Chelsea awoke in the blue light before dawn filled with doubt, missing her students. She loved the small group she met with weekly at Grove, who put up posters around school and gave talks on how to reframe language to be more inclusive. "Can we talk about getting fit instead of getting thin?" Julia Jennings had asked during her disordered eating presentation to the physical education department as part of her senior project. "Can we talk about loving our bodies for what they are and not what they aren't?"

Teenagers often got a bad reputation. Lazy, entitled, self-absorbed. And sometimes that was true. But Chelsea loved them for their earnest belief that they could still change the world. She had thought that once, too.

When Julia was a freshman, she'd called Chelsea out on

body-shaming herself in class. "Ugh, not you, too, Ms. Garden!" She'd flipped her glossy red ponytail in disgust. "It's a body. The only one you've got. Be *kind* to it."

Chelsea had felt her cheeks flare. "Hey, the body started it," she'd tried to joke.

But Julia had only gone on to say, without a hint of cynicism, that the thing she hated most about our culture was its obsession with a certain kind of body, with its bizarre preference for *thinness*. How superficial, she'd spat. Who are we to comment on a body instead of getting to know the important stuff, the inside stuff? The soul! The mind! The heart! How *dare* we? She had quoted Chimamanda Ngozi Adichie and Jameela Jamil's podcast. She had pounded her desk. Chelsea had thanked Julia for her passionate input, had tried to get the class back on track, but she would never forget her student's indignant, disappointed eyes.

If only Chelsea could believe sweet Julia. If only she could think it was just a body, accept it, despite its socially constructed failings. Shrug off the many times she was told she was "a bigger girl" or that her slender brother could "afford" to eat dessert, the fact that she clearly *couldn't* punctuated in the arch of her angular mother's equally angular eyebrow.

In her rare gentler moments, her mother would insist that it wasn't Chelsea's fault; she just took after "that side of the family," never realizing that this sort of explanation only made it worse, that it made Chelsea the loser of a genetic lottery, that it made her body a failure.

Chelsea had spent so many years at war with her body, found herself cutting out the tags in her jeans and Googling the newest diet trend. Still, Julia's words had landed somewhere deep in her, had wriggled into some corner of her psyche and begun to bloom. Somewhere in the last year, Chelsea had felt a slowing of her steady stream of self-shame. *Fuck that*, she could hear the new voice whispering after she deleted a photo that showed too much of her chin, a photo that, despite all his new age-inclusiveness, Stone had insinuated wasn't "the most flattering" picture of her. In it, Chelsea had been caught laughing, a moment of joy. Still, she didn't retrieve the photo from the trash.

A doctor had given a talk at Grove last year about neuropathways, had talked about the metaphorical weight of those ingrained, established childhood lessons in self-worth, and Chelsea had sat in a folding chair in the front row, her eyes on her knees. Her pathways were WWI-level trenches, only instead of covered in tear gas and shit and blood, they were littered with Weight Watchers advertisements and exercise addiction. She couldn't remember a time she wasn't hyper-focused on portion control or food chemistry or fasting or finding the next diet. Those cycles of endless fucking diets, the continual awareness of every tiny thing going into her mouth.

She'd been a vegetarian. A vegan. A raw food devotee. Gluten-free. Paleo. Keto. If it was popular in the Bay Area at some point in the last twenty-five years, Chelsea had tried it. She'd cycled through Atkins and South Beach and Weight Watchers before diets went out of fashion and a new wave of "food mindfulness" just dusted off the same old pain and added glossy new packaging. With each new method, she would find herself more militant, more dogmatic, until finally, last spring, she'd driven straight to In-N-Out Burger, crying in her car for half an hour before stalking inside and ordering a Double-Double and a root beer. She sat at an outdoor table facing the freeway, chewing, thinking, her eyes finally dry. She was exhausted. Wasn't all this obsessive control over her diet, her body, her exercise regimen just her mother's ardent judgment and control wrapped in a new coat? Wasn't this ceaseless wrestling match with her body just another example of trying to please everyone else?

Enough was enough.

Chelsea took a deep breath as people began spilling into the locker room from the FIT HIT class. An older woman with closely cropped silver hair patted her shoulder.

"Don't worry, hon. It gets easier. Come back tomorrow."

* * *

Chelsea parked her car along the curb under a bare-limbed tree. She had driven to Dani's house hundreds of times throughout high school and college, and a few more times during her sporadic visits home, but somehow, being back here, parked beneath this maple, she felt more alien than ever. When Dani texted her out of the blue a few days ago, *heard you were back in town, come to book club*, Chelsea had quickly replied, *I'll be there!* before she could change her mind, but now she wondered if anyone had seen her pull up, would notice if she simply sped away down the street.

She turned off the engine, grabbing the bottle of Sauvignon Blanc that Diego had pushed into her hands as she walked out the door earlier. She ran her hand over the cover of Dani's book club selection, a Reese's Book Club selection she'd found endearing and sweet. Her heart thrummed as she walked the cement path to Dani's door. Silly. She knew how to do the whole book club thing. Had been doing it for years. Chelsea had joined and left more than a dozen book clubs in the last two decades. She knew what was expected of her. Which was, of course, part of the problem.

Because Chelsea had mostly given up talking about what books meant to her with other people. At dinners, at parties, at events outside of school and sometimes inside of school, even at clubs with "book" in the title (those seemed to be more about children or wine, often with accompanying You-

Tube videos about mothering and wine, than about books). In every interaction, Chelsea tried to nod along knowingly (maybe even bemusedly) with what seemed the inevitable joke of her life—that loving something like books was itself a sort of time warp, a failure to modern-up, as her friend Tess liked to joke over her third glass of Cab.

"Chels," Tess would say wryly, "the whole world is about what you can merchandise. Don't be so naïve—the Jane Austen T-shirt sells for more than the actual novel."

Every time Chelsea joined a new book club, it was an act of aggressive hope.

Chewing her lip, she rang Dani's doorbell, the chimes sounding through the house. A moment later, a woman with chunky blonde highlights and intricate make-up yanked open the door with the hand that wasn't holding a glass of red wine. Familiar, but a stranger.

"Chelsea!"

Kristen Rogers. They'd had a few classes together early in high school but never ran in the same social circles once Kristen became more interested in her boyfriends than her own brain. Chelsea shook the judgment away. Jeez, she was starting to sound like Judy.

"Kristen, hi."

"Wow! Come in. Chelsea Garden, what a trip." She ran her eyes over Chelsea's black jeans, gray sweater, white T-shirt, like she was trying to recalibrate this black and white photo blast from the past. "You look *amazing*. Have you heard of *aging*? The rest of us sure have."

Kristin turned on her heel, leading Chelsea into a large living room where several other women stood around chatting, holding wine glasses, sampling a platter of dips, crackers, and veggies. "Look what the cat dragged in!" Kristen sing-songed.

"Meow." Chelsea regretted it the moment it emerged. She

was not the cat in this scenario, but everyone laughed, politely she supposed, as Dani came out of the kitchen carrying something hot and cheesy. She set it next to a bowl of tortilla chips.

"Kristin's famous artichoke dip, y'all. We know this is why you're here. The Whole 30 people are going to want to go to the other room."

"The Whole 30 can kiss my ass." Kristen dove into the dip with a tortilla chip. "Mmmm." Chelsea genuinely smiled at this. The Whole 30 had been the last diet she'd abandoned halfway through.

One night at dinner in Sausalito, Amanda had teased, "Just call it the Half 15 and order the truffle mac and cheese with me!" She had.

"Chelsea!" Dani hurried to hug her. "You came!"

Chelsea hugged her friend. Dani looked the same, maybe a bit tired around the eyes, but with her dark hair swept into a high ponytail, in her casual jeans and sweatshirt, she could easily still have been on the basketball court shooting free throws with Chelsea after practice. It was hard to believe she had three kids, two of them teenagers.

"You look great."

"I look tired." Dani grimaced. "Diana was crying all week. Like the *entire* week. Sobbing." Diana was Dani's youngest.

"How old is she now?"

"Twelve. Middle school. Good lord, you couldn't pay me a million dollars to do that again." The doorbell rang. Dani squeezed her arm. "Amazing to see you." She hurried off.

A woman in jeans and a Santa Cruz sweatshirt standing a few steps away smiled at her. "Chelsea, right? I'm Heather. I was a couple of years behind you. Married Tom Ambrose."

Tom Ambrose. Chelsea hadn't heard that name in years. "Oh, Tom, right. How is he?"

"Oh, you know, he's Tom."

Chelsea hadn't known Tom well, but she nodded anyway. "Is he still working for his dad?" Chelsea thought of the ubiquitous red and black emblem of Ambrose Plumbing—on magnets, on ads in the grocery store, on the side of their fleet of white vans around town. She had seen two just on her way over here, each sighting tugging at Chelsea's nostalgia gene that had been dormant for so long but seemed to be making a steady appearance lately.

Heather shook her head. "Tom's running everything now, actually. Chuck finally decided he liked his bowling team more than his business, thank God. And just in time. I thought they might kill each other."

Chelsea laughed as if she knew the history of this father and son, as if she'd been here this whole time, living this life, instead of away living another one. It dawned on her that this wasn't a second-rate life: staying home, marrying a high school boyfriend, having kids, and sending them to all the same schools these women attended. It was even some people's best life, maybe better than most. She had worried the Bay would turn her into a snob, but maybe she'd always been one. Maybe it was why she'd left? At first she thought her body shivered at the thought, then realized it was her phone in her pocket.

Chelsea held it up to Heather. "Sorry, I have to take this."

In the quiet hall, she stared down at the text from Anson. Chelsea knew she shouldn't text her back. Sheryl Alexander had made it clear in her frosty reply to Chelsea's question about cleaning out her room that she shouldn't have contact with any of her students if she "valued professionalism."

Chelsea had replied by asking her how allowing a teacher to be assaulted was valuing professionalism? No answer. Even so, it felt good to write it, a faint echo of throwing those long-ago beer cans. Now she worried about what she should say to Anson, a quiet junior with massive social anxiety who typically spent her lunch hours huddled in Chelsea's room. When she sent her resignation, Chelsea had agonized over how it might impact students like Anson. Sweet Anson, named after a rose with creamy yellow petals. Somehow, knowing this, Chelsea had always felt even more protective of her, aware that she, like her namesake, could wilt at any moment under the wrong conditions.

Anson: *ur not coming back??!!*

Her hand shaking, Chelsea texted: *family emergency— I'm ok!*

"Chelsea?" Dani stood in the arched doorway. "We're starting."

Chelsea eyed the three dots of Anson's reply-in-progress, but quickly added *long story, sorry – gotta run!* to the text stream and powered down her phone, her stomach knotting with guilt.

She hurried to the high-ceilinged family room off the kitchen where the group of women had brought their wine and appetizer plates, and now sat around a coffee table on an enormous U-shaped couch facing a crackling fire. For its vastness, it was a cozy room, all chocolate browns and plaid throws and thick, creamy carpet worn in places by endless pairs of shoes. Low music played from an unseen speaker. Dave Matthews.

Chelsea couldn't remember the last time she'd heard a Dave Matthews song. A floor-to-ceiling bookshelf took up one side of the room, stuffed with board games, puzzles, books, and some old DVD collections. A card table with three folding chairs sat in a corner, holding a half-finished puzzle of Yosemite. Above the fireplace sat the blank face of a dormant flat screen TV. Chelsea could imagine the hours this family must spend here and was struck with something she couldn't quite name.

What was the word for something you never had, never wanted, but suddenly realized you would never get a chance to have if you changed your mind? Regret? Longing? Maybe a mix of both. The Portuguese probably had a word for it. Or the Germans.

"Chelsea, sit here." Dani patted the sofa next to her. "Do you know Nora Delgado?"

Chelsea nodded as she took a seat between them. Nora smiled. "We met before Thanksgiving. Evan Dawkins introduced us."

Dani's eyes slid to Chelsea. "Oh, really?"

Chelsea rushed to explain. "I ran into him at Imperial Market. Nora was there, too."

Dani smirked. "The plot thickens."

Ignoring her, Chelsea turned to Nora. "It's nice to see you again."

"Are you up for another weekend already?"

Chelsea flushed. "Actually, I'm up here for a bit longer. I decided to leave my job at Grove Prep. It's, er—," she stammered, "a long story."

Nora dusted invisible fluff from her black pants. "It's going around, I guess. One of my English teachers let me know over Thanksgiving weekend that he'll be leaving at semester."

Dani leaned forward, eyes widening. "Who?"

"Dean."

"He's going to work for Carrie's parents." Heather added from where she'd been nibbling cashews and watching them from the other side of the couch. "I ran into her at the post office yesterday." She caught the strained look on Nora's face. "He feels terrible."

"I'm sure," Nora allowed.

Watching her, Chelsea felt certain Sheryl wouldn't be so graceful when discussing her departure.

Dani cleared her throat. "So who liked the book?"

Nora placed a hand on Chelsea's arm, her voice dropping. "Didn't you say you worked in public school before? Is your credential up to date?"

EVAN

"Chelsea?" Evan noticed her hesitate at the door of her car. He'd been on the treadmill when he saw her through the window of the gym, had almost let it go, almost didn't hop off the machine, push through the doors, and call out to her, but she'd told him she'd be in the Bay all weekend.

She turned. "Oh, um, hi." Her lie was all over her face.

Evan knew the socially acceptable thing to do would be to nod and play along. But when had the two of them ever done the superficial thing? "I thought you were heading down to deal with apartment stuff?" He took a few steps toward her, wiping his forehead with the towel he still had around his neck.

She was flushed from her own workout and tucked a sweaty lock of hair behind her ear. "Right. Yeah. I didn't end up going."

"You avoiding me?" he tried to kid.

He watched her almost lie again, saw it flicker across her face, but then she looked at him, her eyes clear. "Kinda, yeah."

He nodded, his mouth going dry. "Okay."

She gave him a nod before opening her car door, getting in, and driving away.

* * *

"Mr. Dawkins?"

Evan was in a hurry, packing up, getting ready to leave. Why did Mondays always seem so long? He hadn't noticed one of his freshman students still sitting in her chair, waiting for him, trumpet clutched in her lap. "Alex?"

"Do you have a minute?" Alex swallowed, her eyes in her lap. She tapped her trumpet nervously against her leg.

"Oh, sure—yeah." He dropped his bag near his desk and pulled up a chair opposite her. Evan had been worried about Alex lately. Not about her music—she was a talented trumpet player—but she'd been withdrawn and shaky the last few weeks, not the laughing kid he'd noticed the first couple months of school. After a minute, he carefully took her trumpet and placed it on the chair next to her. "Alex?"

"Right," she breathed out. "I was wondering—I know the winter concert is in January, and, well, I was wondering—if I could wear a tux instead of the dress the girls wear."

Ah. Evan could feel the moment around him solidify, mattering more than it had a few minutes ago. "If you want to wear a tux, wear a tux."

Alex's gaze shot up to his. "Really?"

"I just want everyone looking polished. Frankly, I hate the whole boys in tuxes, girls in dresses thing. It seems outdated to me."

He watched the color bloom back into her face. "I hate it. I'm not—," she swallowed again, licked her lips quickly, her eyes darting over his shoulder. "It's not like I'm, er—I just hate wearing dresses."

"Alex." Evan waited for her to look at him again. "In this room, you are whoever you say you are, whatever makes you feel safe in your body, okay? No one gets to tell you otherwise."

To his surprise, she flung her arms around his neck, almost knocked him out of his chair with a hug he didn't even have time to respond to. Then she was out of her chair, putting away her trumpet, and at the doorway before turning back.

"Um, my parents might be weird about it. They're—kind of traditional. Kind of, um, religious, and they might be weird."

Evan smiled. "Maybe we should all wear tuxedos. Those dresses are the worst anyway."

Grinning, she hurried away.

Evan looked around the band room, scanning the trophies, the past years of photos (those dresses really were terrible), and felt a warmth move through him. It was an easy pitch, the one he gave people about coming back because this place was a safe harbor, how it was somewhere he felt like he could be himself in high school, and he liked the idea of being the adult for the kids who needed that space. He knew he used it to let himself off the hook about coming home, but it wasn't a lie.

His dad had never understood why Evan needed his music, had always thought his son just couldn't get a real job. But here, in the band room, surrounded by music stands, stray sheet music, plastic chairs, and someone's leftover nachos (he dumped those in the trash), he recognized a familiar warmth moving through him. It was the same as when he'd first realized, all those years ago, that there were places like this one in your life that often felt more like home than home.

* * *

"Ah, shit." Evan watched the hammer topple to the ground. He was trying to hang the ancient strand of outdoor Christmas lights along the front of the house, resting them on the rusted hooks his dad had put in years ago. "Dad? Could you grab that hammer for me?" He looked around. His dad had been there a minute ago, yelling at him to "loop the strand! Loop the strand!" whatever the hell that meant. "Dad?"

Evan scanned the yard. No sign of him. Double shit. This was happening more and more. He'd finally succumbed and put baby latches on the cabinets under the sink when he'd come home to find his dad pouring dish soap into a cup of coffee a few weeks ago. Soon, he'd have to figure out how to keep his dad from leaving the house during the day while he was at school. Their neighbor across the street, Lilly, watched him as best as she could. She was a retired librarian and mostly gardened and read novels on her porch. When he'd first moved in, she'd told him she was happy to watch out for Frank. But he couldn't ask her to do much more than that.

He checked his phone. Nothing from Lilly. He looked up and down the street. Empty.

"Dad!" He did a lap around the neighborhood. Then, another. He couldn't have gotten far.

He was on his third lap when he saw him, sprawled under an oak tree on the street perpendicular to theirs. He was leaning against the trunk, almost completely in shadow, his eyes closed, his legs splayed out. A cold wriggle moved through Evan.

"Dad?" Nothing. "Dad!?"

"For Chrissake, a man can't take a nap under a tree anymore?" Frank hoisted himself to his feet. "This fucking country." He ambled past Evan, toward home.

NORA

"Nora?" Her assistant principal, Mark Weaver, leaned in the doorway. And Mark could really fill up a doorway, still massive and muscular even a decade past his college baseball days. He held up the bright blue folder he reserved for his "Shit You Won't Believe" cases at school.

"Oh no," Nora said, slipping off her bluescreen glasses.

"This one's a doozy."

"The Smiths again?"

Mark shook his head. "Olive Reynold."

Nora sat back. Olive Reynold was a selective mute. A ninth grader. Her brother, Aaron, an eleventh grader, generally did the talking for her at school when he could. Mom lived somewhere in the Midwest. Indiana, or maybe Iowa. Her dad was a handyman in town who didn't always buy into the IEP process for his daughter.

"She talks at home sometimes. Why can't you just make her talk here?" he grumbled at the last meeting.

Their newest special ed teacher, Sally, just blinked at him. "She's a *selective* mute, Mr. Reynold. She's choosing when she wants to talk."

"What's up with Olive?" Nora asked.

Mark shook his head. "You won't believe this, but she talked."

Nora brightened. "She did? On campus?"

"Yeah." Mark came inside and closed the door. "So she has that therapy dog with her, right?" Nora nodded. Some sort of tiny terrier mix Olive kept in a front pack. "Okay, so get this." Mark pulled out a chair at the conference table (theatrically, as he often did), and sat down. "So, I didn't realize it was Olive—I just saw the dog, you know—and so I walked up and said, 'Hey, you can't have dogs on campus.'" He paused for Nora to nod him along. "And she says: 'It's my fucking therapy dog!'"

Nora blinked. "She—? *Exactly* like that?"

Mark broke into a grin. "Exactly like that. Should I let Sally know she might have met one of her IEP goals?"

"Please don't."

* * *

"Remind me why this is supposed to be fun?" Nora asked Dani, blowing on her scalding hot apple cider. They were wandering the aisles of one of the seemingly endless craft fairs held inside the main building at the fairgrounds near any holiday that might warrant a craft fair (all of them).

Dani shoved a churro in Nora's face. "Exhibit A."

"Besides the churros."

Dani shook her head. "Like there needs to be something besides churros."

Nora scanned the booths. Her whole life plan lately seemed to center around trying to get rid of things, rather than adding them, so everything here felt like clutter that would end up in a Goodwill box. She felt a flash of guilt at her judgement. People clearly loved it. Hundreds of them happily perused handmade cards, candles, wooden sculptures, paintings (both small and massive), metal lanterns with glowing innards, pots of jams, infused olive oils. It wasn't the fair's fault she wasn't feeling the holiday-buying spirit.

"Nora?"

Craig stood in front of her, arms laden with bags, still sporting a bit of leftover Thanksgiving tan. What was he doing here?

"Oh. Hi."

He grinned sheepishly at his packages. "Sarah loves a craft fair." His eyes darted around. Nora watched them land on his new wife several booths away, *oohing* over some blown-glass ornaments that were actually quite beautiful.

"But you always hated them," Nora couldn't help but say.

"True. I'm just a pack mule. Buy local, right?"

Nora stared at him, wondering where this version of her ex-husband had come from, this man who said things like *I'm just a pack mule* and *buy local* and carried multiple bags stuffed with crafts. He was unrecognizable. Not that long ago, she could've barely gotten him to window shop after dinner downtown. She hadn't minded, not really; she'd never been one of those women who dragged her partner places against his will.

"We were just going to get another churro!" Dani blurted. "Bye Craig!"

Nora felt caught in an encroaching haze, a fog creeping into her peripheral vision. She felt Dani take her arm and pull her off in the direction of the food court. "That was weird," she finally managed, her vision starting to clear.

"Which part?" Dani asked. "Craig acting like a character from a Hallmark movie or you gaping at him like a zombie?"

"Was I?"

Dani shook her head. "Come on. We clearly need many more churros."

* * *

That night, Nora wrapped herself in her favorite robe and crawled onto the couch. She scrolled through various Netflix options but couldn't decide, instead playing the scene with Craig back in her mind, over and over, his arms becoming laden with what could only be dozens of bags, his eyes, with each replaying, landing more lovingly on the silhouette of his new wife. Why was she doing this to herself? Why had she just stood there, gawping like a goldfish?

Her phone buzzed. Craig again: *great to c u 2day!*

Wasn't it just as easy to type out *today* as *2day*?

It went on: *Sarah and I r going to CO for xmas would love to take Leo can we talk?*

CO? Colorado? They wanted to take her son away to Colorado for Christmas? And why couldn't he use sentences like everyone else their age?

She texted back: *Have you talked with Leo about this?*

Three dots appeared, then disappeared. Then nothing else. She waited a few more minutes. When the phone rang, she assumed it would be him, but it was a number she didn't recognize. She answered it mostly to have something to do.

"Nora?"

"Yes?"

"This is Chelsea Garden. We met at Dani's book group? And with Evan, that day in the grocery store?"

"Of course. Hi, Chelsea."

"You gave me your number?"

Nora remembered giving Chelsea her number, remembered offering her a long-term sub job next semester. Did this woman think Nora had amnesia? "Of course, how are you?"

"Good, good. I've actually decided to stay in town until summer, so I'd be able to take the sub job if it's still available?"

Nora breathed out. At least one thing could go right for her today.

PART TWO

How come when you ask me why,
you don't listen to the answer?

—Sunset Dark

CHELSEA

"Jayden! No headlocks! Or you lose the iPad for the rest of the day!" Kelly was already hollering over her shoulder, her hands full of bags stuffed with wrapped packages, as Chelsea's brother's family made their way out of the rental car and up the path to Matt and Judy's house.

Jayden, their eighth grader, leapt up from where he had pinned his younger brother to the lawn. "I wasn't!"

Kelly caught Chelsea's eye and rolled both of hers. "Like I don't see him, like he didn't do it right in front of me." She blew kisses in Chelsea's general direction. "Hi! Hi! Merry Christmas Eve!"

"Merry Christmas Eve," Chelsea murmured back, her blood pressure already rising.

Chelsea didn't really know her sister-in-law that well. Kelly had been married to Chelsea's little brother Shaun for fourteen years; there'd been holidays and one strange trip to a lake in Vermont where all three kids got the flu, and Chelsea and her parents left early, but even then, she'd never actually *talked* in any depth with her sister-in-law. Kelly mostly existed in broad strokes to Chelsea, always tired, always slightly performative in her stories and gestures or disappearing into another room with a child in tow. Standing there, Chelsea wondered for the first time who this woman was before she was her brother's wife, the mother of her niece and nephews. Who was she now?

Chelsea looked to where her brother attempted to shut the trunk of the rental car with his elbow while balancing the majority of the family's luggage in his arms.

"Here, let me." She hurried to help him, grabbing a battered blue suitcase with the snowman from *Frozen* emblazoned on it before it toppled to the ground.

"Jesus!" Shaun huffed. "Do they think we just magic their bags into the house like Hogwarts? Jayden! Come back here and carry some of this! Kylie, get out of the car!"

When had her brother started speaking only in exclamations? She peered in at her niece, whose little face was pressed close to a large iPhone, something animated whirling on the screen.

"Kylie!" Shaun repeated, louder this time. "Out!"

Chelsea rapped on the glass, then tried the door handle. Unlocked. "Kylie, come say hi to me. I haven't seen you in forever." No movement. "Grandma made sugar cookies for you to decorate. If you hurry, there might be some left before your brothers get them all."

Her niece slid out of the car, eyes still glued to the screen as Chelsea engulfed her in a hug. "You've grown up so much. You must be in high school already?"

Kylie squirmed. "No, silly, I'm nine!"

"Nine! I thought you were sixteen."

"No way!" Kylie ran off toward the promise of cookies.

Chelsea grabbed a few more bags from Shaun when Jayden refused to materialize.

"Jesus!" he repeated as he lost the battle with another suitcase.

Inside, Kelly was shushing the boys in the living room, her voice a harsh whisper. "I don't care; your grandmother went to a lot of trouble to set up the cookie decorating station. Go in there and decorate some cookies right now!"

"But there isn't any candy and only one kind of sprinkles!" Mason whined.

"You'll survive!" Shaun dumped the luggage in the entry way. Both boys skulked into the dining room.

Chelsea caught a glimpse of her mother's set up: a plastic tablecloth, a bowl of white frosting, some silver sprinkles, and a plateful of perfect snowflake-shaped cookies. Her literal mother. A snowflake with anything other than silver sprinkles and white frosting? What a horrifying thought.

"Hey Chelsea," her brother finally breathed. "Place looks great."

"That's all Mom." Her mother always decorated beautifully for the holidays: The tree glowed in the corner, tastefully decorated with glass ornaments that caught the warm, white light. Battery-operated candles flickered throughout the room, and the coffee table held an assortment of red and white roses next to a simple, stained-glass church. Lovely and understated. Chelsea worried she might knock something over.

Chelsea sent Kelly and Shaun to unpack while she headed into the dining room to decorate snowflakes with the kids. Judy sailed back and forth from the kitchen, occasionally commenting on a cookie, "Oh, that's nice, Kylie!" or exclaiming, "Save room for dinner!"

As she spread frosting over each cookie, with her parents' Bing Crosby album playing low in the other room, Chelsea felt her chest loosen. She thought of the Christmases she had spent as a child helping her mother press the ancient mold into the dough, mixing the frosting as the butter smell filled the warm kitchen, and she smiled, humming along to Bing. After an hour, she mopped off most of the frosting from her nephews and niece before sending them to find their parents, so she could clean up and set the table for dinner.

Chelsea brought the plate of decorated cookies into the kitchen, where her mother was checking on the pot roast. "Mmm, smells amazing."

"And it has potatoes." Judy said, her back to Chelsea, the strings of her apron neatly tied in a bow. "So no complaining."

"Thanks, Mom."

They made it most of the way through dinner before things started to wobble.

"Jayden." Judy eyed her oldest grandchild. "You need to eat that roast or no dessert."

Kelly froze next to Chelsea. "Oh, Judy. Actually, Jayden is a vegetarian now. We told him he didn't have to eat the meat." She shot a pointed look at Shaun. "I thought Shaun would have told you."

Judy looked confused. "What do you mean he's a vegetarian? You're vegetarians now?"

Shaun wiped his mouth on the napkin from his lap. "Not the rest of us, Mom. Just Jay."

Judy shook her head. "Children eat what their mothers make them." Chelsea did not miss the glance between Kelly and Shaun.

Matt rushed in. "Judy, remember when Chelsea went through that whole vegan phase?"

"I was twenty-six."

Judy saw this as some sort of confirmation of her point. "Right! An adult. Children don't decide what they eat."

"We feel like Jayden can make that choice if he wants," Kelly said, her voice tight, hand shaking as she clenched her fork. "And I don't mind making more plant-based meals for all of us."

Judy took a bite of meat. "Ridiculous." She eyed the pile

of discarded roast on Jayden's plate. "Now, all that good meat will be wasted."

Kyle leaned across the table and stabbed the pieces with his fork. "There." He scraped it onto his plate. "I'll eat it."

Chelsea couldn't help it. She started to giggle. She knew she should support her brother, but, petty as it was, it felt so nice to have Judy's judgement directed somewhere else for once. And it was just so absurd. Who cared if the kid didn't want to eat his meat? In a moment, she could feel Diego on her other side quietly shaking with laughter, too.

Judy narrowed her eyes at the two of them. "What?"

Chelsea shook her head, tamping down the giggles. "Nothing, nothing."

Shaun put his fork down. "Jesus, Mom."

Judy sent him a wounded look. "You know, no one else ever offers to host!"

"Like you'd let us," Shaun mumbled into his plate.

Judy stood abruptly, dinner clearly over. She started to clear. "Go in the other room and choose your Christmas Eve present. I'll bring out cookies and tea."

Chelsea couldn't move fast enough.

* * *

Chelsea checked the metal tray of the white board, the desk drawers, even the built-in bookcases under the window. No luck. Not a single dry erase pen anywhere.

"Good Lord, my kingdom for a dry erase pen," she muttered, surveying the empty classroom. Almost empty. Dean Moreno still hadn't come to collect most of his stuff or any of the personal posters tacked to the wall: A selection of Shakespearean movies, some Broadway shows. *Hamilton. Dear Evan Hansen.* A series of postcards from famous bookstores. She plucked these from the wall and added them to the box marked DEAN. A UC Davis pennant. Two coffee cups, both chipped. A half-box of English Breakfast tea. A dusty Patagonia fleece that looked like it had been hanging from the back of the desk chair since 2016.

Chelsea paused to take a sip of her coffee, brushing a strand of damp hair from her face. It felt like all she'd been doing since Thanksgiving was cleaning, sorting, packing, unpacking.

Because that *was* pretty much all she'd been doing since Thanksgiving. Well, that and coming up with (not so) clever excuses to avoid Evan Dawkins.

Early the second week of December, she'd driven back to Sausalito and emptied and cleaned her studio. Her car packed, the dumpster she'd hired full, and the studio lemon-fresh, she'd had one bag left to carry out to her car where she found Stone leaning against it like a middle-aged Jake Ryan. Chelsea hadn't been able to shake the image—even if *Sixteen Candles* had aged horribly, according to her students.

"What, no goodbye?" he'd said, his hands in the pockets of his suit pants. He must have come straight from work.

"I said goodbye."

"In a voicemail? It's been five years."

"Six."

"Of course. Right." He'd grinned at her, hoping the crinkles around those ink-blue eyes of his would work their usual magic. Chelsea stared past him at the slice of dark ocean visible from the driveway until he added, "Still, either way, a voicemail?"

Mustering what little strength remained in her reserve, she looked at him. "Let's not do this, okay?" It had dawned on her, though, that the driveway moment might have been a first for Stone. With his wealth and lifestyle and the pair of shoulders he made sure strained against whatever clothing he was wearing, he might never have been at the receiving end of anything resembling Chelsea's voicemail.

Still, he should have been able to figure it out. They'd been fighting nonstop since Thanksgiving. About Chelsea not pressing charges. About Chelsea leaving her job. About Chelsea staying in Imperial Flats instead of joining him for Christmas Eve. About all the ways Chelsea wasn't doing whatever Stone felt she should be doing. She'd finally told him in a voicemail that she was done taking suggestions about her life from Stone Kendrick, effective immediately.

She couldn't have been clearer.

Except, yes, that had been confusion in his eyes as he pushed himself away from her car. Behind the casual hand raked through his hair and a final shrug before he walked down the hill toward his Prius, Chelsea had seen it. Hurt. She had confused and hurt Stone Kendrick, a man who'd always seemed invincible. Watching him maneuver the Prius down the narrow street, she'd both hated and loved the tiny flicker of pleasure it brought her.

"I saw the light on." Nora stood in the classroom doorway in a pair of jeans and a worn Imperial Flats sweatshirt. "Can I help you find anything?"

"Dry erase pens?"

"No big New Year's Eve plans?"

Chelsea shrugged. Dani had invited her to a party at the restaurant. Kyle was having friends over. "My uncle's having a party, but I'll probably just stay here and get organized. You?"

"I'm going to Romano's for some apps and drinks, but I'll be in bed by nine."

"We're living the dream."

Nora studied her. "Come with me. I'm a workaholic, but even I won't be in my office on New Year's Eve."

Chelsea ran her hand over the cover of *The House on Mango Street*, the first book she would be teaching with her three freshman classes. She hadn't read *Mango* in years. "I should probably—"

"Come on." Nora turned toward the door. "But first, let's track down those pens."

* * *

"Champagne?" Evan held out a flute.

Chelsea felt her cheeks flame. "Sure, thanks." When she ran into Evan again, which in this town was highly likely, she had hoped *not* to be wearing a ripped pair of cargo pants and a raggedy SF Giants long-sleeve shirt with a hole in the armpit. Especially to what was clearly a dressy New Year's Eve event at Romano's. Nora had run home to "take a quick shower," but she hadn't mentioned Chelsea might want to do the same. Probably because she assumed Chelsea was a fully functioning adult who had mastered social situations by now.

Evan motioned at her forehead. "I think you have some—dirt?" He offered her a white paper cocktail napkin.

"Dry erase marker," she mumbled, dabbing at the spot. "Did I get it?"

He nodded, scanning her outfit. "Been in the classroom today?" His look seemed to say *or perhaps wrestling with trolls?*

"Yeah, cleaning. I should have gone home to change but didn't want to get roped into Kyle's party." Kyle and Diego had ramped up their Chelsea Improvement Plan in the last couple of weeks, but they were no match for Chelsea the Avoider.

Evan sipped his drink. "It's a bold statement. Besides, everyone here is too busy trying to eat and drink the price of the seventy-five-dollar entrance ticket."

"Oh!" Chelsea glanced around as if she'd been caught out. "I didn't pay anyone?"

"I'm assuming Dani invited you. That's a freebie." He grabbed a few Brie puffs from a nearby table. "Try these. Bert's specialty."

Chelsea closed her eyes as the herbs and cheese melted on her tongue. "Okay, wow."

"I know." Evan snatched a couple more. "Congrats on the teaching gig, by the way. I guess we're colleagues now. How weird is that?"

Chelsea grimaced, licking some crumbs from her fingers. "Long term sub. Is there a sadder phrase in all of education?"

"I don't know. We had that one cool guy. The one with the tattoo."

Chelsea flushed. She hadn't thought about him for years. Fall of her junior year. Algebra II. He was young, maybe twenty-five, and had a dark red tattoo of a tree branch that ran the length of his right arm. The school had obviously told him to cover it, but on certain days he would roll up his blue button-down shirt to the elbows, a shirt that no matter how many times he wore seemed to look new, as if he'd pulled a different one each time from its plastic wrap. Chelsea swore she could just make out the faint impression of holes where he must have plucked the pins from the once-folded fabric. When he rolled his sleeves, she would study the fingers of branch that crept from the cuff at his elbow, skeletal and leaf-less against his pale arm. She would stare and stare at them while he wrote numbers and symbols on the board. She remembered more about those peeking branches than any of the math, remembered the way she used to imagine peeling his shirt from his shoulders so she could see the way the branch wrapped around the width of his back. She wanted to find the place where it began, if that place existed. That branch must start somewhere on the trunk of his body. That fall, she'd wanted to see that beginning place more than anything.

"Chelsea?"

"I was just trying to remember him."

"I'm sure you were," he grinned, and she felt her flush deepen. She'd definitely told Evan all about her shirt-peeling fantasies. Back when they told each other everything. It dawned on her that when she'd first met Stone in a yoga class in Marin, he'd been shirtless, revealing the tattoo of the Tree of Life between his shoulder blades. Had she initially been attracted to him because it had reminded her, even subconsciously, of that substitute teacher she hadn't thought about in years?

Evan squinted at her shoulder. "Oh, I think you might have a—" He plucked off a dust bunny that could likely have its own children.

"Good lord, I should probably go home."

"Or we could go for a drive. You know, if you aren't still avoiding me?" He chose a few more things from the buffet and pulled a bottle of Champagne from one of the many ice buckets stationed throughout the Romano's candlelit dining room, then headed for a side exit.

She didn't miss the sly smile on Dani's face across the room when she and Evan slipped out the door.

* * *

She should have known he would head to the lake.

"A bit late, my friend." He didn't reply, just pulled the car into a spot with a view of the water. He rolled the windows down and began wrestling with the cork. Chelsea couldn't help grinning at his attempt. "You okay over there?"

He popped it loose and offered her the bottle. "I don't have cups."

"Keeping it classy." She sipped at the still-cold Champagne, then handed it back.

Evan took a swallow, his eyes on the water. "Did you get everything sorted out in the Bay?"

After she'd seen him at the gym, he'd texted her one last time to see if she wanted to get a beer. She'd told him she had to go back down to Sausalito again. She hadn't, though. She'd stayed in her room for almost a week, huddled in throw pillows, watching endless videos of tiny octopuses and sloth babies and seasons of old '90s sitcoms she knew she should find slightly offensive or inane but still loved. Chelsea had never had so much December time on her hands before. She'd always been in school or teaching or bartending or tutoring or, for the last few years, in one of Stone and Leila's Holiday Consumer Awareness workshops, which were their own form of consumption, now that she thought about it.

Kyle wouldn't take any rent money. She should have used her extra funds to go on a trip, had even looked up various tours—to Bali, to Ireland, to Patagonia—but nothing felt right, each just more packing, more leaving. She threw in a few applications to overseas jobs mostly so she could tell herself she was at least trying to think about her future, but she hadn't heard anything back. She wasn't even sure she wanted to go overseas, but Amanda had sent her some links with "Have an adventure!" as the subject line, and it seemed rude not to at least half-heartedly acknowledge her friend's efforts.

Chelsea closed her eyes and leaned back against the headrest, letting the sound of the lake move through her. "It's been a pretty crappy month, Evan."

"Or," he angled to face her, his back propped against the door. "It's been a month of liberating changes."

Chelsea motioned for the bottle, thought about it as she took another drink. "Nope, just a shit-show. But I appreciate the attempt at reframing."

"I think we've taken the same workshop."

"I guess I haven't been keeping up with my gratitude lists."

Abruptly, Evan got out of the car, opened the back door,

and started rifling through a pile of clothes he had in the back seat. He shrugged on a sweatshirt over his collared shirt. Back at the still-open front door, he motioned to her. "Come on."

"Oh, no, I don't really—"

"Come. On." He shut the door.

Chelsea climbed out, trading the Champagne for the offered sweatshirt. Zipping up the front, she followed him down to the water, where he was spreading out a blanket on a wide, flat rock. The rock she'd waited on all those years ago. Because of course it was. Chelsea felt momentarily furious with that rock, still looking the same, as if decades hadn't passed. How could it still just be sitting there? Geography could be so smug.

From his sweatshirt pocket, Evan pulled out a slightly squashed wedge of herbed goat cheese and a stack of crackers wrapped in one of Romano's white cloth napkins. She eyed the theft.

"The first step in getting better is admitting you have a problem."

"I promise to return the napkin." He dug a cracker into the cheese. "But in my line of work you turn lifting from the buffet into an art form."

"They didn't have a sharp cheddar?" But her stomach rumble gave her away, and she hurried to accept the cracker with the swipe of cheese across the top, even if goat cheese wasn't her favorite. For a few minutes, they chewed their snack and sipped their Champagne, and they could've been seventeen again, every year in between melting into the unseasonably warm night air. It was almost too much. Chelsea swallowed against the lump forming in her throat and stared out over the dark water.

"Why are you here, Chels?"

She attempted a playful look. "Because you practically kidnapped me and drove me here."

His gaze held hers. "Seriously. What happened to you in the Bay?"

After a moment, she said, "I broke up with some bad life choices."

"Care to elaborate?"

"Not really."

"Judy said something about a married guy?"

"Ugh, Judy." Chelsea collapsed back onto the blanket, the sky above blurry with clouds, no stars tonight.

"Is she wrong?"

"He is married. But they're polyamorous."

"Which means his wife was fine with it?"

"Yep. All consenting adults. Check."

Evan nodded, took another swig of the half-empty bottle. "How long were you with him?"

"Six years."

He chuckled. "Shit, that's so Chelsea. Even alternative, she's the most loyal one in the room."

His words moved through her, a warm wash, even as she wanted to insist that he knew nothing about her anymore. "I quit my teaching job in the middle of a semester, so maybe not so loyal after all."

"Because you were assaulted."

Chelsea sat up. "How do you know that?"

"Dani mentioned it."

"Right. I forgot I was back in Imperial Flats where your life is everyone else's personal property." She hugged her knees to her chest, her head dizzy with Champagne and not enough food and the sheer resentment of the way this town just poked its damn nose in everywhere it wasn't wanted. She didn't know how to explain to him that it wasn't really about what happened in that parking lot. Somehow, that part just seemed inevitable. The way powerful men with money were allowed to operate in the world.

The worst part for her had been everything after it. Sheryl Alexander's response, sure, but also the way the school just went on, as if nothing had happened to her, as if her twelve years there hadn't mattered at all. Just three students had written to her to see if she was coming back. *Three*. And only Amanda had called to make sure she was okay. No other colleagues. After all the meals, and happy hours, and field trips, and staff dinners she'd attended over the years, had she really meant so little to them?

She took a breath. The air had taken on a metal tinge, like it might rain. It wasn't cold, but she shivered anyway.

"Hey," Evan wedged the bottle into a nook by the edge of the rock and scooted closer to her. "Hey." He rubbed slow circles on her back. "It's okay."

She wiped at the sudden tears on her cheeks. "It's not, actually. How can I be this old and still feel like I don't know the things I'm supposed to know?"

"A lot of us feel like that."

"But I'm not even in a normal mid-life crisis, you know? The divorced-with-kids kind. The trying to find my dream job kind. I didn't even get around to any of that. I've never been married. I don't have kids. I don't have anyone in my life who belongs to me. It's not like teaching was my dream job. It just sort of seemed like the next logical step. Don't get me wrong, I really like it. It's steady and meaningful and the kids are funny and great. But I liked bartending, too. If I'm honest, I probably like hiking and reading more than any job I've ever had. What does that say about me? It's like I lack the ability to long for anything that matters. I just drift along, staring at beautiful views, collecting hobbies. Reading. Yoga. Hiking. It's like all I've ever aspired to be is retired! And now I'm back in Imperial fucking Flats still fighting with my mother about all the shit I should have sorted out years ago and teaching at our old high school! How is this my life?"

He nodded, solemn, but his eyes flashed. "You make an excellent point. You are terrible at this whole human existence thing."

"Oh, nice—I'm pouring my heart out and you're making jokes." But she was smiling, shaking her head, wiping her tears. "You know, I broke up with Stone once before."

"Oh, yeah?"

"March 2020."

Recognition lit his eyes. "Ah."

"Yeah, a week before we got shut down for the pandemic. I was packing up that studio apartment. I was moving out. Moving on. And then Covid."

"Most of us completely lost our heads then."

Chelsea sighed. "It wasn't even losing my head. It was just—easier. Stone came over, told me we should try to get through the shut-down together. I remember he just moved around the apartment, slowly unpacking everything I'd put in boxes. Over the next week, he just ferried all the boxes away, telling me it wasn't the right time to make any big life changes, not while the world was imploding. Then, we just—never talked about it again." She hesitated. "But you know the worst part? I was almost relieved. I really, really loved that apartment."

"Housing in the Bay is the worst."

"Believe me, I've always been good at rationalizing the easy choice. It's like an art form."

"So, see—you *do* have a thing."

She gave him a shove but as she did, he caught her, pulled her to him, into the warm comma of his side. The moon came out from behind some clouds, and they both watched the way its light wriggled across the water. Evan stroked her hair and her back, and Chelsea breathed him in, a spice and citrus soap, and something underneath, something that hit the center of her memory, rich and safe and Evan. She found his face with her hands, drew him close, kissing him, pulling him on top of her, tasting the salt from the cracker, the tang of Champagne, and then he was fumbling with the button of her pants, with the zip of the sweatshirt, the clasp of her bra.

"Wait, shit." He pushed away.

She sat up, her breath quick. "What?"

"I don't have a condom."

Chelsea felt the giggle escape before she could suck it back in.

He buried his face in his hands. "I'm just wondering if this could be more like high school right now?" Only he was laughing, too. They couldn't stop if they tried.

* * *

Evan must have washed his sheets recently. The bed emitted a faint whiff of dryer sheet. It reassured her somehow. He hadn't known she would end up here last night. She sat up, blinking into the watery morning light. He'd opened the shade, exposing a patch of patio, a wedge of fencing, a green stretch of trees. She scanned the remains of their New Year's Eve. A congealed slice of the frozen pizza he'd made at two a.m. when hunger won out, the second bottle of wine they'd opened just after that, only an inch or so left in the bottom. Chelsea grabbed her purse from the side table and dry-swallowed two Advil. Her eyes fell on three silver-framed photos on the dresser. All of the same girl. A school photo, toothy and freckled. A cartwheel on a beach. A close-up candid smile, eyes aglow. Evan's eyes. Her stomach fizzed. Did Evan have a kid?

"You're up." Evan carried two ceramic cups into the room. "Sorry I don't have coffee. I can't have it with Frank anymore or he drinks cup after cup and it just ramps him up. We can go out if you want coffee. He's all set now." He settled beside her on the bed and handed her a cup.

She sipped the black tea, creamy and a little sweet. "I'm an equal opportunity caffeine drinker." She tried to sound casual, but her eyes kept darting back to the photos. "Who's the girl?"

"Violet. My daughter."

His *daughter*. "How old?"

"Nine."

"And her mother?"

"Thirty-five." She narrowed her eyes at him. "Sorry. I should have told you. Lauren. We were never married, only together six months when she found out she was pregnant with Vi. We tried to be together on and off for a bit, but Violet's the only good thing about us."

The flash of annoyance wasn't fair. Chelsea couldn't ask him not to have had a life before now, but she couldn't quite tamp it down. Outside, the rain pattered, giving them something to listen to, somewhere to set their gaze for a moment. She blew over the surface of her cup, her eyes slipping back to his mussy hair and stubbled morning face. "This is weird."

"It is that, yes."

"I'm not even sure if it's weird good or weird bad."

"Good, I hope." This was a different Evan than the cocky, defensive boy of her high school years. He looked tired, the filtered light across his face almost green, like they were both underwater. Maybe they were.

"Evan?" Frank Dawkins stood in the doorway in a beige robe, open over a pair of pale pajamas.

"Dad, you remember Chelsea Garden?"

Chelsea felt her face heat. "Hi, Mr. Dawkins."

"The TV's broke!"

"You have to press the button, the top button—hold on." Evan hurried Frank out of the doorway, casting an apologetic glance at Chelsea over his shoulder.

Chelsea set her tea on the side table, slipped out of bed and started getting dressed, trying to slow the pace of her racing heart. She couldn't find her shirt. Where was her shirt?

Evan came back into the room. "Oh, you don't have to do that. You don't have to—"

"I should probably go." Giants shirt. Under the bed.

He watched her pull it on. "Okay, but let's get dinner later."

"Let me see what Kyle and Diego have planned. I've been kind of ignoring them."

"Right."

"Happy New Year."

"Right, okay."

Later, sitting outside Kyle's house in her car, the rain a protective sheet around her, she texted Evan: *sorry to race out of there*

Three dots emerged instantly: *And I thought I was the runner*

Chelsea: *I don't think I should be adding more weirdness to my life right now*

Evan: *I think that might be how life works*

Chelsea: *Deep thoughts*

His dots hovered for a long time before he wrote: *I should have shown up that day after graduation*

Chelsea: *we all should have done a lot of things*

NORA

Nora kept thinking she saw her son in places her son couldn't be. She'd turn a corner in the main hall at school and catch a flash of him, one wide shoulder and flop of black hair, before disappearing into a classroom. Or Leo at the Java House downtown, waiting for the one-room bathroom in the back. Or pulling out of a parking spot at Imperial Market in a blue Corolla. Though, of course not. Of course, it wasn't him. It never was.

Leo was far away, disappearing around corners she'd never see, waiting for restrooms at cafes she'd never visit. At night, she imagined she heard his music playing through the wall only to move through the empty, silent house feeling like a fool. She wondered if there was a word for the feeling of having your child grow up and leave you. Not grief exactly, but something in that general family. Grief's cheerier younger sibling, the one that still dots its 'i's with hearts even as it paints its nails a purple-black. *Get a life*, Leo had once said to her, rolling his eyes. He was maybe eleven or thirteen or one of those ages where kids said those sorts of throw-away, razor-edged comments. How could she explain to him, in his baggy sweats and bare adolescent feet, that she was trying? She really was.

She pulled into a spot at Gold Dust Village, a two-story

crop of white, blue-trimmed buildings housing various services that leaned toward natural healing practices. A holistic chiropractor. A couple of hippie therapists. A yoga studio. She tugged her mat from behind the seat of her car. Two of her teachers had invited her to something called Educator Hour, a special class held once a week at this particular studio focusing on de-stress for teachers. Fifteen minutes earlier, she'd hurried into her leggings and a long tank top behind her closed office door but would still wander in later than she'd hoped. She made her way up the stairs and past several glass wind chimes and strings of prayer flags hanging outside of offices until she found the studio, boots strewn outside its door. She added her own boots to the pile and stepped inside in her socks, a wave of warm lavender air hitting her.

Liane Tabor, one of her math teachers, waved from a corner mat. "We saved you a spot!" she patted the bare patch of wood floor in between her mat and another. "Joan's in the bathroom." Best friends Liane Tabor and Joan Platt had taught in the math department together for thirty years. They were two of the more popular teachers at Imperial Flats, always team-teaching various lessons and bringing in freshly baked bread and homemade jam in mason jars labeled Tabor & Platt. The kids liked to tease that when they retired, they could start their own lifestyle brand. Nora secretly hoped they'd never retire. The younger members of the math department weren't quite as fun, to say the least.

"Thanks." Nora unfurled her mat, creaky from disuse. "Do I sign in?"

"You have to fill out a waiver." Liane nodded toward a reception desk set up on the far side of the studio.

Nora filled out a waiver, paid ten dollars, acquired the recommended props: blocks, straps, blankets, bolsters. It occurred to her that she would likely need them all. She couldn't remember the last time she'd tried to touch her toes.

The teacher was a curvy, snowy-haired woman who introduced herself as a "recovering" elementary school teacher who'd been "in the system" for twenty-six years before finding a "renewed education" in yoga. She began to murmur them through an opening meditation, encouraging them to find their breath, to close their eyes, to listen to their bodies. As much as she tried, Nora couldn't quiet her mind, could feel only the thick rope of ache running from her right shoulder down the length of her back.

After a moment of quiet, the only sound the trickle of an unseen fountain, the teacher's voice filled her ears: "Henry David Thoreau once wrote, 'We must reawaken and keep ourselves awake, not by mechanical aids but by an infinite expectation of the dawn.' I want you to think about this during our practice today, this idea of the dawn, of each day offering a new beginning because of something within us, rather than outside of ourselves. Education is all-consuming and draining. We must reawaken each day and show up for our students. How can we do that if we don't care for ourselves?"

Ridiculously, Nora felt tears well behind her closed eyelids. Self-care was possibly one of her least favorite modern expressions. It felt self-indulgent in a way that got Nora's back up, housed in whatever building also held entitlement and privilege. Or so she'd thought. As she moved into twists, into downward dogs, into tree pose, she wondered how much she avoided spending time on herself because for a while now she hadn't much cared for the company.

* * *

Nora had no idea what she was thinking agreeing to this meeting. Date? Was it a date? It might be a date. Toby Cameron had texted her yesterday: *want to get a drink, see some music?* Her first instinct had been to decline. He was a board member. Weren't ethics a factor? But she had made the mistake of asking Dani, who pushed her to do it. *It's a drink and some music, Nora,* she'd texted when Nora resisted at first, the eye roll implied.

She was early. Not cool. Such an educator habit. Five minutes early, always. But Toby was already there. She could see him across the dim of the room at a table near a window, scrolling through his phone. A flash of something went through her. He was cute. That dark hair graying at the temples, the casual cross of his legs. Shit. She'd felt it at Thanksgiving, too. Attraction. She almost turned and fled. Texted an excuse. He hadn't seen her yet. But she had changed four times. And she loved this dress. Never got a chance to wear it. Too much cleavage for anything work-related. And what else did she do lately that wasn't work or Netflix?

"Hey." She slid into the chair across from him.

He slipped his phone quickly into his pocket, his dark eyes lighting up. "Wow, you look amazing."

She flushed like a teenager. "Thank you." She hooked her purse onto the back of the chair, tossed her jacket over it. "Did you order something?"

"I wasn't sure if you'd like a cocktail or wanted to split a bottle of wine?"

Thoughtful, too.

"I'd love a cocktail."

He handed her the menu. They chatted about the school, about her day, until the waiter returned with their drinks. "Cheers," Toby clinked his glass against hers. She sipped hers, a delicious ginger and gin concoction with some sort of herb infusion.

She let her eyes stray to where the band was setting up. "Have you heard them before?" she asked Toby, before realizing that the guitarist was Evan Dawkins. Her heart briefly sank. Even when she was trying, she couldn't escape her job.

Evan caught her eye and trotted over. "Hi Nora."

She smiled up at him. "I didn't know you were in a band."

"I'm filling in." He glanced at Toby. Nora introduced them, the men shook hands, exchanged a few pleasantries, and then Evan headed back to his bandmates.

Toby studied her face. "We can go somewhere else if you'd like, if you don't want to have to feel like you're on duty."

Touched, she assured him she'd be fine. "It'll be nice to hear him play. I never have."

As the band started their first set, Toby studied them closely. "He's lucky to have something like that. I wish I did, you know, for when I retire. But I don't really have anything."

Nora set down her glass. "You don't have hobbies?"

"Nothing serious, like music or golf or working on old cars. Nothing like that."

Nora realized she didn't know much about his business. Just that he appeared wealthy and busy. Something in real estate, she thought. "I'm sorry, I should know this, but what is it you do, exactly? We've been on the board together for so long, I should know—"

He shook his head. "There's no reason you'd know. It's endlessly boring. I started off in just basic local commercial real estate. But now I work for an international commercial real estate firm which means I answer a lot of emails and spend a lot of time in meetings. And travel quite a bit, which used to be nice." He shrugged, sipped his drink.

"You don't like it?"

"Not anymore. But I'm fifty-nine years old. Not too much longer now."

Like a prison sentence. "Are there things that interest you that could become hobbies?"

"For the longest time, my family was my hobby."

Nora nodded, understanding how something so immersive could suddenly just vaporize.

"What sort of adventures do you have planned for after you retire?" he asked. "Or maybe that's too far off. You're young still."

"Not as young as I used to be." Why did she say that? It didn't even mean anything, not really. One of those verbal placeholders when you don't want to have to say anything real. Nora pretended to focus on the band. What did she want? She'd never been the sort of person to wish for adventure. She wasn't restless by nature, didn't think the grass had a greener glow elsewhere, wasn't much of a lawn person in general. She'd started teaching high school in her early twenties, taken her first job in L.A. at a massive school that had been one of her teenage rivals. Five sections of World History for three straight years. Bored out of her mind, she'd taken the job in Imperial Flats almost on a whim. Maybe that had been its own sort of adventure, city girl moving to a small foothill town half a state away from anyone she knew. But she hadn't thought of it that way. It had been the offer of AP Government/Econ and US history classes that had drawn her. She'd met Craig, had Leo, and when he was just starting preschool she'd filled-in for an assistant principal on maternity leave. Then, she'd been offered the principal job. The years blurred behind her.

So, answering Toby now, she simply said, "I don't always think of what's next. I'm not sure the job gives me a lot of time for that." That last part was a lie. The job was endless as far as thinking about the next thing. Nora just didn't like thinking about what was next for *her*. But everything that had happened with Craig and Leo and their departures, even Dean quitting at semester, had shaken her. She knew she'd better start thinking about it. Because suddenly all those things she used to value—consistency, stability, reliability—seemed almost naïve, like they belonged to a different time.

Nora was fifty-five years old. What *did* she want next?

* * *

Dani rang the doorbell the next morning at eight-thirty, holding up a bag of pastries from their favorite bakery, *Bella's*, and a tray of lattes. She didn't bother to say hello.

"So?" She peered around Nora, who stood in the doorway in her blue-flowered robe. "Is he here? If he's here, I can just hand these off and go."

"He's not here."

"Oh, Nora."

Nora left the door wide and walked back into the kitchen where she'd been reading the paper. "Don't 'oh, Nora' me. We had a perfectly lovely time."

Dani slid onto one of the tall stools at the kitchen bar, setting down the lattes. "You have a perfectly lovely time at a baby shower. You should have been tearing his clothes off." She opened the bag and pulled out two of Nora's favorite cinnamon twists.

Nora took plates out of the cabinet. "Can you imagine?"

Dani arched her eyebrows. "Can you?" Nora tried to hide her smile. Dani sipped her latte. "Well, that's something at least."

Nora poured her latte into a ceramic mug and popped it in the microwave. "Don't you have a family?"

"Everyone's still sleeping."

Nora watched her friend nibble threads from the flaky pastry. "I didn't expect to like him this much."

Dani looked like she might say something, then decided against it. After another moment, she nodded, sipped her coffee, and said, "I know you didn't."

* * *

Nora stepped out of the IEP meeting into the hallway to answer the call from her son. "Leo?"

"Hey Mom. Sorry to call you while you're working. Are you busy?"

Nora's heart flipped at how young and far away he sounded. He almost never called. They texted and Zoomed sometimes, but calls were rare. "I'm in an IEP, but they can manage without me for a couple of minutes—what's up?"

He hesitated. "Dad didn't deposit money this month into my account. And I don't want to bother you. I know it's his month, but I need to buy some things, like for actual school and—"

"Did you try calling him?"

"I left a message yesterday, but he hasn't called back, and I need to get some stuff. We're taking this field trip and—"

"How much?"

"Just like sixty bucks?"

"I'll Zelle you."

"Thanks, Mom."

Back inside, Nora sent Leo a hundred dollars and then shot a text to Craig. "You okay? Leo said you haven't called him back?"

When he didn't reply, she felt a strange niggle in her stomach. Craig was a lot of things, but he wasn't one to ghost his kid, especially when it was his month to put money in Leo's account. She tried to focus on the natural hum and flow of the IEP. It wasn't a contentious one; everyone seemed on board with the plan, so she felt okay spacing out for some of it. Finally, they wrapped up, and she smiled and nodded as everyone cleaned up and left her, alone, at the conference table.

Rain fell against the window, the world a wash of gray.

She drummed her fingers restlessly on the table. Pulling out her phone, she tried calling Craig.

A woman's voice picked up. "Nora?"

"Sarah?"

"Yeah, sorry, sorry. I saw your text. But, well, Craig had a heart attack."

"What!?"

"I'm sorry, I'm so sorry, he's okay. I mean, he's not okay. He's in the hospital. It happened yesterday. I wanted to call you, but I didn't even go home to get things for him until the middle of the night and then I hurried back this morning. His phone was at home."

"How did—?"

"We were hiking, and he just went down. On the trail. Just straight down."

Nora could hear Sarah start to cry and downshifted into administrator mode. "Sarah, that's so scary. Are you okay?"

"Yes, I'm fine. It's just—" She took a deep breath. "It *was* scary. But I should have called you. I should have called Leo. I've been such a mess. I'm doing everything wrong."

Nora tried to make sympathetic sounds into the phone even as she had the same series of thoughts. "But he's okay now, right? He's going to be okay? Should I come to the hospital? I can cancel the rest of my day. Do you need a break?"

"No, no. You don't need to. I think he'll be okay. I'm not sure when they'll let him go home." She paused before adding, "The doctor said he needs to eat better."

"Well, Craig has been eating like a teenager for thirty-five years."

Sarah managed a soft chuckle. "Right? It's disgusting, actually. Even a teenager shouldn't eat that much McDonald's."

"Call me if anything changes or if you need anything, okay? And I'll call Leo and let him know what's going on."

"Okay." Another pause. "Nora?"
"Yeah?"
"Thank you."

EVAN

"Ow!"

"Oof, Vi—sorry." Evan stumbled over the curled form of his daughter at the side of his bed. He hadn't seen her there in the dark. "You okay, honey?"

"I couldn't sleep."

"Is it the bed?" He'd worried the old lumpy futon wasn't going to cut it. Lauren had raised her eyebrows when he'd shown her the alcove he'd turned into a room for Violet, but, miraculously, she didn't say anything.

"It's the shadows."

He picked her up and tucked her into his bed. He knew she was too old to sleep there, knew Lauren would have an opinion about it, but Lauren was back in London. And he was exhausted. Somehow, most nights for the last couple of weeks, Violet had ended up in his room instead of her own. Lauren said she'd had trouble sleeping since they got back from London after Christmas.

Evan had managed to work out from Violet that she hadn't had a particularly good time, had loved the lights and the decorations, but didn't warm to Roman, Lauren's new boyfriend. But Evan didn't think that was causing the sleep issue. He'd Googled a few articles, and most of them said that transitions were hard, that you needed to set boundaries, but he just didn't see why it was that big of a deal if she slept in his room for a few weeks. It's not like he needed the privacy. Chelsea hadn't returned to his bed since New Year's Eve. She'd finally started texting him back but was never available to meet up for dinner or coffee or a hike. Evan was starting to feel like a stalker.

He tiptoed to the bathroom, careful not to step on the creaky spot in the hallway. Frank could be such a light sleeper. He paused at his father's open doorway, listening to the ragged rise and fall of his breath. He'd gone to sleep in his clothes again. On top of the covers. A few days ago, Frank had taken all of his pajamas and cut them into ragged pieces with Violet's craft scissors. And he wouldn't go near the new pair Evan had ordered for him from Amazon.

Evan used the bathroom, but, not sleepy, ended up in the kitchen to make a cup of Chamomile tea. He'd always loved the middle of the night, how it seemed to take all the edges off the world. Everything monochrome. As he filled the kettle, he squinted through the window into the yard. Something there was moving just slightly in the breeze. A ruffle of pale hair, silver or maybe blonde. An animal, crouched. Setting the kettle down, he opened the kitchen door as silently as he could, trying not to startle whatever it was, but it didn't move. Just that same ruffle of air through its coat. Barefoot, he crept across the dark, damp grass.

A cat curled in a heap. Not moving. On closer inspection, Evan could see blood crusted around its mouth. He nudged it with his foot. Dead. His stomach churned. Maybe it had been sick? Hit by a car? Slumped off into the yard to die? Evan stared up at the bare tree branches overheard. Should he just leave it there? What if another animal found the carcass? Worse, what if Violet found it in the morning?

His eyes fell on the shadowed holes Frank continued to dig throughout the yard, the shovel tossed aside. Without thinking too much about it, he scooped up the dead cat with the shovel, dropped it into one of the larger holes, and filled it over with cold earth.

* * *

The signs went up early the next day. Lost Cat. A photo of the sweet tabby currently residing in one of Frank's yard-holes. Evan saw the first one the next morning a few blocks over from his house on the way back from his normal Saturday run. "Shit." He'd stopped, hands clasped atop his head, his breathing ragged, and studied the sign. "Shit."

* * *

Chelsea peered at the sign. "You have to call."
"I know."
"I kind of can't believe you haven't already."
"That's helpful."
"No, it's just—" She pulled out her phone and typed the number from the sign into it. "It's someone's pet."
"Clearly."
Chelsea had her hair pulled into a high ponytail and wore jeans and a beat-up down jacket. She was chewing her lower lip in that way she always had; it made Evan superimpose her teenage-self over her now-self. He probably needed to stop doing that (it wasn't fair to either of them), but something about her brought every old thing he'd ever felt for her to the surface. It was messy and disorienting. Like he'd suddenly been consumed by fire. Until now, that sort of feeling had been reserved for whisky or an exceptionally good set on stage. What was it about this woman, both her now-self and the memory of what he'd felt for her all those years ago, that threatened to burn him to the ground? Did she remind him of all the things he'd once wanted to be? He felt a momentary

flash of anger for what she unearthed in him, for making him remember the ways he'd failed himself. Then he reminded himself that he'd been the one to text her, and what it felt like when she'd texted him back after he'd asked for advice on the cat, those simple words sending heat coursing through him: *be right over.*

"Did you check to see if it had a collar?"

Evan shook his head even though he had thought about that in the early hours of morning, listening to Violet's even breathing next to him. He should have checked to see if the thing had a collar. Still, there was no way he was going to go dig it up and find out.

Chelsea waited a moment, then asked, "Do you want me to call for you?"

He didn't answer, stared across the street at a woman holding a baby peering at them through the white curtains of a blue house. "I mean do we dig it up or what?"

"Well, that would be a question for the owner."

His body gave an involuntary shiver he hoped she didn't notice. "I'll call."

She handed him her phone.

CHELSEA

THANKFULLY, THE OWNER DIDN'T WANT Evan to dig up the cat, but she did want a hug. Standing there on the woman's doorstep, Chelsea watched Evan put his arms around her tiny frame, his eyes wide at Chelsea over her shoulder. Chelsea clenched her jaw; she wouldn't, *couldn't*, laugh right now. The woman must be nearly a hundred years old, had introduced herself as "Bernice, but call me Bern," and Evan had just buried her twenty-one-year-old cat in his yard. No laughing. No matter how ridiculous Evan looked hugging her, no matter how wide his eyes got over the wisps of her swan-white hair.

"I'm so sorry," he kept murmuring.

"He was such a good boy," Bern kept repeating. "Montgomery."

"Great name." Evan stepped back. "Really, great name."

"After Montgomery Clift." She blinked up at him. "You look a little like him."

Evan's eyebrows shot up. "Like your cat?"

Chelsea couldn't help it; she let a giggle escape. "I think she means like the actor. Like Montgomery Clift, the actor." Bern was right now that Chelsea thought about it. He did look a bit like Montgomery Clift. She Googled him to show Evan a picture. "He was known for playing sensitive, moody men."

Evan handed back her phone. "Sounds about right."

Bern blinked from Evan to Chelsea. "Would either of you like some tea?"

Neither of them did, but, really, how could they refuse? Who knew cats even lived for twenty-one years?

Inside, a time warp. Like walking onto a cluttered set of *Mad Men*, if the crew had piled all the set pieces from Don Draper's house into one room. An entire floor-to-ceiling shelf that ran the length of the wall just held a variety of glassware: tumblers, Champagne flutes, high balls, beer mugs, brandy sniffers, coupe glasses. This last row caught Chelsea's eye. Beautiful etched glass, a rainbow of tints, clear. Chelsea tried not to stare, but the woman noticed.

"My husband, Harold, loved antique glassware. Collected it. You can take a few pieces if you'd like. I'm not much of a drinker anymore, but I always thought they were quite pretty, especially in the afternoon light. Even if they are a bitch to clean." She disappeared into what must be the kitchen to get tea before Evan caught Chelsea's eye and they dissolved into quiet giggles.

"I like her." Evan hooked a thumb in Bern's direction.

"I can't really, though, right?" Chelsea asked. "I can't just take some?"

"Sure, why not?"

"You buried her cat."

"Okay, but it's not like I murdered her cat."

"Shhhh." Chelsea shot a look toward the kitchen.

Evan lowered her voice. "Well, I didn't."

"So you say."

"Oh, that's dark." But he grinned, moving closer to the rows of glassware. "I think you should take a couple—she *offered*. These are nice." He held up two of the etched, short-stemmed coupe glasses she'd been eying. "Very Gatsby."

"Those are from the 1930s." Bern set a tray down on a cluttered coffee table. "Harold made the best gimlets." She paused in the memory, her eyes lighting briefly. "Milk or sugar?"

Ridiculously, Chelsea felt tears spring to her eyes. "Both, please."

Bern passed her a cup of tea in a flowered cup with a saucer. "You should take those two glasses. Drink gimlets in them. You can toast my Harold."

"I'd like that." Chelsea brushed at her cheeks. "I'm sorry. I'm being so sentimental."

Bern handed a cup of tea to Evan. "Personally, I think this culture has gotten too hard. Sentimentality is underrated. But I'm an old lady. What do I know?"

* * *

Later, just as the light was leaving the sky, Chelsea opened the door to Evan standing on the narrow, pebbled path that led around the side of the house to her private entrance. He held up a thermos. "Gimlet?" He glanced down at her pants. "Nice PJs. You know it's not even six yet?"

"Did you text?"

"Nope, because you would have said you were grading papers or organizing your socks." He stepped past her into the studio. "Besides, I just buried a cat in a hole my father made because he's losing his mind, so I want to toast to Harold and drink a gimlet."

She pulled the door shut. "You know, a gimlet is really more of a summer drink."

"I don't know about you, but I could use a little summer right now." He grabbed the washed glasses from next to the sink and set them on a tiny cafe table near the bed. He gave the Hydro Flask a quick shake, and then poured two pale green cocktails. He handed one to her as he held the other up, "to Harold."

"To Harold. And Bern and Montgomery." They clinked glasses. She sipped the chilled drink, the lime tart, the simple syrup just right. She studied it, impressed. "This is good."

"I made the simple syrup myself."

"Did you?"

"I might have bartended a time or two in my day."

Chelsea slid into one of the chairs and motioned Evan into the other. "I loved being a bartender. I used to do this silly thing," she paused, shook her head. "Forget it."

"No, tell me."

"I used to get poems printed on coasters to give out, so people would have something to read while they sipped their drinks, especially if they were waiting."

Evan titled his head. "Why didn't you want to tell me that? I love that."

Chelsea flushed. "I don't know. It was sort of a waste of money, but one guy tipped me a hundred bucks once. Told me to donate it to my 'coaster fund.' And I did." She held her glass out for a refill.

Evan poured hers and then refilled his own drink. "Why did you stop bartending?"

"Oh, the usual reasons, I guess. The hours, the grind. And Judy never hesitated to remind me she didn't send me to college to be a bartender." She pulled a face. "It was never fun when drunk guys got sloppy with me."

Evan nodded. "I remember having to escort the occasional gentleman out the door."

"I got my credential because a friend of mine was getting hers and it sounded like something I might like. And I did. I do. I like teaching. Besides, it seemed safer than bartending at the time." She grimaced. "Little did I know. Not once while I was bartending did someone shove me into a door." She stood up to grab a mason jar of cashews from the cupboard, shook some into a bowl, and put them on the table. Mostly, though, she wanted to avoid Evan's darkened expression.

"Did anything happen to him? The guy who pushed you?"

Chelsea popped a cashew into her mouth. "What do you think?"

"That is seriously fucked."

"Yes."

"So you quit. That was brave."

Chelsea frowned. She knew she could play it like that, could act like she'd left with her feet firmly planted on the moral high ground, and maybe she kind of did. But it didn't feel like it. "Not so brave, though. Not really. I didn't sue, I fled. And now I'm living with my uncle in Imperial Flats."

Evan held her gaze for a minute, before letting it slip around the apartment. "Cute place, though. What's he charging you?"

Chelsea dropped her eyes. "He's not."

"Even better."

"Judy said she can't believe I'm okay living here. It's so small."

Evan shook his head. "I like small. How much space does a person really need?"

Chelsea agreed. She'd once dated a man, a biochemistry professor, who told her, in one of the nastier moments of the breakup, that she spent her years trading one small life for another, that she would grow old and realize she'd spent her whole life small. She'd said equally cruel (and mostly true) things about him—his inability to listen, his selfishness, his insufferable ego—until he'd banged out of the apartment. But over the years she'd thought a lot about his accusation. She wasn't sure it had the intended landing he'd been going for, wasn't sure she found it insulting at all.

She had grown to believe that the culture did a disservice to smallness when it came to a life lived. Even as a child, she'd never imagined a large life in the way some of her friends had. Certainly not the life Evan and Denny Bliss had been gunning for. Regular life was enough for Chelsea. She'd only ever wanted to feel like she was loved for being truly herself. Honestly, maybe that had been the biggest ask of her life. So far it hadn't truly happened. But if she could find that, she was certain it would feel like enough.

Maybe she was naïve, maybe she was just small, but that might be what kept her feeling safe throughout the last crazy years. With Covid, and the terrible yearly fires and smoke, with California going on a constant state of alert, losing power, evacuation standbys, with the social unrest they'd been navigating endlessly, small had felt lucky. Each catastrophe brought out a glaring awareness of her own privilege, that gnawing guilt that she'd spent much of her life worrying about trivial things. Over the last few years, the world kept getting bigger and scarier than it had even as a teenager. She'd basked in her luck at wanting (and mostly having) a small, good life. At having enough. A life where she drank chilled wine and had a glimpse of the sea, and graded papers on the weekend in a café that served still-warm cinnamon buns. Even if things with Stone always felt like settling, like something she had to put up with to have that good, small life, she still had it. How many people could say that?

Then Mr. King-Jennings had pushed her into the car door, and Sheryl had essentially pushed her out of Grove, and suddenly she knew those things hadn't been the life she'd always craved. She had been choosing the beauties of a small life over living an authentic one, like an extra in a beautifully lit film who didn't have any lines. Chelsea wanted to stop feeling like an extra in her own life.

Evan split the last of the cocktail between their glasses. "Want to talk about why you've been avoiding me?"

"I've seen you twice today."

"You know what I mean."

"Where's Violet?"

"She got invited to a sleepover tonight. With a new friend. I have her older sister in class, so I promise I'm not sending my kid to some weird house."

"I wasn't worried."

"Sorry, my ex can be a little intense. I always feel like I need to justify."

"Well, if she doesn't like your parenting choices, she shouldn't have moved to London."

He grinned at her gratefully. "Cheers."

They clinked glasses again, and Chelsea felt that bloom of familiarity she associated with Evan. How easy it was to be with him, the air erasing the decades between them. Right now, that ease made her itch like she had hives.

"You're right," she said finally. "I have been avoiding you."

Something crossed his features, a ripple of something that could be mistaken for insecurity if Chelsea didn't know him as well as she did. "I've been wondering if maybe—it wasn't what you'd hoped or imagined."

"What, the sex?" When he nodded, she sighed, almost exasperated, "That part was great!"

"Well, I thought so."

She shook her head. "How did you not tell me you had a kid? Right from the start?"

He flushed. "I apologized for that!"

"It was obviously *not* the sex."

"Okay, okay. Sorry. But you never know—maybe we'd both built it up too much over the years."

There. An admission that she'd been on his brain all this time, too. Her entire body heated with it. He'd always been able to do that, turn up her internal thermostat without even trying. It made her irrationally angry. "Not the problem."

"So, what is?"

She waved her hand generally at the tiny room, the even white tiles by the kitchenette, the blue-gray walls, the endless throw pillows. "My life is the problem."

"This again?"

"What do you mean?"

"I'm just wondering when you're going to stop thinking there's some other version of life you're supposed to be living."

"I will when you will."

"Fair enough."

* * *

Chelsea pushed her cart down the cereal aisle, furious with herself. Gimlets had turned into wine and Thai food and then they'd ended up back in bed together before Evan had to leave to go check on his dad. The worst part was it had been even better than the first time. Sweet and slow and then not. Perfect. *Shit, shit, shit.* She'd wanted New Year's to be a fluke. She couldn't do this right now, not when her life felt so wobbly, not when she'd just ended things with Stone, not when the intensity of teaching this new group of kids kept her up through the night. She tossed granola, tea, and a box of frosted strawberry Pop-Tarts into her cart before heading toward the produce section.

"Chelsea?"

"Oh." Chelsea's stomach dropped. "Hi Mom." Her mother looked perfectly put together as usual. Trim navy slacks, an ivory cashmere twin set, her make-up flawless. Chelsea felt Judy's gaze drink in her own yoga pants, the ratty Grove sweatshirt with the holes near the kangaroo pocket. Why did so many of her clothes have holes?

Luckily, the box of Pop-Tarts took the brunt of Judy's attention. "Oh, Chelsea, Pop-Tarts? You aren't eight."

As if Chelsea had somehow forgotten her age. "They're for Evan's daughter." Why did she just say that? She hadn't even met Violet yet. She and Evan had talked about possibly meeting up for a movie next weekend and then going out for pizza so she and Violet could get to know each other, but she certainly wasn't providing breakfast for his kid yet.

Her mother brightened. "I heard you two were spending time together."

Chelsea peeked in her mother's hand cart. Plenty of leafy greens and a plastic-wrapped package of chicken breasts. And some orange juice for her dad. Judy wouldn't even drink juice when they recommended it after donating blood. "We're teaching together now, so logically I would see him."

Judy put a thin hand conspiratorially on her arm and gave her an uncharacteristically playful squeeze. "I think it's wonderful."

Chelsea couldn't hide her surprise. "You used to think he was aimless, that he spent too much time on his music."

"Did I?" Judy waved to someone over Chelsea's shoulder. "I remember thinking he was a lovely boy. And so handsome." She leaned in, wiggling her perfectly groomed eyebrows. "Still so handsome."

What was actually happening right now? "Okay, well, I should get going. Good to see you, love to Dad."

"Chelsea, come to dinner next week. You're living too close to be such a stranger. I'll even buy bread."

There she was.

In the checkout line, Chelsea tried not to run their conversation over and over in her mind, that terrible habit she'd always had of over-analyzing everything her mother said. How she'd said it, where she'd put her inflection, where she'd let her gaze settle as she'd inflected. It was a ridiculous pastime and Chelsea hated to think of the endless, wasted hours she had eaten up in its pursuit. But she couldn't help it, couldn't fight back the troubling thought that she had spent too much of her life living in opposition to her mother, in direct pursuit of whatever her mother might frown at or find unappealing, possibly in direct harm to her own life.

Chelsea had once been home during her mid-twenties when her parents had some friends over for dinner. They'd been chatting in the living room when Chelsea had come in from a run. One of the friends, the husband, had asked what she was doing for work, and she had answered, "I'm bartending."

Her mother had hurried to say, "But she's not a bartender!" It was possible that Chelsea had bartended for a few extra years than she might have otherwise just to spite her mother. Okay, that definitely happened. Her mother always insisted on telling people that Chelsea was "rebelling" during this "bartender phase," but it wasn't actually rebellion if you were an adult, right? It was just living your life and having someone else disapprove?

Standing in the check-out line, she wondered how many of her choices had been made simply to piss off her mother. One of Chelsea's successful take-aways from her years of therapy was the realization that she'd always longed for a certain kind of mother. She remembered one day in her early thirties sitting in a stylish office (this had been Jonathan, late forties, closely trimmed beard, sweet), listening to the sound machine play ocean waves, and, somehow, they'd ended up discussing the phrase, "A face only a mother could love." Chelsea had never understood that phrase.

"Well," Jonathan said, shifting in his chair. "It implies the sort of unconditional love that mothers have for their children." Then, he corrected himself. "Some mothers."

For Chelsea, it had felt completely foreign, had implied that mothers were the least of our critics instead of the central one. Her mother loved her face only if and when it was washed and properly moisturized.

Still, though, even as she longed for a mother who would love her no matter what, Chelsea made decisions entirely because she knew they would fall short of her mother's approval. If she wanted this love so desperately, she had asked Jonathan that day, why did she work so hard to impede it? Perhaps, he'd offered, it was easier to already know the outcome than to try for what might feel out of reach? He'd hit on something there, sending a burst of recognition through her and one of the messiest crying fits she'd ever had in therapy. She'd gone through most of his box of tissues.

This, Jonathan had insisted in between her hiccupped apologies, was *loss*. And it was. Chelsea had always felt she and her mother had somehow misplaced something special, let it slip carelessly down a storm grate like a bobbled set of keys.

Early in their relationship, Stone had insisted that Chelsea take a workshop called "The End of Loss" with him. Ostensibly, the workshop was about how we never truly lost anything, that if we allowed ourselves to view each loss as a practice of non-attachment, as a gift of expansion, then we eradicated loss from our lives. They'd sat in a circle in a room with hardwood floors and pale gray walls overlooking the ocean and the leader had asked them each to share a loss they then reframed as a gift. Chelsea had instantly thought of her mother, but it had seemed too private and scary, so she made something up. Something about a friendship from college. She said all the things she knew she should, used all the buzzwords everyone else was using, and she hadn't even felt bad about it later like she usually did.

Mostly because Chelsea had thought the workshop was total bullshit.

In middle school, she'd lost her favorite journal, one with a blue fabric cover, that held everything she'd written in fifth and sixth grade. There was no growth there. No gift. Just a loss of all those childhood words that meant so much to her, that she could never get back. It was just fucking lost. And then, at dinner later that evening, she'd thought again of her mother. How she'd felt such a loss of what that relationship might have been. She tried to talk to the leader about it over the vegan curry they all ate for dinner, a tip-toe into asking if something could simply just be a loss, if perhaps there was beauty in that, too, owning that absence, but he'd told her over his lifted spoon that she wasn't working hard enough to see its gift. She had eaten the rest of her curry in silence.

Later that night, Stone told her if she didn't stay open to new ideas, she would remain stuck. Why hadn't she thought to ask him then a question she should have asked so many times since: why when those new ideas originated within her, when they contradicted whatever workshop leader they were paying for insight, why didn't *those* new ideas count?

"Is that everything?" A man named Thomas with kind eyes and a comb-over scanned her Pop-Tarts and set them into her canvas bag.

She hurried to swipe her credit card. "Oh, sorry—spacing."

"Do you need help out?"

"I don't need help, thanks."

Even if she knew she did. Seemingly endless supplies of it.

* * *

Chelsea was about to lock up her classroom when she

heard someone clear a throat behind her. Turning, she saw Ashleigh O'Hare with a half-dozen other girls standing outside.

"Ms. Garden?"

"Yes?"

"It's our Civil Issues Club today."

Chelsea searched her memory for a meeting she was supposed to attend. Civil Issues was not ringing any bells. "Sorry?"

Ashleigh flipped her beautifully lightened hair over one shoulder. "Mr. Moreno was our advisor for this club. Where we discuss civil issues—you know, like anti-racism and sex positivity and body politics and climate change? I thought you might be taking over since he left?"

"Oh!" She hurried to open the door again and usher the girls inside. "I can do that." She dropped her bag back by her desk and helped them push some desks into a small circle.

Ashleigh opened a spiral folder and flipped it to an empty page. "We used to have separate clubs for each of the things, but we basically just kept stealing each other's members, plus my mother *freaked out* when I mentioned being sex-positive, so we just rolled them all together into one club and gave it an innocuous name."

Chelsea blinked. This girl reminded her of her students at Grove. "Oh, right—great idea."

"Also," Ashleigh added, "we might just roll the Queer Alliance in, too, since their advisor is going on maternity leave."

"Except Adam said Mr. Dawkins offered to be their advisor," another girl added. She had a cello case and too-long bangs that didn't seem to be that way on purpose. Chelsea couldn't help but smile at the mention of Evan. *Mr. Dawkins.* His high school self was lighting himself on fire right now.

Ashleigh made a note of it. "Fine. Okay, let's get started."

* * *

Chelsea always cried in animated movies. Pixar. Disney. Miyazaki. She must have watched *My Neighbor Totoro* a dozen times. Cried every time. And *Inside Out*? Waterworks. So she was relieved when Evan suggested they go see a live action movie with Violet Friday evening. Something based on a video game Chelsea'd never played. Not that she thought crying was bad; it wasn't. It was a beautiful thing, crying. It was more the *way* she cried. It wasn't a sweet trickle, eyes welling and spilling like a heroine in a Jane Austen remake. Chelsea blubbered. She grew red as a tomato and choked out sobs. It was embarrassing.

On a second date with a man whose name had since slipped her mind, during the opening of *Up* at a movie theater in San Francisco, she'd had to excuse herself and hide in the bathroom. A woman in the next stall had asked if she needed to go to the emergency room. So not wanting her first introduction to Violet to include an unhinged sob, Chelsea was relieved to know this movie would feature live kids and a video game she couldn't care less about.

Chelsea waited for Evan and Violet in the dim carpeted lobby of Imperial Cinemas, Imperial Flats' old Art Deco movie theater, one of the few truly lovely buildings in downtown. The same family had owned the theater for years and had restored much of the original tile and ceilings. They almost lost the entire business during the pandemic when everything shut down, but thanks to local fundraising efforts and grants, they'd reopened. Chelsea was so glad they had. She'd always loved this building. She'd had her first kiss in Theatre 3 in sixth grade. Jake Coles. As she stood in the popcorn-infused air, waiting, she wondered what Jake Coles was up to now. With that name, she always thought he should be an FBI agent or someone else who flashed a badge.

"Chelsea!" Evan waved to her as he crossed the lobby, Violet at his side. Chelsea felt her breath catch. In the photo he kept of her, Violet looked more like her mother, auburn-haired and a small, intricately-shaped nose. But she walked like Evan, same stride, same quick smile and wave. And those eyes.

"Hi!" Chelsea thought her voice sounded too high. "Violet, nice to meet you." Better.

"Hi, you, too." Violet replied, confident. She wore jeans with rips in the knees and a jacket cooler than anything in Chelsea's wardrobe. Navy canvas, with an army-like cut. And a T-shirt that read: "Trust Women." Chelsea liked her instantly.

Evan smiled, rubbing his hands together awkwardly. He was nervous. "Did you get snacks?" He stared at Chelsea's empty hands. "Of course not, you obviously don't have snacks. Can I get you snacks? Something to drink?"

Violet's eyebrows shot up. "Whoa, Dad. Breathe."

They all laughed. "Good advice." He put a hand on Violet's shoulder. "What do you usually get, sweet girl?"

"Milk Duds and popcorn. And an Icee. Cherry."

Evan gave an impressed nod. "Okay, not your first rodeo. Chels, you?"

"I'll take some Milk Duds, too. No popcorn. And I brought a water bottle."

"You can have some of my popcorn if you want," Violet offered. "But I like to dump my Milk Duds in while it's still warm, and shake it around. My mom taught me that."

"Your mom sounds like a smart woman."

"She is. She's in London."

"I bet you miss her."

Her eyes followed Evan to the concessions counter. "It's nice to see my dad so much."

"I'll bet."

"And my mom says we work each other's last nerve, so breaks are good."

"Okay."

"You teach with my dad, right?"

Chelsea watched Evan trying to balance all their stuff as he headed back over. "I do. We used to go to high school together, so I've known him a long time."

"Right. My mom says you're the one who got away."

"Oh, well—"

"Here we are." Evan gave the popcorn and Icee to Violet, then pulled the candies out of his coat pocket. "Milk Duds." As he handed them over, he caught what must have been a strange expression on Chelsea's face and glanced quickly between her and Violet. "What?"

"Violet was just telling me about how she adds her Milk Duds to her popcorn while it's still warm."

"Your mom does that," he said to Violet.

"Duh, where do you think I learned it?"

Evan raised his eyebrows at Chelsea. "When do you think they grow out of the 'duh' phase?"

"Do we ever grow out of it?" She smiled, as they followed Violet into the theater.

* * *

Later, after they'd eaten pizza, Evan gave Violet a pile of quarters and sent her off to the game room. He picked a stray piece of pepperoni from the almost empty pizza pan, giving Chelsea a hopeful look. "So?"

"She's an amazing kid."

"She really is."

His relief made Chelsea smile. She wasn't lying, but it's not like she would tell him if his kid were an asshole. Across the restaurant, she could see Violet through the glass of the game room, hunkered down over an old Ms. Pac-Man game. Violet felt her watching, glanced up, and flashed a smile. Chelsea's heart thrummed. Evan had asked her something else, but she hadn't heard him. "What?"

"I asked how school is going."

Chelsea sipped her wine, trying to ease her heartbeat. "Well, yesterday a boy was eating an entire roast chicken in my first period class."

"Gross."

"And when I asked him to put it away, he said, 'But Mr. Moreno let us eat breakfast in class.'" She tried to laugh but she was definitely feeling off, like she was trying too hard, and she couldn't quite catch her breath, felt sweaty on the small of her back, behind her knees. Somehow, Violet's quick smile had worked its way under her skin and sitting here, across from Evan, with Violet near, both of their proximity felt suddenly dangerous. She took another gulp of wine, her hand shaking.

Evan didn't seem to notice. "Teaching is so weird. Once a kid brought an entire smoked trout to a band event. Wrapped in foil. Head still on. The bus reeked."

Chelsea tried to laugh, but, again, her breath kept catching. This time, Evan noticed. "You okay?"

"I don't know." She reached for her recently filled water glass, drinking more than she should probably drink in one swig. Coughing, she tried to set it down, but it landed on the side of the empty pizza tin and spilled in a whoosh into Evan's lap. "Shit—sorry!"

"It's fine." He dabbed at his lap with a wad of paper napkins.

Chelsea pushed her chair back abruptly, grabbing for her purse, which kept getting stuck on the back of her chair. "I'm so sorry," she said again. "I'm sorry, Evan. I can't do this. Tell Violet how great it was to meet her, but I can't do this. I have to go."

NORA

Nora had been meaning to check in with Chelsea Garden for weeks, but something kept coming up. Nora had walked by her classroom during the first week back after the holidays and she'd seen Chelsea moving through small groups of students, nodding and talking with them, while they worked on some sort of group graphic. She had looked entirely relaxed in the room, a pair of readers pushed into her hair, a pale gray jacket over a white T-shirt and a pair of dark jeans and boots. On the board, she had written in crisp, neat writing: *What is memory?*

Nora couldn't believe how lucky they were to get a teacher of Chelsea's caliber on such short notice. She was inclined not to worry much about her, but she still wanted to check in. These kids weren't prep school kids. Some of them were lucky if they made it to school at all. Which was why she couldn't seem to get back over to Chelsea's classroom again for that check in. Since second semester started, every time she'd scooted her chair back to head that direction, a call from an angry parent rang through, or a teacher on prep period came to her door, or a discipline issue popped up. Last week, Mark Weaver had poked his head in to report that the ag department was missing a pig. An actual live pig. "Operation: Where's My Bacon?" Mark had joked before heading out in search of the roving porcine.

And this morning had been awful. A freshman girl had been jumped at the bus stop by a group of other girls who'd been harassing her on social media. She'd spent most of the morning on the phone with the terrified parents, the police, and a mental health counselor who sadly said they had seen an uptick in these sorts of "jumpings" in the last few months, especially among girls. Nora opened her desk drawer and rummaged around for her Advil.

"Nora?" Elaine Frink stood in the doorway. "You said to tell you if I saw Ashleigh O'Hare's mom on campus. I just saw her head toward the gym."

Nora tipped out three amber pills instead of two. If Sue O'Hare was on campus, she'd need anti-inflammatory reinforcements. "Are we at graduation yet?"

"Only ninety-two more school days."

"Is that true?"

Elaine shrugged. "A rough ballpark."

"Under a hundred is good."

* * *

When Nora made it into Chelsea's room a couple of days later, it was almost five on Friday afternoon, so she was surprised to find the teacher at her desk, head bent over a stack of papers. "Still here?"

Chelsea looked up. "In-class essays. These kids really don't want to write anything by hand anymore, do they?"

"Not if they can cut and paste something instead." Nora leaned into the doorframe. "I've been meaning to check in, see if you had any questions or concerns, but each day keeps swallowing me up. So, here I am, finally, checking in."

Chelsea rolled her head on her shoulders, massaging a muscle in her neck. "I think I'm okay. They're good kids. Different from the ones I've been teaching for so long."

Nora nodded. "They're the whole spectrum." She took a chance. "Want to talk about it over a glass of wine somewhere?"

Chelsea perked up. "Really? That's my kind of check-in."

Twenty minutes later, they sat in the window of a new downtown Bistro called Shade, two chilled glasses of white wine in front of them. Chelsea's gaze traveled over the bare brick walls, the chalkboard menu, the tiny fairy lights strung across the ceiling. It made Chelsea feel old. "This is so much nicer than anything we had while I was growing up here."

Nora liked the place, but she also had a soft spot for the ancient bars around town with their cracked vinyl booths and neon Budweiser signs on the walls. She hoped Imperial Flats wouldn't change so much that she no longer recognized it.

"It's changing, I'm sure like everywhere else."

"My students at Grove told me everything now has to look good on Instagram to be profitable."

Nora sipped her wine. "They seem savvy, your old students."

"Or at least good at parroting whatever their parents say around the dinner table."

As they both finished their first glasses and ordered seconds, Chelsea talked about her old school: the privilege, the wealth, the stress of expectation so many of her students endured, their endless pursuit of first-tier colleges.

Here, Nora told her, just getting some of them to graduate was a huge triumph. "We coax more than our fair share across the finish line. And by coax, I mean drag."

Chelsea studied a car trying to parallel park in too-small of a space on the street outside. "I don't know, maybe I'm romanticizing it, but I might like this more. It feels more—genuine, more like what I thought of when I first went into teaching. I mean, don't get me wrong, the kids at Grove could be great, but sometimes trying to be a teacher within that whole system just felt like being the pool boy." Her gaze snapped to Nora. "Sorry, that sounds terribly elitist of me. There is obviously nothing wrong with being a pool service technician."

Nora grinned. "I know what you mean—and there is something quite different between being a pool service technician and being *treated* like the 'pool boy,' which I think was your point."

Chelsea visibly relaxed. "Exactly, thanks."

Nora thought about something she hadn't remembered in years. "My first year of teaching was in L.A. I had this amazing mentor teacher; she'd been in the history department for a thousand years but hadn't tired of it, you know the type?" Chelsea nodded. Nora remembered her mentor's vibrant classroom, her enthusiasm for teenagers, not just history. "The kids loved her. I remember asking her what her secret was."

Chelsea leaned forward. "What did she say?"

"She said no matter the type of school or students you teach, you have to remember they are all other people's kids. Each one, someone else's child. You are only borrowing them for a short blip in their lives."

Chelsea sipped her wine. "I like that."

"I did, too. I think we get very invested and think of them as *ours*, you know? *Our* kids. But at the end of the day, they belong to someone else. And I think that can help us not take things too personally, but also remember our cargo is very precious." Nora raised her glass again. "Okay, that's enough edu-philosophy from the admin in the room. I just wanted you to know that whatever brought you here, we feel lucky to have you."

Chelsea raised her glass too, her expression growing almost watery. "Thank you for saying that." Her eyes slid toward the window again. "It was just time for a change."

Watching her, Nora wondered how much Chelsea knew about her own changes in the last few years: Craig's affair, the divorce, her son leaving for college. Years ago, Nora thought she'd learned everything she could about how to wall herself off from the small-town gaze that often followed her through the grocery store or at the county fair or home basketball games. As the high school principal, she was a prominent (and, at times, unpopular) figure about town. She thought she'd grown accustomed to keeping all of that at arm's length. People made up their minds about so many things without knowing any of the actual circumstances. She tried not to give it a second thought. But the last few years had made that difficult.

During the pandemic, when Nora felt her job morph into a blur of crisis-management, when she'd been forced to run a school from her living room or sequestered in her office on the empty, lonely campus, enduring endless hours of Zoom meetings; when, later, she'd been trying to reopen the school and was mostly hit with rage from both sides demanding masks or no masks, vaccines or no vaccines, when she'd just been trying to stay afloat—Craig had been joining a hiking club, meeting Sarah for long walks, planting the tiny seeds of his future life. It all still felt so *unfair*.

"I think it's great you knew it was time for a change," she told Chelsea, realizing as she said it that she wasn't sure she would recognize when she herself was ready for more change. Maybe that ship had sailed.

She remembered visiting Craig the evening after she found out about his heart attack. He'd waved off her concern with a glib, "It happens." It felt much like the way he'd waved off their marriage.

"I just realized that I don't know anything about you," Chelsea said. "Are you married? Have kids?"

"I have a son in college. And I'm divorced." She hated how easily she could sum that up.

"So you understand change, then."

"You know," she said to Chelsea, signaling their waitress for the check. "Not once during my entire marriage did my ex-husband buy packing tape." At Chelsea's odd look, she smiled, "Sorry, that was out of left field. But all this talk about change for some reason made me think about how much Craig would order and ship back, and order and ship back, and I'm not really an online shopper, but not once did he ever buy any packing tape. He just expected it to be there, in the closet in the office, where I kept him in endless supply."

"Okay." Chelsea was still trying to follow her.

"I wanted him to change, to just once think about buying some stupid tape! But you know what? I never once asked him to, and I never let him run out."

She'd always just made sure there was enough.

* * *

Nora'd had a piece of beef jerky stuck in her teeth since ten-thirty that morning. All day, she'd tried to find a quiet snippet of time alone to dislodge it, but she'd had two IEPs, a high school review board, and a sprinkling of other meetings. So, when she finally, at four-fifteen in the afternoon, stood by the sink in her office, it wasn't surprising that Toby walked in to find her with a finger jammed in her mouth.

"I'd have thought you'd be one of those people who keeps floss in her desk." He pulled back a chair, the one he always chose for board meetings, and flopped into it, his long legs crossing at the ankles. She'd always thought Toby had a bit of a scarecrow quality to him, those long limbs, but the more time she spent with him, the more she realized how graceful he was. Like a dancer, almost. Craig wasn't graceful.

Ever. More like a plodding linebacker. She bit her lip, trying to shake the comparison from her mind. She had to stop doing that, constantly lining up a mental compare/contrast list of both men. It didn't help anything.

"The board meeting isn't for another two hours," she told him.

"I was thinking we could grab a quick bite to eat?"

"It's four-fifteen."

"Long agenda tonight. Wanted to spare you from that frozen burrito defrosting in the mini-fridge."

It was a Samosa wrap, but point taken. "I actually have a four-thirty call I have to be on."

"Shall I go get us something, then?"

Nora could feel the skin across her back and arms prickling. "I brought something."

Toby studied her. He wore tortoise-framed glasses and favored sweaters with a half-zip in the front over a plaid collared shirt. She'd never gone for preppy guys. And yet, here she was, her stomach flipping at the sight of that sweater, at the man underneath it.

"What's going on, Nora?"

"What do you mean?"

He leaned forward, elbows on his thighs. "Look, I'll admit, I've been out of the game a long time. And I only dated a couple of other women before Liz. But even I can tell when someone is pulling back. Shouldn't we talk about why?"

Nora had spent the majority of her marriage trying to get Craig to talk to her, to delve deeper into what he was feeling and thinking about their relationship. She'd taken enough trauma-informed and social-emotional workshops to know how important it was to have access to feelings, especially when trying to sort out any kind of educational challenge. Turns out, any challenge, really.

Of course, when faced with it on a Thursday afternoon, with a piece of jerky in her teeth, she felt herself doing what Craig would do, pulling the metaphorical garage door closed over her own interiority. "I really have to get on this call."

Toby nodded, his mouth pulling into the beginning of a frown. "Okay." He stood up, his hands finding his trouser pockets. "But I'll keep asking. I'm annoying like that."

"Not annoying," she managed. "I'll see you at six, right?"

"You will." He paused at the door, looked as if he might say something else, but decided against it, and pulled the door shut behind him.

* * *

Dani poured another splash of wine into her glass, groaning as Nora recounted the earlier conversation with Toby, the awkwardness of the board meeting where he wouldn't meet her eyes. "Why are you like this?"

"He's a board member."

Dani rolled her eyes. "Nice try. This is Imperial Flats. If you didn't date people you might cross paths with professionally—"

"Say what you want. It's an actual conflict of interest." Nora popped an olive in her mouth, running her hand across the polished bar at Romano's, enjoying the hum of chatter and clinking forks on plates behind her. It was pretty busy for eight-thirty on a Thursday evening. Dani often talked about how lucky they were they hadn't lost the whole place during the pandemic, had squeaked through with their take out and home delivery food service. Nora helped herself to more olives.

Dani frowned. "Did you even eat?"

"I had most of a lukewarm Samosa wrap."

Dani grimaced. "You eat like a fourteen-year-old boy. I blame Craig." She motioned to Barry, who'd been at Romano's since essentially the dawn of time. He didn't blink before disappearing toward the kitchen, coming back five minutes later with a bowl of steaming pasta in some sort of creamy red sauce covered in freshly grated cheese. He set the bowl and a fork on a crisp white napkin in front of Nora.

Nora breathed it in. "You're too good to me, Barry."

Smiling, he went back to stacking glasses at the far end of the bar to give them at least a semblance of privacy. She'd had Barry's oldest son in her history class years ago. Jason. She'd heard somewhere he had two kids now. Somewhere out of town, if she remembered correctly. She bet Barry was a terrific grandfather.

Nora swirled noodles. "This looks great, Dan, thanks."

"Don't change the subject."

"You changed it first."

Dani studied Nora over her wine glass. It struck Nora that this was the second time today someone had watched her like that. First Toby, now Dani. Better to just come out with whatever she could manage to explain. Dani had that carefully honed instinct that came from her special combination of mother-of-three-restaurant-owner-small-town-girlness. There was no fooling Dani. Not for long, at least.

"It's a problem that he's a board member."

Dani narrowed her eyes. "And?"

Nora dropped her eyes to her food. "I am so busy right now."

"And?" Dani pressed.

"And I don't—" Nora set her fork down. "I don't know what the next step is. And I don't like how that feels. That uncertainty."

"But you genuinely like him." It wasn't a question.

Nora felt her face heat, those same prickles that spread before across her back and arms. "I do."

Dani leaned over and forked a mouthful of Nora's pasta. "Then it can't be that hard to find a new board member, right?"

EVAN

"Chris, I'm wondering if you'd be interested in, you know, joining us today?" Evan paused the rest of the group to wait for the dusty-haired sophomore who could never seem to find his music, backpack, chair, music stand, and certain days, trumpet. Once, shoes.

"My trumpet's gone!" Chris stood at the back of the room, near the cubbies, fists on hips. "Who took it?"

"No one took your trumpet, dummy." Caroline rested her tenor sax on her lap. "Why would anyone *do* that?"

"Thanks, Caroline," Evan told her. "I got this."

"I brought it this morning and put it right here and then I went to the bathroom and now it's gone." Chris hiked up his baggy pants. He probably lost his belt.

"Here!" Ava held up a black instrument case near her piano. "It's here, Chris."

Chris hurried to get his trumpet and join the rest of the jazz band for their early morning practice. Evan's phone buzzed again. Lauren. Even if she was eight hours ahead, she knew he was in school early. He took the kids through a few measures, trying not to notice when it buzzed a third time. His bass player, a tall shaggy-haired boy named Rodney, shot him a glance. "You need to get that, boss?"

"Nope, not now. Okay, let's try that again at measure four. A-one, two, three, four."

* * *

By that afternoon, Evan knew he couldn't keep ignoring Lauren's texts and calls. She'd start thinking something was wrong with Violet. But four texts and two calls in under eight hours? His stomach turned sour. Something was wrong.

He texted: *With a student. What's up?*

He waited until the three little dots turned to: *when do you pick up V?*

He checked his phone. Three-thirty-five. Vi had her basketball practice after school today until four. He texted her back: *4*

I need to talk to you. Call me en route to V. Thx!

Ugh. Lauren could entrap like no other human he'd ever met. He was actually already in the parking lot of Violet's school planning out some new charts he wanted to try with the jazz band in the morning, but he waited ten minutes to make it seem plausible that he'd walked from his classroom to his car. He scanned the lot of Violet's school, dotted with the cars of other parents waiting for practice to finish, turned on the car so his Bluetooth would engage, and called his ex.

"Evan?" Lauren sounded breathless and faraway over the speakers in his car.

Who else would it be? "Yep."

"Listen, I know that we talked about Vi staying with you through the end of the school year, but I miss her too much. I want her to come to London."

Evan blinked. The bare branches of a maple blurred through the windshield. "You can't be serious, Lauren. She just got here."

"It's too hard."

"Maybe for you. But it wouldn't good for her to be bounced back and forth and you know it. She's made friends here."

He could hear traffic sounds in the background of the call. He imagined her walking down a busy London street wrapped in one of those capes she thought made her seem artistic, the Thames a gray sheet in the distance.

"Like you said yourself, she just got there. How good of friends can she have made?"

"She's on the basketball team."

Lauren didn't even try to hide the snort that rippled through the phone. "She's nine, for fuck's sake. They don't even know which direction to run at that age."

"She knows which direction to run."

"We need to talk about this, Evan. I'm sick, literally sick from missing her. It's not working. This was a terrible idea."

"Again, for you."

"Well, yes."

His heart hammered. Why hadn't he anticipated this? "Why didn't you just take her with you to begin with?"

"Jesus, Evan. That's beside the point."

"Is it?"

"I'll call you tomorrow. We need to get it sorted." Did she have the edges of a British accent already?

"Lauren—" But she'd already clicked away.

The door to the multi-purpose room burst open and a spill of fourth grade girls made their way to the cars waiting in the lot around him. Violet wore her team sweatshirt and a pair of too-big shorts that hit below her knees. She'd pulled her hair into a messy ponytail and walked as she chugged water from an empty Vitamin Water bottle he'd filled for her that morning before he drove her to school. His heart turned over.

She yanked open the passenger door. "Hey Dad! I made two baskets."

"Two! Wow, that's great, kid." He gave her a fist-bump.

She eyed him. "Why does your face look funny?"

"I just have a funny face."

"No, it looks squishy."

Evan tried to smile. "Just a long day at school, I guess. Shall we get burgers?"

"Yes! And pesto fries."

"And pesto fries, of course, of course." Evan swallowed over the emerging lump in his throat and pulled the car out of the parking lot, Violet already fiddling with his iPhone to change the music.

* * *

After dinner, he settled Violet on the couch next to his dad to watch *Onward*. For some reason, this particular movie relaxed his dad almost into a trance. They'd tried a few other movies, but they didn't have the same effect. Evan had been abusing it, and likely Violet's patience, lately.

"You sure you can stand this movie again?" he asked her.

She chewed a bag of microwave popcorn, her eyes never leaving the screen. "I love it."

He shrugged. "Okay, but call me if he gets weird."

Her eyes darted to Evan. "He's sitting right here. He can hear you."

"Just call if you need to."

"Got it."

Evan made sure the sliding door was locked, checked that his phone was on, then turned the lock on the front door on his way out. He needed to run out his conversation with Lauren. Thirty minutes. As he ran the quiet streets, watching carefully for ice already forming, he felt his anger rising. How could she do this? For all of her shit, Lauren had been a good mom and fair to Evan. He knew he'd been more distant than he should have been, knew that she had done the lion's share. *Lioness*'s share. But did this give her the right to make this kind of sudden change? It seemed erratic and cruel to tell your nine-year-old she could live with her father for a semester and then yank her to another country. Would the law see it the same way? He hoped it wouldn't come to that.

He stopped at the corner of Anderson Drive, waiting for some cars to pass before crossing. He itched to text Chelsea, but he didn't want to dump this on her. She'd made it clear at the restaurant she couldn't do this, whatever *this* was. But he couldn't help himself. She would know what to do.

He texted: *Lauren's trying to move Violet to London ASAP.* He added a sad face emoji.

She quickly responded: *WTF!?!*

Good, good. He wasn't overreacting. *Right?!* He sent back.

Should I come over?

Can you meet after work tomorrow?

Yes. Just tell me when and where

He took a deep breath and headed home.

CHELSEA

"Did you sign something? Some sort of agreement? What's the custody situation?"

Evan frowned into his beer. "To be honest, Lauren and I have never done anything legal about our arrangement. After we split, she just said we should avoid all that legal shit. I was always traveling for my music anyway. I sent money when I could, showed up when I could. She left Violet with me whenever she needed to, and I could make it work with my schedule. I mean, I'm on Vi's birth certificate as her dad, but we don't have anything legal."

Chelsea looked like she was choosing her words carefully before she settled on, "I think you might need to."

"Lauren would flip."

Chelsea picked at the fries neither of them seemed to really want. Gold Rush Brew was dead. It was a Wednesday afternoon. They were the only ones in the place. They'd ordered fries because it seemed rude not to give the pink-haired waitress something else to do besides deposit two beers on their table.

"Maybe she's just freaking out. You said she could be sort of—" Chelsea searched for a more flattering word than *erratic*.

But Evan didn't need her to finish the sentence. "Yeah, she can be. And she can also be insufferably stubborn once she decides something."

It was hard to believe under a week ago, they were sitting with Violet at Lucky's Pizza, eating a deep-dish pepperoni and olive pie drizzled in garlic olive oil, watching her play video games. Chelsea's cheeks flushed at the memory of her speedy exit. "Have you told Violet?"

Evan shook his head. "She's been so happy these past few weeks. Sleeping well. Inviting a friend over after school." He caught her eye. "She loved you, by the way."

Chelsea dropped her eyes to her beer. "Anything would seem good after that movie."

He grinned. "That was truly terrible."

"When a nine-year-old calls you out for plausibility, you have a problem, Hollywood." Chelsea fished around her brain for a change in the conversation. She didn't want to have to explain her awkward exit, or the distance she'd been keeping all week. Suddenly, she thought of something: "Do you want me to call Kyle? Ask him? Maybe there's something legally you can do to keep her from taking her out of the country but that won't seem too threatening."

Evan frowned. "I'm not sure I can afford a lawyer right now."

"I can at least ask him."

Twenty minutes later, Kyle slid onto the bench next to Chelsea. "Look this isn't my area," he told them, nodding at the waitress who dropped off his wine. "But I called a good family law guy I know, ran the situation by him on the way over, and he had some thoughts."

Evan glanced at Chelsea and then back at Kyle. "Wow, thanks, Kyle."

Kyle took a sip of his wine and helped himself to a few cold fries. "Look, she's being unreasonable, but the only real legal action you can do is file a case to create an actual custody agreement."

"Lauren won't want that. She doesn't believe in all the

legal stuff. It's why we never got married. Well, one of the many reasons."

Kyle wiped his fingers on a napkin. "I don't want to tell you how to live your life, and I get that maybe coming from a lawyer, this will be taken with a grain of salt, but it's better for Violet to have some legal structure in her life, some rules her parents have to follow."

Chelsea nodded along with what Kyle was saying. "It's not right to take her out of school and across an ocean right now, Ev. It's really not."

He drained the rest of his beer. "I can't believe she would do this."

Kyle studied him. "Look, filing a case like this would at least mean you'd get a temporary automatic restraining order, which wouldn't let your ex take Violet out of the state. It would give you some time to sort things out."

Chelsea saw Evan wince at the sound of a restraining order. She reached across the table and squeezed his hand. "I don't know a whole lot. And I'm not a mom. But shouldn't Violet have a say in this? Maybe you two should both talk to her at the same time, over Zoom or something? Have a family meeting about it. She told me she loves being here with you."

He brightened. "She did?"

"When we were at the movies."

Chelsea didn't miss the look on Kyle's face as he watched her with Evan. She almost told him that smug *I knew it* expression made him look a lot like his big sister. But he'd come here to help, he'd called his friend, so she cut him a break. Only she gave him a soft kick beneath the table anyway.

He feigned surprise. "What?"

"You know what."

He sipped his wine. "I haven't the faintest."

* * *

Chelsea nodded to the students streaming out of the classroom. As they left, they added their portfolio cover sheets to a stack in front of her on the desk. Chelsea sniffed.

"Wait, Natalie, what is this?" She held up a paper, stained a deep, unsettling yellow.

Natalie shrugged. "Oh, yeah—that's cat pee. Sorry."

Chelsea handed it back to her. "Could you reprint that and bring it back tomorrow?"

Another shrug, but Natalie took it, stuffed it in her backpack, and disappeared out the door. Chelsea shook her head in disbelief. That was new. She sorted the haphazard papers back into a reasonable-appearing pile, breathing out. School had just ended, and she always needed about fifteen minutes to let the dust settle.

"Ms. Garden?"

One of her seniors, Matthew, stood with his backpack hooked over his shoulder. "I was hoping to talk to you about the reading circles?"

"We'll start those in the next couple of weeks."

"I might have trouble getting a book."

She gave him what she hoped was an encouraging smile. "Oh, don't worry, I can check one out for you if you need me to."

"My mom can be—," he shifted uncomfortably, his gaze out the window, "kind of intense about what I read."

Chelsea tried not to let her surprise show on her face. He was almost eighteen years old. Was his mom still checking up on what he was reading? "I'm sure we'll find you something you can both agree on." Her phone buzzed. Kyle. "I'm sorry," she said to Matthew, "I have to take this."

"Oh, right, okay."

She watched him shuffle from the room before answering. "Kyle?"

"Now I'm the one who needs a favor."

"Okay."

"Diego's in jail."

"What!?"

"It's a long story. I'm due in court five minutes ago and he needs you to come down there. We really don't want to call Judy."

"What happened?"

"I can't get into it. It's a whole thing with the recycling."

She fumbled to toss things into her purse. "They're arresting people now for not properly sorting their bins?"

"Can you just get down there? And maybe leave the jokes for now? He's not in the mood."

"Right." She locked her classroom door behind her.

* * *

On the drive over, Chelsea realized she wasn't completely surprised to hear things had spiraled with Diego and that bin. He'd been going slightly bat-shit around it for the last month. Usually so calm and steady, he'd become almost unhinged, the recycling turning into an obsession. Not the bin itself, but whoever was throwing their empty chip bags, fast food wrappers, and half-eaten sandwiches into it all the time. Chelsea had found him more than once, the bin on its side, sorting through well-washed jelly jars and empty wine bottles, picking out loose bits of burrito or cellophane from donut packs.

"Wrecks the whole thing," he'd mumble as he worked furiously to decontaminate the bin. "Assholes! I'd rather they just dumped their trash in my front yard!"

She'd offered to help him once, but it had been like going to someone else's church, the faith unfamiliar. She'd only been in the way, her standards clearly not high enough. He'd finally snapped, "It's actually better if I just do it myself!" and she'd slunk back inside to her room, her ego momentarily bruised. He was apologetic afterward, brought her a mug of mint tea and three chocolate wafers. Diego was nothing if not self-aware. He knew he was being a nut. But he couldn't help it, staring out the half-curtained front window at regular intervals when the bin was on the street, moving it from the carport to the side of the house behind a gate.

"It's like he seeks it out!" he'd bellowed last week after discovering a Taco Bell bag stuffed inside.

What Chelsea didn't know until she was driving him home from the police station was that he'd set up a camera. The kind used to track wildlife. He'd figured it was the twenty-something down the street who'd been living in his parents' basement since the pandemic started and he wanted to catch him in the act. Turned out, it was a forty-something real estate agent who'd decided to empty out her car each time she checked on one of her listings down the street. She'd been dumping her trash (and the trash her three sons managed to leave in her car) for months. They'd arrested Diego yanking one of her For Sale signs out of a nearby yard. It was the fourth one he'd upended before they tucked him into a cop car.

Chelsea glanced at him. "You could have just asked her to stop throwing her crap in your bin." He didn't say anything, just watched the world move by outside the passenger window. "Or, you know, your way works, too, I guess." She pulled the car onto Macintosh.

"I know it's completely insane, okay? I just—I don't know what got into me." He took a deep breath, his head still turned toward the window. "What's happened to people? It's like they just kept getting more and more awful each year." Diego quietly gathered his things, his hand on the door handle before they'd come to a complete stop.

Chelsea pulled the car along the curb and turned off the engine. "I think maybe they've always been awful. We're just getting old enough to hit the tipping point on examples."

He sighed. "Right. Okay, thanks for picking me up."

"Fridays are never interesting enough anyway," she tried to tease, but Kyle was right; he wasn't in the mood. "Diego?" He paused outside the door, leaned back down. "At least you did something about it. Most people wouldn't."

He drummed his fingers on the top of the car. "Well, thanks for that, I guess."

She watched him walk into the house, his shoulders hunched. She'd meant it, though. Diego had passion. He fought for things.

Sitting here, Chelsea wondered if she'd fought for enough things in her life. She wasn't much of a fighter. She worked hard, but she often worked the hardest to avoid conflict. Which was why these last few months had been so strange. Not that Chelsea minded who she was in the world. She felt safe in her quiet ways. And she felt like she contributed through her teaching. She held doors open for people. She thanked service workers. She believed those small things mattered, that doing your part mattered. But was it enough?

All her life, she'd been a role-player. In basketball, her team had been great, but she'd been just okay. She was a terrible shooter, but could play defense, was a good passer. No matter what, she could hustle. She'd realized somewhere in her late thirties that she'd relied heavily on this hustle instinct for much of her life. Wherever she didn't quite measure up, she could offset with hustle. Which was really just a fancy word for stubbornness. All those diets. That stressful year of getting her teaching credential while waiting tables. Her relationship with Stone. *Hustle.*

A few years ago, the educational buzz word had been "grit." Chelsea hated that word. It sounded like the stuff you found between your toes after a day at the county fair. Of course, she'd come to hate the word "hustle," too. Hustle was just another word for scam. Better to be a fighter, she was beginning to think. At least when it came to your own life.

But she had stood up to Grove. She had ended things with Stone. Maybe it wasn't too late for her.

Chelsea hadn't packed up her room before she left, so she waited until Diego had gone inside before heading back toward school. As she neared campus, she passed one of the signs from the real estate agent who'd been tossing her trash in Kyle and Diego's bin. Alyssa Barker. Chelsea pulled the car over again, idling. She recognized that face. Alyssa Barker used to be Alyssa Jones. The same Alyssa Jones who had thrown Chelsea's school clothes into the showers of their seventh grade PE class. That day, she'd been forced to wear her PE shirt and her friend Erika's sweatpants all day instead of the cute Esprit skirt and cropped sweatshirt that had ended up soapy and soaked in the back corner of the mildewed middle school showers. What was it about a seventh-grade memory that could bring gooseflesh to the surface so quickly?

Thing was, Alyssa hadn't turned out to be a bad person. In a cruel twist of small-town fate, she'd ended up as Chelsea's chemistry lab partner junior year of high school and after a couple weeks of curt answers on Chelsea's part, Alyssa had come right out with it.

"Look, I'm sorry about your clothes," she'd said over a Bunsen burner on a late-fall afternoon. "That was shitty of me."

Chelsea remembered freezing behind her too-big pair of safety goggles, her eyes on their experiment. "Oh, okay. Well, I'm sure you had your reasons."

"Not really. You just looked cuter than I did that day, and my mom wouldn't drive me to the Esprit Outlet in San Francisco. That was it, basically." She shook her head as she took down some data in a chart. "I was such a little bitch in middle school."

Chelsea had stood there, stunned. "Oh. Well, thanks for saying something." And that had been it. They'd had different classes senior year, and she hadn't really seen Alyssa again until just now, staring out of a Coldwell Banker Realty sign with bright-white teeth and a trendy haircut.

Maybe Chelsea could ask her to drop any charges against Diego if she bought her a cute outfit? Did Esprit still make clothes?

* * *

The last person she expected to see sitting on the curb when she got back from school was Stone. Honestly, after the week she'd had, she didn't have the energy for this, for him continuing to turn up like the lost love interest in a mid-range eighties rom-com. Why couldn't he just text like a normal person? Make an appointment. See if she was available. For a man who made her take more than one workshop on consent and boundaries, this was bordering on harassment.

She got out, closed the door, but kept the car between them. "Stone."

"I know, I know. I should have called."

"Yes."

"But I was at a conference in Sacramento of all places, and it was just too close."

"Sacramento's not that close."

"Closer than the City."

"Sacramento's a city, too."

Stone grinned, stood, and brushed some dirt from the seat of his expensive dark Chinos. "Cute little town."

"Try not to be patronizing. It's been a long week."

"You're teaching again?"

"Who told you that?"

He nodded at her school bag that she had rested on the hood of her car, stuffed, a few papers spilling from the top, and she shrugged.

"I took a long-term sub job at my old high school."

He tried not to do that thing with his head, the pity-tilt, but he wasn't a very good actor. Sort of like most of the mid-eighties love interests. "So, you're not planning to come back anytime soon? I haven't rented the cottage yet." That Stone always referred to the studio she lived in all those years as "the cottage" was part of the actual problem, wasn't it? His pretension disguised as charm.

"Have you eaten?" she asked. "We could grab something." Mostly, she didn't want to have to do the whole Kyle and Diego dance. They'd met him a few times in San Francisco back when she was still smitten and defending his every move. Even then, Kyle had barely tolerated him, and Diego had done that thing with his face that looked like he was sucking on a lemon wedge.

"You're the local. Tell me what's good."

Obviously, she would take him to Romano's. The food was great, and Dani would provide both emotional back-up and the kind of familiar small-town attention that Stone would find endearing. Plus, they had a bar. She was very much in need of a bar right now. "I'll drive."

* * *

Dani widened her eyes behind Stone's back as she seated them at a corner booth tucked away in the back of the warm, busy restaurant. "Hot," she mouthed at Chelsea.

Chelsea gave her an almost imperceptible head shake. "Dani, this is my ex, Stone. He just stopped by for dinner before heading back to the Bay." To Stone, she said, "Dani and I played basketball together in high school."

"And now we're in a book club." Dani handed them both a menu.

"This place is too much." Stone's eyes perused the checked tablecloths, the polished wooden bar, the tables each glowing with an ivory glass-orbed candle. "Old school."

Dani shot Chelsea a quick look of understanding before asking, "Can I get you two anything from the bar?"

"Vodka soda with two lime slices," Stone said, picking up the menu, and pulling a pair of readers from the breast pocket of his blazer.

"I'll take a glass of red, whatever you recommend." Chelsea didn't need to look at the menu. She would for the rest of her life only order the lasagna when she was at Romano's. It was made out of magic. And cheese. Lots of cheese.

Stone flipped his readers onto his menu and leaned back against the booth, resting a long arm across the back of the padded seat. "So what? I'm here for a carb fest and then you're kicking me out?"

"That sounds about right."

"What did I do to make you so mad at me?"

"You being here unannounced isn't helping."

"What, we're not friends?"

"Were we ever?"

He pulled a white envelope out of an inside pocket and slid it across the table to her. The candlelight cast his face in a warm glow. "I think we're friends."

Inside, something legal. Her stomach clenched. An agreement with Grove to pay Chelsea her remaining salary for the school year. The place for her signature was blank. "What is this?"

"I told you Leila was good at her job." Stone nodded to the bartender who dropped off their drinks. He squeezed in the two lime wedges and took a sip. "Ah, that's good."

"I didn't ask you to do this." Her fingers shook as she tucked it back into the envelope. On one hand, it felt good to see Sheryl's prim signature agreeing to pay her. On the other hand, she felt sick that they'd gone ahead and done this without her approval or involvement. Like she was a child. "But I resigned."

Stone leaned forward, his forearms resting on the table. "You were basically threatened and forced to resign. Leila made sure Grove knew she would take much more from them than your salary if this went any further."

Chelsea took a too-big gulp of her wine, but managed not to choke. "I don't know what to say."

"Say thank you."

"Did either of you stop to think I'll never get a recommendation from Sheryl now? I might need one if I, you know, ever want to work again." Dani reappeared before Stone could reply. Chelsea handed her the menu. "Lasagna, please. It's still your grandmother's recipe, right?"

"Of course."

Stone picked up the readers again and made a show of analyzing the menu. "Can I have the chicken marsala made without butter?"

Dani raised her eyebrows but said, "I'm sure we can figure that out."

"And no polenta."

"Do you want extra veggies? They're steamed."

"Fabulous."

Chelsea didn't miss the eye roll as Dani made her way back to the kitchen. She scanned the restaurant. About three-fourths of the tables were full, probably normal for a Friday evening, and the room hummed with the collective blend of low conversations. The warmth, the hum, the wine made her drowsy and she wasn't sure how much more of this conversation she could stomach. She thought of Kyle and Diego at home, sitting out in the sunporch, unpacking Diego's arrest, his time in the cell today. They'd be drinking wine and eating a pizza Diego had thrown together.

She'd texted Kyle to say she was out with a friend, to which Kyle had replied: *not your mama*. Still, she felt like she should be hiding this dinner. What if Matt and Judy chose tonight of all nights to go out? What if one of their friends saw her here with Stone? But that wasn't even the point, was it? She didn't want to be sitting here with this envelope in front of her. Or this man for that matter. She tried to focus on something Stone was saying now, something about a trip to Patagonia he and Leila were planning, but she couldn't stop thinking about Diego and his bins. If he could care that much about *recycling*, she could stand up for her own life, her own ideas.

"I'm disappointed you did this without asking me," she interrupted.

Stone looked momentarily confused, perhaps thinking she was talking about his trip. "Wait, you mean the Grove money?"

"You should have asked me."

Stone's face reddened. "You know what, Chelsea. Leila went to a lot of trouble for this. You know what she bills per hour. She didn't have to take the time to do this."

"I never asked her to, but I'll pay her back."

He shook his head, his features softening. "No, no, that's not what I meant. It's not what I meant at all. Don't turn it around. I thought you'd be happy. I know money's always been a struggle."

She felt her face heat. "I wouldn't say that."

"Well, I've been spotting you most of your rent for six years."

"I always offered to pay more, I tried—" Chelsea stopped, leaned back, as Dani approached with their steaming dinners.

Dani gave her a questioning glance as she set the plates in

front of them. "You need another one?" she nodded at Chelsea's nearly empty wine glass.

"No thanks. I'm driving."

Dani looked at Stone who shook his head.

Chelsea ate a bite of her lasagna. It was even more delicious than she remembered, the Béchamel and red sauce creating just the right blend of cream and tart tomato. But she knew most of it would end up in a to-go box. She put her fork down and wiped her mouth on her napkin. Then, she slid the envelope across the table. "I'm not going to take this."

Stone didn't bother to hide his frustration. "Jesus, Chelsea. In the real world, people take the money. You're not some heroine in a Jane Austen novel."

Chelsea clenched her napkin in her lap. "First of all, you've never read a Jane Austen novel in your life." He held up his hands in mock surrender, then went back to his butter-less, polenta-less chicken. "Second, I don't want this. I didn't ask for this. It was never about money; it was about how they *treated* me. Why can't you understand that? Stop doing things for me that I don't ask for and then getting annoyed when I don't throw myself at your feet in gratitude."

You don't have to be so dramatic—" he started.

"Finally, I don't want to see you again, okay? I need to move on from you and I can't do that with you showing up on my uncle's doorstep. I'm not even sure how you got the address. But we're not friends. We've never been friends. We're done, you and me. It's a boundary I need to set. I didn't take all those workshops with you and learn nothing."

He chewed slowly for a moment, his eyes on his plate, before finally looking up at her, his eyes serious. Dani stopped by en route to another table. "Do you two need anything else?"

Stone kept his gaze on Chelsea. "Just the check, thanks."

"And a to-go box," Chelsea added, giving Dani a weak smile, then slid her eyes back to Stone. "For my carbs."

Stone pushed the envelope back across the table. "I'm going to leave this with you. For when you're done with your theatrics and realize the moral high ground looks a lot like poverty."

* * *

Sunday morning, Chelsea waited outside her car near one of the irrigation ditches favored by walkers in Imperial Flats. Earlier in the week, Dani and Nora had invited her to go for a walk and then have brunch at one of the newer restaurants downtown. It was warm for February, already in the low fifties at nine-thirty a.m., and after a few minutes of waiting, she stripped off the vest over her flannel shirt and tossed it back into her car. A moment later, Dani's minivan turned down the gravel road and pulled in behind Chelsea's Volvo.

"Okay," Dani said instead of hello. "I'm going to need some details on that tall drink of water from Friday night."

"Do people still say 'tall drink of water'?"

"I'm retro." Dani propped her foot up on her front tire and adjusted one of her laces.

Nora parked her shiny Acura behind Dani and climbed out, looking fashionable and sporty in her leggings and North Face tech shirt. "Sorry, running a little behind."

"You're fine." Dani said and the three of them set off along the ditch trail, the pale winter light filtering through the bare branches of the surrounding oak trees.

They chatted aimlessly as they walked, mostly Dani filling them in on her kids' morning antics: neither of her sons would be out of bed before noon, and what was it about the sixth-grade brain that reverted back to toddlerhood?

"Diana can't even remember to brush her teeth right now without me reminding her. And last night, she left the burner on after she made an egg sandwich, didn't even notice when the pan started smoking and the fire alarm went off."

Nora nodded. "Leo once put laundry detergent in the dishwasher. He actually had to go into an entirely different room to get the detergent. And heaven forbid they ever close a cabinet they open. Or empty a trash can instead of just piling more and more on top of it. Who knows what goes through their heads?"

Chelsea nodded and put on what she hoped was an understanding expression. She often felt out of the loop in kid-driven conversations, but she always tried not to be weird about it. She knew people didn't mean to make her feel left-out when they talked about their kids, and the endless pressure she'd gotten in her thirties to have children infinitely down-shifted once she'd reached her forties, so she didn't feel defensive the way she used to. It rarely came up anymore. And she felt pretty comfortable talking about teenagers in general; she'd worked with enough of them over the past fifteen years to have some ideas and stories to share, but she knew it was nothing like having your own child.

It made her crazy when people had too many opinions about teenagers when they didn't have them or work with them, so she imagined it was even worse for mothers when non-mothers started in on theoretical parenting. "Everything's easier in theory," one of her former Grove colleagues once told her, leaning against a counter in the staff room, adding cold water to a steaming Cup Noodles to cool it down in time to eat it before her next class. "Everything is different when you do their laundry for the better part of two decades," she'd said, slurping noodles. This same colleague had also said her entire teaching style had changed in the years after having her kids. She'd started seeing her students differently, as someone else's baby or sticky toddler or little leaguer. Being a parent was hard. Even being a mediocre parent was hard. All that aforementioned laundry and cooking and permission slip signing and science fair projects and doctor visits.

"Just doing a basically decent job saps all your energy," she'd said, dumping the half-eaten soup in the garbage before heading back to class. Chelsea had just nodded and tried to look sympathetic. She didn't even suggest that maybe some protein might help with that energy issue.

Because, of course, this was the same colleague who'd always made her feel vaguely apologetic for her life anytime she mentioned doing something that the mother of a child might not be able to manage.

"A whole weekend!" she would exclaim when Chelsea mentioned that she'd been to a workshop with Stone somewhere along the coast. "I can't remember the last time I had a whole weekend to myself."

That was the hardest part of mothers for Chelsea, that thin layer of martyrdom so many of them seemed coated with. But she never said this out loud. No, she understood right away, even in her early twenties, that mothers got to do that. They got to share and show pictures and complain and be wistful about their lost independence, but there was an unwritten understanding deeply embedded in the culture that she was never, ever to remind them that they could have made different choices.

"Poor Chelsea!" Dani said, casting her a side-long glance. "We're rambling on and on. I want to circle back to my previous question about the dreamy guy you brought to Romano's Friday night.

Nora perked up. "Dreamy guy?"

"My ex," Chelsea explained. "And, yes, he is dreamy on the surface."

"And by dreamy, I mean hot," Dani added.

"Except that is a huge part of the problem," Chelsea told them. "That outside is part of what kept me tethered there when I should have broken things off a long time ago. He is very handsome and charming, and I feel superficial for saying it, but it is much of the reason it took me six years to stand up for myself."

Dani nudged Chelsea's arm with her water bottle. "Has he always been butter-free? And no polenta? That should have been a warning sign right off the bat."

"Sadly, I've only recently started paying attention to most of the warning signs in my life."

Nora chimed in. "You and me both. And I'm a lot older than you. I'd say you're ahead of the game." Chelsea glanced at her, surprised. Nora was one of the most put-together people Chelsea had ever met. Nora caught her look and elaborated, sharing about her divorce, her ex-husband's affair, her son, Craig's recent heart attack.

"And work has been strange lately." She stopped herself, realizing, Chelsea thought, that she was talking to an employee. Or maybe just talking too much in general. Nora seemed more a listener than a talker.

Chelsea glanced sideways at Nora. "I'm sorry work's been hard. I hope I'm not adding to that. I can barely find the copy machine."

"Oh, God, no—we're tremendously lucky to have you. No, it's really just that the parents have gotten harder for me. The students, too. More entitled. Angrier, more distracted. Less interested in whatever social contract we supposedly have with them when it comes to their own education."

Dani snorted. "Bert said the other day that so many parents lately are confusing pandering with love."

Nora grinned, weakly. "Sure, sure. That's part of it. And I do truly think that most of that behavior is rooted in love. But just because people love their kids, doesn't mean they know how to parent them."

They walked in silence for a moment, perhaps each of them mulling over the way they'd reached an age where they felt the need to make blanket statements about the generation behind them.

Nora continued, "I'm sympathetic, I really, really am. I mean, who can blame this generation, right? They've been doing active shooter drills since they were in kindergarten. They got dragged through a pandemic that wasn't their fault. *Of course* they're sick of school, of the system, of all of it. It just feels like more of an uphill battle than ever before." She went a couple of paces before adding, "Or maybe I'm just getting too old for it all."

They walked the trail in silence for a few minutes until Dani leaned in and put her arm around Nora's shoulders, squeezed, then let go.

"I feel the need to add that they could all also spend a bit less time on Instagram and their PlayStations and a bit more time on their homework."

Chelsea shot Dani what she hoped was an admiring look. "That sounds dangerously like good parenting!" Because listening to Dani made her think about that cozy room where they met for book club, think about Dani's three children, her job at the restaurant, the sweet ease between her and Bert. Chelsea couldn't help blurting out, "How do you do it?"

Dani looked surprised. "Do what?"

Chelsea wasn't sure how to articulate it without sounding judgmental or envious, even if she was a bit of both. "Manage it all! Three kids. Your job. Your marriage. And still, you always seem—so at peace. Sorry, I know no one actually 'has it all' or whatever, but you seem pretty damn close to it."

Dani burst out laughing. "Do I?" She shook her head. "I'm sure that whole seeming-at-peace thing is really just exhaustion." The filtered light through the pines above cast shadows across her face. "I think my sense of humor gets me through most of it," she added. "It's all such a constant juggle. Maybe when you're always dropping things, you get used to the floor around you being messy and full of tripping hazards."

"You do make it look easy, Dan," Nora agreed, sipping water from a glossy bottle.

Dani frowned. She walked a bit more before saying, "Okay, truth: I am a raging accommodator and people-pleaser, so I repeatedly put the needs of my family before my own. That's how I do it."

Nora's eyebrows shot up. "I didn't know you felt that way."

Dani shrugged. "Look, we've got three kids and we're trying to run a restaurant together and mostly succeeding, but even when the kids were little, Bert just seemed less capable of multi-tasking, so I ended up doing most of the kid stuff, filling in the gaps. Don't get me wrong, I love the guy, but he didn't think about things like vaccine schedules or permission slips or baking cookies for a fundraiser or buying dog food. And if I brought it up, he would say he was too busy with his work; he would get flustered and honestly act like a pill. But I was working full-time too, in theory. Sometimes, I would get mad, and we'd get in these stupid fights that were exhausting, so it just got easier to do it myself than get mad at him for not noticing what needed to be done." She gave a little salute. "Captain Accommodator at your service! And then it just sort of solidified into our roles. I just got used to it."

Nora was nodding vehemently. "Same with Craig. Jesus, Leo was ten before he knew where the kid's dentist was."

Dani gave her a knowing look. "Right? I can count the appointments Bert has taken them to on both hands and that's only because I ask. Even the fun stuff—piano or dance or swim team or soccer—he honestly doesn't offer. I thought I was so progressive hyphenating our names when we got married, Romano-Jones." She sighed. "Not as progressive as I thought, apparently."

They rounded a corner on the path, passing a pair of women in their late-twenties each with a small child tucked into a carry-backpack, little heads bobbing along the trail. As they passed them, Chelsea caught a snippet of their conversation, and it was the basically the same one Nora and Dani were having.

"—just throw a load of her clothes in the washer—"

"—why can't he just think about what we might have for dinner—?"

Chelsea had sometimes romanticized having a family, but she wasn't sure she would have liked the daily reality of it. "Do you regret it?" She asked Nora and Dani, hurrying to add, "I mean, I know you love your kids, of course, but—"

"You know what I regret?" Dani interrupted. "I regret not just sitting Bert down right at the start and saying, here's how this is going to work: you're going to do these things, and I'm going to do these things, and if we ever feel lopsided, we're going to fix that. I regret that I just accepted this whole beleaguered-mom thing, the extra work, and then the grumbling about it over wine with girlfriends. I bought into that. That's on me."

It was Nora's turn to put her arm around Dani. "Not entirely on you. Culture is an actual thing."

Dani shot her a grateful smile. "You know what Diana said last night at dinner? She said no woman is exempt from being a woman in a patriarchal world." She chuckled. "I'm sure she saw a meme somewhere. But, who knows, maybe her generation will do better."

Chelsea tried not to let the doubt creep into her voice. "Maybe."

* * *

On a whim Monday after school, Chelsea drove to her parents'. Her mother had made not-so-subtle hints over the past month that it was *incredible* that Chelsea lived so close, yet they still *never* saw her. Her mother never just called her or actually invited her to something, but the message was clear: Chelsea needed to make more of an effort. The one time she'd said, "You can call me, you know? You can invite me over," her mother had told her she didn't want to be a burden.

Chelsea parked her car and walked the short path to the door, hesitating when she realized she had never dropped by unannounced before. Should she knock? Would that be strange? Would it be stranger just to barge in? Before she could decide, the door whipped open.

"Good grief." Judy stood blinking at her. "I thought you were a murderer, lurking out here."

Chelsea slouched through the doorway. "Get a lot of murderers around, do you?"

Judy closed the door behind her. "You shouldn't joke about murderers. It's not funny."

"Right, murder not funny. Check." The house smelled like cinnamon and Chelsea was struck with a memory of coming home after school to a platter of snickerdoodles. How old had she been? Eight or nine, maybe. Her mother used to bake more. "Did you make cookies?"

"I'm making preserves."

Chelsea followed her mother into the kitchen where she watched her screw lids onto mason jars. "Smells wonderful."

"Here." Judy handed her a still-warm jar. "The last of my frozen apples from Betty's tree." Chelsea had no idea who

Betty was. She was about to ask when her mother turned to her again, wiping her hands on a dish towel. "What're you doing here?"

"I'm just dropping by."

"But why?"

"To say hi."

"Hmm." Her mother turned to the sink, filling it with hot soapy water.

"I don't have an ulterior motive. You said you never see me."

Judy busied herself washing a large silver pot. "Well, we don't."

"Where's Dad?"

"He has a Monday class."

"Oh." She studied her mother's back, so straight. "How are you?"

"I'm fine, of course."

Chelsea waited for more, but there was never much more, was there? Why did she always think there might be?

NORA

Sarah Crocker lived in the flagship house of her parent's subdivision: Crocker Estates. The Crocker family had never been shy about pasting their name on the various projects they'd built around the community and the maple-lined subdivision overlooking the downtown of Imperial Flats was no exception. It was their crown jewel. The dozen or so homes, all some version of a woodsy cabin-Tudor hybrid, sat on leafy two-acre lots with wide lawns, backyard pools, and outdoor kitchens.

Nora drove her car the requisite fifteen miles an hour through the wide streets. She was always struck by the sheer volume of the houses in Crocker Estates, none of them less than 5000 square feet. She'd remarked to Craig once that she wouldn't want to clean houses like these to which he'd smiled and said, "They don't clean their own houses." Right. Of course.

Nora pulled her car through Sarah's open gate, parked in the guest lot (labeled with an ornate metal sign that read, "Guests"), and made her way up the landscaped path to the front door. As she rang the doorbell, she noticed another metal plaque, smaller than the last one, that read, "Black," over the doorbell. Craig's last name. The one she'd decided not to take all those years ago. She cleared her throat as if she could clear the memory, adjusting the cooler bag of heart-healthy meals dangling from one arm so it wasn't cutting off her blood flow. Sarah and Craig Black. Sarah had taken his name. Sarah apparently didn't share her parents' need to slap the Crocker name on everything. Didn't matter. People knew who she was.

Sarah threw open the door—"Nora!"—dressed casually in designer jeans and a cashmere shawl sweater, her feet in tasteful indoor/outdoor shearling slippers. "Come in, come in. This is so kind of you."

"Thanks." Nora felt her pulse quicken as she stepped inside the foyer (because it could only be called a foyer, *holy shit this house was huge*!). "Wow, this house."

It was the best she could do. It *was* a gorgeous house, if you liked massive spaces: wood ceilings, polished floors with thick ivory area rugs, plush furniture. Every lamp looked specifically chosen and intricately placed. Not like the lamps Nora hurriedly grabbed at Home Depot because she suddenly found herself squinting through the dimly lit living room. Sarah either had a design-eye or hired someone who did. Probably both.

Sarah waved off Nora's compliment. "It's a mess right now." Nothing anywhere in the house could be described as a mess. Except, perhaps, Nora's ex-husband, sprawled on a Merlot-colored sofa facing an enormous TV. Nora tried not to let her surprise show on her face. The heart attack had aged him, his skin ashy, his dark hair mussed and grayer than the last time Nora had seen him. Sarah motioned to the cooler bag. "Can I take that?"

Nora handed it to her. "It's enough meals for a week. All can be frozen."

"You're an angel. I'll just get these tucked away so I can get you your bag back." Sarah disappeared through an arched doorway.

"Did you bring beer?" Craig joked, pushing himself up against the pillows stuffed behind him. He pulled a charcoal gray blanket from the back of the couch and spread it over his lap. His socked feet stuck out the other end. She recognized that blanket. They'd bought it together years ago at a store in Napa. A rare weekend they'd taken. Her stomach twisted. She'd actually spent about an hour a few months ago looking for it.

She bit back the instinct to say something about it. "You always said it would be worth it, the heart attack eating all those burgers would cause. So, was it?" He gave her a thumbs up. "Liar."

"Yeah, no—I should have listened to you years ago. But Sarah won't let me near red meat for the rest of my life, so you win in the end."

Nora didn't respond. They both knew this wasn't true.

Finally, she asked. "Did you talk to Leo?"

"Yeah, I called him. Sweet kid. Asked if he should get on the next plane."

"Well, I should hope so." Still, Nora felt an internal bloom of pride that her son had shown some compassion for his father. He'd been so angry at him when he found out he was leaving her.

"I told him he could just come home during spring break."

Nora felt a shameful twinge of pride that Leo had shared his spring break plans with her and not his father. Petty. But she was starting to feel her skin itch. No matter how mature she tried to be, it was too strange to be here with Craig, to see him on the couch where he and Sarah curled up to watch TV. Her stomach soured. She hoped Sarah liked terrible American cop shows with bad writing. She started to inch her way toward the front door. "Okay, well I just wanted to drop off some food, see that you're okay."

He glanced toward the archway Sarah had disappeared through earlier. "Sarah was going to bring your bag back."

"It's fine, really. Keep it. I have too many of them. School fundraisers you know." Then, she turned and fled before Sarah could return, before Craig could say anything else, her palms damp, her heart beating wildly under her jacket as she fumbled for her car keys.

* * *

"Nora?" Toby sounded worried. Of course he did. He was a decent human being and she'd barely managed to choke out a greeting when he picked up. "Where are you?"

She let out a shaky, sob-filled breath. "In my car."

"Driving?"

"Parked." She broke down again, trying not to sob directly into the phone. She was in the empty lot of Gold Dust Village, of all places. Near the yoga studio. It had seemed the easiest place to pull into as she headed home from Crocker Estates. "I just dropped off some dinners to Craig. And Sarah. At—their house."

"Where are you? I'll come to you."

Ten minutes later, Toby slid into the passenger seat of her car. It was after seven and dark; a lone streetlamp edged the parking lot with a spill of pale light. She'd managed to pull herself together, but her face was swollen and tear-stained.

"Did something happen?" Toby asked, his voice gentle. "Did he say something to you?"

"No, no—nothing happened. It was just—" she searched her spinning thoughts. "Their *home*."

Toby put his hand on her thigh, resting it there. "I can't even imagine how I'd feel if I had to see Liz and Mr. Yoga in their Hawaiian apartment. It makes me sick just thinking about it. I hope it's infested with geckos."

Nora tried to smile. It actually helped a little, to hear that.

"He was on the couch with this blanket. And the thing

is, we bought that blanket together. For watching TV. It's big enough for two people. We bought it in Napa on a weekend away. A weekend where I thought we were good, you know? It was one of those clear, bright weekends where we drank wine and thought, wow, we've raised a great son and done right by our careers and we're good and then a few weeks later he was gone. And now he's recovering from a heart attack under our blanket on *their* couch." She wiped at a stray tear and looked at him sheepishly. "Childish, right?"

"Who cares if it's childish?" Toby shrugged. "Why shouldn't you feel like that right now? We're allowed to feel petty or frustrated or hurt. It's allowed."

Nora noticed the set of his jaw, the way he probably hadn't been allowed to feel most of those things in any sort of genuine way. Not publicly. Probably not in front of his children. No, Toby struck her as the one who was expected to be the strong one, the tough one. Her role, usually. Only, she wasn't so sure it made you strong to act like you were fine when you weren't. Maybe it was the opposite.

He gave her thigh a quick squeeze. "He shouldn't have kept that blanket."

"Thanks."

"Let's go steal it."

She laughed, at first, because he sounded so serious. Then, sobered up when she realized he might be. "Are you serious?"

He grinned, the light of the streetlamp reflecting in his eyes. "It's not that kind of movie."

"What kind of movie is it?"

"The kind where we go get a drink and talk about how we both got screwed by the people who were supposed to love us the most."

※ ※ ※

Monday morning, Nora's heart sank when she saw she had a meeting scheduled with Sue O'Hare at eleven. Sue meant well, she really did. She served on several school committees, almost single-handedly ran the Cross-Country Boosters, and always remembered a box of candy or candle for Nora at the holidays. But she was one of the most irritating parents Nora had ever encountered. Nothing she did for the school came without strings, without the implicit assumption that she was owed something in return. And the sun rose and set with her youngest daughter. Gratefully, Ashleigh would graduate soon.

The phone on Nora's desk buzzed. Her secretary. "Hi Elaine."

"Did you have a good weekend?"

"It was fine—you?"

"Yeah, good." Elaine hesitated. "I was calling because I just talked to Joan. Someone is airdropping pornographic images onto people's laptops in G-Wing."

Just what Nora needed on a Monday morning. "On the Chromebooks?"

"No, just to people with MacBooks. Or iPhones."

Nora closed her eyes. Usually her IT guy could nip these sorts of things in the bud. "Can you send Jamie down there?"

"He's heading down now. Mark's already there. I just wanted you to know."

"Thanks." Nora reached for her Advil. "Oh, Elaine, remind me why I'm meeting with Sue O'Hare at eleven?"

No hesitation this time. "She wants the school to subscribe to the National Youth Scholars Association."

"And why would we do that?"

"They provide all graduating seniors above a certain GPA with a certificate." She could practically hear Elaine smirk through the phone when she added, "and a sticker for their diplomas."

"So, this is so Ashleigh can have an extra sticker on her diploma commending her as a National Youth Scholar?"

"Yes."

"But it's something we pay for?"

"It is. It's a private organization. $75. For the stickers."

Nora sighed, watching the morning frost melt on the windows of her office. "And having a sash from the National Honor Society isn't enough for our Miss Ashleigh?"

"Apparently not. Or at least not for her mom."

"Did I already say no to this?"

"You did. Twice."

Nora checked her email. 114 new emails. "If I say yes, will she cancel this meeting?"

Elaine paused, clearly surprised. "I'm sure she would."

Nora chewed her lip for a moment. "Okay, I'll pay for it myself, though. Not out of school funds. Send me the link."

"Are you sure, Nora?"

"Best money I'll spend all day."

EVAN

Evan passed the basketball back to Violet, who dribbled it twice, then took a shot, missing by a mile. He watched her chase it down. They'd all been up earlier than usual for a winter Saturday, so after a quick breakfast, Evan bundled them up and drove them to the high school for some fresh air. He looked out across the basketball court to where Frank wandered the nearby football field with his metal detector. Evan had read somewhere that having a specific, simple task could keep him focused, and, so far, the metal detector had been a nice distraction.

Violet took another shot. This one at least hit the rim and clanged back to her. She watched it rolling toward her but made no move to grab it.

"You okay, bug?"

She shrugged. Her eyes studied the black asphalt at her feet.

"What's up?"

"Mom said I'm moving to London soon."

Evan's limbs went liquid. "What?"

A couple of weeks ago, Lauren had freaked out when he told her he was considering filing a court case for custody, had screamed at him over the phone. "How dare you?" she'd shouted. "I'm her mother!" But in her fury, she'd gone silent for the better part of two weeks, and he'd made it through the rest of February attending Violet's final basketball games for the season, teaching his classes, and pretending Lauren had forgotten about everything. He'd felt a normalcy start to settle in. He'd even felt Chelsea warming to him, joining him for an occasional walk or drink after school.

Then yesterday, Lauren had texted and asked if they could please work this out, without lawyers, the way they always had, and his body shivered with goosebumps. "We'll make something work for all of us," she'd texted diplomatically. He didn't trust her. Still, they'd set up a Zoom for later this morning to talk with Violet about whether she'd even want to move. They'd agreed to include her in the decision, but Violet wasn't supposed to know anything yet.

When Violet didn't say anything else, he cleared his throat. "Where'd you hear that, bug?"

She passed the ball to Evan so he could take a shot. "Mom called me. Yesterday, after school. She sent a picture of her and Roman, that *man*." Evan couldn't help but grin, as if he didn't know who Roman was. "It was in his flat, in the room where I would live. Why is it called a flat?"

Evan tried to keep his voice neutral. "That's what British people call an apartment." He scooped up the basketball. He'd vowed not to let his anger with Lauren impact his decision to go through legal channels, but she was making it hard to honor that. She'd promised not to breathe a word of this to Violet until after their Zoom today. Swore to him she wouldn't. And now she was calling and sending photos? "They have a lot of words that are different from ours for the same things. Did you notice that when you were there at Christmas?"

Violet looked at him for the first time. "They call elevators *lifts*."

"Right." Evan took another shot. It bobbled on the rim and dropped away. "And they say boot for the trunk of a car."

Giggling, she brushed a stray wisp of hair from her face. "Like, put the groceries in the boot?"

"Yeah."

"That's funny. I thought they just spoke English." She chased after the ball.

Evan signaled for her to shoot it. "Well, it is English. We speak American English and they speak British English, which, technically, was English before ours was." He rebounded her shot, holding the ball tight to his chest. He waited until she looked at him again. "Violet, we're going to work this out, okay? Nothing is decided." When she only nodded, he took another shot, bricking it off the backboard. She trotted over to where the ball had come to rest against the fence. "Vi?"

She was watching her grandfather through the chain link. "What's Grandpa doing?"

Evan followed her gaze. "Oh shit." He took off at a run. "Dad! Dad!"

Frank had apparently decided the metal detector made a decent shovel and was digging at a spot just before the closest ten-yard line. He wrestled it free of Frank's clutches. "You can't dig here."

"Those damn deer," his father mumbled, before wandering back toward the basketball court.

* * *

Lauren was breathless, talking too fast for either Evan or Violet to get a word in. "Oh, you'll love it, Vi. You didn't get to see their amazing parks when you were here in December because the weather was crap, and we'll go see castles and get high tea at the Savoy and see a play at the Globe and you'll just love living here."

Evan scooted his chair closer to Violet, let his shoulder touch hers. They had the computer on the kitchen table. Outside, the early March day seemed too bright, too blue.

Finally, Evan broke in. "Um, Lauren? I thought we decided to let Violet think about what she wants?" He knew Lauren could read through his fake-adult voice, but he didn't care. He honestly was glad they were on Zoom, so he couldn't strangle her.

Lauren leaned in, her face looming. "You want to come here, right, sweetie? You want to be here with me?"

Violet glanced at Evan. "It sounds nice."

"It's so lovely, sweetheart! You would meet so many interesting people!"

Evan's body tensed. Two could play this game. He put an arm casually across the back of Violet's chair. "Does this sound like a place you want to move to right now, bug? Or would you rather wait until the end of the semester, so you can finish up with your friends at school? It's just a few more months." Even through the screen, even out of the corner of his eye, he could see Lauren's expression sour.

Violet looked pale and small in the wooden chair. He hated that they were doing this to her. Why couldn't Lauren just stick to the plan? She'd known Roman for two weeks before agreeing to move to London with him. Two weeks! She was having some sort of identity crisis, which was fine, it was, but dragging their daughter across the ocean because of it was not. He waited for Violet to answer, felt his stomach churning. What must it be like to live a life where you weren't always paying for your bad choices?

Violet let out a long breath. "Actually, Mom. London sounds great. I'm so happy you love it." Lauren beamed and started to say something, but Violet pushed forward. "And I can't wait to come visit in April liked we talked about. We can do all those fun things you said. I don't much like tea, but that sounds fun anyway. But—" She licked her lips, and

Evan felt her small body shaking slightly. He squeezed her shoulder. "If you don't mind, I'd like to stay with Dad for a bit longer. If that's okay with you?" Under the table, she pressed her knee into his, left it there. Evan's whole body lightened, like his heart might explode and float away into the bright March light.

Lauren looked shocked, but she recovered, downshifted. "Well, of course, honey. Of course, we don't have to decide anything right now. You think about it, okay?" Her voice wobbled, "I just miss you so much."

Evan almost felt sorry for her.

Until she texted: *I won't let you turn my daughter against me* as soon as they'd logged off. Evan closed the laptop screen and waited until Violet had run off to get her art supplies before he let himself put his forehead down on the table.

* * *

Sunday afternoon, he left Violet and his Dad with *Onward* and went to meet Chelsea. Lately, his life still felt like *Groundhog Day*, but in a steady way, a way he'd never have wanted at thirty, but, at forty-five, felt somehow comforting deep in his bones. On the drive over, though, Evan couldn't quite believe how fucking tired he also felt. It was three-forty-five on a Sunday, and he was pretty sure he could pull the car over, lean the seat back, and sleep for about six hours. Instead, he pulled into a spot at Gold Rush Brew.

He pushed through the door to find Chelsea eating a burger. "You ordered without me?"

"Sorry, I was starving. I've been grading in-class essays for the last two hours."

He noticed the pile at her elbow, next to a half-empty glass of water and an empty bowl that looked like it might have been sitting there for the duration of that grading. "Here?"

"Yeah," she followed his gaze. "I also had the soup. Navy bean." She pushed her plate toward him. "I'm like a Hobbit. Second lunch."

He picked up a cucumber slice and dipped it in a blob of balsamic dressing. "I'm not sure a Hobbit would order salad."

"I'm sure Hobbits eat their veggies. They're so agricultural."

Evan ordered himself a burger and beers for each of them. "So Violet told Lauren she wants to stay."

"Evan! I can't believe you waited to tell me that!"

"Well, your story about grading was so interesting—" He laughed as she flashed her middle finger. He ran a hand through his hair which he was pretty sure he forgot to brush today. "Honestly, it hasn't really sunk in. Besides, I don't trust it. Lauren might just make her go anyway."

"After asking her?" Chelsea shook her head and forked some salad into her mouth. "No way."

Evan gave her a funny look. "Because your mother has never asked your opinion, then did it her way when you didn't give her the answer she was after?"

Chelsea grimaced. "Fair."

They both waved at a colleague from school being seated at a far table, one of the PE teachers and his wife, their two small kids in tow. The younger one, maybe three, was dragging a stuffed dragon behind her on a leash. Evan felt a pang at the sight of her tiny backpack, her mismatched socks. Had Violet ever had a pet dragon? He'd missed too much when she was little.

"So, you're not going to file the case?"

Evan leaned back to let the waiter set down his food. He was suddenly ravenous and ate the burger in five quick bites. Chelsea watched, saying nothing. Finally, he met her eyes. "I'm so tired."

She nodded, stole a fry.

He stuffed a few fries into his mouth and chased them with some beer. "I just don't know if I can do one more thing, you know? My dad tried to dig up the football field with a metal detector yesterday. My students aren't ready for the Mountain Jazz Festival next weekend, and now I might have to file a lawsuit against my ex-girlfriend because she can't pull her head out of her ass? But the worst thing? She spent so many years tolerating me with my own head up my ass that I'm not sure it's fair of me to call her out on it."

He watched Chelsea take it all in, glancing quickly at the PE teacher and his wife because he'd likely said "ass" one too many times for a family establishment, but they didn't seem to have noticed. Both kids were watching an iPad with headphones.

Chelsea dragged another fry through his ketchup. "Okay, we're going to put a pin in that metal detector story because I want to loop back to that, but first, you don't have to apologize for wanting to keep your child close to you. It's not like she's moving to Reno."

"True."

"You deserve to have a relationship with your own daughter."

He felt tears prick his eyes. Problem was, though, even as he nodded, he wasn't sure he did deserve it. "Can you not push on this, Chelsea, please?"

She looked hurt. "I'm just trying to help. I mean, honestly, Evan, how much longer can you do all of this? It might be time to start finding some more help for your dad—"

"I really don't want to talk about it." It came out angrier than he meant it to.

"Don't get mad at me; I'm worried about you."

"Maybe it's not your job to worry about me. You're the one who keeps pushing me away!"

She gave him that cold look she could drop into at a second's notice. "Fine."

"Chelsea, I'm sorry—"

His phone chirped.

Violet: *u should probably come home*

He texted back: *Is it grandpa?*

Violet: *no some guy is here i don't want to let in a stranger*

Evan peered at the picture she'd sent with her text, clearly taken through the hallway window: a figure hunched on the front porch. Evan had to squint at first, not believing, but it was him, looking sheepish, hands in the pockets of his trendy jeans.

He held out the phone to Chelsea. "You've got to be fucking kidding me."

She leaned in. "Is that who I think it is?"

"Yep."

"Well, shit."

PART THREE

You look familiar. Go away.
—Sunset Dark

CHELSEA

Denny Bliss didn't look like he did on his album covers. Gone was the arrogant chin tilt, his heavy-lidded eyes bored but piercing. Gone was the haircut that seemed to be some sort of hybrid homage to both David Bowie and Tom Petty in its bright-blond shag. Gone was the smooth, line-free face photoshop and Instagram filters produced. A beat-up blue hoodie covered the mess of tattoos on his muscled arms usually on display. As he sat slumped on Evan's couch, a bag of frozen peas pressed to his face, he looked every bit of his forty-five years. Tired and worn-out.

The peas were for the bloody nose Evan had inflicted fifteen minutes ago, and Denny winced as he applied the bag gingerly, then pulled them away to check the blood flow. Chelsea hadn't seen the blow coming, had been shocked to see Denny go down so quickly on the front porch, had hissed, "Your daughter's inside!" at Evan, like she was breaking up a fight between two sulking teenage boys. Which, essentially, she was. When she'd hurried inside to find some ice, she'd found the peas.

Violet perched on a chair in the corner of the room, her eyes wide, her legs tucked up under her. "Ohmygodohmygodohmygod," she kept repeating. "I can't believe it—you're Denny Bliss. You're Denny Bliss!"

"He knows who he is," Evan grumbled from the wooden chair where Chelsea had told him to sit and stay in a few minutes earlier.

"Do you need a doctor?" Chelsea asked Denny, narrowing her eyes at Evan, who pretended not to notice, who looked pointedly out the window at nothing.

Denny gave his nose a tentative once-over. "Naw, I'm sure I had that coming. Not the first time. Probably won't be the last."

"What're you doing here, Denny?" Evan glared at him.

"I got your email."

"The email I sent last June? That email?"

Denny shot a sheepish grin toward Chelsea, then back to Evan. "Yeah, sorry, man, I'm terrible about getting back to people. I have people for that now, so I just, I dunno, don't do it."

"Yet here you are."

For the first time, Denny looked uncomfortable. "I need a favor."

Evan let out what could only be described as a guffaw. "From me?"

Denny set the sweating bag of peas on the coffee table. "Yeah, man. I know, I know, why would you help me? But, I'm not really sure where else to go. I'm in some trouble."

"It's not true, right?" Violet asked him from her chair. "That girl? It's not true."

Chelsea and Evan locked eyes. "What girl?" they asked at the same time.

Denny's gaze slipped between them. "She said she was nineteen."

Evan leaned forward, his forearms falling to his thighs. "Oh, shit, Denny. What did you do? How old was she?"

Violet, the nine-year-old in the room, the one who probably followed all sorts of Instagram accounts her parents didn't realize she followed, chirped, "Sixteen."

Chelsea's stomach turned. It took everything in her to not be the one to hit Denny this time.

* * *

Chelsea knocked at the doorway of Nathan Tan's classroom. He was staring at his computer screen intently and hadn't noticed her standing there. "Sorry, am I interrupting something?"

He smiled at her, pushing away from his desk and starting to stand. "Just Google Classroom. What's up?"

"Don't get up." She leaned against one of the front row desks. "You'll never believe who showed up at Evan's house yesterday."

"I'm intrigued."

"Denny Bliss."

"You're kidding."

"Not even a little."

Nathan gave a low whistle. "Wow, reunion year."

Nathan had been two years ahead of Chelsea, Evan, and Denny. She hadn't known him well. He was one of those quiet, brilliant kids who took computer classes and advanced science and steered clear of the performing arts wing. With his dark hair and liquid eyes, she'd always assumed he'd be a late bloomer, and she'd been right. He'd gone to UCLA for undergrad and law school, practiced for a few years, then moved back to Imperial Flats for a history job at IFHS. He coached tennis, had a daughter at Cal, and attended school events with his wife, who was a chiropractor in town. He was handsome in the way of television character actors, favored cardigans with elbow patches, and his students worshipped him.

Chelsea could see why. His walls were papered with photos of civil rights activists, enlarged copies of original documents like the Thirteenth Amendment, and movie posters like *Do the Right Thing*, *Selma,* and what appeared to be half of Ang Lee's oeuvre. He radiated contentment in a way that Chelsea found intimidating, and, if she was being judgmental, suspicious.

On the board, he'd written in sharp, black pen:

It is privilege to think you're exempt from history.

"Who said that?" she asked, nodding to it.

He followed her gaze. "I did."

"Want to come for a drink with us?"

"With you and—?"

"Evan and Denny."

He grabbed his coat. "Count me in."

* * *

They chose Charlie's Bar because it would be dark and peopled with the type who wouldn't give a shit about Denny Bliss. Even so, they picked the table in the empty back room, Denny tucked into the farthest corner. He'd insisted no one followed him to Imperial Flats, no one knew he was here, but with the amount of paparazzi that had been hounding him the last few weeks, stalking his New York apartment, his home in the Hollywood Hills, well, he couldn't be a hundred percent sure.

Out of some latent habit perhaps, Chelsea took drink orders. An IPA for Evan and Nathan, but Denny said, "My nutritionist won't let me drink anything with color. Vodka rocks, I guess."

Chelsea groaned. "Jesus, Denny, you're in Imperial Flats running from a sex scandal. Get the drink you want."

"Right. A Manhattan. But don't let them use shit vermouth."

"I'll make it myself, but I'm wondering if you actually hear what an enormous douche you sound like?"

She didn't miss his smile as she headed to the bar, where the guy watching poker on TV didn't seem to mind when she offered to get the drinks. He waved her back, and she made herself at home. It all came back to her and she found herself wishing she'd never given it up.

Last night, she'd Googled Denny Bliss for the first time in over a decade. She used to follow his career closely, still listened to his music, but his life had stopped being interesting to her after the second album and the third wife. He'd really stepped in it this time. A sixteen-year-old after a concert in Miami. Denny had turned into a cliché years ago, when each of his new girlfriends or wives kept getting younger, but this was a new low for him. That the girl had told him she was nineteen, that she was apparently admitting that to the press didn't help alleviate the sick feeling in Chelsea's stomach, or the flurry of Internet shame being leveled on him. Well-deserved, in Chelsea's opinion. Denny had been dancing too close to the sun for years.

Which meant he hadn't changed at all. As she made the drinks, she couldn't help but flash to all those afternoons in Denny's garage where he'd waltzed in late by forty-five minutes or an hour to a rehearsal *he'd* called. Evan would glower at him over his guitar.

"I guess we can finally get started," he'd say pointedly at Denny's back, who would just grin and flip him off.

Back then, Chelsea had wanted to think all that swagger, the shaggy blonde hair and sunglasses indoors, all the bad grades and cheap tricks to talk teachers out of detentions, had been hiding something insecure in Denny, something darker he was trying to outrun. Maybe, though, he had just always been an asshole who hid it behind talent and charm. Chelsea was tired of this particular brand of man showing up in her life unannounced, and, yet, here she was making him a drink.

She found a tray and returned with a couple of Manhattans for her and Denny and the beers for Evan and Nathan. Denny broke off his conversation with Nathan to take a sip. He held up the drink appreciatively, winking at Chelsea.

"Wow, Chels. Lady knows her way around a cocktail." It was the first dose of Denny-charm she'd seen since he'd been here. She was sure it wouldn't be the last. He'd always had treasure troves of it.

Evan wasn't buying it. "So, what's the plan, Denny?"

Denny didn't answer, just sipped at his drink, scrolling on his phone. "Cuz the couch you slept on last night was a one-off. You can't stay with me."

More scrolling. Evan looked like he might punch him again.

After yesterday, Evan had lasted about an hour before asking Chelsea if she wouldn't mind taking Violet while he went for a run. She knew this was how he'd clear his head, so she'd agreed, taking Violet to Main Street for a hot chocolate while Denny watched *Onward* with Frank. The whole thing might have been worth it to see Denny settle in on the couch with Frank Dawkins and a bag of microwave popcorn if Evan hadn't looked so miserable.

Denny had loathed Frank in high school, mostly because Frank rotated a series of offensive names for him, all unoriginal versions of questioning Denny's sexuality in only the way men of the last century could. Sometimes Chelsea thought all those young women were just Denny proving a point to the small-minded jerks he'd grown up with. But she knew that was generous of her, and overly simplistic.

"Denny?" Evan pressed. "I have Frank and Violet. I can't babysit you, too." He shot a glance at Chelsea. "And Chelsea's in the smallest Airbnb in Northern California."

Denny tucked his phone into his pocket. "I can stay in a hotel."

"Why can't you stay at your parents'?" Chelsea asked.

He flicked some hair from his eyes. "They moved to Arizona years ago. They live in one of those places, you know, Sedona Vista or Red Rock Heights or some bullshit? I don't know, I just pay for it."

"You will last two minutes in a hotel once they figure out who you are," Nathan said. He hesitated. "You can stay in our guest cottage. It was supposed to be for Steph's mom, but she won't move out of L.A. so it's just sitting there."

Denny blinked at him. "Seriously? Thanks, man."

But Nathan wasn't charmed either. "Look, I have a daughter who's actually nineteen so don't think for a second I approve of any of this."

* * *

"Evan?" Chelsea sat up in Evan's bed, listening for signs of him, but everything was quiet. Frank had turned in hours ago; Violet was at a sleepover. Chelsea pulled on a sweatshirt and leggings before padding through the house. Frank snored through the door of his room. She found Evan in the kitchen with a cup of tea, lit only by a distant streetlamp through the window. "Hey."

"Oh, shit, did I wake you?"

"I had to pee." She took a minute to drink in his mussy night hair, his hands cupped around the mug, the faded plaid of his robe, and her body heated with the realization that she was starting to love him again. In honest moments, she knew she had never really stopped.

He stood to fetch the kettle and a mug, another tea bag. "You want some?"

She accepted the steaming cup and slid into the chair next to his. Denny had been at Nathan's for the last week and they hadn't much heard from him, but it was strange to think of him a mile away, sleeping in Nathan's guest cottage. She knew Evan had bigger problems than a long-lost band member, but it was too weird. One more thing.

"You okay?"

He sat back down. "I don't know what to do about Lauren."

"Did you hear from her?"

"She texted earlier. Said she'd fight me over a custody agreement. That if I push this, she'll make it impossible for me in the future. I'll get what I want now, for a few months, but I'll be 'entering a war' with her. That's how she put it." He studied a beam of headlights from a passing car moving across the kitchen wall. "Maybe she's right."

"She's wrong not to consider what Violet wants."

He sipped his tea. "Vi's going in a few weeks. What if Lauren just refuses to send her back?"

"Well, that would be a dick move."

A slight smile. "Yes."

Chelsea drank her tea for a moment, savoring the warmth. "Again, I know I'm not a parent. But it seems to me that everything she does right now is establishing her relationship with her daughter for the long term. She's accusing you of being short-sighted but maybe so is she. Each time she denies Violet her own agency in this—and in anything, really—she erodes their relationship."

Before Chelsea could even set her mug down, Evan leaned forward into her, his face against her chest. Tea sloshed onto his shoulder. "I don't deserve you," he murmured into her.

She managed to choke out a sarcastic, "True," even as she blinked back tears.

NORA

Mark Weaver leaned on the table across from the sophomore boy slumped in a chair in Nora's office. "Here's the thing, Andrew. We know you took the vodka, so I'm just giving you a chance to come clean here, now, with us. Because you're a good kid who made a stupid choice, and we'd rather not involve the police if we can avoid it."

Andrew shrugged, his hands folded in his lap, his foot tapping against the chair leg. "I found it in a bush. By the baseball diamond."

Mark sighed, leaned back. He adjusted his tie, flipped through his folder on the desk in front of him that Nora knew was just his Shit You Won't Believe file, but he made sure Andrew thought it held *things that mattered*. It was a prop. Mark watched a lot of detective shows. Nora wasn't sure she had the energy today for his usual show.

Mark sighed theatrically again. "You *found* it?"

"Yeah."

"In a bush."

Nora checked her watch, her patience thinning, and decided to step on Mark's toes. "The reason we know you took it, Andrew, is that Imperial Market has a camera, so we have footage of you taking the vodka."

Andrew's head jerked up, his eyes darting between them. Nora nodded at him. Mark flashed her a look of annoyance, but she was the boss, so he nodded, too. "You hear that, Andrew? You're on camera taking it. Not from a bush. From the store."

"I didn't drink any of it."

Mark drummed his fingers on the table. "Not really the point, though, is it? Whether you drank any of it?" Another shrug from Andrew.

Nora's office phone rang, and she went to her desk to answer it. "Elaine?"

"Andrew's grandfather's here to take him home. Is Brian pressing charges?"

Brian was the general manager of Imperial Market, had been the general manager for most of Nora's tenure at the high school, and she often wondered if she should have him on speed dial. He was always far kinder to the kids who messed with his store than Nora would have been, but even he had his limits.

"He hasn't decided," Nora said to her secretary. "We'll send Andrew down. He's going home for now." She leaned heavily on the last two words, replacing the receiver, but noticing the impact they had on Andrew, the increased tapping of his foot. He looked one part relieved, one part terrified. Which was what she was going for.

"Your grandfather's here."

Mark stood up. "Head straight to the office and have grandpa take you home. You'll hear more from us soon."

Andrew slunk from the room.

Mark eyed the bottle on the table and grinned at Nora. "Kid can't even swipe the good stuff?"

Nora sank into her desk chair. "Sorry I hurried us along. He was getting on my last nerve."

Mark waved her off, already over it. "He's not a bad kid. I used to coach him in Little League. He's gotten in with a rough group is all."

"Yeah, well at some point, getting into a rough group and staying there means you've become part of the problem."

Mark tucked the file under his arm, shaking his head. "Found it in a bush. Didn't realize we had a vodka tree on campus."

"That's my kind of tree." Nora shook her head, added her notes to the appropriate file on her computer.

Mark took a final sip of his coffee before rinsing the mug in Nora's sink. "Want me to check in with Brian?"

Nora massaged her neck, distracted. "That'd be great, Mark, thanks."

He paused in the doorway on his way out, turned back to her. "You okay, Nora?" Mark was a sweet guy. Classic small town. Grew up here. Played baseball. The kind of local star that makes you love the town that made you shine. Went to Chico State. Came home. Coached baseball, married a local girl, had a couple of kids. He was reliable, funny, and, even if too soft most of the time, one of Nora's biggest assets at Imperial Flats. He was not, however, someone who would likely relate to an existential crisis.

"Just not a lot in the tank today."

"Ah, sure. We all have days like that."

Only, if he did, she'd never seen one.

* * *

Nora had already changed into her pajamas when the doorbell rang. She pulled on a robe, and opened the door, surprised and, yet, somehow not, to see Craig standing there. He was dressed in jeans, an Imperial Flats High sweatshirt, and a Giants hat. He held up the bag she'd brought his food in. "I was just returning your bag. Were you already in bed?"

"Not yet." She opened the door and he followed her through to the kitchen.

Inside, his eyes scanned the room, landing on the half-finished glass of wine on the counter. "Got another glass?"

"Should you be drinking?"

"Red wine's good for the heart, right? Just a small glass."

She pulled out another glass and poured him an inch of wine. He sank onto one of the stools, his eyes closing as he sipped. "Damn, that's good. Sarah's a fucking food-Nazi right now."

Wincing, Nora kept the counter between them. She didn't have the energy to give Craig another lecture about how maybe it wasn't good form to refer to his new wife as any sort of Nazi. He wouldn't listen, thought she'd been forced to take one too many sensitivity trainings.

"I'm sure that's not true."

"It is. I can't eat anything, I can't drink anything. We can't have—" He caught himself, his cheeks reddening. "I can't go to the gym. Just stupid short walks."

"What are you doing here, Craig?"

He swallowed, met her eyes. "Just wanted to bring back your bag. And say thanks for all the dinners." Nora frowned. This. This was all the problems in her marriage encapsulated into one annoying moment. She'd told him to keep it, that she didn't want it back, but he didn't listen. Instead, he showed up at a bad time, with a bag she didn't want back, and drank her wine. He drained the wine and poured a bit more. "You ran out of there pretty fast."

Nora felt her throat tighten. "I didn't *run* out of there."

"I don't want things to be weird, Nora."

"Really? Because, generally, if you don't want things to be weird, you probably shouldn't have an affair and then leave without trying to fix anything between us. But that's what you did, so, yeah." Nora tugged at the belt of her robe, her hands shaking. She crossed them over her chest.

Craig held the empty wine glass in both hands, cradled there. He rolled it between his big hands for a minute. "It doesn't have to be like this. We don't have to keep rehashing things."

"I don't think that's what I'm doing."

"It's best to move forward."

"Funny how the people who dump all the shit in the past in the first place are always the ones who want to move forward."

He studied her face. When she didn't say anything more, he nodded, set down the glass, and let himself out.

* * *

Nora walked the campus sometimes as the school was just waking up, as staff and students arrived, as the light came into the sky. She loved to see the kids huddled by their lockers, joking around, scrolling their phones, the couples tucked into each other, holding on for dear life before the day's schedule cleaved them apart. She loved seeing the teachers move through the hallways with their coffees and lanyards, calling out good mornings. She loved the mothers in their down jackets over pajamas pulling through the drop-off lane, eyes bleary, a smaller child or two often in the backseat. She loved the way the buses moved through the lower lot, the spill of bodies and backpacks. All these lives humming around her.

She stopped at the top of campus near the library, taking in the sprawl of the baseball field and football stadium in the background. Tears pricked her eyes and she tried to shake them away. She was losing it, clearly. But something about these mornings felt temporary all of a sudden. Ephemeral.

She couldn't stop thinking about Craig coming to the house with that stupid bag, couldn't stop thinking about how easily he'd tossed aside their marriage, all those individual moments and memories, all the holidays and shared television shows and vacations and meals and home projects.

A life shouldn't be disposable.

She knew she wasn't alone. The pandemic had created chaos in so many relationships, people had gone down dark tunnels during those endless months of not knowing what might happen. So much loss of livelihood, of friendships, of love, of hope. She and Craig had been casualties, really. The terrible reality was she thought they'd been made of stronger stuff.

Truth was, she missed their little family. All those vacations and weekends and pajama-clad Netflix binges and inside jokes. Nora had never been a sentimental, nostalgic person. She hadn't made a scrapbook of Leo's baby years, never needed holiday traditions or for Leo to do the same sports year to year. She'd never wished for him to stay small. She'd been shocked by the number of mothers she knew who bemoaned their children becoming teenagers, as if somehow this was the first act of teenage rebellion, this unavoidable shedding of their childhood selves. She hadn't been sympathetic enough, she realized now, when those mothers had expressed sadness, loss, fear. Hadn't realized until perhaps this moment that they weren't trying to keep their children little, not really, but rather voicing a primal sorrow at the inevitable march of time.

Her phone rang. Mark Weaver. She picked up. "Morning."

"One of the buses hit a power pole."

"On campus or off?"

"On."

"I'll be right there."

EVAN

Evan and Violet maneuvered their bikes across the graveled section of Lookout Point. "Want to stop here for lunch?" he asked her.

She stepped off her bike, wheeling it to a bench. "Here?"

"Great." Evan pulled off his helmet and dangled it from his handlebars. Violet imitated him, and he felt a pang again, watching her. He brushed some dirt from the bench and sat down, Imperial Flats spilling out in front of them. "Look," he told her. "You can see the high school, and our house."

She sat down next to him, brushing some hair from her eyes, and followed his gaze. "What's for lunch?"

"Cheese bagel?" He held up the bagels he'd toasted with cheddar and wrapped in foil.

"Yum." She took hers.

"And baby carrots."

"Less yum. Did you bring chocolate?"

He held up a Kit Kat. "Always."

They ate in silence for a few minutes, eyes on the view. Clouds were beginning to roll in, a staggered layer of pale gray and white. "The sky looks like frosting," Violet said, and Evan felt her shiver next to him.

He hugged her to him. "It might rain. We should head back."

"I like rain."

"It rains a lot in London." When she didn't respond, he opened the Kit Kat and snapped her off a stick.

She ate it in slow, steady bites. Licking some chocolate from her fingers, she told him, "Mom called me."

"When?"

"Yesterday, after school. She says she knows it might seem scary, but I have to move to London. If not now, then at some point. She's not coming back to California."

Evan pushed aside the bubble of frustration with Lauren. He was tempted to tell Violet exactly what he thought of her mother's phone call, but he remembered Chelsea's words and asked instead, "How does that make you feel?"

"Like she's not listening to me."

Hm. Maybe Chelsea was onto something. "Did you get along with Roman when you were there at Christmas?"

"That's a weird name. Roman. I thought that's what people from Rome were called."

"It is. It's also a name."

"A stupid name."

Evan tried not to smile. "Maybe. Your mom sure seems to like him."

She shrugged and accepted another stick of chocolate. "He seems like any of the guys she says she loves. But then they leave, and then she doesn't love them anymore. And things go back to normal. We've just never had to move to London before."

Evan felt his chest tighten. How could a nine-year-old girl sound so jaded? "I don't think I realized she was dating these guys. I only met Joe. And Miles."

"Joe was nice."

"Was he?"

"Yeah. He remembered I don't like mushrooms and so he always left them out of things he cooked. He was nice."

"You don't like mushrooms?"

"I hate them."

"So does Chelsea."

"She's nice, too."

Evan took a breath, considered what he should say, then decided for honesty. "Listen, bug, I don't know what's going to happen with your mom. Who knows if this thing with Roman will stick or not? But I'm always your dad, no matter if you live here or in the Bay or in London. Always. When you're nine or twenty or fifty. I'm your dad. Geography doesn't change that." What he didn't tell her was that he was sorry he hadn't shown up for her more before now, that he didn't much deserve the loyalty she was currently showing him.

Violet stared straight ahead with serious eyes. "I'm going to tell her that I'm staying through the end of the year. Here. I'll visit for spring break, but then I'm coming back here to stay until summer. It's not just up to her. It's my life, too."

Evan pulled her closer, in awe of his tough kid, his strong girl, but aware, too, that Lauren was mostly to thank for that. Strong girls came in many forms. "I think you should try to tell her that."

* * *

The studio was tucked behind the house at the edge of Nathan's property with its own short gravel driveway that passed by the main house. As he'd driven down it, Evan could just make out Nathan and his wife, Stephanie, sitting down to eat, the yellow glow of light from their window spilling into the yard beyond. Denny had texted earlier and invited Evan for dinner at the studio. At first, he'd said no, he had to be home for Violet and Frank, but Chelsea said she'd have dinner with them, that she thought it was a good idea for Evan to go see Denny.

"I know you're angry with him," she'd said, standing at the door of his classroom earlier. "But it's just dinner. It's not a Forgiveness Summit. You could always spit in his food should you feel inclined."

He knocked at the door of the cottage. It was painted white with green shutters, and he stood beneath a trellis that held gnarled twists of a bare-branched vine that probably flowered in the early summer. The cottage seemed far too sweet, too gentle, to hold the likes of Denny Bliss.

He knocked again, louder this time, and Denny called out, "It's open."

Inside, Evan was surprised to see a small pine table set with candles and two wine glasses. Denny had laid out cheese and crackers and some olives. Music played from hidden speakers. Not Sunset Dark, gratefully. Something more Americana, mellow.

"Cute place." Evan realized it was a stupid thing to say even as he said it. It wasn't like it was Denny's place.

Denny looked around as if noticing his surroundings for the first time. "Yeah, I guess it is." He wore a pair of sweats and a flannel shirt over a white T-shirt that looked like it had been washed a thousand times.

Evan couldn't help but grin at the shearling booties on Denny's feet. "Nice slippers."

"It's fucking cold up here, man." Denny poured red wine into a glass. "You drink red?"

Evan popped an olive into his mouth. "Thought you weren't drinking alcohol that had color?"

"Wine doesn't count."

"Classic Denny. Still making your own rules."

"Only way to live."

"If you're a narcissist."

Denny sipped his wine. "You would know." He moved to

the narrow counter and started unboxing some food. Caesar salad, a tub of pasta, garlic bread. "Got this stuff from that Shade Bistro. Chelsea recommended it. Smells good. Want to dig in?"

Evan pulled out a chair, trying not to let it bother him that Denny had talked to Chelsea. They busied themselves filling their plates, not making eye contact, taking sips of wine.

Finally, through a forkful of salad, Denny said, "Look, let's just come out with it. I know you hate me."

"I don't hate you."

"I think you do."

Evan shrugged.

Denny set his fork down. "Whatever, man. But you left us."

Evan moved some pasta around on his plate. "That's not how I remember it."

Denny got up and crossed the room to the squat gas fireplace in the corner, fiddled with the dial until a short flame flickered. He wiped his hands on the thighs of his sweats. "Whatever. I remember an ultimatum that they either kick me out or you'd leave. That's your choice to leave in my books."

Evan frowned. "That's a simple version of it."

"Maybe, but it was a long time ago, Evan." He sat back down, filled his wine glass almost to the top. "Water under the bridge."

"Only your water is gold-plated now and I'm living with my dad, so, yeah, you get to say that."

Denny studied Evan for a moment. "I know you don't want to hear this, I know it won't help anything, but my life isn't all you think it is. It looks like it to people on the outside. We pay a lot of money to people who make sure that it does, but it's not real, all that public shit. I mean, look at me—I'm in fucking hiding right now."

"Oh, please spare me the it's-so-hard-to-be-a-rock-star speech. I'm eating." Evan stabbed at a piece of penne. "You're in hiding because you couldn't keep your dick in your pants."

"Speaking of simple versions of things."

Evan set his fork down with a clink. "Fine, Denny. Explain it to me. Explain how having money and success and fame is so terribly hard for you. How it makes you do stupid things like sleep with underage girls. Poor Denny. It's fame's fault, right? So fucking entitled." He picked up his fork again, but his stomach had soured.

Denny leaned back in his chair and folded his arms across his chest. "My therapist thinks I'm attracted to young women because I'm trying to relive my youth, that I'm not happy with the way my life turned out, and I'm trying for some sort of do-over."

"How much does that cost you?"

"I think she might be right."

"I'm not sure 'do-over' is a clinical term."

"I am sorry, Evan. Not that you give a shit."

Evan narrowed his eyes. "You're sorry?"

"I'm sorry for what happened with you. I'm sorry we couldn't just make it work all those years ago and you felt you needed to leave us, because of me. I should have tried to work it out with you, talked to you, listened to you, or whatever, but I was young and stupid. I'm sorry I never wrote you back when you emailed. I should have apologized years ago. I should have sent you a check for your jazz band. I should have," he fumbled, "done better."

Evan toyed with his salad, took a sip of wine. He knew it was his turn to atone, but he wasn't feeling it. He didn't want to just say the obvious next thing. It wasn't that easy. It couldn't be, right? He'd imagined this conversation for a long time, and it hadn't gone like this. Somehow, Denny had even managed to beat him to the bigger man portion of the event, with a speech his therapist probably fucking wrote for him.

Evan poured more wine. "I'll still take that check for the jazz band if you're offering."

* * *

When he climbed into his bed next to Chelsea that night, bleary, she had her back to him, so he thought she might be asleep.

Then, she murmured, "How'd it go?"

Flat on his back, he pulled the covers to his chin. "He's still Denny."

She rolled over. "Okay."

"Except he apologized."

"Did he mean it?"

"How can you tell?"

"You can tell."

"How?"

She scooted up until she was resting against the headboard. She pushed some hair from his eyes, her fingers trailing across the side of his face. "Someone either seems genuine or they don't. Either it sounds real or it comes off as a robotic response. Like, they know they're *supposed* to apologize, but they don't actually buy into the reason for apologizing. Stone always knew he *should* apologize, and he could sound pretty convincing sometimes, but at the end of the day, all of his apologizing was self-serving, nothing more. It was what he knew needed to happen so we could stop talking about whatever I felt like he should be apologizing for."

Evan propped himself up on his forearm. "Is that why you left?"

"One of the reasons. After a while, if they keep apologizing but the behavior doesn't change, then either those apologies are shit and they're refusing to grow, or they're an idiot, and neither of those are good long-term options."

Evan blinked into the dark, the streetlight edging the blinds in pale light. "I meant it when I told you I was sorry about not meeting you after graduation."

Chelsea slid back down under the covers. "I could tell." He was almost asleep before she added, "I just wasn't ready to hear it."

CHELSEA

CHELSEA HAULED THE TWO BAGS of soil she'd told her mother she'd pick up across her parents' front yard, through the gate, and around to the veggie beds out back. It was still chilly, and the sun was thin this early in the morning, but that didn't stop Judy Garden from donning a fleece jacket and some thick jeans for planting carrots, broccoli, cauliflower, and whatever else she put in the ground this time of year. Her father always teased her that she married him for his last name.

"Thanks, you can just put those there." Judy waved a spade toward the edge of the nearest veggie bed.

Chelsea's nostrils filled with the scent of turned earth. It was a smell she'd always associate with her mother, a pleasant one.

"Can I do anything?"

"I'm done." Judy stood up more slowly, more methodically than Chelsea was used to seeing. "Would you like some tea?"

Chelsea almost said she needed to get back, that Diego was helping her with a cake for book club later, but she saw her mother's hands shake slightly as she peeled off her gardening gloves and found herself agreeing to tea. She'd been trying to stop by more often, even for a few minutes at a time. Her mother seemed most interested in proximity. Chelsea just showing up once in a while seemed to tick an invisible box for Judy, even if they never much said anything that mattered.

Inside, her mother put out a pot of English Breakfast with a tiny pitcher of milk and a dish of sugar cubes on the small table in the corner of the kitchen. Chelsea helped herself, watching the dark liquid steam into the cup. "This is such a pretty tea pot."

"It was my grandmother's. Did you not know that?"

"I'm sure you told me, but I didn't remember." She sipped her tea, milky and sweet, the way she liked it. The kitchen was warm, and Chelsea watched her mother wash up at the sink.

"So Denny is back in town, I hear." Her mother toweled off her hands and poured herself a cup of tea. "The prodigal son returns." When Chelsea didn't respond, Judy pulled out a chair and sat down. "Bev saw him downtown picking up dinner last night from that new place, the one with the strange name. Shake?"

"Shade."

Judy grimaced. "She told me this morning." Bev was their neighbor. She'd spent many an hour leaning over their back fence. Treaties and contracts had been signed and annulled over that fence.

Judy tasted her tea, then added a minuscule splash of milk. "Have you seen him?"

Chelsea couldn't help but smile. The call this morning to grab a couple bags of soil had been a ruse. It wasn't just proximity. Her mother wanted information. Chelsea got up and searched the cabinets for something to go with the tea. Some cookies or maybe a granola bar. No luck. She sat back down to Judy's waiting gaze. "He came to Evan's when he first got here. We found him somewhere to stay."

There went the famous eyebrow. "He should be in jail."

"Probably."

She brushed at a stray fleck of dirt on one of her hands, before examining her nails. "It was terribly unfair what he did to Evan. I'm surprised he showed his face there."

Chelsea felt a momentary wash of warmth that her mother would stick up for Evan, but she also felt an old, strange stab of defensiveness for Denny. Judy had never liked him, had never thought he'd deserved his fame. Try as she might to hate him, Chelsea would always feel a warm bubble of admiration for Denny, that he'd come from this place, had such deep roots here, and yet had so crisply left it behind. Until now. She set down her cup. "He didn't know where else to go."

Judy's expression looked like she might have a few ideas, but in a rare show of reserve, she didn't elaborate.

* * *

They read *The Searcher* for March book club. Chelsea was glad they didn't just read literary novels, though, as far as mysteries went, this one was on the literary side. She had lost herself in its rich sense of place, and it made her want to move to Ireland. Sometimes, she dreamed about just succumbing to a faraway endless landscape of green and sky. It comforted her. Every once in a while, late at night, she would scroll through Airbnb listings for coastal places in Ireland, Scotland, Norway, Iceland. Something about a rugged northern coast had always called to her. At least it would be far away from Imperial Flats. Although, even as she thought it, she felt a strange sense of—not guilt, something else. After spending most of her adult life avoiding it, would she miss it here if she left?

After parking along the curb at Dani's house, she reached for her bag and the massive Tupperware holding the Irish apple cake with custard sauce Diego had helped her make. The entire car smelled of nutmeg. Kyle had also tucked a small bottle of Irish whiskey into her bag on her way out. Inside, she unpacked the cake in the kitchen and pulled out the tub of sauce. "Can I borrow a knife to cut this?" she asked Dani, who was plating tiny quiches.

Dani leaned in and took a deep breath. "Mmm, smells yummy."

"Diego helped me."

She added her cake to the array of snacks on the dining room table, left Kyle's whiskey on the bar, and poured herself a glass of Sauvignon Blanc. Stone used to tell her it was a wimpy wine, even for summer, but she didn't care. She liked it.

Nora arrived with another bottle of whiskey, unwinding a scarf from around her neck. "Great minds," she said, setting it down next to Chelsea's. Then, she leaned in close. "Anything to the rumor that you and Evan have Denny Bliss stashed somewhere?"

Chelsea's stomach sank. First her mother, and now Nora. She knew it would get out sooner or later, but she was already tired of Denny Bliss taking up all the air in the room. "Ugh, I don't want to talk about it. I'm here for *The Searcher*."

Except, it turned out, no one wanted to talk about the book.

They wanted to talk about Denny Bliss.

Kristen Rogers and Heather Ambrose were tucked under blankets on one of the big couches in Dani's family room, next to a crackling fire, and didn't waste time peppering Chelsea with questions when she walked through the door. "All right, where is he?"

Chelsea feigned innocence. "Where's who?"

Kristen groaned. "Oh, please, out with it. We know you're hiding him."

Chelsea settled on a couch next to Nora. "Hiding him? That's a little dramatic."

"Chelsea," Heather whined like a middle schooler. "Where is he?"

"She's not telling you!" Dani exclaimed, setting down snacks on the square coffee table. "You'll stalk him!"

"I won't!"

Kristen scoffed. "You will."

Heather smiled. "You're right. I will."

Chelsea shook her head in disbelief. "Do any of you care that he slept with a sixteen-year-old girl?"

Heather helped herself to a mini quiche. "She said she was nineteen!"

Chelsea couldn't hide her shock. "Seriously? She could be his daughter."

Dani swirled her wine in her glass. "Well, to be fair, the lot of them could be his daughter, right?"

Kristen shrugged. "He's a rock star. Aren't they all like that?"

Nora spoke up. "I don't believe in giving artists permission for behavior we wouldn't accept from an accountant."

Chelsea squeezed Nora's arm in solidarity. "Exactly. Thank you."

Heather popped a salt and vinegar chip into her mouth. "I slept with an older guy when I was in high school."

Kristen gaped at her. "You did? How much older?"

"He was twenty-two."

Kristen rolled her eyes. "That's barely older. Who was it?"

Heather grinned. "Tad Archer."

"No!" Dani and Kristen said in unison, exchanging a glance that Chelsea could only interpret as impressed.

Awareness dawned on Nora's face. "I had a Tad Archer in class. In my first year or two at Imperial Flats."

Dani elaborated. "He was truly gorgeous. Tall, dark hair. Basketball player. I always thought it was sad he didn't go to college with how good he was."

"Not much of a college guy, our Tad," Heather said, not unkindly. "But, damn. So pretty."

Dani shook her head at Heather. "This is complete apples and oranges. Tad was twenty-two. Denny is *old*."

"I'm older!" Nora interjected. "But yeah."

As the women took turns speculating about Denny's whereabouts, Chelsea was struck with a memory of Denny from high school: It had been early in the morning at Evan's house. They'd all slept over in the living room the night before, eating pizza, playing video games, watching *Saturday Night Live* until, at one point, Frank had wandered out and told them to shut the fuck up. That morning, Evan and Tommy and Julian were dead to the world on the floor, wrapped in quilts, but she'd heard someone moving around in the kitchen.

She'd slid from the couch and crept through the doorway where she found Denny making coffee. He was in gym shorts and a ripped IFHS band sweatshirt and his feet were bare.

He'd turned, "Morning, beauty," he'd said to Chelsea and poured her a mug of hot coffee. As she'd added milk and sugar, she'd felt strangely warmed by the sight of him, leaning against the counter, stripped of his usual big energy (because Denny always seemed to be performing, no matter what he was doing), but not then; there, he had just been Denny, and they'd sipped their coffee in silence. It was her favorite memory of him.

Chelsea wondered what it would be like not to know Denny Bliss as a real person. For him to be just some random celebrity on the cover of *Entertainment Weekly*. Maybe then she could stop being so angry with him. It was personal with Denny. Not just because of their history and what he did to Evan, but because it brought everything that happened at Grove, and with Stone, straight to the surface. These entitled men running around the world wreaking havoc, making demands, and people, even women, just excusing it. She felt Nora watching her and knew she was thinking the same thing.

"Come on, Chelsea!" Heather pressed again. "You're really not going to tell us where he is?"

* * *

But nothing stayed secret in Imperial Flats for long, especially when the town stood to benefit from the news. The local paper had soon sniffed out his arrival and, by the following weekend, barely disguised their glee with the headline:

LOCAL SUPERSTAR RETURNS HOME AMID SCANDAL!

Sunday morning, Diego read it out loud over crepes:

HE IS KNOWN WORLDWIDE AS the lead singer of the band Sunset Dark, but Imperial Flats knew Denny Bliss and two of his bandmates (Tommy Langer and Julian Bertolone) long before they blasted to stardom. All three were born in Imperial Flats and members of our own Imperial Flats High School Jazz Band, along with former bandmate Evan Dawkins, who now runs that program.

IN RECENT YEARS, MR. BLISS has come under scrutiny for his controversial romantic entanglements. Last week, he was accused of an inappropriate relationship with a sixteen-year-old Miami, Florida high schooler. While he insists the girl never disclosed her age, it still sent the Grammy-nominated artist into hiding. And where did he choose to hide? Right here in Imperial Flats. While both Evan Dawkins and former high school friend Chelsea Garden (who both now teach at IFHS) were not available for comment, several sightings of Mr. Bliss around town have confirmed that he has, indeed, come home.

Diego looked up. "You were friends with him?"
"I was friends with Evan, so I spent a lot of time with Denny."

"And you were not available for comment?"

Chelsea rolled her eyes. "I'm not getting involved." Chelsea squeezed some lemon over her crepe. "But what do they mean 'controversial' romantic entanglements? Like it's a political theory and not sex with an underage girl?"

Diego snorted his agreement, drizzling melted honey-butter over his crepes. "Why did Evan leave the band?"

Chelsea glanced at Kyle who looked up from the *New York Times*. She chose her words carefully. "The short version is that Evan and Denny had a falling out, Evan told the band it was him or Denny, and they chose Denny."

Diego winced. "Ouch."

"Yeah."

Kyle sipped his espresso, his eyes still on his paper. "They knew they couldn't replace that voice."

Chelsea stared at her uncle. How had she never realized that before? But now that Kyle said it, of course that was it. Denny had one of those distinctive rock voices recognizable anywhere, soulful and gravelly. It was the cornerstone of the music. Evan was a beautiful songwriter and talented guitarist, but at the end of the day, there was no replacing that voice.

She bit into her crepe. "Obviously, Evan took it personally."

Diego nodded. "But why did Denny come back now? Wouldn't he expect Evan to chuck him out?"

Chelsea dropped her eyes to her plate. "Sometimes the only place to go when nothing makes sense anymore is somewhere that knew you before you fucked it all up."

* * *

On Monday afternoon, Chelsea looked up at the gentle knock on her classroom doorframe to find her dad standing there. "Chels-bells."

"Dad?" She hurried to her feet. "Is everything okay?"

He stepped inside, his eyes scanning the room. "Oh, sure, sure. Just wanted to come see where you're spending your days."

Chelsea felt her chest tighten. When had he gotten so old? He'd turned seventy last year, but still taught one class at the college, and she never thought of him as old, never thought of either of her parents as old. In her mind, she had frozen them somewhere in their early fifties even if she was closer to that age than they were. But standing there in his baggy navy parka, his sweater seeming a size too big, his pants hanging a bit loose, he seemed suddenly like an elderly man. His hair had thinned and paled, not gray really, but not the dark blonde of her youth. It was like he'd been washed too many times.

She tried to see the classroom as he might see it, all the posters and too many desks crammed into a tight space. "It still has most of the stuff from the last teacher since I'm just filling in for the semester."

He clocked her mug and laptop and sweater hanging over the desk chair. "Seems you're fitting right in."

"I like it." And she did, she realized, her skin tingling. Actually, she might love this work.

"I am most myself in a classroom," her dad said. He ran his hand over a front row desk, then gave her a thin smile. "Sorry, I'm sure that sounds strange. I'm sure home is supposed to be the place where I feel most like myself."

Warmth bloomed in her belly. "You don't have to explain anything to me." He swallowed, almost nervous, but didn't respond. "You okay, Dad?"

He blinked behind his glasses. "Sure, sure." He wandered for a bit, his hands in the pockets of his parka, taking in the white board, the bookshelves. "It's just, you know your brother left so quickly at Christmas. They were just here a few days, we barely had time to see them. Who knows when he'll come again? He used to come so often, when the kids were tiny, but then—"

"His kids are that age where they each have a thousand activities. They barely see each other anymore, much less have time to travel out here." Her brother had bought into that particular brand of suburban culture that spent countless hours and thousands of dollars on extra-curriculars for their kids in a frenzied race to see what they might excel at in the thin hope it might get them into the right college.

Grove had been the same way. Chelsea couldn't believe the schedules her students had kept sometimes. She waited for her dad to say more, but when he didn't, she added gently, "Shaun's always just done his own thing, though, hasn't he? I mean, since he went to Boston, we never much saw him after that."

Her dad nodded, cleared his throat, his gaze settling on her. "Your mother loves you both, you know? I mean, I know she can be sharp. I do know that. She's always been too hard on both of you, but it's mostly her being hard on herself. I'm not sure that's visible from where you're standing, but it's the truth."

Chelsea felt tears pool in her eyes. "That's a hard thing for a child to understand."

He blinked at her. "But you get it now, right? That she just wants you to be happy."

Chelsea felt familiar unease move through her. It had always seemed to her that when her mother told her she just wanted her to be happy, it was mostly because Judy was unhappy with Chelsea's current choices. It had never felt like a wish. Only a judgment. She didn't want Chelsea's version of happiness; she wanted her children to choose her own specifications.

"I have been the same amount of happy as most people, I'm sure. Even if she never seems to believe me."

He looked pained, distracted himself from having to look at her by scanning the bookshelf of novels near the door. His back to her, he said, "I don't like conflict. Never have."

"I know, Dad."

He turned, surprised. "Did you? I hadn't realized it until recently. That conflict thing." He ran his hand through his hair. "At the college, they had us take this social-emotional professional development class. I didn't have to take it; I only teach one class, but it seemed interesting, and the days are long now, so I thought, what else would I be doing? So, I signed up for it. All this stuff about trauma and personality types. Made my head spin. It was interesting, though. It's where I realized that thing about me, about conflict. How I avoid it. All this talk now, all this talk about feelings and vulnerability and active listening, well, we didn't know much back then, did we? Back when we were raising you and Shaun. Maybe we didn't know the things we should have."

Her sweet dad. Chelsea took a step toward him. "You listened Dad. You tried."

"There was so much we didn't know."

"I'm not sure Mom would listen to it now."

"She loves you so much."

Chelsea felt an instinct bubble up—to ease his mind, to tell him it was okay, that she knew her mother loved her—then realized she was doing the same thing he'd been doing, avoiding conflict, avoiding anything uncomfortable, so she tried to articulate some of the swirl in her brain, even if maybe she was saying it to the wrong person.

"I love her, too, Dad." The inside of her mouth felt like sand, but she pushed through. "It's just that, well, I think that if we don't know how to reflect and take responsibility for when we hurt people, even if it wasn't intentional—if we don't try to change, if we don't simply listen and hear the way we've made someone feel, well, I'm not sure love is enough."

* * *

Chelsea went for a long hike through the hills a couple of miles outside of Imperial Flats. It was a chilly afternoon, gray, with low clouds and the thinnest sunlight could be before calling it something else. March could flip in a moment, turn bright and sunny and spring-like, but for now winter still had a hold on it and the trail was cold and full of shadows.

For the last few days, she'd been thinking about the conversation with her dad. It was something she always did with conversations, picking back through them, turning them over, holding them up to the light. She had been in her mid-thirties before realizing other people didn't necessarily do the same thing. Stone had given her a mug once that read: *Hold on, let me overthink this*. She'd laughed, of course; it was funny—and true, but she'd also been embarrassed. Like he'd caught her picking her nose.

In the last few years, though, Chelsea had grown weary of a culture that saw the things she valued as weaknesses or deficiencies: her sensitivity, her overthinking, her desire for depth and quiet. Especially when their opposites seemed undesirable. Should we be insensitive, shallow, noisy?

Her dad wanted her to understand and accept that her mother loved her, that she was sharp-tongued and critical, true, but that she didn't know how to be anything else. It was sweet of him to try to talk to her about it, but wasn't his explanation part of the bigger problem? If she was to have any sense of peace with her mother, would it once again be her job to accommodate a person who couldn't see herself, who couldn't apologize or be accountable for her own role in the problem?

Chelsea understood she had inherited her father's tendency to make allowances, and that in some ways this had made her life richer, this ability to try to live in other people's skins once in a while, to forgive them for not seeing beyond themselves. She knew there was value in a growth-mindset, in flexibility, in her ability to see outside herself, but it was just fucking exhausting sometimes to always be the one yielding to empathy. Didn't the massive amount of time spent accommodating other people's rigidity cause its own issues? There was an entire group of people, selfish people, who didn't want, crave, or even have the capacity for introspection, for self-reflection, for attempting to contemplate what it might feel like to live in *her* body for a change, and yet somehow it was her job to try to understand *them* while they just moved about the cabin, knocking into the back of her chair? Honestly, Chelsea was jealous of them sometimes.

Years ago, when she'd first started seeing Stone, she'd taken a weekend empathy-building workshop in Santa Barbara with both him and Leila, one of the few she'd done with the two of them. They'd sat near an open window, the beach-breeze fluttering the gauzy curtains, and, at one point, the leader, a woman in her sixties, had broken down in tears, listening to the story of one of the other participants. Chelsea hadn't missed the look exchanged between Stone and Leila, the smug glance. Later, over wine on their private ocean-view terrace, they'd complained they hadn't thought her tears were professional. Chelsea had pointed out it was a workshop in *empathy*, after all, and they'd both laughed and clinked their glasses.

"Then we've gotten our money's worth," Leila had said wryly.

Chelsea had let them think she'd been joking.

Accommodation was its own sickness.

Like so many times in her life, Chelsea found herself at a crossroads. She understood that her mother would never change. And she knew that, yes, forgiveness was for her own well-being, her own sense of peace much more than for anyone else. Still, what happened when each time you tried to forgive a person, they picked at the very scab you kept attempting to bandage over with that forgiveness? It wasn't like she could hook up some sort of forgiveness IV and drag it behind her like an oxygen tank, constantly giving herself hits through a plastic mask.

So she'd stayed away from her mother and as a result she'd caused pain. For her father, and, seemingly, for her mother, too. As Chelsea came to the peak of the hike, the flat place with a view of pines and bare maples and rolling fields, and the winding sheet-metal glint of river in the distance, she thought that maybe being an adult was mostly accepting that things might never be what you want in certain relationships. Maybe adulthood was a perpetual state of settling for an inevitable absence of epiphany in other people.

She pulled out her phone and, on a whim, called her brother.

"Chelsea?" He sounded worried.

"Hi!"

"Dad's okay? Mom?"

"They're exactly the same."

"Right. So, you're just calling—to say hi?"

She felt a pang of guilt for the confusion in his voice. "Is that okay?"

She heard papers rustling, keyboard keys clicking. "Of course."

"How are you?"

"Busy. Kelly's pulling her hair out with Jayden."

The vegetarian. "What's going on?"

"It's like he's allergic to any sort of ambition or organization."

"He's thirteen."

"He'll be fourteen next month."

"He seemed passionate about the whole vegetarian thing."

"Oh yeah, that's over." More paper rustling. "He realized he'd have to give up pepperoni pizza."

Chelsea laughed. "Sometimes it just takes certain kids longer to find their path." Sometimes, forty-five years, apparently.

Her brother sighed through the phone. "That's what I tell Kelly, too, but he bombed those tests you take for private school and she worries he'll drown in public. He's so sensitive. I'm not surprised he bombed them, though. He spends all his time playing video games."

"Why don't you take the video games away?" She broke her own rule before she could stop herself.

"We tried that. It just made him sulk around the house and break things."

"Break things?"

"It's a long story. Anyway, I have to run to a meeting. You good?"

She hesitated, then just told him what he wanted to hear. "Yeah, I'm good."

"Great catching up with you. Gotta go." He clicked off before she could say goodbye.

Chelsea stared at the phone. Every conversation she'd ever had with her brother felt like the small talk at the beginning of a job interview. For him, though, this was a relationship: the occasional catch-up had always been enough for him. The truth was her brother didn't know her, not really, and she didn't know him. Not in a meaningful way. The harder truth was it would always be this way, no matter how much Chelsea wished it wasn't. Just like her mother would always comment on the Pop-Tarts in her cart. And her dad would always try to explain why. And she would never be able to change a goddamn thing about it.

It was all that annoyingly, infuriatingly simple.

NORA

IF NORA HAD TO SIT through one more IEP or discipline or safety meeting today, she felt she might truly explode. Headline: *Local School Administrator Combusts during Safety Protocol Meeting.* This summer would mark the end of her twenty-seventh full-time year in education and she had officially become one of the educators she swore she would never turn into: exhausted, jaded, counting the days until the next break.

For a while she had blamed the pandemic, of course. What educator didn't feel like they'd been vaulted back into the fatigue of their first year of teaching during that unruly time? Truthfully, it had been more grueling than her first year of teaching—her first year had been so buoyed with optimism and adrenaline. The pandemic had just been upsetting, fear-riddled, and exhausting. But it had been in her first year of teaching that she'd learned to avoid the staff room, that sauna of martyrdom. Haggard lifers standing around with lukewarm mugs of coffee, calculating the days until their pensions kicked in. She had loathed them, had met her fellow newbies for margaritas in the late afternoon, and vowed to never turn into the crusty old trolls populating the staff room. She still found most of them insufferable. Dreaded the kind of faculty gathering that would put her face to face with the ones who'd been talking retirement since they were in their tenth year. The ones who for some reason had chosen a career with teenagers when they didn't seem to like them very much.

Only now, Nora realized, she found herself relating to them. She found herself nodding along when someone bemoaned how much education had changed, how much kids had changed, how frustrating parents had become, even as she tried to joke that it had always been thus. Didn't Plato complain about *kids these days*? Every generation thought the one following it was making things worse, had shorter attention spans, lapsed values, a lack of appreciation for actual learning. She *didn't* think that, actually. She found this particular generation of teenager rather inspiring. They were more political and empathetic than she remembered being as a teenager. Their levels of anxiety kept rising, but they also talked openly about mental health and kindness and pluralism in a way that inspired Nora, made her think the kids would be all right.

But Education was another story. It started years ago with all the testing. Then, each year, it seemed more things kept being heaped on the educational plate: mental health intervention, active shooter drills, power outage and fire protocol, relentless data-gathering—testing, testing, testing. All so politicians could throw around words like "accountability" and "grit" and "transparency." Both sides of the fence, guilty.

Somewhere along the way, the idea of teaching as an artform had been replaced with teaching as a procedural act. No longer teachers, but technicians. It broke Nora's heart, on days she paused long enough to realize how long it had been since she'd thought about her school in a holistic, creative, programmatic way. Her life had become filling out state forms and writing accountability documents and responding to crisis after crisis after crisis. She'd found herself grumbling about it to Toby on a walk recently until she realized she sounded just like them, those long-ago staff room martyrs, and she snapped her mouth closed in shame.

"Nora?" Elaine stood in the doorway.

Nora made sure her mic was muted and waved Elaine in. "County safety meeting," she told her. One of the rare good side effects of the pandemic was certain meetings stayed on Zoom even after things settled back in. It saved her the time of running around the county all the time, making small talk, drinking bad coffee, nibbling stale grocery store cookies.

Elaine handed her a slip of paper. "Kerrianne is worried about this one."

Kerrianne Day was their visual arts teacher, mostly painting and drawing, but she also covered the one section they'd managed to keep of ceramics. Nora glanced at the paper, then back at Elaine. "Does she think she's suicidal?"

Elaine nodded, her expression saddening.

"Let me get off this call." Nora glanced back at her screen. Elaine hovered in the doorway until Nora looked up again. "Was there something else?"

Elaine bit her lip. "It's not urgent, but—" She held up a slip of paper in her hand. "We've had a parent complaint about a teacher."

Nora rolled her eyes. "Jack again?"

Elaine paused. "Chelsea Garden."

"Chelsea?"

"Yeah."

Nora sighed. "Okay. I'll just get off this call."

* * *

Nora made Chelsea a coffee and set it down on the conference room table where Chelsea fidgeted in her chair. Flipping open the notebook where she documented parent complaints about teachers, she dated the new entry. "We've had a parent complain."

Chelsea's brow furrowed. "About me?"

Nora nodded. "About a book you're reading in class. It happens all the time. Which one are you teaching right now with your seniors? *The Handmaid's Tale*? *Snow Falling on Cedars*?"

"We're actually doing reading circles right now. The kids chose books and are in groups of three or four with the same book."

"Right, okay." Nora slipped on her readers and studied the paper Elaine had handed her earlier. "This says *Dreaming in Cuban*." Nora frowned. "When did the department add that one?"

Chelsea shifted in her chair. "Um, it's not on the reading list. For this project, I wanted them to choose books that featured women of color and other marginalized voices."

"So, it's not on the board approved reading list?"

"It was a finalist for the National Book Award in the nineties."

Nora took her readers off. "I wish that mattered."

Chelsea sighed. "Nora, the reading list here is basically from 1987. It's almost all the same stuff I read when I went here. With the exception of *The Handmaid's Tale*, which was already checked out by the way, the senior reading list is basically white guys. Mostly dead ones. I mean my choices for this unit were *1984* and *Beowulf*. How can we justify that?" When Nora didn't respond, she added, "What did the family complain about?"

Nora glanced down. "Smuttiness."

"Did they use that word? *Smuttiness*?" When Nora nodded, Chelsea let out a puff of annoyed air. "It's a beautiful novel about families and the complexity of the immigrant experience."

"It's not board approved. Please tell me you at least got a permission slip from the families."

Chelsea's eyes fell to her lap. "I didn't even think to get permission slips. I've never had anything I've taught questioned before."

Nora leaned forward, her forearms on the table. "You taught in the Bay Area at a private school. Liberal, educated parents."

"Not all of them."

"Most of them. And culturally, it's just different than here." Nora could see tears pooling in the corners of Chelsea's eyes. "Chelsea, I'm sure it's a beautiful book. I'm sure these kids would benefit enormously from reading it. But we have to be careful. We have a deep Christian community here, a vocal conservative vein. They have a right to know what their kids are reading."

"They have Shakespeare on the reading list! It's like sixty percent dick jokes."

"Board approved smuttiness."

Chelsea met her gaze. "It's a white, male-centric reading list. What kind of message does it send to students—girls, boys, white and otherwise—when all they read is the straight white male narrative? When all they see of women or people of color or queer writers is thrown in as poems or short stories or essays as 'supplemental' to the 'real' books?" Chelsea stabbed the quote marks into the air with her fingers. "It prioritizes the heteronormative white male experience."

"I agree."

"Then—" she threw up her hands, "then, what the heck?"

Nora leaned forward. "I agree with you. And we fought for a long time to get some women on that list. You should have seen the board meeting to approve *The House on Mango Street* and *The Handmaid's Tale*. You would have thought we were trying to get them to approve *Lolita*. Or soft-core queer porn. You know how it is. You grew up here."

Chelsea managed a smile. She sipped some of her coffee. "Since I've been back, the town seems like it's changed so much, I guess I just assumed it would be okay."

"And you've had one complaint. *One*. But you have to get a permission slip if you stray from the list. People have to be given a choice. They have to be able to say, 'No, thanks, we want the dead straight white guys,' even if they haven't realized that those can be the smuttiest of all. I mean, we teach *Of Mice and Men* to our freshman. Curley wears a glove with Vaseline. For his wife. Who doesn't even have a name in the book. She's just Curley's wife."

Chelsea's face brightened. "Exactly. You get it."

Nora closed her notebook. "Look, it's not personal. It's just public school in a rural community. You have to cover all your bases. I once had a complaint from a parent because Dean suggested *The Golden Compass* as an independent reading book and a mom called to complain because she didn't believe in her son reading books with talking animals." She took a beat, then said. "Because they are the work of the devil." Chelsea blinked at her. "Yep. But Dean sent home a slip with a spot for the parent to agree to the outside reading book and it was signed."

"So she'd agreed to the book and then complained about it?"

"Nope, the kid had signed it for her."

Chelsea shook her head. "Wow."

"Right? But, suddenly, it's not our problem. We have the form to show her. With the forged signature. That becomes a parenting problem. Without the form, it's a school problem."

Chelsea set her mug down. "So how do I fix it?"

Nora waved her off. "Let me do that. We'll say you've been reprimanded, that you're a long-term sub, that you didn't know the rules. We'll offer another book instead. We'll give him *1984*. Let them deal with Orwell's brand of board-approved smut." Nora stood up and moved to her desk, leaning against its side. "Nine out of ten times, they just want to know someone heard them."

Chelsea made her way to the doorway before turning back. "They see smuttier things on Netflix all the time. And in their video games."

"Of course they do."

* * *

Toby was on the East Coast for a week, and, somehow, they'd become the person in each other's lives who helped out when one got in a bind, so Nora had Toby's Golden Retriever for the week. Moonie was the sweetest dog Nora had ever met. A feathery, white-blonde eight-year-old who mostly just draped herself over Nora's couch for the daylight hours. Even so, Nora ran home at lunch to take her on a short walk and let her use the facilities.

As Nora circled the block for the second time, she quite literally almost ran into Dani. Or rather, Dani almost ran into her. Dani pulled out her AirPods, huffing, and bent over, hands clutching her knees. "Sorry—didn't—see—you."

"Should I call an ambulance? Since when do you run?"

"Just—started—last—week," Dani gasped.

"Going well?"

Dani took a deep gulp. "I hate it with all of my soul." Nora just shook her head. Moonie sat down on Nora's feet, aware they might be awhile. Dani finally took stock of her. "Did you get a dog?"

"This is Moonie. Toby's dog." Dani shot her a confused look. "He's gone for a week back east for work, so I have a houseguest."

Dani finally stood upright. "Oh, really?" She ruffled the dog's ears. "What a cutie."

"She is."

Dani titled her head. "So, let me get this straight. You're not sleeping with him, but you're babysitting his dog?"

Nora felt her face heat. "Who says I'm not sleeping with him?"

Dani's jaw actually dropped open. "Nora Delgado!"

"What?"

"You have been withholding essential information! We're meeting directly after work today. At the restaurant."

Nora gave Moonie a soft tug and set off down the street. "If you say so." She waved goodbye to Dani, who put her AirPods back in, and reluctantly jogged off in the other direction.

* * *

Nora thanked Barry for the gin and tonic and found a seat at a nearby table. Dani had given her a quick hug, then rushed off to deal with something in the kitchen, so Nora perused the specials board and sipped her drink, not eager for Dani to begin her inevitable interrogation.

Nora had never been the sort of woman who talked openly about sex. She didn't think she was a prude. And she certainly liked sex; she just didn't like elongated conversations about it in that *Sex and the City* way so many of her girlfriends seemed to favor. It still felt like a sacred, private thing to her and she'd never enjoyed airing it out over cocktails. But she knew Dani well enough by now to know that this sort of disclosure was important in their friendship.

Dani slipped into the seat next to her. "Bert's making us something with cream and veggies. He'll bring it out." She reached across the table and grasped Nora's hand. "I'm so happy for you! Remember when you thought Toby was obnoxious?"

"You're enjoying this."

"I am."

"And he *was* obnoxious. Sometimes." She sipped her drink. "I'm assuming he still will be." Honestly, though, Toby had been a board member for years, and always a good (albeit sometimes infuriating) one. Strong attention to detail, vocal, and professional. Even if she was quite sure they'd compromised that last one. At least a half dozen times now.

And Dani wasn't buying her casual snark anyway. "This sounds serious, Nora."

Nora held her friend's gaze, her stomach whirring. "I think it might be."

Dani squeezed her hand, then leaned back so Bert could deposit two steaming bowls of pasta in front of them. Nora breathed in, and without preamble, burst into tears.

Bert put a big hand on her shoulder, joking, "It might not be my finest, but I swear it's edible."

Nora attempted to get herself under control. "Ohmygod, I'm sorry. I'm so sorry. I have no idea why I'm crying. It looks beautiful, Bert." Even through her watery vision, she didn't miss the look exchanged between Dani and Bert. "What?"

"Well, it's just—" Dani twirled a loop of pasta around her fork. "It's about time, is all."

"What is?"

"Have you had any good public cries yet? Through all of it?"

Nora looked horrified. "Of course not!"

Dani looked at Bert, who gave Nora's shoulder a squeeze, then let go. Dani balanced her fork on the bowl's edge. "You need to let it out." Dani handed Nora a clean white napkin.

Nora dabbed at her eyes. "But things are good with Toby. Really good." As she said it, a fresh round of tears betrayed her. "This is ridiculous!"

"He's a good guy, Nor," Bert said. "I'm in Rotary with him. A really good guy."

"I know!" Nora choked out. Other diners were starting to watch her, put their forks down, pay attention. Jesus, she had to pull it together. This wasn't about Toby, was it? She had no idea what this was about. She took a staggered breath. And then another one. Then, she gazed up at Dani's enormous teddy bear of a husband.

"Bert, this looks delicious. Could you, by any chance, pack it to-go for me?"

"Give me five minutes. I'll have Marco run it out to your car."

* * *

"Nora?" Elaine hovered in the doorway.

Nora slipped off her readers and glanced up from the LCAP document she was working on. "What is it?"

Elaine licked her lips nervously. "I was just wondering if you're okay."

Nora's eyebrows went up. "Why wouldn't I be?"

"Did you not—see the Facebook post?"

Nora's stomach dropped. "What Facebook post?"

"Oh."

"Elaine?"

Ten minutes later, Nora had watched the video. Twice. The video of her sobbing in Romano's. Someone had "shared" it with the caption: "Is this who should be leading our kids?"

She was in the process of swallowing two Advil when her phone rang. Dani.

"Nora?"

"I saw it."

"If I find out who took it, they will be banned from the restaurant for life."

Nora couldn't help but smile. "No need to track the source—I won't give it that much of my time." But her stomach felt like someone had backed up a truck and filled it with cement.

Dani paused on the other end. Nora could hear her breathing slow down. Finally, she said simply, "I'm sorry, Nora."

EVAN

Evan had popped out to the bathroom before school but bolted on the way back to his room when he heard the scream. "What the—?" He froze in the doorway of his classroom. Caroline stood white-faced in the middle of the room, clutching her sax to her chest. He followed her stare. Denny.

Sitting, feet up, at his desk. "Morning, teach!"

"You're—you're—," Caroline couldn't seem to get other words out, still couldn't seem to move.

"What're you doing here, Denny?" Evan let his gaze slip to Caroline. "You okay, Carrie?"

"Ohmygod, Denny Bliss," Caroline finally managed.

Other jazz band students started to trickle in, sleepy, clutching coffee and instruments. They, too, froze when they noticed Denny, though Evan was grateful none of them had Caroline's vocal reaction. His ears were still ringing, and he'd been outside.

Denny scanned the walls: the years of group photos, the various trophies lining the cubbies (most at least a decade old), the racks of costumes and instruments. "Man, this place hasn't changed. I practically lived in here for four years. What a trip."

"Right, glory days and all that." Evan walked to his music stand, motioned his students to start setting up. "We have class in," he glanced at the wall clock, "three minutes."

Denny held up his hands. "Don't let me stop the magic. I'll just observe."

Evan turned to him. "Right, because an international rock star won't be distracting at all."

Chris blinked at Denny. "Do you just carry around a ton of cash, like, all the time?"

Denny grinned. "You plannin' on robbing me, kid?"

Chris blanched. "No!"

"Chris, why don't you go get set up?" Evan walked to the desk and leaned in close to Denny. "You really can't be here."

Denny pantomimed zipping his lips. "Church mouse." He winked at Caroline, who gave a yip, but still didn't move.

Evan tried again. "You need to go. Now. I'll come over after work."

Denny made a show of wheeling the chair back, standing up, hands in the air again. "Okay, okay, I can tell when I'm not wanted."

"Clearly not," Evan mumbled.

Eleven sets of eyes followed Denny Bliss as he made his slow, sauntering exit from the band room.

* * *

Evan closed the classroom door behind him and leaned against it. Chelsea looked up from her desk. "You okay?"

"What am I going to do with him? He showed up at jazz this morning."

"Denny?"

"Who else? I thought Caroline was going to have a stroke."

Chelsea grinned. She had Caroline in her one junior section, so Evan knew she could picture it. "He can't possibly stay in town for much longer, right? At some point, Nathan and Steph will kick him out."

Evan flopped into one of the front row desks, wincing. "These are not comfortable." He kicked his long legs out into the aisle. "I had to unplug Frank's landline. The journalists alone. Not to mention the crazy fans. I've found three bras on my front lawn. Just tossed there. Different sizes, so I'm assuming three different people. I mean, what do they even expect him to do with them?"

Chelsea slipped off her readers. "Are they cute bras?"

"I didn't actually check for style." Evan hated to admit it, but he was starting to feel the smallest bubble of sympathy for Denny. It couldn't be easy, the relentless attention and scrutiny. Or maybe Denny loved it. He always had.

Chelsea leaned back in her chair, stretching her arms over her head before dropping her hands in her lap. "Maybe you should give him a project?"

"What sort of project?"

"You said you were having trouble with ticket sales for An Evening of Jazz, right?"

Evan didn't like where this was heading. The jazz band's biggest annual fundraiser was an event called An Evening of Jazz in April. Cafe tables, appetizers, a wine bar for the adults. A silent auction while the jazz band played their tunes. This was Evan's second time in charge of it since he'd come in the middle of last year, and he was nervous. They'd only sold twenty tickets so far and all of them were to band families. The event was weeks away. He eyed Chelsea. "We've sold about twenty tickets, one of them to you."

"Maybe a surprise guest would help sell more tickets. Everyone will know you mean Denny Bliss."

"I don't want him upstaging the kids." Mostly, Evan didn't want the liability. "Besides, he'd never agree to it."

* * *

Evan stood with Violet in front of the travel-size section at CVS, their handbasket filling up with tiny toothpaste, mini shampoo, a travel pack of antibacterial wipes, and, inexplicably, deodorant. "Do you use this?" Evan plucked out the tiny tube of something lavender-scented and claiming to be organic. He held it up.

"Dad." Violet had a way of turning single words into eye rolls. "I'm turning ten in a week."

"Do ten-year-olds stink?"

"You should spend five minutes in my math class."

Smiling, Evan tossed it back into the basket. "Fine. Won't your mom have shampoo?"

"I like that one." She held up two containers of lotion, scrutinizing them, then selected one. She held up a canister, peering at the small print. "Do I need Evian spray to stay refreshed on the plane?"

"Absolutely not."

"Why?"

"Because you're not on a reality TV show."

Outside, Evan tossed the bag into the backseat where Frank waited for them. "Don't go through that," he told him. "It's not yours."

Frank ignored him, picking through the purchases. He held up the deodorant, uncapped it, sniffed. "Smells like the stuff you spray when you poo." Violet giggled from the front seat, which only encouraged Frank. "Like when you take a big poo."

Evan started the car. "No potty talk, Dad. You agreed." He pulled out of the parking spot as his dad, just faintly, whispered, "Poooooo," from the back seat. Violet tried, and failed, to stop giggling, turning her head toward the window.

Certain days, Evan couldn't believe this was his life.

* * *

"I'm in."

Evan blinked over his beer. He and Denny lounged in front of the fireplace, their feet kicked up on the coffee table, each with a bottle in hand. "So you're sticking around for a bit?" He clocked the room: the piles of take-out containers, the empty wine bottles lined up on the counter, the heaps of dirty clothes. Denny's guitar sat propped against the double bed. Evan wondered if he'd been playing it or if it was just sitting there for show.

Denny kicked off his slippers, warming the soles of his bare feet. Evan noticed he had unusually hairy toes, middle-aged toes. When did they both get so ancient? "I'll stay at least another few weeks," Denny said. "Nathan and Steph said I can crash here as long as I want. I offered to pay them, but they wouldn't accept it, said they'd advertise that 'Denny Bliss' stayed here if they turn it into an Airbnb. I told them to knock themselves out. I'll even get them one of those dorky photos together where I sign it for them to hang on the wall."

"Lucky them." Evan sipped his beer. "Even so, you don't have to do this, Denny."

"Hey, it was my band once, too."

Evan hesitated. "I'm going to say 'surprise guest' on the announcement. That way, if you've got to split, I can sub in someone else."

Denny cut his eyes to Evan. "I'm not going to flake on you."

Evan shook his head. "I'm not saying that. I'm saying in case you have to leave. For whatever reason."

Denny stared glumly into the fire, the fingers of his free hand tapping along to Miles Davis on the speakers. *Kind of Blue*. Evan thought it was a bit on the nose, another problematic male musician. "They're not pressing charges. The girl's family. But my publicist thinks I should lay low for a while anyway."

So, Evan thought, once again, Denny would get to act without consequence. The Denny Bliss Lifestyle Method. "How much did that cost you?"

Denny drained half his beer, his expression darkening.

"Just because you got away with it, doesn't mean you didn't fuck up."

Denny shot Evan a wounded glance. "No one really talks to me like that anymore."

"Maybe that's part of the problem." When Denny's pout deepened, Evan couldn't help adding, "Hey, can't help it if I'm immune to the Denny Bliss magic."

Denny clinked his bottle against Evan's. "Cheers, brother. Believe it or not, that's part of the reason I came back here. Because I knew you would be."

They drank in silence. Watching the flicker and shadow, Evan had a flash of the last time he saw Denny, peeling out of the parking lot of that shit club they'd been playing. Where had that been? Somewhere upstate California with a name that sounded like a tractor company. He couldn't remember. They'd had that horrible fight. Evan had made his ultimatum, standing there in the neon glow of a graveled parking lot. Tommy and Julian had watched him, huddled against the brick siding of the club, smoking cigarettes, shaking their heads. They'd told Evan not to decide anything, not to make decisions at two a.m. when they'd all been drinking, when they were on the last leg of a shit string of gigs.

But Evan wouldn't budge. How would life have turned out if he'd just agreed with them, piled into the van with them, forgiven Denny for the thousandth time? What if he'd just gone home? He wouldn't have Violet. He wouldn't be here in Imperial Flats where he woke up most mornings next to a sleeping Chelsea Garden, to a job he might actually be starting to care about. A strange question creeped in. Was it possible, given all evidence to the contrary, that Evan might have done something right for once?

* * *

Evan found Chelsea in tears on the bench outside the administration building. "Hey." She sat with her elbows on her knees, her fists in her eyes, her hair spilling forward, almost completely covering her face. Evan put a hand on her back. "Chelsea?"

"That—was—bad."

Suddenly, the door to the main office burst open and a woman and her son emerged with Nora trailing behind. Evan recognized the kid. Matthew—something. He'd been in band for a hot second last semester before his mother yanked him out of the program. Nora cut her eyes to Evan and Chelsea and tried to divert the woman and Matthew away, but it was too late.

The woman charged over to Chelsea. "You should be ashamed of yourself. How do they let you work with children?"

Nora hurried to put herself between them. "Okay, that's enough. Everyone needs to go home and cool off. I understand you're upset, Mrs. Hill, but I won't tolerate you talking to one of my teachers like this. We've figured out a solution."

Evan was impressed. Nora was using a voice he'd never heard from her before. A voice he, personally, would not want to fuck with. Evan waited to see if Mrs. Hill would contradict her, but just as she looked poised to respond, her son tugged at the sleeve of her shirt.

"Let's go, Mom. *Please.*" He looked as if someone had been slowing sticking pins along the undersides of his arms.

Evan moved closer to Nora, just in case she ended up needing back up. She didn't. The woman and her son turned and crossed the parking lot, climbed into a squat green sedan, and peeled away.

"Jesus," Evan breathed.

"Yes," Nora sighed. "That is primarily who she was quoting the whole time. Though, I'm not sure which part of Jesus's philosophy encouraged abuse of civil servants."

As if they both thought of her at the same time, they turned in tandem to check on Chelsea. The bench was empty.

"Not the best meeting?" Evan frowned at Nora.

"They rarely are lately," she sighed, before yanking the door open and disappearing back inside the building.

Evan pulled out his phone, texting Chelsea: *You okay?*

After a few minutes, she replied: *I'm going to take a nap. For the rest of my life.*

CHELSEA

EVEN WITH ALL THE LIGHTS off and the shades pulled, Chelsea's migraine wouldn't stop blinding her. She could only see red behind her eyelids. Bright, hot red. She'd taken three Advil and Diego had lit a candle, peppermint and lavender, and they were helping a little. At least the air smelled lovely. But she hadn't touched the cup of Chamomile tea he'd left by her bed. She squeezed her eyes against the red. Nora had said that nine out of ten times, parents just wanted to be heard. Nine out of ten times, she could make a call and it would go away.

Why did Chelsea keep beating the odds lately?

Mrs. Hill wanted her fired. Over a book. Over her kid reading a book. Nazis, apparently, were all the rage again. Nora had called her a few hours ago, encouraging her to take tomorrow, Friday, off. Matthew would read *1984*. It would also be offered to the other students and a permission slip would be sent home. Once those were signed, Chelsea could continue with her reading groups. Any child (parent) who wanted a board-approved text would get Orwell.

"She's being ridiculous," Nora had insisted when she called, but it was hard for Chelsea not to feel that sting of Thanksgiving all over again. Of Mr. King-Jennings. Of Sheryl Alexander. But Nora had stood up for her; she had tried.

So Chelsea called a sub for Friday, her hands shaking.

She closed her eyes again, her head spinning. What were parents so afraid of? When did it become better for your son to cheat than get a B in a class? When did it become the answer to shove your child's teacher into a car door? Or want your child's teacher fired over a book assignment you didn't agree with? Resting there in the dark, she wondered if things had gotten scarier, stranger since they'd started back after the pandemic. Had all the lockdowns and distance learning and attempts at hybrid models made people nuts? Was it the smoke from the relentless California fires? Initially, Chelsea had assumed parents would be grateful to have their kids back in school full-time after Covid, but it had ended up feeling like they'd just gotten more paranoid, more demanding, more myopic with each passing month.

She heard a faint knock on the outside door. "Come in," she called, weakly. Through her eyelids, a sheen of light. Then, darkness again.

"Chelsea?" Evan's voice. "I brought food. Courtesy of Dani." She felt his weight settle next to her on the bed. "You okay?"

"Migraine."

"You're probably allergic to asshole parents."

She felt suddenly so grateful for Evan she started crying again, tears leaking through her closed eyelids.

"Hey, hey," he said, "it's going to be okay. Nora's great. She's got your back."

Chelsea nodded, sitting up, attempting to open her eyes. "What'd you bring me?"

"Spag-bol and wine. But I'm thinking no on the wine with that migraine." She watched him fill a glass of water at the sink. The Advil was finally starting to work, and her stomach rumbled at the tart garlicky smell of the pasta. Evan piled some on a plate and handed it to her with a fork, set the glass of water next to her on the table. "You need anything else?"

"This is perfect." She swirled some noodles. "What time is it?"

Evan checked his phone. "Almost eight."

"I'm taking tomorrow off."

"Nora said. I ran into her in the parking lot when I was walking out. For what it's worth, that mom does this with everyone. She pulled Matthew out of band last year because we played a Black Sabbath song. She's the type of parent who thinks she can bubble-wrap her kid from the world, who believes the world exists to align itself with her values."

Chelsea felt the tendrils of pain chew at her neck. "I can't believe I didn't think to send home permission slips."

"Not sure it would have avoided this."

"Some of it."

"Sure." He chewed on a piece of cheese toast. "But she would have found a way to kick up a stink. She clearly lives for it."

Chelsea forked another bite into her mouth. "My parents used to side with my teachers. No matter what. It would never have crossed their minds to challenge something a teacher sent home with me."

"Frank had no idea what I was doing in school. Or if I even went to school."

"He would have cared if you didn't go to school."

"Maybe." Evan watched the flicker of Diego's candle. "I guess some people think it shows their kids how much they love them when they make other people's lives miserable on their behalf." He glanced back at her. "I have to say, I'm pretty sick of that particular brand of person."

"Is it just me or does there seem to be more of them scurrying about the planet these days?"

"I think it's just you."

"Thanks a lot."

Evan borrowed her fork and helped himself to some of the pasta. "Denny said he'd be my 'surprise guest' for the event."

She took her fork back. "Really?"

"He won't show."

"Maybe he will."

"He won't."

* * *

"Chelsea?"

"Hi Mom." Chelsea closed her car door and leaned against it, the phone to her ear. She was meeting Evan and Violet at the park. She could see them over by the swings, Violet's long hair streaming like a cape behind her as Evan pushed her higher and higher.

"What happened at school? In book club last night, Margaret Downs said you'd been fired."

Chelsea sighed, connecting the dots. Margaret Downs was the attendance secretary. And, apparently, she was in a book club with Judy Garden. "I haven't been fired."

"She said you assigned an inappropriate book to a child!"

"I assigned a National Book Award Finalist to a twelfth grader."

"It's not like the city here, Chelsea. We don't expect our kids to grow up before they're ready."

"Or at all."

"What?"

"Nothing."

"You're mumbling, Chelsea. Dad and I are worried. That you've lost another job."

Evan walked toward her, saw she was on the phone, and gave her a wave. Chelsea waved back, started walking toward the swings. "I haven't lost anything. I left Grove. And I'm teaching here now. I haven't been fired."

"Do you need money?"

"No! Anyway, we worked it out with Mrs. Hill. Her son will read something else. These things happen."

"Wait? Is this *Tara* Hill?"

Chelsea frowned. "I think so. Her son is Matthew?"

"Oh, for goodness sake. That woman has a lot of nerve! She had an affair—*an affair*! When Matthew was in elementary school. And she has the nerve to question your morals? I should call her mother."

"Please don't."

But Judy didn't seem to have heard. "The next time I see her—how dare she threaten your job?"

Chelsea couldn't help but smile. Evan caught it and gave her a hopeful thumbs up. She gave him one back.

"Thanks, Mom, seriously, I appreciate that, but," she paused. She hadn't planned on telling her mother—hadn't told anyone yet about the email she'd gotten last week—but she couldn't stop herself. "It might not matter anyway. I was offered a job overseas. In Ireland." Her body tingled thinking about it. She still couldn't believe it. She wasn't sure she even wanted to teach overseas, not really, but it was nice to be offered, to have options. And she missed rain; they had so much of that in Ireland. "I might take it."

Judy sighed into the phone. "Don't be ridiculous. You're not moving to Ireland because Tara Hill rode her high horse to school. Maybe you should come by the house later. Dad is really worried. He's been in his workshop all morning."

"Neither of you need to worry, I promise. Tell Dad it's safe to leave the workshop. I have options."

Her mother didn't respond. They were clearly done talking about Ireland. Chelsea could hear clinking. She imagined her mom in the kitchen, bending over the sink, her rubber gloves plunged into soapy water, the phone on speaker on the counter.

"Anyway, I can't imagine what Margaret was thinking telling all of us you'd been fired. I should have told her to mind her own business."

"Wouldn't that have been something."

"What?"

"Nothing." Chelsea untangled herself from the call by promising to come by when she was done at the park.

"Could you pick up some of that good cheese at Brewer's on your way, the kind your dad likes? It's right near you."

* * *

Chelsea hurried down the sidewalk to hug Amanda, who'd just driven up from the Bay to see her. Downtown Imperial Flats hummed with busy Friday night energy, people spilling out of bars, sitting outside under patio heaters at restaurants, wandering in and out of shops. She tried to imagine it through her friend's eyes: the Victorian shopfronts, the antique store with the weird gold-mining supplies in the window, the Mercantile with its bright candy counter.

"This place is so cute!" Amanda gazed around, a silly smile on her face. "Like I'm in a Hallmark movie." She glanced at Chelsea. "Sorry, that's horribly patronizing. It's not like San Rafael is the height of urban cool."

Chelsea laughed. "Anything is cooler than Imperial Flats." She drank her friend in, her jeans and boots, the cute cropped leather jacket almost the exact ink color of her eyes. "How are you? It's been way too long."

Amanda shook her head. "I'm so sorry not to make it up here before now. I wanted to come for New Year's, but I kept getting sick. And then, whoosh—third quarter raced by."

"Same for me." Chelsea linked arms with Amanda, strolled with her down the sidewalk for a block, chatting. Teaching was so immersive for periods of time, whole months lost to grading, planning, recovering from constant interaction with students, Chelsea was always grateful to have this friend who understood its rhythm, who could laugh with her about all the random things that made teaching special and strange without needing too much context.

"Drink?" Chelsea motioned to Shade Bistro, its white twinkle lights casting a warm glow over its doorway. Amanda followed her inside to an empty, tall two-top near the window.

While Amanda fussed with hanging her coat on the back of her chair, Chelsea ordered a bottle of white wine and some olives.

"So," Amanda said, situated. "Tell me everything about your life here."

"Well, I almost got fired again."

Amanda widened her eyes. "What!? First of all, Grove didn't fire you. You left. So, none of this 'again' business. And what do you mean you almost got fired? What happened?"

"A parent went crazy over a book I assigned her son to read. A 'smutty' book." Chelsea made the necessary air quotes.

Amanda grinned. "You know the rule—no pornography until senior year at least."

"It was *Dreaming in Cuban*." Chelsea nodded at the waiter as he poured their wine. She popped an olive in her mouth. "And he *is* a senior. My principal, Nora, couldn't believe this mom freaked out as much as she did. In the end, he is reading *1984* instead." She paused for dramatic effect. "Because nothing bad or sexual happens in *1984*."

Amanda groaned. "Why do parents immediately assume old things are harmless."

"The elderly should obviously commit more crimes."

They clinked glasses. "Cheers," Amanda said. "Here's to teaching: where parents want you to watch their kids all day but only if you follow all of their rules individually."

"Cheers." Chelsea took a sip of the cool, crisp wine. "I miss you."

"I miss you, too."

"What's new at Grove?"

Grove sounded pretty much the same. They'd hired a guy to replace Chelsea. Young, a few years out of a potted-Ivy college back east. Worked for a year before deciding it was time to "give back" while staying with his parents in Marin. Amanda told Chelsea everyone called him Mr. Haircut behind his back because he was always perfectly coifed.

"He worked one year in D.C. after college in something government adjacent, so, you know, he has *a lot* of opinions." Amanda rolled her eyes. "He tried telling Sheryl that our reading list didn't have enough classics. He won't be there long. I'm pretty sure we're a stepping-stone to law school anyway. But, yeah, just what Grove needs: more young white guys who feel slighted by the lack of Hemingway on our reading list."

"He should come teach in Imperial Flats. He'd be delighted."

Amanda swirled the last of her wine in her glass before asking, casually, "Do you like it here?"

Chelsea used a napkin to wipe olive oil from her fingers. "I do. I mean, it brings things up. My mother's here." Amanda nodded knowingly. Chelsea and Amanda had bonded early over their distant, critical mothers. "But I like my job more than I'd expected to. It's different from Grove. These kids aren't privileged like that. They're mostly sweet, even if most of them don't like English, or reading, or school for that matter. But I like it. I mean, not all the kids at Grove liked school, either, obviously, but they'd pretty much bought into the system that said they should do whatever they needed to do to get into a certain university. Which, as you know, has its own issues."

"You had the bruise to prove it." Amanda seemed to realize it came out more angry than funny, and, for the first time, a silence bloomed between them. Amanda had never been good with subtext or brushing things under the rug. It was one of the things Chelsea loved about her. And she knew exactly where Amanda stood on Stone's envelope revelation.

She refilled her friend's wine glass. "I'm not going to take the money."

Amanda reached over and squeezed Chelsea's hand. "I'm sorry if I was pushing you about that. I was just so mad at Sheryl, at the whole thing. You should do what feels right for you, even if I want you to get every dime out of them you can and then kick them in the throat."

Chelsea squeezed back and then refilled her own wine. She'd been trying to explain her thinking to Diego and Kyle the other night, too. She'd finally landed on the following: "I guess because money is how they solve everything, it just feels like letting them win. Again. Stone gets to feel self-righteous. Sheryl gets to feel absolved. I still feel gross."

Amanda nodded, her face a little sad. "I get that, I do. You're just a better person than I am. I would want to hit them in a language they understood. Since they clearly don't care about how this made you feel."

Chelsea stared out at the darkening evening. "I'm not a better person, I promise. I'm living in my uncle's Airbnb for free and was basically handed a job without trying. I don't want to push my luck. Of course, Stone said I'd change my mind when I realized my moral high ground feels a lot like poverty."

Amanda's eyes widened. She shook her head. "Seriously, what you ever saw in him is beyond me."

"He had really nice abs."

"Fair. He was very, very pretty." Amanda raised an eyebrow. "Speaking of cute boys, you promised to fill me in on your Evan status."

Chelsea warmed at the thought of Evan. She'd tried to keep her feelings in check, but at the same time she kept being pulled to him in a way that was scarily out of her control. She decided Amanda would see through her immediately, so she went for honesty. "It's kind of freaking me out."

"Your great love."

Chelsea titled her head. "Why do you say that?"

Amanda avoided her gaze by fiddling with her napkin. "It's just, when you told me about him, he sounded like someone very special."

Chelsea glanced around the restaurant, searching for familiar faces. She was getting used to scanning the vicinity like a spy for anyone who might report back to Judy. "When did I talk about him?"

"Remember that night after finals?"

Chelsea groaned. "Margaritas."

"That's the one."

"I vowed to never eat guacamole again. That didn't last long."

Amanda smiled at her. "I think it was about the third one in, you told me about Evan, about how it felt to feel that close to someone. How comfortable you two were just hanging out, watching a movie, or listening to music. How you felt like he cared about you in a specific way that let you be yourself. You said you'd never found that again."

"Oof. Margaritas make me earnest."

Amanda leaned forward. "But was it true?"

Chelsea's cheeks flamed. "The thing is, everyone tells you that teenage feelings can't possibly be lasting feelings—young love, and all that, you know?" Amanda nodded, so Chelsea continued with a theory that had been swirling in her mind since she first saw Evan again at Imperial Market and all those feelings came crashing back into her.

"I think I always accepted what adults told me about high school, that it was, you know, *high school* and whatever you felt then was temporary or foolish or unformed, that it somehow didn't hold validity in the adult years. Problem is, when you have a closeness with someone in high school, like what I felt with Evan, and it's also the first time, you think maybe it will always be like that, that these powerful connections will just continue to show up for you, that the world will keep handing you people who really see you, and when it doesn't, well, then what?"

Amanda shook her head. "I didn't have that in high school. I had it in college, but it's the same idea. We both went our separate ways for grad school and decided it wasn't the right time for us." Amanda turned, gazing out the window, her eyes glowing with twinkle lights, then said, "He's married now."

"Do you still talk to him?"

She shrugged. "Not really. Honestly, it's too painful. It's like what you're saying. I expected it to happen again. So far, it hasn't. And he moved on."

"You still have plenty of time. You're like twelve years old."

"Ha! I feel ancient." She picked at the remains of the olives. "But *you*. Reconnecting with your great high school love? You're a Nicholas Sparks novel."

Chelsea grinned. She and Amanda had also bonded early over their mutual love of romance novels, something you're decidedly *not* supposed to love as an English teacher. "Hopefully without whatever trauma he uses to up the stakes in the third act." She took a sip of wine. "Not that things are easy. He has a kid who's living with him now. But her mother just moved to England and wants her to move there, too."

"Ouch."

"Yeah. He's really sad about it, and not sure what to do. And it doesn't help that Denny Bliss is back in town, complicating matters."

Amanda plonked down her glass. "Wait, Denny Bliss as in Sunset Dark Denny Bliss? Is here. In Imperial Flats."

"Did I not tell you that?"

"Uh, no."

"You know I went to high school with him, right? Evan used to be in a band with him?"

Amanda reached her hand across the table in a mock shake. "Uh, hello, I'm Amanda—and you are?"

* * *

"Denny, this is my friend Amanda. Do *not* sleep with her."

Amanda, having gone giggly at the sight of Denny in the doorway, shushed her a bit too loud. "Chelsea! Like we would!" Only, if body language was any indicator, she seemed like she most definitely would.

Denny was eating it up, all dimples and blonde hair flopping across his forehead. He motioned them into the cottage, the fire glowing behind him, wine open on the table. "Nice to meet any friend of Chelsea's. Come in, have some wine."

"Great!" Amanda could only seem to speak in exclamations or giggles. Which was unlike her. Evan stood up from where he'd been sitting on the couch, exchanging a bemused look with Chelsea. They were almost getting used to this reaction from people. Almost.

"Amanda, this is Evan. Evan, Amanda," Chelsea tried. And to Amanda's credit, she mostly said hello, even if she couldn't quite unstick her eyes from Denny.

"Thought you were having a ladies' night?" Evan kissed

Chelsea, quickly, as he brushed by her to pull a couple more wine glasses from the cabinet.

"We were." Chelsea poured the wine as Evan fished out some cheese and crackers, poured a bag of mixed nuts into a bowl.

Evan watched Amanda hanging on to whatever Denny was telling her. "Right. I'll order some pizzas."

Denny collapsed into the overstuffed armchair next to the couch, kicking his slippered feet onto the coffee table. "So, Amanda, you teach English like Chelsea?"

"I do." She settled on the end of the couch closest to Denny.

Denny accepted the glass of wine Evan handed him as Chelsea placed the plate of food on the coffee table and took a seat next to Amanda. "Evan told me." He chuckled. "Three high school teachers and me on a Friday night. What a trip. Must be weird to hang out with teenagers all the time."

Evan took a seat at the far end of the couch. "It's not when you don't try to sleep with them."

Amanda's jaw visibly dropped.

Denny frowned into his wine. "Man," he said. "You're not going to let that go."

Chelsea tried to catch Evan's eye, but he wouldn't look at her, was busy typing in a pizza order on his phone. They sipped their wine in awkward silence for a moment. The fire became riveting. Finally, Denny cleared his throat and turned to Amanda.

"Evan also told me you coach water polo. Is that like soccer except people try to drown you?"

Amanda laughed gratefully. "Yes, basically."

Evan tucked his phone away. "Pizzas will be here in forty-five minutes." He picked up a cracker but didn't eat it, tapped it absently on his thigh, then he looked at Denny. "Sorry, okay?"

Denny gave him a quiet look, then shrugged. "Whatever. Nothing I can do about it now."

"Well—" Evan began.

Chelsea cut him off. "This cheese looks delicious." She smeared a cracker with triple-cream Brie and handed it to Amanda. "You love Brie, right?"

Amanda widened her eyes at her, but asked, "Who doesn't love Brie?" She glanced between the two men. "So, you've known each other since high school?"

Since they both seemed fully committed to a who-can-stare-harder-at-the-fire contest, Chelsea answered for them. "They were in jazz band together. Evan sort of folded me into the music group even though I don't have a musical bone in my body."

Evan put his arm along the back of the couch, grazing Chelsea's shoulder. "She often made sure we ate something other than Taco Bell and sour straws."

"Aw, don't listen to her," Denny added, smiling at Chelsea. "She also had some sweet pipes when she'd trust them."

Amanda shot her a surprised look. "You sing?"

Chelsea shook her head. "I'm not sure you could call it that."

"Not true," Denny said, slathering a cracker in Brie. "She could be very Taylor Swift à la *Evermore* when she wanted to be."

Amanda turned to her. "Oh, really? I think you should sing something."

"Now?"

"Why not? Wine, fireplace, famous musician. It seems perfect."

Chelsea didn't miss Evan's face darkening at the famous musician comment. "I don't know."

Denny hopped up and grabbed his guitar from where it rested next to the bed. "Come on. I'm booooored. Please."

She glanced at Evan. Speaking of Taylor Swift, he'd been

noodling around with Violet the other day, playing "State of Grace," a song Chelsea had always loved, especially the acoustic version. "Evan? 'State of Grace'?"

Denny handed him the guitar and he took it, albeit grudgingly, and moved to a kitchen chair. Chelsea found the lyrics on her phone. Evan played some opening chords and then nodded to Chelsea. As she sang, Denny added some light percussion in the background, the top of a bookshelf filling in for the drums. Chelsea closed her eyes and as she sang Taylor's song about grace and worthwhile fights, she was vaulted back to the days of curling up on the ratty couch in the garage where they played, Denny pushing her to sing duets with him, Evan scribbling lyrics on the pad of paper he always carried with him. The hours she spent there had seemed endless.

Toward the end, Denny sang along with her, and she felt her skin ripple with goosebumps. When they were in high school, Denny had always seemed partly committed to a Bruce Springsteen impression, not in a bad way, but in a way that didn't feel entirely him. Over the decades he'd found a rugged, soulful voice all his own, the one that made him a star, and hearing it up close like this, she could feel it in every cell. Somehow, he only made her amateur fumblings better. When they finished the song, her heart thrumming, Chelsea opened her eyes to Amanda's own glossy ones.

Amanda breathed out. "Jesus, that was beautiful. High school must have been different for you than it was for me. When we sang, it was mostly terrible Karaoke to bad eighties songs."

Evan didn't respond, just leaned the guitar back against the bed. "The thing is," Denny began, "we had something back then. I know it sounds corny, but it was special. The whole world in front of us. It doesn't happen very often anymore. Those type of moments. The ones that feel like magic."

He watched the flames shift. "You don't get as many of them as you think, and they are pure. Like when you take a really good shit, and everything just feels flushed out and clean and perfect for a minute."

Chelsea cut her eyes to Amanda who looked horrified. Evan shook his head, but he was grinning. "See, Amanda. High school wasn't as great as you might think."

NORA

Toby flagged her down from across the restaurant, an open bottle of white wine and two glasses in front of him. "Wine?"

"Please." Nora sank into her seat. What a day. Sue O'Hare had been on a rampage about prom ("These kids deserve a boat on Tahoe, not some grimy hotel ballroom!"), about graduation ("Something needs to be done about those horrendous honors sashes!"). Months away, and Sue was already making demands, eating up too many hours of Nora's week. Nora couldn't wait for Ashleigh to graduate and take her mother's educational hostage situations with her.

Toby watched her gulp half the wine in her glass. "That sort of day?"

"I am growing increasingly weary of entitlement."

"Yeah, well, you might need to move to a hut on the edge of a cliff somewhere to avoid it these days."

"You're in real estate—find me one."

Toby scanned his menu. "Claire Wilson asked me to step down from the board."

It took Nora a moment to register. Claire Wilson was new to the board this year and probably shouldn't be the one asking him. "Okay."

"She's right."

Nora nodded, eyes on her menu, but not really seeing it. She should have insisted Toby step down months ago. "I know."

"I'm sorry to leave you hanging this late in the school year—"

"No, it's okay. We'll figure it out. Of course, you should step down. I should have said something sooner."

Toby leaned his forearms on the table, tried to catch her eye. The candlelight flickered across his features, warming them. "I wasn't going to be there much longer anyway. The Arts Center keeps asking me to join their board and it would be interesting to be a part of that, lots of changes coming up for them with the new construction."

"Sure."

"And it's been so contentious these last few years. It will be almost relaxing to do something else for a while."

"Right."

"Nora?"

She managed a smile, reached across and squeezed his forearm. "It's fine, Toby, really. I think I'll get the pasta special. What about you?"

He was about to answer when they both became aware of a hushed whispering at a table behind them. Nora had a view over Toby's shoulder, but he had to turn to see what was happening. A couple whisper-argued at the table, the woman with her hand on the man's arm, and he was half-in, half-out of his seat. "No, I'm going to say something—"

"Cliff—" But the woman couldn't convince him to sit back down.

The man's eyes were suddenly on Nora and in two strides he was looming over the table. "Maybe you should spend more time on our kids, and less time drinking and having meltdowns in restaurants," he huffed, hands on hips like a middle-aged Superman impersonator.

Nora blinked, all the blood in her body turning instantaneously molten. That fucking Facebook post. In all of her twenty-seven years, she'd never been accosted in public by a parent. At school, sure, at sporting events, a half-dozen times, but never out in the world while she was just trying to order the pasta special. After the day she'd had, after all of the days she'd been having for *years*, this guy had the nerve to come over to her table at a restaurant with this shit? She cut her eyes to Toby, who looked as shocked as she did. He started to stand, but Nora beat him to it.

"If this is about the Facebook post, shame on you for not getting the full story. And if it's simply about thinking that as your child's principal, I'm not entitled to personal time, that I'm some sort of indentured servant who is chained to her desk waiting to serve you twenty-four hours a day, then double shame on you."

Okay, *double shame on you* was pretty lame, but Nora couldn't think straight with the blood pounding in her ears as her limbs turned to jelly. She yanked her coat from the back of the chair and headed to the front door, vaguely aware of Toby opening his wallet, tossing bills on the table, and hurrying after her.

* * *

"How much longer until you hit thirty years?" Dani asked as they crested the hill. Dani stopped to scan the view, taking a swig of her water bottle.

"I'll have twenty-seven full years in June. I should be able to do three more years, no problem." Nora couldn't believe she was having this conversation. She'd always assumed she'd be a lifer, one of those educators who had to be gently moved along after forty years of service.

Suddenly, she could barely imagine making it until June.

"Would it be so terrible to leave now? Three years is still three years of your life. Let yourself off early. For good behavior."

"I'm fifty-five! What would I even do with myself?"

Dani started back down the trail. "You could work for us."

Nora knew Dani was half-joking, but she thought about it, about a job that you left behind when you clocked out. She'd only had a job like that once in her life, waiting tables the year after college, and that had always just felt like a gap before her real life began as she saved up money for her teaching credential/Master's program. What would it be like now to have a job with set hours? That was done when those hours ended?

Last night, the alarm company had called her at three a.m. and she'd driven to school to make sure no one was stealing computers again. What would it be like to have a job where you didn't get three a.m. calls because there were people in this world who stole computers from schools?

"I couldn't afford the health insurance," she finally mumbled, following Dani down a narrow stretch of trail that spit them out near an irrigation ditch. Dani didn't say anything, but Nora knew her friend enough to know she wanted to. "What?"

"Nothing."

"No, what, Dan?"

Dani stopped, turned to her with worried eyes. "You just don't seem to like your job very much anymore. And you used to. Actually, you used to love it."

"That's just middle age. Who likes their jobs in middle age?" When Dani didn't respond, she added, "Besides you, I mean."

"There's a difference between not liking work and having it grind you into a nub."

Nora picked up the pace, forcing Dani to keep up with her. One of the things she'd always loved about her job was how hard it was. The job was *education*, but it was so much more than just programming and filling out forms and sitting in meetings. Over the years, she'd spent so much time with a front row seat to other people's tragedies. She'd lost students to car crashes and suicides and eating disorders and cancer. She'd watched families struggle through alcoholism and debilitating depression and jail time. So much loss. But she'd also watched students graduate and go to college and get married and have children and find jobs that they loved. Life at a school was being immersed in a microcosm that reflected the world. It was a rich, intense job that never failed to teach her something, to remind her to be grateful for whatever small, good thing was happening in her own life at any given moment.

Their footsteps crunched over the graveled ditch path. Finally, Nora said, "Look, it's a tough job. Some years are better than others. Remember that crazy dad who showed up in my office and threatened to kill me? Thank god, Elaine saw him coming and called the police, right? I got through that year, I can get through this one. I'm not a nub yet."

"Only the difference is," Dani pressed, "you knew what that was. That was a deranged man who ended up in jail. That was a thing you could point to and say, 'Well that's fucked.' Wrong place, wrong time. This is different, though, isn't it? I'm not sure you know what *this* is. How can you get through something if you don't know what it is you're getting through?"

Nora studied the March light filtering through the pines, the glint of it on the water rushing through the canal. Hadn't she been here before? She'd felt done during the pandemic. That had felt endless and exhausting and uncertain. And she'd gotten through it. She'd managed. She'd lost Craig and she'd managed. Leo had moved on and she managed. Was Dani right? Was this something else?

"I don't want to get to the end of my life and wonder why I couldn't just suck it up for three more years."

"Maybe by then you'll be old enough to realize that sucking it up is fine for something like a workout, for an impossibly boring meeting. But you shouldn't have to do it for your actual life."

* * *

"Leo?" Nora set her book on her bedside table. She checked the clock. It was past one in the morning for Leo. "You okay?"

"Yeah, no—sorry, were you sleeping?"

"Not yet. Reading."

"I just wanted to check in. Um, is Dad doing okay?"

"He's on the mend. Did you ask him?"

"You know how he is. He's always 'fine' no matter what I ask him."

Nora smiled. Over the years, she and Leo had often discussed his father's tenuous relationship with his own feelings. Leo's generation was different. They didn't see having a range of emotions as weakness like so many did in the generations before. It was one of the things Nora loved about this particular group. She hoped being adults didn't beat it out of them. She took a sip of lukewarm tea.

"What about you? Getting excited for break? You still going to Florida with Elana?"

"Yeah."

Warning flags began flapping. "You don't sound too thrilled."

"I think she's cheating on me."

A shiver moved through her, even beneath the warmth of her favorite flannel sheets. She studied the empty room she had shared with Craig for so many years. The same pale green walls, the same honey wood floor. "Why would you think that?"

"Don't freak out."

"Always the precursor to freaking out."

"Mom."

"Okay."

"I saw them once."

"Elana?"

"No, sorry. I saw Dad and Sarah once. Right at the end of that second big lockdown during Covid. When you were in meetings all the time trying to get the school to move to hybrid."

Nora's mouth went dry. "You saw them? What does that mean?"

"They were standing by Dad's car outside his office. I was driving to work, and I saw them, standing there. They were just talking, but it was too close, you know. Too, I don't know how else to say it, *close*. I asked him about it, and he said she was picking up some paperwork for a new development. He said they were friends from that hiking club. But, you know, it didn't look like just friends."

Nora felt the familiar rage. The hot, white flash of it. She kicked off the duvet. It was bad enough that while she was trying to keep a school from collapsing during a pandemic, her husband was traipsing through the woods with Sarah fucking Crocker. But it seemed he was also standing in parking lots with her, too close. In full view of their son.

"Oh, Leo." She tried to keep her breathing even. She hated that even after so much time had passed, the feeling still came surging back. "I'm sorry he lied to you. I'm sorry he lied to both of us." Was it her responsibility to apologize to her son for his father's cowardice?

"It's just, what if I ask Elana, and she lies, too?"

Nora hesitated. These kinds of conversations could turn to quicksand. "Have you seen her with someone?"

Leo sighed. "Just this one guy. From her creative writing class. I got that same feeling, like the one I got with Dad that day I saw him in his parking lot."

"Oh, honey."

"Mom, I think I'm just going to come home for break. Can you send me a ticket?"

"Of course. Yes, of course. But Leo. Talk to her first, okay?"

"Maybe."

EVAN

Evan stepped outside his classroom to take the call. "Lauren?"

"Is there a way to transfer Violet's ticket into my name?"

His stomach dropped. "What, why?" He could hear echoing sounds of traffic, the murmur of a crowd in the background of her call. "Where are you?"

"Covent Garden."

"What happened?"

"I'm coming home."

"What *happened*?"

Her voice broke. "He has a family, Evan. Like an entire family. Wife, kids, a fucking dog named Rupert."

"Shit, Lauren."

"What is actually wrong with me? How could I fall for this?"

"I'm going to call you back as soon as this class is over, okay?"

But, when he called, she let it go to voicemail.

* * *

Evan stopped to grab a sandwich before heading back to school. He'd left Frank and Violet in front of their most recent fixation, *Ratatouille*, with bowls of soup, a box of Ritz crackers, and his number at the ready on Violet's phone. Chelsea said she'd check on them in a couple of hours. It should be okay; they couldn't seem to get enough of that little rat and his chef hat.

He pulled into the parking lot. He had a meeting in a half hour with some of the band moms to finalize all the plans for An Evening of Jazz and was actually looking forward to having some time to eat a sandwich and scroll through his school email. After they'd announced the "special guest," they'd sold the remaining sixty-five tickets almost instantly. Sadly, it was too late to change the venue so they could have more people. Still, they'd never sold eighty-five tickets before.

As he got closer, he noticed the lights on in the band room. He didn't think he'd left them on. Soon, he could hear the lonely strains of a piano, a beautifully rendered melody, melancholy, unrecognizable. He pushed open the door. Denny sat at the piano on the far side of the room, his eyes closed, his fingers moving across the keys. He hadn't heard Evan come in.

"Denny?"

Denny whirled, genuinely startled. "Oh!" He turned back to the piano. "I know, I know, I'm not supposed to be in here. I thought maybe it didn't count if it wasn't school hours."

Evan dumped his sandwich on his desk. "Didn't count as breaking and entering?"

"The janitor let me in." He flashed Evan a smile. "He's a fan."

"Of course he is."

"I missed playing. I don't understand people who don't have pianos in their homes."

"Probably because they're not musicians."

"Like I said, I don't understand that." Denny stopped playing and turned toward Evan. "What are you doing back here?"

"I have a meeting. With some band moms."

Denny nodded. "Ah, band moms. The best." His gaze scanned the room. "I miss those days sometimes. The band bus parked in a parking lot somewhere for a comp. Goofing off. The moms serving us tacos or pizza or whatever."

Evan rolled his eyes but secretly he agreed with Denny. He'd loved his high school band days. They'd been his family. It had brought him back here. But he wasn't about to let Denny start playing the good ole days' card. Especially because it wasn't true. "Yeah, a private jet doesn't hold a candle to the hot blacktop of a high school parking lot."

Denny shrugged. "It was different. Pure. That was back when the only thing that mattered was playing music with your friends."

Evan groaned. "There aren't any cameras, Den. You can cut the sentimental artist shit."

"Laugh if you want, but I mean it." He motioned at the room. "This was all back before we wanted it to be anything else."

"You always wanted it to be more than it was, Den."

Denny shot him a wounded look, then caved. "You're right." He noodled a quick bit on the piano before he stood. "I did."

"And you got everything you wanted."

Denny shrugged on the jacket he'd tossed over a chair. "If you say so." He sauntered toward the door. "See you later, Ev. Have a good meeting."

"Wait, do you need a ride?"

Denny hesitated at the door. "I don't mind the walk. It's a nice night." He tapped the doorway once before setting off.

After the meeting, Evan arrived home to find Chelsea, Violet, and Frank asleep on the couch, empty soup bowls and a half-finished sleeve of Ritz on the coffee table in front of them. Chelsea heard him come in and stirred. "What time is it?"

"Only eight-thirty."

She slipped off the couch and helped him clear the debris of their dinner. In the kitchen, he told her about Denny's sad piano, his revisionist history. She loaded the bowls into the dishwasher. "Now as I was young and easy under the apple boughs."

"What's that?"

"'Fern Hill' Dylan Thomas. I taught it today. To my seniors." He handed her the soup pot to dry, and she ran a towel over it.

"I don't know it."

"He's a Welsh poet. 'Time held me green and dying / Though I sang in my chains like the sea.'"

"Uplifting."

"It's about not realizing the magic of childhood while we're in it, about how Time makes sad sacks of all of us. About the realizations we have later in life."

"So a midlife crisis poem. I'm sure your seniors where thrilled."

Chelsea grinned, placing the dried pot back on the stove where Evan kept it.

Later that night, she texted *Fern Hill* to him with the caption: *But we sang in our chains. We sang. Sometimes, it's not revisionist; it's just epiphany.*

CHELSEA

Violet didn't go to London for spring break. She didn't seem to mind that Lauren had cancelled the visit. When Evan told her over burgers and curly fries at the Burger Barn, Violet had chewed thoughtfully for a moment before washing down her bite with a gulp from her frosted root beer. "Okay," she'd said, then reached for some of Chelsea's fries since she'd already eaten all of hers. Evan had widened his eyes at Chelsea, then shrugged and picked up his own burger.

Chelsea had been hoping for some sort of break, though, so she'd found a place where they could stay for a few days in Bodega Bay during the break, Frank and Violet in tow. She'd been there before with Stone, had taken some workshops in Big Sur with the owner, and he was more than happy to rent it to her since it was just sitting empty, something that never failed to strike Chelsea as incredible and unfair. A place with that view sitting empty most of the year.

The two-story house looked out over an upscale housing development, a stretch of beach and ocean glimmering beyond it. Violet squealed when she saw how close to the water they were and begged them to go play in the sand. Over the next few days, they ate clam chowder, built sandcastles in the chilly air off the water, played board games during a rainy afternoon, and hiked through the damp hills, turning back when they'd had enough of Frank's grumbling.

The second afternoon, Evan played guitar for them on the beach, working through some Tom Petty and Aimee Mann covers, and some of his own songs. Watching him, Chelsea thought how wonderful it would be to play music, to be able to pick up an instrument and make it sound like that. He scanned the waves as he played, his eyes unreadable. Chelsea worried about him sometimes; she knew he saw himself as a failure in his music, saw his teaching as a consolation prize, if that. She knew some people felt that way, like teaching was something to settle for. Those who can't, and all that shit. She'd always hated that expression.

She felt teaching was an art all its own. She'd always valued the relationships with her students over the content she was teaching them. She loved books and words and language, sure, but truly she loved the astonishing construct of the teaching world: each year, the universe dropped brand new humans in front of her, and they started out unknowable, names on a list, and then, slowly, over the course of a year or two, they revealed quiet intimacies about themselves, through their journals or what they said in class or just in what T-shirts they wore. Each class had its own atmosphere full of inside jokes, absurdities, and mood. It was as if each year her students wrote a novel that only she got to read. She wondered if other teachers felt like that, if Evan knew he could create that specialness in his band room, that he already had.

On their last evening, the sun came out, sending spangles of light across the water, and Evan and Chelsea left Frank and Violet to play Uno downstairs while they took a bottle of wine to the upper deck of the house.

"Well, this doesn't suck," Evan said, clinking his glass against hers. It was windy and they both zipped their jackets against it. Still, that stretch of sparkling water, that endless piece of sky. "Thanks for organizing this."

"Of course."

"How do you know this guy again?"

Chelsea studied the blur of horizon. "He's a friend of Stone's, actually." She sipped her wine. "And he and I took a workshop on toxic positivity together in Big Sur."

Evan hesitated, then, "Can I ask you something about that?"

"About toxic positivity?"

Evan laughed. "No, I meant, well, about Stone."

Chelsea felt the back of her neck tingle. She'd had this conversation a number of times over the years, had been surprised she and Evan hadn't had it sooner. "Sure."

"I just don't think that I could ever do that."

"Do what exactly?"

"Share you with someone else."

Chelsea felt the warmth of that spread through her, even as she felt defensive. "Then you're likely not polyamorous."

"But you'd be okay with it?"

Chelsea thought about it. No, she realized. She wouldn't be fine sharing Evan. What worked with Stone didn't apply to what she felt for Evan. "It's hard to explain. It was fine with Stone and Leila. It worked for what I needed during that time. I don't feel that way about you."

"Leila is his wife?"

"Yes."

He cleared his throat. "Did you, um, have a relationship with both of them?"

She grinned at the pink in his cheeks. "I did have a relationship with both of them, but I didn't sleep with Leila. I'm sadly, boringly, straight as a fucking arrow."

He sipped his wine. "So you don't want more partners than me right now?"

She shook her head and he looked visibly relieved. "Honestly, I'm not sure I was ever truly polyamorous. Stone was safe because I never felt fully invested in him; I loved the excitement of it all more than I loved him. And it pissed off Judy Garden. Added bonus." She held up a hand. "Don't say anything." She stared back out over the water.

"You know, something I came to love about their community was that it encouraged the idea that everyone had a say in what was happening. It was all about consent, about transparency. I sometimes felt jealous of Leila, but it wasn't about sex. It was about how easily she moved through that world. How confident she was about her choices, how easily she shared Stone with me. They had a very different relationship than we did, and that was, well, that was kind of the point. That all relationships are and should be different, should be discussed and agreed to and determined by the people within them, not the ones outside of them. There was something liberating about all that *communication*. Fucking annoying at times, too, don't get me wrong. But for me, it was so much better than the alternative."

Suddenly, she realized what had drawn her in for so long: that ability to say, 'Love me as I am *unconditionally*.' And have it, for the most part, feel like that was what was happening. She shared her realization with Evan.

"You hadn't felt loved unconditionally before that?"

She chewed her lip, watched the water. "I feel like my dad mostly does, even though he doesn't stick up for me. I've never felt like my mom loves me unconditionally, no. Her love feels very conditional." Chelsea felt his gaze shift back out to the water. "I know you sometimes struggle with the way I talk about my mom, because, at least, I have a mom, here, alive, but sometimes she's—"

"A judgmental jerk?"

She burst out laughing. "Yes! And sometimes, that's just hard, you know? Having a mom who you feel only loves you when she approves of you, who has to weigh in on every single choice or appearance or idea as if her opinion matters just a little more than everyone else's, and especially more than yours. As if there is only one way to live."

"Hers."

"Yeah. Anyone doing it any other way is a fucking idiot."

He filled her glass again before topping off his own. "I'm sorry if I made you feel like you couldn't talk honestly about your mom."

She shook her head. "I think I'm finally starting to just accept things the way they are. This is who my mother is. This is who I am. And these two things are sadly not a great fit. I can't change it, no matter how many workshops I take."

Evan leaned forward to kiss her just as Violet appeared at the glass door to the deck, struggling to open it. Evan moved to help her slide it open. "Okay, bug?"

"Grandpa's cheating," she said, tearfully.

Evan shot Chelsea a knowing look. "Right, we'll come down."

* * *

Chelsea screamed loudly enough for Diego and Kyle to come running, both in their pajamas, both rubbing sleep from their eyes. She stared at the snake. In her shower. There was a snake in her shower.

"Chelsea!?" Kyle burst into the room. "Are you—what is it?"

"Snake," she breathed, pointing. Kyle recoiled. Diego came closer. "That?" he asked, pointing to the small curl in the corner. "That is what you're screaming about?" His face broke into a wide smile.

Chelsea gaped a him. "It's a *snake*."

"Barely." Diego grabbed the garbage can and, to both Kyle and Chelsea's horror, picked up the snake and dropped it in. "Come on, little guy. You took a wrong turn." He disappeared out of the bathroom.

Kyle and Chelsea exchanged shocked looks. Recovering, Kyle said, "You're up early for a Sunday."

"Breakfast with Judy."

He tugged the tie of his robe closer. "Whose idea was that?"

"I invited her."

Kyle's eyebrows shot up higher than they had with the snake.

"I'm trying to accept her for who she is and not who I want her to be."

"Good luck with that." At her pained expression, he added, "At least let me make you a cup of coffee first. I'll put some whiskey in it."

* * *

She met Judy at Rachel's, a favorite family breakfast spot that Chelsea hadn't been to in over a decade. Chelsea loved Rachel's; the food was always delicious, and it was housed in a cute country cottage next to a creek lined with leafy shade trees. Chelsea remembered piling into a booth with her brother after church on Sundays, ordering pancakes with bacon, the wedge of orange and grapes arranged on the plate to look like a smiley face. As she pulled into a parking spot, she wondered if they still did that. She and her brother would wolf down their food, then beg to go play by the creek while her parents discussed whatever sermon they'd just listened to. She would always stuff her grapes in her pocket so she could eat them down by the water. As she studied the outside of the restaurant with its vines and empty patio, Chelsea realized those had been truly good mornings.

She took a deep breath.

Inside, Judy was already at a booth, a cup of steaming tea in front of her. Chelsea slid in across from her. "Morning."

Judy tilted her head. "Are you alright? You look pale."

"I found a snake in my shower this morning."

"Gracious! Those boys." She shook her head, picking up one of the two menus, more for something to do than because she'd order something other than an egg white omelet.

Chelsea picked up her own menu. "Well, they didn't *put* the snake in the shower."

Judy ignored this. She lifted her mug, blew gently across the surface. "They have the most delicious Chamomile tea here."

Chelsea skimmed the specials board over Judy's shoulder. "So, I assume you're getting the French toast stuffed with mascarpone cheese?"

Judy blanched as if Chelsea had suggested she snort coke for breakfast. "I'm certainly not!"

A young waitress came by the table. "Can I get you something to drink?" she asked Chelsea.

"I'll have a Chamomile tea."

Judy nodded approvingly. "And I'll have an egg white omelet with steamed veggies. Please have Eddie fry it in olive oil and not butter."

The waitress was clearly familiar with this request. "Of course."

Chelsea handed her the menu. "I'll have the omelet of the day, please."

"Hash browns or fruit?"

"Fruit."

Chelsea studied the restaurant. They'd updated their booths to a rich green and put in beautiful dark wooden tabletops. When Chelsea commented on it, Judy explained that Rachel had retired and passed the restaurant to her daughter, Tabitha, who had been a few years behind Chelsea in school. Tabitha, according to Judy, could be "a bit big for her britches."

"I think the changes look nice."

"Cost Tabitha a pretty penny, according to Rachel." Judy shook her head. The waitress dropped off Chelsea's tea, and Judy changed the subject to her brother's offspring and their various activities. Jayden continued to disappoint everyone, Mason had recently become involved in some sort of martial art that Judy found baffling, and Kylie was moving up a level in gymnastics. "They're still working on that speech problem of hers."

"She has a speech problem?" She hadn't noticed it at Christmas, but now that Chelsea thought about it, she did sound a bit like she had a Jersey accent, in that charming way little kids often did.

"They waited too long to deal with it." Judy leaned back so the waitress could set down their plates. Chelsea's oozed with cheddar cheese and chicken apple sausage. "Good heavens," Judy remarked, "You could feed an entire family." She sliced off a delicate piece of egg white with the edge of her fork.

Chelsea tried to take small bites and deep breaths. This might have been a terrible idea. She should have invited Kyle and Diego too. And her dad. She should have buffers. "I wish I could see them more," she said finally through her first mouthful.

"Well, they never visit." Judy set down her fork after two bites and picked up her tea.

"Christmas was nice," Chelsea tried.

"You know, your father and I invited them to Disney World for spring break, but they said no. We even offered Disney World because it would be so much closer for them."

Chelsea swallowed. "Maybe they already had plans?" Was it her imagination or did her mother look teary? "Mom?

Are you okay?"

Judy dropped her eyes to her purse, fiddling with the clasp. "They didn't have plans." She pulled out a handkerchief and discreetly patted under her eyes.

"Mom?"

"I'm sorry to get emotional."

Chelsea had never seen her mother cry in private much less in the middle of a restaurant. It was like watching a strange animal perform a sex act at the zoo. "It's okay, really. It's fine."

Judy took a breath and returned her hankie to her bag. She lifted her fork and took another small bite of omelet. "Kelly doesn't want to travel with me."

"What? She said that?"

Judy picked up her tea again. "Shaun said Kelly finds me too judgmental. That they don't want to spend vacations with me anymore. Can you imagine? I'm not judgmental!" Chelsea shoveled in a large bite of omelet. Judy narrowed her eyes at her. "What is that face?"

Chelsea felt the cheese congealing in her belly. "Well. Um. Sometimes you can be blunt with your opinions."

"Everyone has opinions! I don't mean anything to be judgmental."

"When I said I might take the job in Ireland, you told me it was ridiculous, and I wasn't moving to Ireland."

"It is ridiculous!"

"That's judgmental!"

"It's not judgment. It's pragmatism. Do you want to move to Ireland?"

"I'm not sure. Maybe I'll go just because you don't want me to!"

Judy pursed her lips in distaste. "That is incredibly immature."

"Yes, I know that." Chelsea felt her own tears beginning to pool. "But the problem is, Mom, that just once, I wish you'd start by asking a question about what I think or want without leveling a judgment first."

"I don't mean it as a judgment!"

"Maybe it doesn't matter how you mean it. Maybe it matters more what I feel. Or what Kelly feels." Judy waved her off. "You don't care how Kelly feels?"

"She needs to toughen up. She's too sensitive."

Chelsea felt suddenly close to her sister-in-law. "Another judgment."

"Oh, please." Judy motioned to the waitress for the check.

Chelsea set her fork down so her mother wouldn't see her hand shaking. "Maybe she isn't built to let things go. Maybe she doesn't think that's healthy, actually. Not everyone wants to just brush things under the rug, Mom. Some of us think being sensitive is a good thing, that it's important to consider what other people might think or feel about something we've said. We try not to hurt people."

"Honestly, I worry about your generation. You've all had it too easy. You could all do with a little toughening up." She took the check from the waitress, who seemed to be avoiding eye contact.

Chelsea blinked back her tears. "Right. Because we all haven't gone through a global pandemic, climate change, or school shootings, and social justice protests. We've all just been sitting by our pools drinking Starbucks."

Judy rolled her eyes. "Don't give me that. I lived through the sixties."

"That was almost sixty years ago! Do any of you actually remember the sixties or do you just like to reference being there as if it lets you off the hook for the next five decades?"

Her mother glared at her. "What's gotten into you? You've

been spending too much time in the Bay Area. Bunch of liberal nonsense."

"See, that! This is why Kelly doesn't want to travel with you!"

They both froze. Chelsea knew she'd gone too far, but Judy pulled her purse onto her lap and said stiffly, "Well, I think that's enough of that for one day. I just wanted to have a nice breakfast out with my daughter. *You* invited *me*, remember?"

"I'm sorry, Mom." Chelsea eyed the majority of her breakfast still on the plate. She thought about every workshop she'd ever taken about empathy or conflict, tried to find a way to connect with her mom. Finally, she said, "It must have been hard to hear Shaun say they didn't want to go. That must have been very painful."

But her mother was already pulling her armor back on. "It's not *painful*! Don't be dramatic. I just don't understand it. Who turns down a free trip with three kids?" She pulled the check toward her, then riffled through her purse for her readers. "No one ever offered a free trip to your father and me, you know?"

"I know." She watched her mother calculating the tip (fifteen percent to the penny), her readers slipping down her thin nose, and she felt a sudden warmth of sadness move through her. For the first time, she saw her mother as someone else. Someone who had her own history filled with grief and fear and maybe even regret. Even if she would never in a million years share any of it out loud, especially not with Chelsea.

And no matter what, Chelsea couldn't change her. She would always be a woman who took pride in all the ways she limited herself, as if there was some reward for her austerity. She would always speak in directives rather than ask questions or offer support. But, from where Chelsea sat, she also seemed like a woman who, when it came down to it, appeared deeply lonely. Chelsea reached across the table and squeezed her mother's hand.

"Chelsea, stop! I'm trying to sign the check, for heaven's sake."

NORA

Nora pulled her car behind the unfamiliar truck idling in Toby's circular driveway. Its bed was heaped with furniture, boxes, and a few stuffed black trash bags. A man sat behind the wheel. Nora could just make out his left hand tapping to unheard music on the steering wheel. Suddenly, Toby burst from the front door, holding a lamp aloft. He shot in front of the truck, crossing the patch of winter-beaten lawn beyond the driveway. Behind him, a blonde woman gave chase. Liz. Nora recognized her from her Christmas cards and from various school functions of the past. Only now, she was disheveled, dressed in yoga pants, and very, very tan.

Nora scrambled out of her car at the same time as the man in the truck.

"Toby!" Liz came to a stop about twenty feet from him, a lock of hair coming loose from her ponytail, hanging across her face. "You're being ridiculous. Give me the lamp."

"I found this lamp! In Venice! I had it shipped across an ocean. It's my lamp!"

Nora exchanged a look with the guy from the truck, realizing, belatedly, that he must be The Yoga Instructor. They both took a step back, watching Liz advance slowly on Toby. Toby's eyes looked wild. For some reason he was only wearing one shoe. One of his sock feet had a hole in the big toe.

Was this the same guy who had told her not to worry about the Napa blanket Craig kept?

"Toby?" Nora asked, tentatively.

Liz shot her a pleading look. "He won't give me my lamp."

"I see that." Nora couldn't seem to get Toby to look her way. "Toby?" she tried again. "Why won't you give her the lamp?"

"It's just a lamp, dude." The Yoga Instructor added with a shrug.

Toby didn't even glance in his direction. "Seriously, Liz. I'm not sure what's worse: you coming here expecting to ransack the house before I got home from work, or the fact that you're sleeping with someone who says 'dude.'"

"Dude," The Yoga Teacher muttered, climbing back into his truck.

Liz threw up her hands (something Nora was sure she'd never actually seen before, only read about in books), and stalked back into the house.

Toby turned a pained, but sheepish gaze on Nora. He lowered the lamp.

Watching him, it dawned on Nora that they used to be better at being grown-ups. Once, they'd had family dinners, and sent Christmas letters, and taught teenagers how to drive. They had functioned as couples, keeping their voices (mostly) lowered during arguments so they wouldn't wake the kids, and as parents, attending little league games and driving small children to doctor's appointments with a bowl in the backseat in case they threw up again. When had that changed? It was as if those earlier functions no longer had purpose, had become historical appendixes.

Maybe it was a relief. They weren't modeling anything for anyone anymore.

But she didn't really know how she felt about any of it. She just knew she was tired. She couldn't actually believe how fucking tired she was. Nora crossed the lawn to Toby, brushed away some lint that must have fallen from the lampshade onto his shoulder. Clearly, no one had dusted this lamp in years.

"Do you want to hide the lamp in my car?"

* * *

Later, Nora and Toby sat on his couch drinking white wine and studying the lamp where it sat aglow on a low table, providing the only light in the room besides the fire Toby had lit. Nora tucked up her legs and pulled a cashmere throw over her lap. "It's a beautiful lamp."

They both started laughing. Toby shook his head. "Her face when she came out and there was no lamp."

"It was pretty funny."

"I'm so embarrassed you saw that."

"Saw it? I participated in that!"

"After my sanctimonious blanket advice."

"Advice is easier to give than to practice."

"We're supposed to be at the place in our relationship where you only see my good qualities."

"Besides the snoring, you mean?" At his stricken expression, Nora grinned. "I snore, too. Don't worry about it. Besides, I'm pretty sure we sat in enough board meetings together to reveal some of our less-than-stellar personality quirks."

The timer beeped and he went to retrieve the appetizers currently baking in the toaster oven. "I'm more interested in why you were only wearing one shoe."

He blanched as he lifted tiny puff pastries onto a plate with a spatula. "I was really hoping you hadn't noticed that."

"In my line of work, you look to the details. This seems like an interesting one."

As he settled on the sofa next to her, he explained that Liz had ended up chasing him down the stairs and, at one point, he'd scrambled over the couch they were currently sitting on. As he'd gone over the back of it, she'd tugged off a shoe, sending him sprawling across the coffee table, and onto the floor. Then, he'd grabbed the lamp and fled out the door.

"You're lucky you didn't break something," Nora told him.

He stared into his wine. "We haven't fought like that since our early twenties."

"So you were due."

"Did you and Craig fight?"

"Every couple fights." Except Nora and Craig had always been silent fighters. Stewing, keeping score, avoiding. Nora wondered if that was possibly worse than blow-ups. At least with a blow-up, the fight has somewhere else to go other than sinking back into their own bodies. But Craig hated conflict. And Nora had enough of it at school. It was easier to just keep pushing things into the past. Until it wasn't, of course, and they had ended up buried by it.

Toby turned and kicked his legs up on the couch so that his toes were just touching her thigh. He bit into a crab puff. "These aren't half bad for frozen."

Nora agreed and helped herself to another one. Maybe she had reached the age where finding a delicious frozen crab puff was enough to call it a good week? Especially paired with a cold white wine. They chewed in silence for a moment, until Nora squeezed one of his sock feet.

"Are you sure you're okay?"

Toby sighed, his eyes searching the room. "So many years in this place. Christmases, birthday parties, school projects, puppies that grew into dogs, Friday night movies with pizza and piles of teenagers." He sighed again. "It feels empty now."

Nora nodded. Leo hadn't come home for spring break, had gone with his friends to Florida after all, and somehow her house felt even emptier than all those months of him away at school. "We spent years so busy our heads might explode and then, *poof*, empty rooms."

He scooted closer to her on the couch, tucked a lock of hair behind her ear. "Except, not completely empty." He kissed her, tasting of crab and butter and wine, and behind that, tasting of him, something she realized with a flip of her stomach, she recognized and longed for. Nora slipped her hand to the back of his head, kissing him back in a way that felt lucky for that, at least.

* * *

"Leo?" Nora squinted at the clock next to her bed. "It's four a.m.—is everything okay?"

"Oh, shit, Mom, sorry, forgot about the time difference."

Toby shifted in his sleep, groaned, and rolled onto his side. "Hold on a minute." Nora tip-toed out of the room. When she got to the living room, she pulled a blanket over her lap. "You're up early, though?" It would be seven a.m. in Florida. "How was your week?"

"Eh. I'm taking a walk on the beach. The place we got is a pit. I needed some air. Thought I'd watch the sunrise."

"Is Elana with you?"

Her son breathed into the phone, or maybe it was the wind. She imagined his feet trailing through sand at the edge of waves, the sun turning the water a swirl of orange and pink. "She didn't come." He paused. "We broke up."

"Oh, honey. I'm so sorry." She crossed her legs and pulled the blanket to her neck. "I guess that means you talked to her?"

"She says she wasn't cheating. But she told me she couldn't be with someone who would accuse her of that. I didn't accuse her, I just asked! I shouldn't have said anything."

Nora felt a stab of defense. After all, she'd been the one

to tell him to talk to her. "I don't know, Leo. It seems like an overreaction."

"Well, that's Elana."

Nora didn't really know the girl very well, didn't know if that was a fair assessment of her. She could hear the pain in her son's voice. He'd been smitten. Not like the couple of girls he'd dated in high school. It had been easier, though, when Nora had known the girls, known the parents. She'd had more to contribute when things went south or just ended. "Do you have class Monday? You could come for a couple of nights at least?"

"Naw. It's not terrible. We have one more night here anyway." He sounded hungover, was likely drinking too much.

"Be safe, though."

"Mom."

"I'm still allowed to say that; I can worry."

"I know." He paused and she wished she could pull him to her, hold him the way he might have let her when he was younger and had fallen and skinned a knee or banged his head. It was strange to think those years were long gone, where the weight of his body was something she took for granted as a daily experience. "I'm going to go find some coffee, maybe grab an egg sausage sandwich."

She smiled. Craig's solution for a hangover, too. Genetics were funny. "Sounds like a good plan."

"Mom?"

"Yeah?"

He hesitated. Maybe he'd tell he missed her, that he loved her. "Sorry I woke you up."

Close enough.

EVAN

"Lauren?" Evan opened the door wider.

She stood shivering on the porch in the gathering shadows of late evening in a too-thin jacket. "I'm sorry I didn't call first."

"No, it's fine. Come in."

She followed him into the kitchen where Violet was doing a craft kit with yarn balls and scissors that Chelsea had bought her in Bodega Bay, but they'd never opened.

"Hey, Vi."

"Mom!" She jumped from her chair and ran to her mother, almost knocking her over. "What are you doing here?" she muffled into her stomach. Evan was glad Violet asked so he didn't have to.

"Things didn't work out with Roman, sweetie."

"He has a weird name."

Evan watched Lauren smile, rock their daughter, smelling her hair, breathing her in, cupping her face in her hands. He put the kettle on for tea.

Frank wandered in from watching TV. "Who are you?"

Lauren glanced at Evan, worried. They'd met many times. "I'm Lauren. Violet's mom. I used to be Evan's girlfriend."

"His girlfriend is Chelsea." Frank said, gruffly.

"Oh?" Lauren's gaze darted to Evan. He hadn't filled her in on Chelsea yet.

"I'm tired." Frank shuffled off to his room.

"Isn't he the sweetest?" Evan joked.

"When did you and Chelsea decide to upgrade?" Lauren asked. She tried for casual, but Evan knew her too well, knew how jealous she could be, even if she'd projected that onto him throughout their entire relationship. Lauren had many good qualities, but she saw other women as competition. Always.

"I'm sure I told you?"

"You didn't."

"Chelsea bought me this yarn kit!" Violet showed her the poodle she was making from purple yarn. One of its googly-eyes was sliding down the glue Violet had sloppily applied.

"You seem a bit old for that, I think."

Violet frowned at her poodle.

Evan congratulated himself on handing the teacup to Lauren, rather than hurling it at her head.

* * *

Somehow, they only had half of the mini-baked potatoes they would need for the evening. Lisa, Ava's mom, was trying to get in touch with the woman who was supposed to be bringing another seventy-five. She eyed Evan from behind the silent auction table, nodding at something on the other side of the call.

"Yikes, sorry. No, of course. No, thanks for doing that." She tucked her phone in her back pocket. "Her oven isn't working so she's taking them to her mother-in-law's. They'll be here."

Evan rubbed his temples, closing his eyes for a moment. One of the most difficult things for him about teaching was having to be in charge of all the things he was used to other people being in charge of when he played at events in the past. He had some wonderful parents who helped out with band logistics, but ultimately he had to make sure everything happened. Not just the music. The food, the tables, the stage, the bartender. He needed to figure out a way to delegate more. Other schools he'd seen at jazz festivals had boosters. He'd ask Nora how to make that happen for next year. He paused at the thought. It might have been the first time he'd ever thought of this job as having a next year.

Diego came through the main door with a platter, Chelsea trailing behind him with another. "Did someone order 150 mini-crepes with sausage and cheese?"

"Oh, excellent—thank you, Diego." Evan hurried to help him arrange the platters on the enormous warming trays Dani had provided, his mouth watering. Each crepe had been carefully wrapped around a sausage slice, and oozed with cheese, a sprig of fresh dill added as garnish. They were possibly too beautiful for a high school jazz night.

"Wow," Evan said. "You really don't do this as a job anymore?"

Diego waved him off. "You're too kind." But he beamed at them; he knew they were gorgeous.

"Kyle's parking." Chelsea smiled, her eyes soaking in the warmth of the twinkle lights, the café tables, the stage where the kids warmed up. "It looks fabulous, Ev."

He swallowed nervously. "I need to tell you something." He tried not to notice her expression cloud when he mentioned Lauren, that she'd be here shortly with Frank and Violet.

"When did this happen?"

"Last night. She just showed up on my doorstep."

"Okay."

They both turned at a crashing sound from the stage. Chris had just dropped his trumpet. Into the drum set. They watched him scramble to right the cymbal he'd clearly tripped over, to extract his trumpet from between the drums. "Sorry! Sorry!"

Chelsea sighed and gave his arm a squeeze. "We can talk later. You've got your hands full right now."

"Chelsea!"

Chelsea's friend from the Bay Area, Amanda, crossed the venue toward them. "She was way too nice to come to this," he told Chelsea.

She waved to her friend. "It might have something to do with the special guest."

"Ah." Evan hurried to the stage to help Chris, who had somehow also managed to catch his sequined jazz jacket in the kit. After Evan untangled him, he sent him to get the other members of the band for warm-up.

Over the next half hour, people began to stream in. Evan waved to parents of students and a few other teachers who came to support students from their classes. He noticed Mrs. Eklund speaking with one of the parents who always seemed to be around school, Sue O'Hare. It was nice of them to come. He waved to Nora Delgado and the tall man with her. Chelsea had told him Nora was dating a board member. As people collected plates of food, ordered wine, found tables, and scanned the silent auction items, Evan felt something loosen in his chest. So far, so good.

At seven, when almost all of the presale tickets were accounted for, he dimmed the main lights and sorted his band into their places, his stomach fizzing again. No sign of Denny. No sign of Lauren, Violet, and Frank. Using one of the stage mics, he welcomed the crowd to An Evening of Jazz and his students began to play, a bit wobbly at first, but they soon found their footing, and Evan left the stage to mill again through the tables, welcoming people, thanking them for coming, his eyes repeatedly on the door.

At seven-fifteen, Lauren entered with Violet and Frank, her face drawn. Frank was wearing his pajama bottoms. Evan hurried over.

"He wouldn't change into pants or get in the car," she told him, looking flustered. "So Violet told him she would wear her pajamas, too, if he'd get in the car." Violet's jammies were at least a black satin with a white piping down the side. Frank's had pelicans on them. His father had to pick this night of all nights to start wearing pajamas again?

But Evan just nodded. It didn't matter. He'd be at a table most of the night anyway. Evan ushered them over to the side table he'd saved for them. Chelsea was on the other side of the audience, sitting with Kyle, Diego, and Amanda, but Evan could feel her eyes following them. Sweat beaded his upper lip.

Between songs, he hopped back onstage to introduce the members of the band. Lisa gave him a wave from behind the silent auction tables and he let people know that the bidding was officially open. He went to check on the food and to see if the bartender needed anything before heading to the back room where Denny should be waiting. Still no sign of him. His phone buzzed. He slipped it from his pocket, ready for a Denny excuse, but it was Lauren: *Your dad won't use this bathroom. He wants to use his own bathroom.*

Jesus.

He hurried out to the audience where his dad sat straight in his chair, arms crossed defiantly. "Dad?"

"I'm not going to the ladies' room with her." He hooked a thumb at Lauren.

"I wasn't going to take him in—" Lauren started.

"I know." Evan crouched down next to his dad. "You can come with me to the *men's* room."

"Okay." He stood and followed Evan.

While his dad urinated into a toilet with the door open, Evan texted Denny again: *where are you?*

His phone pinged back: *in your shitty green room*

He made it. Evan couldn't tell if the wash of emotion flooding him was more relief or fear. Probably both. He didn't want to assume the worst, wanted instead to imagine Denny had the capacity to show up and do right by him, even if doubt threatened to swallow him whole.

Evan ushered his dad back to the table before locating Denny in the makeshift green room, where he found him lounging on a threadbare couch, a mug of red wine balanced precariously on the seat beside him, absently strumming his guitar, eyes closed.

"Thanks for being here, Den. I'm going to have you go on in about ten minutes if that's okay?" Evan winced at the deferential sound of his own voice, but something about Denny's ease brought it bubbling up.

"Sure thing."

Back in the main room, Evan watched his band from behind the silent auction tables. They looked snazzy in their blue sequined jackets and black shirts and jeans. And they were doing a passable version of "Straight No Chaser." His body thrummed with pride; they could barely play the first two measures a few weeks ago.

When they finished, Evan stepped back onstage, waiting for the murmur in the audience to die down. "Hey, everyone—thanks again. How about another hand for these jazz musicians!" He clapped along with the audience. "I'm going to give this crew a break and bring out the special guest we promised you."

The room went instantly silent. The band members shuffled off the stage and found their parents or friends in the audience who had saved them chairs. Evan waited until everyone was seated. "As you have all probably guessed, our guest tonight is an Imperial Flats graduate himself who has made something of a name for himself out in the wide world." He paused as titters moved through the tables. "In fact, he truly needs no introduction. So without further ado, I give you our hometown boy: Denny Bliss from Sunset Dark!"

The audience went crazy: hooting, cheering, clapping, stomping their feet. Denny came out through the side wings, holding his guitar by its neck, waving nonchalantly to the audience with a casual grin. He was dressed in expensive jeans, worn Converse, and a faded Bleachers T-shirt. Even Evan had to admit that his star power didn't need any accessories. No one could take their eyes off him.

Denny chatted into the mic as he fiddled with his guitar. "Hey, thanks, thanks, everybody. It's such a trip to be back in The Flats. So cool of you to come hang out with me tonight." He waited for the next round of cheers to die down. "Aw, you're too kind. I'm really here to support these kids. Music saved my life in high school. So, tonight get those wallets out and give this band your money, because we know the arts don't get the money they need or deserve."

He started to play the opening of one of Sunset Dark's biggest hits, "Dress Code," only whereas the original radio version was pop-y and quick, he'd stripped it back to a mellow, slower acoustic version. His trademark voice filled the room. Evan noticed people whispering the lyrics, swaying along. With raucous bouts of applause in between, Denny played three more songs before stopping and scanning the room. "Where's my boy? Evan? Where ya at?" Evan gave him a wave from near the auction table. "Hey, come up here. We need to do a duet."

Evan shook his head. "No, we really don't," he laughed nervously, waving Denny off, his eyes darting over the crowd who were clearly wanting him to jump on stage.

"Ah, come on. Who wants Ev to come up here and play with me?"

Evan hadn't thought the audience could get louder, but they could. He hurried on stage, mostly to quiet everyone down. This was rolling out longer than he'd meant it to. "Okay, okay. One song. And then let's get the kids back up here."

Denny grabbed a second chair and handed Evan his guitar. He stood, holding a mic close. "For those of you who don't know, Evan and I used to be in a band together." Evan's stomach soured. "He wrote a few great songs back in the day and I thought we'd share one with you if we can both remember it."

Evan shook his head. "I don't know, man—"

"It's called 'Sunlight Girl,' and he wrote it about a very special girl who happens to be right here in this room. A Ms. Chelsea Garden. Chelsea, where are you?" Denny peered out into the crowd, catching sight of her, and giving her a salute.

Evan found Chelsea's startled face in the dark haze of tables. He'd never told her the song was about her, but before he could say anything, Denny began to sing, just that Denny Bliss voice melting across the suddenly silent room.

She moves through the dark,
through the park,
through the world,
This sunlight girl.

Evan grimaced and then caught up with him on the guitar, acutely aware of how cloying the lyrics sounded, how full of his teenage self he'd been to write them. Still, with Denny's grit and buttery voice, with the guitar beneath him, even Evan knew it was probably the best song he'd ever written. He saw Lauren scanning the room, Violet pointing Chelsea out to her, Lauren's eyes narrowing. Uh-oh.

Evan slid his gaze to Chelsea, who was staring at her hands in her lap.

When they finished, the crowd sprang to their feet, stomping and clapping and whistling. He realized, briefly, how unfair it might be to pull his students back on stage after this, how he probably should have saved Denny for the end of the show. But they seemed energized, hopping back on stage, jogging up the stairs. Chris high-fived Denny and Caroline beamed at him. Denny thanked everyone and turned to Evan, who handed him back his guitar, even managed an awkward hug with his old friend for the audience's sake.

"Thanks, Den."

"Yeah, I'll be in the back."

Evan introduced the first song of the next set, and people began settling back into their seats, or wandering off to survey the auction items or the dessert table that Lisa had set up while Denny was playing. Evan glanced again to Chelsea, but her seat was empty. Amanda leaned on her forearms, chatting with Diego and Kyle.

Evan went to check on his dad. When he reached their table, he found Frank slumped in his seat, eyes closed, arms crossed over his chest. Violet was reading to him quietly from her fantasy novel, her knees turned toward him, the book in her lap. Evan felt an intense wash of love for his daughter. "Hey, bug. Where'd your mom go?"

"Bathroom."

For a reason he couldn't quiet put his finger on, his stomach twisted, his gaze catching on Chelsea's empty chair. But before he could move, he saw Chelsea hurry back into the room, grab her bag, whisper something to her tablemates, and head toward the door, Amanda on her heels. "Thanks for being so good to Grandpa," Evan told Violet, then followed Chelsea and Amanda outside.

They'd already made it around the side of the building when he caught up to them. "Chelsea!"

Amanda put an instinctive hand on her back. Chelsea half-turned, and the streetlamp caught the sheen of tears on her cheek. "I'll call you tomorrow, Evan."

"Is this about the song?"

She clutched her bag close to her chest with both hands. "Don't worry about me, Evan. Amanda and I are going to go get a drink. Seriously, we can talk tomorrow."

"Let's talk now. The kids are dialed. We can find somewhere quiet."

"I'm going to wait in the car," Amanda said to Chelsea. "No hurry, okay?"

Chelsea shook her head, but Amanda walked off anyway. She looked back to Evan. "I don't want to do this now."

"Do what?" Evan's stomach gave that strange twist again. "Did Lauren say something to you? In the bathroom?" At the look on her face, Evan knew he'd hit on it, and he tamped down the flash of anger that surged through him. "What did she say?"

"Really, Evan. I don't know what's going on. I don't want to get in the way of you three being a family again."

"Wait, what?"

Chelsea froze, looking confused. "Evan, maybe we better—"

"Just come with me, please. I don't know what you're talking about." He found the side door of the building, the one that lead to the other side of the green room. "Let's go talk, okay? Please?" He held the door open to her, stepping in behind her into the narrow, dimly lit hallway. "Here, just here." He fiddled with the door to the green room, letting Chelsea in first.

"Oh!" She stopped short, Evan colliding with her back.

"What?" Evan peered around her, registering a beat too

slow what had stopped her, taking in the shadowed forms on the couch.

Denny Bliss untangled himself from a half-dressed Ashleigh O'Hare.

Chelsea's shoulders slumped. "Ashleigh?"

Ashleigh shrugged her dress back on. "Oh, hey, Ms. Garden. Um, er—" She gathered up her tights, her shoes, her bag. "I should probably go—"

"No, you wait here." Chelsea's teacher voice kicked in.

Evan couldn't speak, was choking on rage. He'd never wanted to murder Denny Bliss more than he did in this exact moment, and he'd spent years planning out ways to murder the man.

Denny ran a hand through his mussed hair, his eyes darting from Chelsea to Evan and back. "She's eighteen!" He pushed himself up to sit on the arm of the couch, cut his eyes to Ashleigh. "You're eighteen!"

Before Evan could process any of it, he heard a deep, guttural cry—not a scream; it wasn't high enough to be a scream—and he watched Chelsea lunge at Denny.

"You selfish fucking asshole piece of shit!" She hit him in the chest with both hands—Ashleigh screaming, ducking behind the sofa—and he toppled backwards, and then Chelsea was straddling him, pummeling him with her fists.

"What is going—?" Nora appeared next to him, Toby at her side. "Evan?"

"Jesus, Chelsea, stop!" they heard Denny choke out as he dodged more of Chelsea's punches. He finally managed to wriggle free of her and made a beeline for the open door that led outside.

Chelsea chased after him, followed by Evan, Nora, Toby, and Ashleigh.

By the time the group, now joined by Amanda who had

been sitting in the car when they rushed by, caught up with Denny and Chelsea, Denny had made it inside the public pool area behind the venue and Chelsea had him cornered near a pile of stacked kickboards and coiled lane ropes.

"She's not eighteen, you fucking moron!" Chelsea was screaming at him and throwing one kickboard after the next at him. He dodged most of them, but one hit him squarely in the back when he turned to avoid it. "We are throwing a birthday party for her at the end of the month in the fucking Civil Issues Club!"

Denny cut his eyes to Evan, his arms up protecting his head. "Evan, man. She told me she was eighteen."

Chelsea chucked another kickboard. "Because that worked out so well the last time, you absolute fucking idiot!?"

Nora looked shaken. She had her arm around Ashleigh's shoulders, who couldn't stop sobbing. "Okay, let's just all take a breath. Chelsea, you need to, well, you need to stop—" She winced at the final kickboard—"Stop throwing things!" Chelsea stopped, panting. She had run out of kickboards anyway. "And Denny, you should leave immediately."

"I'm trying to!" He pointed at Chelsea. "She's lost her fucking mind." His Bleachers T-shirt had a long tear down the side, his hair stuck up in every direction, and his lip was bleeding.

"I've lost *my* mind? Me!" Chelsea made a jab as if she was going to have another go at him, and Denny let out a yelp.

"Chelsea?" Nora warned. A light wind sent ripples across the dark water of the pool.

Denny inched away from them, closer and closer to the group. Watching him, Evan felt his stomach twist with rage— *how could he fucking do this!?*—and before he could stop himself, he shot across the pool deck, caught Denny around the shoulders, and they both plunged headfirst into the pool.

The swirl of water caught him off guard and he felt his throat fill with it. Coughing, sputtering, he clasped both hands over Denny's head and pushed him under the water. Denny kicked at him, pulled at Evan's hair, and for a moment they were a tangle of wet limbs and clothes, but then Toby was between them, pulling them apart, pushing Evan back toward the side of the pool. "Enough!" he said in the kind of voice a man acquires from raising three children. "Enough!"

And the three of them slogged their way toward the pool stairs.

PART FOUR

> That guy who said
> hell is other people,
> never met the ones
> who feel like home
>
> —Sunset Dark

NORA

"Nora?" Elaine knocked on the doorframe. "Sue O'Hare is calling again."

Nora sighed, her hands pausing over her laptop keyboard. She had two documents to finish for LCAP and WASC and didn't have time for Sue O'Hare. Again. Besides, her lawyer said it might be best to just let him communicate with Sue. "I can't talk to her right now."

Elaine nodded; she looked drained. Sue had called six times yesterday, too. "No problem. And still no comment for the newspaper?"

"There's nothing to say."

Except that wasn't true. A seventeen-year-old student had been caught half-naked with a forty-five-year-old musical guest at a school event, and then he, in turn, was assaulted by two of her teachers. And there was some gray area around how they gained access to the public pool area, and the school would have to pay for the damage to the kickboards. That Denny wasn't pressing charges against them didn't help the fact that any guests who hadn't gone home, plus the jazz band students, had seen them slink back inside the building, three of them dripping, and in Denny's case, bleeding.

And she didn't even want to think about the way Sue O'Hare had started screaming at all of them. Yes, there was plenty to say. Nora just had no interest in saying it to the local paper.

Elaine closed the door behind her. Nora slipped off her readers and wondered how much Advil she could take before it ate away the entirety of her stomach lining. She looked around her office: the scrawled notes from the last board meeting on the whiteboard, the photos of graduating classes lining the walls, past WASC reviews, past safety plans, endless binders of endless forms packed onto dusty bookcases. How long had it been since those shelves had been dusted?

She clicked over to the email she'd been working on earlier addressed to Rick Aaronson, their superintendent. Her resignation. She hadn't sent it yet, but she knew she would. Soon. She couldn't go the distance, wouldn't make it to thirty years. Not because she couldn't, but because she didn't want to. Come June, she would host her final graduation, pack up her things, and move on. People would think it was because of what happened with Denny Bliss and Ashleigh O'Hare last weekend at the jazz event. Let them. It almost made it easier.

Mark Weaver knocked at her door. "Did you want to talk about the review board for the Roberts kid?" She nodded and he settled into a chair at the conference table, the same one Dean Moreno had slumped in all those months ago. Nora joined him, knowing she would recommend Mark to the board for her job next year. He'd be perfect. Mark loved this school. And she simply didn't have room for that sort of love anymore. She was done.

She remembered one of her mentors in L.A. many years ago announcing her own retirement, one that had come seemingly out of the blue. "It's time," she'd told Nora over a lukewarm cup of Chardonnay in a plastic cup at her retirement party. "You just know."

Nora hadn't believed her until now. Suddenly, the idea

of starting another new school year, sending out calendars, organizing the schedule, watching a new batch of kids spill in from the parking lot seemed impossible.

She had nothing left in the tank.

Twenty-seven years of classrooms, and discipline, and curricula, and testing, and sporting events, and professional development, and infuriating and hilarious teenage antics, and wonderful and difficult colleagues, and meetings (too many meetings), and thousands of teenagers. Good years and bad years. Bizarre pandemic years and average, easily forgotten years. And years where your band director tackles his former-bandmate-turned-rock-star into a pool. What a note to go out on, right?

But she would miss the rhythmic, (mostly) predictable nature of a school year. For much of her life, September had meant the start of school. New backpacks and blank notebooks. Text-book check-outs and clean whiteboards. June had meant graduations and locker clean-out. Her students had gone on to be doctors and plumbers and therapists and grocery store managers and mothers and fathers and cancer survivors and victims. Some had travelled the world. Some had been in and out of jail. Too many had died. And she had been witness to their lives, had been part of something larger than her.

It was enough.

* * *

When Nora first heard the honking, she'd been annoyed at the disturbance. She was staring down a leaky faucet with a DIY YouTube video playing on her laptop on the kitchen counter, one of those projects she'd been putting off for months. She wore baggy sweats and had her hair tied back in a bandana. The honking persisted.

"Okay!" She hurried outside.

Toby waived from the driver's side of an enormous silver sprinter van.

Nora's heart flipped. Over the past couple of weeks, during hikes, over dinner, sitting in front of a movie, they'd discussed what started as a crazy idea of Toby's, just casually at first, and then it had grown into a plan that might not be as crazy as they first thought, especially after the incident with the angry parent at dinner and then what happened at the jazz event. Come June, they would put their houses on the market, pack things into storage, and go explore the country. In the meantime, he would keep his eyes peeled for some kind of used RV, for eBikes they could strap to the back. He would talk to some friends of his who were already out on the road. Toby would work remotely for the next year and Nora could take a year and read all the books she hadn't had time to get to in the past decade that had piled up on her Kindle. She could stare at mountains or the desert or the ocean without feeling guilty for not working on the school safety plan or suicide prevention program. They'd hit the road like they were twenty-two again, he'd said. Only at twenty-two, she'd been living in a crammed house in Silver Lake with three other women from undergrad, waiting tables, saving up money for her eventual credential and master's degree. The only time she hadn't been in school or teaching or working in administration had been that time after college and a year's leave with newborn Leo, which had been a sleepless blur.

Toby motioned to the van. "A friend of a friend in Marin bought it new at the start of the pandemic for himself and his wife," he explained, getting out and slamming the heavy door. With his hair mussed and his cheeks pink, standing there beaming at the van, Nora got a sense of how he must have looked as a young man. He grinned at her. "Now, they barely use it, so they sold it. To me!" He noticed her face. "I know it's fast, but it was a screaming deal. Honestly, I could turn around and sell it tomorrow for more than I bought it."

Nora stared at the van, her body filling with what could only be panic. Her mouth went dry. She couldn't feel her feet. Could she seriously be considering leaving everything behind and living with a man she barely knew in a van? It might seem like being twenty-two, but they weren't. Not even close. Where would Leo stay when he came home? What would Craig think?

Toby frowned at her lack of response. "Do you want to see the inside?"

She let him lead her around to the sliding door. As he pulled it open, her breath caught. The interior was beautiful: hardwood floors, and honey-colored woodwork in the slim kitchenette with stainless steel appliances, a double bed set high in the back, with a table that pulled out from beneath it to form a dining space for two bench seats. Toby studied her face.

"He's a carpenter, the husband. Everything is custom." This wasn't a twenty-two-year-old's van. They stepped inside and he showed her all the secret storage spots beneath the bed. The built-in drawers, the hidden shelving, the fully stocked kitchen, the mini-espresso machine. "This was a complete labor of love for him. He had to go inside when I wrote the check. I got the sense his wife was never really into it, but you know how people were during the pandemic; they needed their pet projects."

"It's gorgeous." Nora ran her hand over the intricate tile backsplash behind the sink and gas range, imagined her favorite duvet and a set of soft sheets covering the bed, imagined a row of novels on the tiny bookshelf near the bed.

Stepping outside again, he showed her the storage area in the back. "They included their whole outdoor set-up, too:

chairs, a folding table, a rug, an awning. Even the bistro lights!" Toby beamed at her. She knew Liz hadn't much liked to travel and would only stay in hotels when they did. Toby had wanted something like this for so long. But she had to be careful; she had to want it, too.

Or maybe she was making it harder than she needed to. She'd always done everything for the long haul. Maybe it was time to try something *for now*. She could just *try* it. If she hated it after a few months, if she and Toby weren't compatible or she found she didn't like being nomadic, she'd come home and buy a condo. She gazed behind her at the house she'd raised Leo in.

She hadn't even wanted it at first. Craig had insisted on the two-story layout with the wide stretch of back lawn where they could put a playset and trampoline. And it had been a lovely home, but without Leo and Craig, it had stopped being that a while ago. She would always have the memories of Leo running downstairs at Christmas, his feet padding the stairs, the hiding spots for Easter eggs in the back yard, the pizza parties with his friends in the open kitchen. She'd grown to love it because of Leo and Craig and everything they'd been within its walls. It was the last thing she needed to say goodbye to.

"Let me drive it," she told Toby, and reached for the keys.

EVAN

ON SUNDAY AFTER THE EVENING of Jazz fiasco, Evan woke wondering which of his crises he should face first. Lauren. Or Denny. He chose Lauren. Partly because he knew which fire needed extinguishing before it turned into a blaze. They packed a lunch, slathered Violet with sunscreen she probably didn't need, and headed out for a hike. Lauren wore leggings with elaborate cut-outs up the side, a North Face jacket, and a trucker hat. She looked the part of active-weekend-mom, her hair in two short caramel braids that matched the tone of her aviator sunglasses. Evan had always thought Lauren lived like she was being followed around by a camera crew. Maybe he just attracted performative people like this in his life? First Denny, then Lauren. What did it say about him?

During the walk up to the lookout, Lauren insisted she'd been nothing but gracious in the bathroom with Chelsea. "Girl to girl," she insisted as they watched Violet skip ahead of them, pausing to collect smooth pebbles to weigh down her pockets. "It was very civilized."

"She seemed upset."

Lauren feigned innocence. "I can't help how she seemed!"

Evan wasn't buying it. He knew Lauren could be ruthless when she saw something as a competition. He'd once found it charming, sexy even. She'd once gotten into a full-out brawl with a woman at one of his events who wouldn't stop buying him drinks. So he wasn't about to argue with Lauren now. No one could hold the line like Lauren, especially when her pride was at stake.

When they reached the top, they found the bench occupied, so they laid a blanket on a patch of dirt off the trail and settled down to eat their picnic. They chewed quietly, studying the view of Imperial Flats below them. The wind had come up and Evan went searching for a rock to weigh down Violet's peanut butter and jelly bag before it could blow away, so he didn't hear the first part of Lauren's conversation with Violet, but as he sat back down, he caught a question that sent his stomach churning.

"What do you think, Vi?" Lauren handed her a bottle of Vitamin Water. "Do you think I should stay and live with you and Daddy for the rest of the year?"

For a moment he wondered if he'd imagined it, but Violet's confused face told him he'd heard it loud and clear. "Dad?" she looked at him. "I thought Chelsea might come live with us?"

Lauren brushed at some dirt on her leggings. "Why would you think that?"

Violet gave her mother a strange look. "Because Dad loves her."

Lauren laughed awkwardly. "He loves all of us, sweetie. He loves you and he loves me, too."

Violet took another bite of her peanut butter and jelly sandwich. "But not like with Chelsea. It's not the same."

Lauren reached out and touched Violet's knee. "I just thought it might be fun for us. You know, we could be a proper family."

Evan hadn't seen the tears start, had always been alarmed at how quickly they could spring from his daughter's eyes.

She'd always been like that. One minute, practical and calm. The next, waterworks. Violet shot to her feet.

"Why do you have to ruin everything?" she shouted at Lauren, who drew back from her as if slapped. Violet threw her sandwich to the ground and sprinted back down the trail. Evan had to admit, the stricken look on Lauren's face made him feel terrible for her, even if she'd brought it on herself. He told her to pack up the picnic and then he chased down the trail after Violet.

* * *

"Shit, Nathan. Clearly, he's used to maid service." Evan surveyed the inside of the cottage Nathan and Stephanie had so generously offered to Denny and allowed himself to be furious with Denny Bliss again, that familiar rage where, had the man walked through the door, Evan would have happily tackled him into ten more pools, one after the other. Of course, he wouldn't be walking through the door anytime soon.

Denny had skipped town on Monday evening, took a private jet to Hawaii, leaving the usual mess in his wake, and not just the emotional kind. An actual mess. Take-out containers and empty wine bottles lined the counters. Half-eaten bags of chips and cookies crowded the small table. The bedsheets were wadded into a twist. The floor and couches were littered with magazines and printed sheet music. The floor was grimy with muddy footprints and various crumbs.

"The bastard went to Hawaii on a private jet," Evan grumbled. "And left us with this."

"He did leave a thousand dollars in cash on the counter." Nathan looked mostly amused, though his expression faltered when he lifted a pink bra out of the kitchen sink. Evan took the bra and stuffed it into the black garbage bag he was already beginning to fill. Nathan added a half-eaten yogurt container. "You sure you want to take this on? We can hire a cleaning service." Evan shook his head. Nathan nodded. "Okay, I'll bring the recycle bin close, so you don't have to make too many trips." Nathan disappeared out the front door.

Evan moved through the room, muttering, "Fucker, fucker, fucker," as he collected magazines and sheet music and take out containers, separating what he could recycle and what he could throw out, stripping the bed, tossing whatever was left in the fridge, emptying the garbage in the kitchen and bathroom. He shut his eyes to that last one as he emptied it into the bag. Bathroom garbage always felt the most intimate: wasted floss, used condoms, acne pore strips. It held the most secrets. Evan plucked the thinning bar of soap from the shower and tossed that in, too.

He scanned to see if he'd missed anything. "You're a pig, Denny Bliss," he said to the empty room, but he felt his anger already losing its heat.

Part of him was glad Denny had left. Not the circumstances, sure, but the exit. Evan didn't have the time or patience for him, but he felt grateful for the realizations Denny had left him with. Evan had mostly blamed the pandemic for what happened with his touring career—the gigs dried up; there weren't as many studio options—but if he was honest with himself, he'd started to hate the life long before Covid sidelined the music industry. He'd been sick of living out of a suitcase, tired of spending time with other musicians who treated Airbnbs and hotels like dorm rooms. He didn't want to sleep on friends' couches anymore.

When Evan had accepted the band director job, he'd felt shame spread through his body. In certain circles, high school music teacher had always been code for the place failed musicians went to die. But soon, Evan had discovered what a load of shit that was. Musicians could be sanctimonious bastards sometimes.

Somehow, he'd always been most afraid to face Denny. For Denny to see him taking crappy gigs in bars or teaching jazz to a bunch of teenagers instead of out in front of thousands of adoring fans. The thought of it had kept him up some nights. Nothing, he'd thought, would ever measure up to what he'd lost when the band chose Denny. Now, though, looking around this room, he was glad Denny had seen him with his students, with Chelsea, with Violet. Had seen him at home. There weren't enough chartered jets in the world to make Evan want Denny's life ever again.

Once Evan got rid of most of the debris, he hauled the recycling out to the bin Nathan had left by the cottage, then set about cleaning the bathroom and living area with the supplies Stephanie had left out for him. As he sprayed and wiped and scrubbed and vacuumed, he tried not to think about Lauren back at the house, making herself far too comfortable in his opinion. He'd have to tell her to pack her bags soon, to head back to her parents', or to a friends' house. She couldn't keep staying with him.

He scrubbed hard at the glass on the fireplace. He was not looking forward to that conversation. Instead, he ran through possible pieces they could take to the Reno Jazz Festival next fall. The kids had sounded surprisingly together at the jazz night; they might even move up a class. Evan let himself feel proud of them, proud of how far they'd come.

He turned at the knock on the open doorframe. Chelsea stood there, in jeans and a baggy sweatshirt. "Wow, you've done so much already. Am I too late? I had a couple of students stop by after school."

"I haven't done the kitchen yet," he told her, tossing her a rag and a bottle of lemon cleaner. "And Stephanie left some stainless-steel cleaner, too. Over there," he motioned to the counter.

Chelsea studied him for a moment, then got to work. He watched her scrubbing the sink, her ponytail bobbing. Last night, he'd stayed over at her house, leaving Lauren and Violet to keep an eye on Frank. His anger still boiled at the thought of Lauren confronting Chelsea in the bathroom last Saturday, even if Lauren kept insisting she'd been nice about it. What had she been thinking? And he wasn't sure she was all that diplomatic. Chelsea had pulled back, even after he'd told her it was just Lauren being Lauren. She'd done this before, decided they would be a family again when a relationship went south. But Chelsea didn't know that. He'd tried his best to explain.

"Do you need me to do the bathroom, too?" She stood holding the cleaner, her hands in a pair of yellow rubber gloves.

"Do you mind?"

She gave him a faint smile and headed toward the bathroom. He was pretty sure he could read what was beneath it; somehow, they both knew this would be the last time they cleaned up a Denny Bliss mess. He knew it would feel good to scrub it clean.

* * *

Saturday afternoon, Evan took a walk with Lauren, Violet, and Frank around the neighborhood. Frank had taken to collecting things: rocks, bottle caps, stray pieces of twine. He kept them in a blue canvas grocery bag from Imperial Flats Market. Evan thought it was disgusting, but the one time he'd tried to empty it into the garbage, Frank had lost his shit, screaming and crying and clutching the bag to his chest. At least he wasn't digging holes in the yard anymore or cutting his pajamas to ribbons.

"You should find a place that can take care of him. He's not getting better." Lauren nodded to where Frank had found an empty, flattened Junior Mints box and was adding it to his collection. Violet was blowing bubbles around him from a bright pink container. They caught the April light, iridescent and shimmering.

Evan tried to tamp down his own bubble of annoyance at Lauren's words. He knew she was right. Chelsea had told him the same thing, and a few weeks ago she's sent him a list of local options she'd researched. Only Chelsea was back to being distant, not returning his texts, and he wasn't feeling gracious toward the women in his life right now.

"I'm already looking into some."

"Don't wait too long."

"Got it, Lauren."

They rounded the corner near where he and Chelsea had told Bernice about her cat. He thought of the gimlets in the glasses she'd given them, could almost taste the tart lime juice. It seemed hard to believe they'd already made memories, less hard to believe he'd already messed things up.

He stopped walking. "You have to leave, Lauren."

She made it a few more paces before turning back. "What?"

"You can't stay here. This isn't going to work."

She took a step toward him. "You don't know that."

"I do."

He watched the muscles twitch around her mouth the way they did when she was about to cry. Or yell. But she licked her lips, took a breath. "Please don't do this, Evan. Think about Violet."

"I am."

"We're her family."

"That won't change."

Lauren slipped off her sunglasses, her eyes searching his. "You're serious about Chelsea?"

"This isn't about her. This is about us. This *never* works, you know that. We're best for Violet when we're apart. She knows she has two parents who love her. What more does she need?"

Lauren's face crumbled. "What am I going to do, Evan? I can't move back in with my parents again. I'm thirty-five years old!"

He pulled her to him, stroking her hair, letting her sob into his chest. "Hey, hey, you'll figure it out. You always figure it out. You're the toughest person I know. Besides your daughter. And look at me! I moved back in with my dad and I'm in my forties. You're ahead of the game!"

She stepped back, wiping her eyes, and they both looked to where Frank was using a stick to pry a piece of gum from the ground, Violet squealing next to him, "Ewwww, Grandpa, ewwwww, that's chewed gum! Grossssss!"

Lauren shot Evan a wry look. "Yeah, that's going well."

CHELSEA

Chelsea was almost to her car Tuesday afternoon before she remembered she needed the stack of essays from her seniors that she'd left on her desk. She often made the kids turn in their work via Google Docs, but this particular assignment had to do with editing, so they'd marked up their papers with a pen in a color she could easily see in response to a series of questions she had given them. She loved reading the notes they wrote to themselves in the margins. Dropping her bag inside her classroom door, she hurried to her desk.

As she picked up the stack of essays, a folded square of paper fluttered to the floor. Probably a note someone had been passing in class that got caught up when they passed their essays forward earlier.

Except it had her name on it: *Ms. Garden*, scrawled in purple ink.

Ashleigh O'Hare always used purple ink.

Yesterday, Sue O'Hare had marched Ashleigh to school, all the way to the door of Chelsea's classroom to deposit her for English. "I will pick you up after class," she'd said to her daughter's downcast stare. Chelsea hadn't made eye contact, had pretended to be busy reading something on her computer. Red-cheeked, Ashleigh had slumped in her seat in the front near the window until about halfway through class when she'd raised her hand. "Can I use the bathroom?"

Nodding, Chelsea had watched Ashleigh pack her entire bag, hoist it over her shoulder, and cross the room to leave.

"Ashleigh." Chelsea's tone had stopped the girl at the door, but she hadn't turned around. "He's not worth it."

But apparently, he was.

Apparently, Denny had chartered a plane to Oahu, and about-to-turn-eighteen Ashleigh O' Hare, who'd months before argued for extra rough draft points on her *Hamlet* essay, had been on that plane with him. Mahalo, Imperial Flats. Aloha.

Chelsea opened the note. It was from Ashleigh. She must have dropped it on Chelsea's desk before leaving class yesterday:

Dear Ms. Garden,

Denny said I should write you and explain some things before we leave. Maybe you'll have more luck getting through to my mother, but I won't hold my breath. Denny said you're the best, that you care about people, and you think people should live their own lives and not do things just because other people think you should. I told him I totally felt that from you as a teacher. I loved your class and our Civil Issues meetings. You made us think about things and you cared what we thought. That was cool. Not many people do that. Anyway, not that I need to explain my choices to you, and I don't think you'd even want me to, but for the record I know it's crazy what I'm doing. I know he's old and I know he's got a reputation, and I know that people will say I'm throwing my life away, but I'm not an idiot. I already checked to see if I have enough credits to graduate and I do. And if they don't let me just graduate with the credits I already have, I'll just take the stupid test that lets me get my diploma. Or I'll go to community college. Maybe in Hawaii. Point is, I'm done living my life so my mom can brag about me to her friends. I don't want any of the things she wants and I'm tired of trying to be perfect. Denny said you would understand. Maybe you will. I'm glad you were the last teacher I saw before I walked out of Imperial Flats forever.

Anyway, thanks

Ashleigh

Chelsea couldn't help but smile at the dramatics of the last line. And at the note as a whole. Like so many girls of her generation, Chelsea admired how confident and sure of herself she sounded. Even if it all went to shit, even if she ended up back in her teenage bedroom by the end of the month, apologizing to her mother, she'd taken a huge risk. Chelsea read through the note again, marveling at its intelligence, at its self-awareness. Ashleigh hadn't left for a man, as so many people would frame it; she'd seen an opportunity and seized it.

* * *

Chelsea had clearly reached that point in life where everything landed as metaphor. From a bench overlooking the town, she chewed her sandwich and stared out at the rare late morning fog breaking apart over Imperial Flats. The deli had forgotten to put cheese on her sandwich. She'd asked for provolone. And there was mayo when she'd said no mayo. Not too much, though. She peeled back the sourdough bread and peered at it. She'd spent most of her life claiming she hated mayo, but she liked it on this particular sandwich. It tasted good. It was tangy and mixed nicely with the mustard and peppers and pickle.

She took another bite, realizing with a low ache of sadness that she had denied herself mayo for as long as she could remember because somewhere along the way her mother had said it was just empty calories, had stitched the concept of withholding-as-virtue into every seam of her childhood. And Chelsea had let her, had carried so much of that imprinting into her adult life.

Sandwich metaphors.

She blinked back tears, trying not to think about metaphors in terms of the current Evan and Lauren situation. She tried not to draw connections between not getting what she'd asked for and finding out she'd loved something she had denied herself. Except the harder she tried, the clearer the metaphors became. A byproduct of too many years teaching English. Metaphors could be relentless.

Fact was, she had loved Evan Dawkins for most of her life. Had likely held every other man against the litmus test of him. She'd been to some beautiful places in her life, met some truly wonderful men, but she'd never felt as safe with them, as wholly herself, as she had with Evan in high school when they'd spent hours talking, sitting on opposite sides of the couch, socked-feet knocking against each other, or not talking, just listening to records on Frank's old player, Evan splayed out on the floor, eyes closed. Maybe she'd chosen to teach high school partly because it reminded her of a time in her life when she'd had that, even if she'd taken it for granted then.

Her phone buzzed in her pocket. Evan. She'd hiked up here to clear her head after the rollercoaster of last week. In theory, to be alone. She should have left her phone in the car. It felt impossible to be alone with the buzzing reminder of Evan texting every hour or so. She knew she wasn't being fair, ignoring him like this. He wasn't doing anything wrong. He'd even stayed over at her place Tuesday night to talk things through. Early Wednesday, long before heading to school, she'd curled up next to him as rain-drenched morning light spilled across them, as he'd apologized for everything that had happened since the jazz night.

Denny.

Lauren's ambush in the bathroom.

Jesus, what a mess.

Lauren had found Chelsea in the bathroom washing her hands and had casually introduced herself. "You're Chelsea, right?" She'd said, moving close into the mirror to wipe a stray bit of mascara from beneath one eye. Chelsea had toweled off her hands, using the opportunity to study her. She'd read countless articles about the patriarchal construct of female competition, understood how damning the tendency to compare could be to women, but she couldn't help it. Lauren was gorgeous. Brown eyes, auburn curls. And naturally waif-like in a backless, draping, slate-gray dress Chelsea couldn't help but think was a little much for a high school jazz event. Chelsea had stood there, feeling ashamed, and let herself compare and judge and all the shit she had been working on for thirty years and couldn't quite seem to kick.

Lauren had turned and leaned against the sink, her arms crossed across her chest. "Listen, girl to girl, I came back to talk to Evan about trying again as a family. I don't want to step on your toes, but this is my family, okay? I'll fight for them."

Chelsea hadn't said anything, had been too shocked at this woman's candor, at the seeming conviction that she deserved whatever she decided she wanted. Without waiting for a reply, Lauren had given her a stony look and pushed through the swinging door of the bathroom, leaving Chelsea staring after her.

Evan told her he'd taken a hike with Lauren and Violet the Sunday following the jazz night, and Lauren had told him she wanted them to be together again. To be a family. For Violet, she'd said. She'd said it on this very hill, in fact. In front of her daughter. Apparently, Violet had burst into tears and they'd had to chase her down the mountain. Evan said it was just Lauren being Lauren. He was furious with her. Lying next to Chelsea in bed, he'd told her that when Lauren felt lost and hurt, she would free-fall through the air clutching for any branch to grab hold of. Metaphors again. Evan as tree branch. It bothered Chelsea that Lauren had announced her plan in front of Violet, had folded her into the proclamation, before talking to Evan. What kind of person used her daughter as leverage in that sort of emotional deal?

Even Judy Garden wouldn't stoop so low.

Chelsea's head pounded with the sort of headache she hadn't had since Mr. King-Jennings. Somehow, everything now felt lumped together with that mess, with the shove into the car door, with her exodus from Grove, with her breakup with Stone, with Denny's terrible behavior, with Lauren's demands. Chelsea felt tumbled in the wake of all of it, water-logged with uncertainty. Chelsea had long ago given up on thinking the world would ever be fair, she really had, but it didn't stop her from being exhausted by how shitty it could consistently be. Her phone buzzed again. She should probably just power it down.

"Chelsea?" Nora stood a few feet away, a sweatshirt tied around her waist, a water bottle in her hand. Nora pulled her AirPods out and smiled. "You had the same idea I did."

Chelsea made room for her on the bench. Sitting, Nora drank some water, her eyes on the view. Chelsea waited for her to finish before saying, "What a week, huh?"

Nora let out more of a groan than a sigh. "You know,

I thought I'd reached the point in my career where I pretty much had a blueprint for most situations. But I don't seem to have one for when your Valedictorian skips town on a chartered plane to Hawaii with a rock star."

"After being pummeled by two of your teachers." Chelsea added, taking another bite of her sandwich.

"Right. That, too. No rulebook for that one." Nora screwed the cap back on her water. "Of course, he's not pressing charges, so you two should be okay."

"What about you?"

Nora frowned. "They were found at a school function. At some point, someone will have to take responsibility for it. I'm still waiting to see what Sue O'Hare decides to do." Nora slipped her sweatshirt on over her head against a chilly wind that had just come up. "And we know she's not—a pushover parent."

Chelsea burst out laughing. "Understatement of the year. She found me Tuesday morning before school, told me I should never have let Ashleigh leave class on Monday. As if that would have stopped her from boarding a plane."

Nora shook her head. "That woman would have authorized us chaining the kid to the desk if we could."

"Probably most of the problem right there."

"You know it. I know it. Mom wants to point the finger anywhere but at herself."

"What a disaster." Chelsea sighed. "Personally, I don't envy anyone who falls for Denny Bliss."

Nora pulled her sweatshirt sleeves over her hands. "Was he always like this?"

Chelsea shook her head. "Not when I knew him, not in high school. I've always thought most of his exploits have been vengeance for all the girls who wouldn't give him the time of day until he became famous."

"Poor Ashleigh. She won't know what hit her."

"Oh, I don't know," Chelsea said. "I think we might not be giving Ashleigh O'Hare the credit she deserves on this one. I think she saw an exit hatch and took it."

"You know, I wondered the same thing. No matter what, she'll have a great story to tell at dinner parties someday." Nora mistook Chelsea's expression for surprise. "Sorry, that's not fair of me."

"You're not the only one thinking it, believe me."

Nora gave her a grateful smile. "Thanks for that. Because I'm a principal, people think I'm all rule books and proper thoughts, but this job has not made me the biggest believer in the goodness of humans, you know?"

"I really do."

"And with a kid like Ashleigh, I can't help but wonder if she needed to do something like this, something this drastic, to get out from under that iron thumb she's been pinned under her whole life."

Chelsea thought of Ashleigh's note. "I think you're right about that."

"Who knows?" Nora said, stretching her arms over her head. "It might do her mother some good in the long run, too."

Chelsea nodded, but she wondered if women like Sue O'Hare were capable of growth when it came to their daughters. She wasn't sure her own mother would ever see beyond her own version of things. She imagined Sue was cut from a similar cloth. They didn't grow to see the other side; they felt betrayed. Maybe that betrayal felt safer than having to admit they did anything wrong in the first place. "It might take Sue a long time to see a silver lining in this story."

Nora gave Chelsea's arm a quick squeeze. "This sure hasn't been the easy semester I promised you back in December."

Chelsea folded the brown paper around her sandwich

and shoved it into her bag. She tried to discreetly wipe a stray bit of mayo from her leggings. "I never expect teaching to be easy. It's one of the things I like about it."

"The challenge?"

"That, and maybe the drama, too, sometimes." Chelsea grinned at Nora's raised eyebrows. "I know, I know, I don't like drama in my own life at all. I avoid it at all costs." She motioned to the bench. "I'm avoiding it right now! But I love working with teenagers. Everything with them is so raw and emotional and immediate. They live like they're feeling everything for the first time: fury, love, excitement, jealousy. They are deliciously alive."

"That they are." Nora nodded. "They're exhausting." Chelsea remembered Nora had a son in college. She'd often wondered what it would be like to work with teenagers all day and then go home to one. "So does that mean you're coming back to us next fall? Dean sent in his official resignation. It's yours if you want it." When Chelsea hesitated, she added, "Or are you going to take that job in Ireland?"

Chelsea's stomach dropped. "How did—?"

"Small town."

"Of course." Her mother had probably told someone in the produce section. Or taken out an ad in the newspaper. "I'm not totally sure about Ireland. I honestly haven't even told Evan about it yet." At Nora's surprised look, she said, "I kept waiting for the right time, and then there just wasn't a right time. I'm trying to sort a few things out."

Nora pointed to the bench. "Do these things have anything to do with what you're avoiding right now?"

Chelsea's cheeks burned. "Yeah."

"Evan? Oh, ignore me—I'm being so nosy!"

"No, it's okay. It does have to do with Evan."

"Telling him about Ireland?"

"I wish that was all." Chelsea stared out over Imperial Flats. "His ex-wife came back from London. She wants them to 'try again' as a family."

"Ah." Nora took another short sip of water. "And what does Evan think about that?"

"He said she does this after a failed relationship, said he's not interested in going down that road again."

"You don't believe him?"

Chelsea shifted awkwardly on the bench. "I don't want to come between him and his family."

"I don't get the impression he thinks that's what you're doing."

Chelsea's phone rang, Evan's picture flashing on the screen. Nora nodded at it. "Speak of the devil. I should probably head back anyway. Consider the job offer. Maybe let me know by the end of next week?"

Chelsea nodded, made like she was answering, but as Nora retreated back down the path, she let it go to voicemail instead.

* * *

After the hike, Chelsea drove through Imperial Flats, taking side streets, avoiding the highway. She drove past Dani's house, past homes of childhood friends, through the downtown, past Charlie's Bar and Faraldo's Hardware, past the tattoo parlor and the library and pulled into the far side of Burger Barn's parking lot. She didn't want to go back to Kyle's, and she didn't want to try to find Evan.

His last text read: *okay, I'll wait for you to reach out.*

Somehow, that was worse, the ball in her court now. She couldn't seem to shake something Nora had said. *I don't get the impression he thinks that's what you're doing.* Chelsea knew Nora was right. Even as it hurt her to think it, she knew there was a small part of her who found Lauren's urgent words in the bathroom last Saturday a sort of relief. Okay, then, she'd thought, even as her face heated in defiance, it can't go anywhere with him because I can do a moral thing; I can step aside, move to Ireland, and let him choose his family.

Which was, of course, total bullshit. Chelsea needed to stop hiding behind her imagined moral compass. It didn't make her a good person. It made her a coward.

Chelsea wasn't coming between a family and she didn't want to move to Ireland. Lauren was manipulating things, and, even worse, Chelsea knew Evan *knew* that. He *told* her he knew it. Yet she grabbed the first excuse to run away. Which was what she always did. Her entire life. She ran from anything with a whiff of settling her down, forcing her to face the difficult things she'd rather avoid.

Teaching at Grove had been her longest relationship and, even then, she'd fled at the first sign of trouble. She hadn't turned and fought. She hadn't asked Sheryl Alexander to fight for her. Her mother had told her she had been like this as a child, too. That she'd hidden at the first sign of conflict. Maybe Chelsea had spent so many years trying not to listen to Judy Garden that she hadn't heard any of the true things she'd told her. Over the years, she'd even, ironically, left any therapist who'd landed too close to forcing her to admit it: Chelsea kept the stakes low so she couldn't be let down. She'd made it a lifestyle choice.

And if she didn't do something this time, she'd lose Evan. Again.

She backed out of the parking spot and pulled into the drive-thru. Drops of sweat beaded her top lip. She wanted French fries dipped in a vanilla milkshake. She wanted to eat and cry and eat and cry. So she ordered from the crackle-voice over the speaker, and, minutes later, with her fragrant sack of salty fries and the too-cold shake, she pulled back into a far parking spot and let herself have almost all the things she needed in that moment.

* * *

Chelsea found herself on Evan's porch, the afternoon sun just starting to warm her back. She'd been standing there too long, not knocking. Just lurking, trying to get her tears under control. The last thing she needed was some sort of *I'm-just-a girl-standing-in-front-of-a-boy* situation on his front porch, looking like a bloated, middle-aged fish. I mean, honestly, she loved that rom-com shit, but she was no Julia Roberts.

Suddenly, the door opened. Violet blinked at her, holding a dripping paintbrush. "What are you doing?"

Chelsea stumbled. "Oh, um."

"You've been standing out here for, like, five minutes. Do you want to come in or what?"

"Is your dad here?"

Violet nodded. "He said he was going to go out to the backyard to regret his life choices. You should come in."

Chelsea followed Violet into the kitchen. She was sitting at the table with Frank and they were both filling in one of those paint-by-number books you only need water for. Violet was halfway through a sleeve of Thin Mint Girl Scout cookies. Chelsea watched them for a minute, her chest tight. They were so beautiful.

She found Evan flat on his back in the middle of the back yard next to a bucket filled with ice and beer.

"Are you changing your latitude?" She settled on the grass next to him.

"Lauren just left." He propped himself up on his elbows, eyeing her. "You have something—" He motioned to the white blob on her sweatshirt.

"Vanilla shake. Listen, I'm sorry."

"For not texting me back? For pummeling Denny Bliss?"

"The first one. Not the last one. Kinda proud of the last one."

He sat up all the way, opened a beer, and handed it to her. She took a swallow. He peered at her face, worried. "You've been crying."

"I've never been better."

"Okay."

She set her beer down next to her, leaned into him, and kissed him, first on the side of his face, then on both eyelids, then his cheeks, then his mouth. Pulling back, she held his face. He hadn't shaved and she loved the rough feel of his scruff beneath her hands. "I want us to be together. I want to be here and teach and live our life, here, together. I can't imagine myself anywhere else. We can go to Ireland on vacation sometime."

"Ireland? What are you—?"

"It doesn't matter. I want to be here, with you. I want to try."

"Chelsea, so do I! I've been trying to tell you—"

"I know. It was me. I freaked out. Lauren—"

"Lauren doesn't get a vote."

Chelsea dropped her hands from his face, scooted so she was facing him, and clasped both of his hands in hers. "All my life, I've kept things small. And distant. I've kept the stakes as low as I could so I wouldn't get hurt. Coming back here was supposed to be a break from life. It was never supposed to become my actual life. But then, here you were, and being with you felt perfect and simple and I worried that it was once again me rationalizing the easy choice the way I always do. So I freaked out." She shook her head; she was rambling.

The afternoon felt suddenly full of sun and cold at the same time, the bare trees casting splintered shadows over them. Her whole body shook.

"Sorry to get all last-scene-of-a-rom-com with you, but it's true. I don't want small; I don't think I ever wanted small. What I wanted was something special. Something I had a long time ago with you. It was easy and quiet, and it was ours and then it was gone. I have missed you my whole life. I'm done missing you." She was crying again, the tears spilling down her cheeks.

Evan pulled her close, whispering into her hair, "It's okay, it's okay. I've always liked a good rom-com. Too bad it's not raining. This would be a really good scene in the rain."

Chelsea smiled into the fabric of his shirt, into the Evan-smell of the flannel. Pulling back, she looked at him. "Are you sure about this? It's a lot to take on. I'm a mess."

Evan gave her that slant-smile of his she had loved for so long, the one that managed to be weary and hopeful and knowing all at the same time. "We're old. If life wasn't messy, then what the hell have we actually been doing all this time?"

Enjoy more about
Other People's Kids: A Novel
Meet the Author
Check out author appearances
Explore special features

ABOUT THE AUTHOR

Kim Culbertson is the award-winning author of five YA novels with Sourcebooks and Scholastic as well as the author of the Heinemann teaching guide *100-Word Stories: A Short Form for Expansive Writing*. She lives in Northern California where she has been teaching high school since 1997. Somehow, through it all, she still adores teenagers and feels lucky to work with them but that's probably because she spends as much time traveling and hiking in Tahoe as possible. *Other People's Kids* is her first novel for adults. Visit her at www.kimculbertson.com.

ACKNOWLEDGMENTS:

THIS BOOK ALMOST DIDN'T HAPPEN. Years ago, I was burnt out on the publishing industry and wanted to return almost entirely to my teaching, somewhere I've always felt safe and nourished. But I woke one night, longing to remember why I started writing in the first place. To figure that out, I returned to school: the MFA program in Fiction at the Rainier Writing Workshop. I want to thank everyone at RWW (my mentors and classmates) for reminding me during those next few years why I first fell in love with writing: because I love characters and stories and grappling with them on the page. Chelsea, Evan, and Nora came out of the writing I did in that program, and I will be forever grateful to the people there who brought me back to the work.

I want to also thank these early readers: Darien Hsu Gee, Scott Nadelson, Tabitha Lawrence, Josh Weil, Sands Hall, Loretta Ramos, Kirsten Casey, and Jaime Williams. You all encouraged me to keep revising, keep exploring. I wouldn't have finished the book without you. Peter and Ana, you read more drafts of this book than we can count. I'm so grateful.

A special thank you also needs to go to my amazing agent Melissa White at Folio Literary. She believed in this book early on and worked tirelessly to find it a home. She is one of the things I treasure most in this industry. Which brings me to Sibylline Press and Vicki DeArmon and Julia Park Tracey. Thanks, ladies, for what you're doing with this press. Thank you for the amazing people you have around you (Alicia, that cover is gorgeous! Suzy, you saved me on a wobbly day!) Sibylline is a beautiful home for *Other People's Kids*. The true gift of being in publishing is the people you meet along the way.

I had a few logistical questions while writing *OPK* and am grateful to Alison Cohen for pointing me to Jim Lazar for legal guidance. Any mistakes I made are mine, not his, when it comes to Violet and her situation with her parents. This is also true for anything relating to therapeutic work with teenagers. My go-to person has been Emily Gallup for the better part of two decades. Thanks, Em. Also, thanks to Mary Volmer who long ago helped me come up with the name for Imperial Flats. And a special thanks to Ana and Tenaya for their diligent market research ☺

Education has always had my heart. My parents and grandfather were educators. My husband is heading toward thirty years in teaching and administration, and my daughter is about to embark on her own journey as a teacher. I've spent most of my professional life learning from some of the best educators in the industry. There are too many of you to name here. You know who you are. I am especially grateful for everyone (and I mean *everyone*) at Forest Charter School. I am so lucky to be part of this community of people who care about working hard to create a safe place for teenagers and children so they can attempt to face this difficult world knowing a bit more about who they are and what they want. The work you do can't be measured. You inspire me every day.

A NOTE FROM KIM

I'VE BEEN IN EDUCATION FOR twenty-seven years (and counting). Jeez, it feels like fifty. My grandfather was an educator. Both my parents were educators. And now my daughter wants to be an educator (break the cycle, Ana!). All jobs are challenging. Education, though, brings with it the unique responsibility of being charged with caring for other people's kids, even on days I can't even find my car keys. I teach in the same small rural town I grew up in. My students still act like they're seeing a zoo animal when they catch me in public (and not even an exotic one, the kind you forget lives at the back of the zoo in its own little hollowed out cave). I know way too much about certain people's families and have to pretend like I don't when I see them at the post office. This job makes me cry at least once a week. It's emotional and rich and exhausting and interesting, and I love it with all of my heart. This book was born from that teacher heart, but it is for all of us in middle age just trying to make sense of where the years have gone. Seriously, the other day one of my students didn't know who Steven Spielberg was. And when we Googled him, she said, "that *old* guy?"

Give me strength.

STUDY GUIDE QUESTIONS:

I WAS LUCKY TO HAVE five amazing authors write testimonials for this novel and I think what stood out to them in the book is worth discussing in a Book Club or, casually, among friends. Or just in your own head after reading. We all have our own ways of reflecting on whatever we've just read. I will let them guide you:

Scott Nadelson writes: "Kim Culbertson gives us an intimate view of a profession and its practitioners so often taken for granted. With precise detail, subtle drama, and surprising humor, she creates complex characters we want to spend time with and learn from, both in and out of the classroom; they may not want their students to know it, but her educators are fully alive and frustratingly, stubbornly, lovably human." **Do you think teachers are often taken for granted? Why might that be? How did these teachers in particular strike you as human?**

Loretta Ramos writes: "Kim understands our desire for connection, and that sometimes real connection comes from the people who knew us first." **How is this true for Chelsea, Evan, and Denny? Has this been true or untrue in your own life?**

Darien Hsu Gee writes: "*Other People's Kids* offers a moving, hopeful story of what it means to come home." **How is this book an exploration of home—both leaving it and coming back to it?**

Sands Hall writes: "The pages of Culbertson's winsome and wise novel turn swiftly, even as they offer ongoing and profound ideas about life choices. Choices that may have led to dead ends—or to surprising places." **What specific choices do you see these characters make that end up as dead ends or that lead them to surprising places?**

Josh Weil writes: "The greatest magic of this novel is the glow that growing to know [these characters] will cast over your own life, making you view those around you—and maybe even yourself—with a bit more generosity. Did any characters in particular do this for you?**

Sibylline Press is proud to publish the brilliant work of women authors over 50. We are a woman-owned publishing company and, like our authors, represent women of a certain age.

ALSO AVAILABLE FROM
Sibylline Press

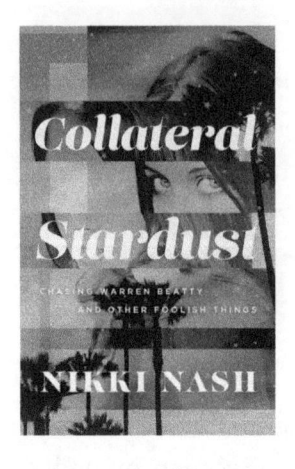

Collateral Stardust: Chasing Warren Beatty and Other Foolish Things
By Nikki Nash
MEMOIR
280 PAGES, TRADE PAPER, $19
ISBN: 9781960573421
ALSO AVAILABLE AS AN EBOOK AND AUDIOBOOK

Raised in a chaotic, bohemian Hollywood household, teenage Nikki Nash becomes fixated on a bold mission: meet and win over Warren Beatty. With determination and a detailed plan, at eighteen, working in a restaurant near the Beverly Wilshire, her long-shot dream collides with reality. While Warren remains ever present in her life, this is really the story of one woman navigating Hollywood as a producer, comedian, and actor in the eccentric fringes of L.A., brushing up against fame, danger, and dysfunction.

Seeds of the Pomegranate: A Novel
By Suzanne Samuels
HISTORICAL FICTION
416 PAGES, TRADE PAPER, $22
ISBN: 9781960573445
ALSO AVAILABLE AS AN EBOOK and audiobook

After illness derails her dreams of becoming a painter in Sicily, Mimi Inglese immigrates to New York, only to be dragged into her father's criminal underworld. When he's imprisoned, she turns to counterfeiting to survive, using her artistic gift to forge a path through Gangland chaos. As violence closes in, Mimi must risk everything to escape a life built on desperation and reclaim the future she once imagined.

You Could Be Happy Here: A Novel

By Erin Van Rheenen

FICTION
280 PAGES, TRADE PAPER, $19
ISBN: 9781960573476
ALSO AVAILABLE AS AN EBOOK and audiobook

When Lucy loses her mother and discovers her real father may be a man from her childhood summers in Costa Rica, she sets out to find him—and herself. But the village she returns to is no longer the paradise she remembers, and her search raises more questions than answers. *You Could be Happy Here* is a story of identity, belonging, and redefining home in a world that no longer fits the past.

The House of Cavanaugh: A Novel

By Polly Dugan

FICTION
248 PAGES, TRADE PAPER, $18
ISBN: 9781960573469
ALSO AVAILABLE AS AN EBOOK and audiobook

In 1964, Joan Cavanaugh has a secret affair that leads to the birth of a daughter whose true paternity she takes to the grave. Fifty years later, a Thanksgiving reunion unearths the buried truth, shaking the foundations of two tightly connected families. *The House of Cavanaugh* is a gripping story of hidden pasts, unraveling loyalties, and what it really means to be family.

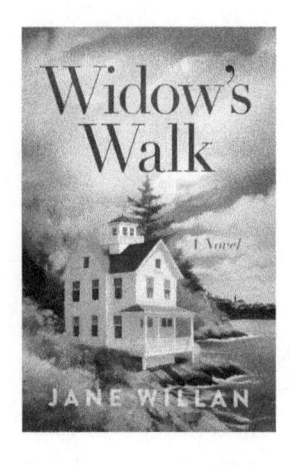

Widow's Walk: A Novel
By Jane Willan
FICTION
336 PAGES, TRADE PAPER, $20
ISBN: 9781960573452
ALSO AVAILABLE AS AN EBOOK and audiobook

When new Reverend Miranda McCurdy brings progressive change to a tradition-bound coastal church in Maine, her efforts spark fierce resistance—especially after she challenges the town's beloved Thanksgiving pageant. As the congregation splinters and a woman seeking sanctuary raises the stakes, Miranda must choose between fleeing back to her old life or staying to fight for the community she's slowly come to love. A stray dog and a mysterious stranger may tip the scales in this story of conviction, belonging, and second chances.

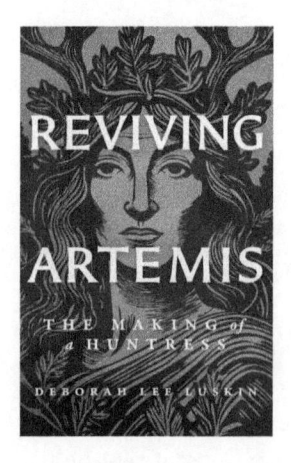

Reviving Artemis: The Making of a Huntress
By Deborah Lee Luskin
MEMOIR
280 PAGES, TRADE PAPER, $19
ISBN: 9781960573759
ALSO AVAILABLE AS AN EBOOK and audiobook

At sixty, longtime writer, gardener, and teacher Luskin feels a wild new calling: to leave the safety of her garden and learn to hunt deer. *Reviving Artemis* follows her late-in-life transformation as she confronts fear, embraces the forest, and reclaims a primal connection to nature. Blending humor, vulnerability, and myth, it's the story of a woman choosing to age on her own fierce terms.

For more books from **Sibylline Press**, please visit our website at sibyllinepress.com